Master of the East Fork

A Novel by

CARROLL C. JONES

Master of the East Fork
Carroll C. Jones

Published October 2014
Little Creek Books
Imprint of Jan-Carol Publishing, Inc

Front Cover Painting: Jeff Pittman
Design: Tara Sizemore

ISBN: 978-1-939289-50-6
Library of Congress Control Number: 2014954186

You may contact the publisher at:
Jan-Carol Publishing, Inc
PO Box 701
Johnson City, TN 37605
publisher@jancarolpublishing.com
jancarolpublishing.com

In memory of the brave and hardy souls who first settled the wild lands surrounding the forks of the Pigeon River.

Letter to the Reader

A few years ago, I began dabbling in family and Civil War history and ultimately found myself the proud author of three award-winning nonfiction books. I had never entertained thoughts of writing fiction—until a chance discovery provided the seeds from which grew my first fictional tale, *Master of the East Fork*.

While researching and writing *Captain Lenoir's Diary*, I learned how Thomas Isaac Lenoir was uprooted from his studies at the state university just prior to the American Civil War and relegated to the wild mountains of western North Carolina. Living in a lonely log cabin and with little farming experience, Lenoir was expected to manage the business affairs of his family's 5,000-acre farm and its passel of slaves. It was his *familial duty*, his father had impressed on him, and Thomas could not rightly refuse.

Thus the fictional young slave master, Basil Edmunston, is born, and danged if the poor boy does not immediately fall victim to African vexations and the enchanting allure of two beautiful mountain belles, Julia and Altha. For sure, Basil needs your backing to help find his runaway slaves, sort out romantic intrigues, and deal with the ominous threat of the antagonist, that no-good, Sam Beck.

Good reading,
Carroll C. Jones

Author's Note

The scenic valleys along the upper Pigeon River and its tributaries have a rich and intriguing history, extending back to the end of the eighteenth century when white settlers first penetrated the wilderness setting. Reliable historical resources have provided the inspiration to create fictional characters and imagine fanciful stories based on some of the region's actual pioneering families, who tamed the wilds surrounding Forks of Pigeon (present day Bethel, N.C.) Specific names of individual characters portrayed in the book, although common to the area, for the most part have been fictionalized. And no representations made, or tales told within these pages, should be construed as anything other than historical fiction.

Acknowledgements

The historical structure of this work of fiction is based on extensive study and research supporting my three previous publications: *The 25th North Carolina Troops in the Civil War*, *Rooted Deep in the Pigeon Valley*, and *Captain Lenoir's Diary*. Primary source materials used to develop these books included collections of Lenoir-family documents held by Hugh K. Terrell and Ike Forester, and the vast assemblage of Lenoir-family letters and documents contained in the *Southern Historical Collection* of the University of North Carolina's Wilson Library.

Special recognition goes to Edie Burnette—a wonderful writer and historian in her own right—for taking the time to read the original manuscript of *Master of the East Fork* and making her valuable suggestions to improve it. She was, also, kind enough to contribute the "foreword" for this book. Thanks, Edie!

Lastly, I could never dream-up and create a fictional character as strong or as special as the real one who stands by me every day, and makes everything seem worthwhile. With no better words to express my appreciation, let me just say, "Thanks, Maria, for allowing me to read all those chapters to you!"

Foreword

By Edie Hutchins Burnette

Carroll Jones and I are double-second cousins—our maternal Hargrove grandfathers were brothers who were fortunate enough to find themselves two Shook sisters to marry. We spent many childhood days on adjoining North Carolina farms in the heart of Haywood County's Pigeon Valley, relishing the heritage and natural beauty of a rural setting bequeathed to us by our great-grandfather, William "Hack" Hargrove. Not only do we claim this unique kinship and common ancestry, but we also share a kindred love for local history. As a result, Carroll writes books and I compose newspaper columns about the history of Haywood County.

Master of the East Fork marks a transition in writing for Carroll—a successful transition, in my considered opinion—from historical nonfiction to fanciful stories born of an inspired imagination. His previous books are scholarly works that reveal endless hours of research and facts meticulously gathered. One offers an accounting of the service rendered by a regiment of Rebel soldiers from western North Carolina during the Civil War—the 25th N.C. Infantry Troops. Another records and annotates a handwritten diary faithfully kept by the captain of a Confederate company known locally as the Haywood Highlanders and formally as Company F, 25th N.C. Infantry Troops.

In making the leap from nonfiction to fiction, Carroll hesitantly undertook this first novel with no little degree of unease. Turns out his concerns were unfounded. Borrowing ideas from the historical circumstances of the Pigeon Valley's early settlers and their primitive settings, he proceeded to create characters and invent lively tales of his own. These characters, particularly one named Basil Edmunston, became very real people in Carroll's descriptive literary style. Writing with passionate feelings and keen insight for the whimsical actors who dance through his story and using appropriate period dialogue in the portrayal of their interactions, he succeeds in bringing to life people from a bygone era—along with the challenges, tragedies, satisfactions, and even romances they might have experienced.

Brushstrokes oozing with close attention and deliberate detail paint the wild scenery and settlement along the upper reaches of western North Carolina's Pigeon River. Readers are comfortably transported back to the pioneer days. There they stand with the reluctant protagonist, Basil, beside his rustic cabin styled the "Den", surveying from that lofty vantage point the surrounding rugged mountains, fields of corn worked by slaves, and the distant East Fork River. Basil's romantic dilemmas and vexing trials of managing his family's immense mountain farm and its little band of bonded Africans soon become burdens readers readily shoulder.

I suspect those who read *Master of the East Fork* will come to understand how seemingly normal double-second cousins could become so infected with a fondness for their heritage. Hopefully, for the readers' sake, this condition will be catching.

Edie Hutchins Burnette–a graduate of Wake Forest University, former Asheville Times page editor, and retired teacher–has written literally hundreds of newspaper columns for Asheville's Citizen-Times concerning the history of Haywood County. She is a lifelong resident of Canton, North Carolina, and historical sleuthing and literary projects still top the list of events in her active schedule.

Contents

Chapter 1

A Fateful Reunion

"Whoaaa, girl! Whoaaa! Steady now," encouraged the young horseman as he reined the chestnut mare to a halting stop. Rearing on tired hind legs, the steed's head jerked back from the unexpected and unpleasant tug of the hard steel bit lodged in her mouth. With one gloved hand stroking and patting the horse's sweat-lathered neck and the other deftly clenching the reins, the rider cocked his head upward and strained to see through the gloomy darkness. His anxious eyes scanned the hillside, searching for a familiar sight. In just a few moments he spotted it—firelight spilling through the forest from the window of a crude log cabin. There in that rustic shelter his elderly father anxiously awaited his arrival. And theirs was to be a fateful reunion.

In the low doorway of the cabin, Thomas Edmunston embraced his youngest son with a stout hug and an affectionate kiss to the side of a scraggly unshaven face, "Basil, my boy! Thank God you made it."

The father was noticeably relieved from a distressing anxiety now that Basil had arrived safely. Theirs was indeed a loving father–son relationship. Although Basil Edmunston was twenty years old, the unabashed reverence he held for his father had not diminished with the onset of manhood. He would do anything for the man. And his arrival that night at the forlorn log cabin on the family's Haywood County farm, located in the remote western mountains of North Carolina, was a testament to his filial devotion.

The year was 1846, and winter's waning frigid blasts had not yet abated. Basil had traveled for three days over poor mountain roads through rain, sleet, and snow to get to the Haywood cabin. At six feet and a few inches tall, the boy had to duck his head to pass through the doorway as his father ushered him into the warmth and comfort of the humble quarters.

"Come on in, son, and let's get you dried out some and warmed up. I'll get one of the boys to take care of your horse," offered the elder Edmunston, alluding to the male members of the band of slaves that worked the farm.

"Hello, Father. It's real good to see you," Basil responded in a raspy voice as he proceeded to shed his sopping hat and coat.

Spotting a strange dog in the still-open doorway, the father quipped in astonishment, "Well now, who might this be?"

Turning to look behind him the bushed Basil offered, "Oh, him—just some ole cur that took up with us down about Pigeon River Ford. Tried to chase the thing off but couldn't discourage him atall from tailing us."

"Well, he looks as if he could stand a bite to eat," Thomas observed. "I'll ask Patsy to find him something," again referring to one of the African servants. Turning toward a slight figure lurking in a dark corner he directed, "Now, Patsy, would you see to this mangy dog of Basil's and get someone to come and take the horse away?"

The first thoughts of the elderly slave cook were that this young Master was a mighty handsome specimen for a white man and that now she had another mouth to feed—and not necessarily in that order. Gray hair poofed out from under the edges of a scarlet scarf that wrapped her head, and her big eyes shone white as she stared at Basil. It had been a right good spell since she last had seen the boy, and he sure had grown a sight.

"Yessa, Massa," Patsy respectfully responded as she moved toward the doorway and the dog. "Good to see you's agin, Massa Baz," she said as she lurched by, shooing the dog in front of her.

"You too, Patsy!"

"What about you, son? You hungry? How about a drink of brandy?" the father asked as he closed the heavy planked door behind Patsy and the ravenous, whimpering dog.

"No, no, thank you, Father. I'm awful worn out. It was a long hard ride today. But some water would do nicely, though."

"Sure enough—coming right up," Thomas replied as he hustled to the water bucket and offered up a dripping ladle to his son. "Now, Basil, how was your trip? I want you to sit down and tell me all about it," the inquiring father asked as he carefully hung Basil's floppy felt hat and great wool overcoat, both sodden and heavy from the weather, on a wall peg near the roaring fire. The hot, yellow blaze was confined within a gaping fireplace constructed of local river rock. And on a mantle beam above the conflagration, two candles affixed in tin holders flickered like miniature torches. Yet the warm hearth barely illuminated the cabin's dim interior, and the father and son strained to get a good look at one another.

Before Basil could even reply to his father's query about the trip, another question came his way, "Better get out of those wet boots, son. Did you have any trouble with the river crossings?" The elder Edmunston stepped over to a dim corner of the cabin, took down a crude chair hanging from yet another peg poking out from the log wall, and placed it in front of the fire for his son.

"Ahhh," Basil unconsciously uttered after gulping down the water and exhaling deeply. Handing the gourd dipper back to his father, he removed his boots and soggy woolen socks and placed them before the fire to dry out. Then he collapsed heavily into the wooden chair, stretching his long legs and cold feet toward the yellow blaze of burning locust logs that were noisily hissing and popping. Running both hands through an unruly shock of long black hair and pulling it back from his face, Basil finally breathed a great sigh of relief.

Thomas scooted another chair from the small dining table and plopped down next to his son. Looking expectantly at the weary sojourner, he waited anxiously to hear a full account of the trip. Basil then set about recounting his journey, knowing that his father was interested in every last detail, including accidents and unusual occurrences along the way.

Basil related how the roads from Caldwell County, the origination of his trek, were tolerable for the most part. However, to the west of the tiny settlement of Old Fort, where the winding trace pierced the formidable Blue Ridge Range, he had encountered trouble. At that high altitude, the road was covered in snow and ice. Basil avowed to his father that never before had he experienced such treacherous going on horseback. As it happened, his horse had actually slipped and fallen once, skidding rump first into a laurel thicket crowding a creek bank. Luckily neither horse nor horseman was hurt, and they suffered no more such upsets along the way.

Basil had slept the previous night on the tavern floor of Alexander's Inn on the Swannanoa River. Lying on a cornhusk-filled tick, he had unfortunately found himself tucked between two other boarders. They were a rough sort, he explained to his father. Both were ill-clothed and suffering from the effects of the innkeeper's ardent spirits. One of these men was fat as a sow at killing time, and the other snored a sight. Basil bemoaned the miserable sleepless experience. He reported to his father that he had arisen early and was astride his horse and well on the way to Asheville before the last traces of darkness had given out.

"Did you stop by to pay respects to Colonel Deaver?" his father broke in. The Colonel Joseph Deaver that Thomas spoke of was the first citizen of Forks of Pigeon, the Haywood settlement embracing the rich farming grounds at the juncture of the east and west forks of the Pigeon River. Because Deaver was held in such high esteem by the local folk, he was reverently referred to as "The Colonel" and was one of their most popular political leaders. He was also proprietor of a mercantile store and a grain mill, both flourishing enterprises located just a few miles below the Edmunstons' place.

"No, I didn't stop. Didn't have time, it being late and all. I thought it best not to tarry," Basil replied. "But I ran into Columbus Hartgrove on the road thereabouts. He said to give you his regards and that he'll come up to see you sometime later this week, before you head back to the Fort."

Basil was referring to Fort Catawba, the moniker favored by the Edmunston family for their plantation home in Caldwell County—a magnificent manse and estate located on the site of an early frontier bastion of the colonial Indian fighters and patriots. And the inference from Basil's message was that his father aimed to return to Fort Catawba sometime soon. You see, Thomas Edmunston did not actually live at the Haywood County farm. Years ago, he had turned over control of the God-forsaken place in the heart of a mountain wilderness to overseers. As an absentee landlord, Thomas travelled to Forks of Pigeon only once or twice a year to settle outstanding debts, dun his debtors, and deal with issues that were beyond the authority or capacity of overseers.

Upon hearing Columbus Hartgrove's name, the elder Edmunston's eyebrows arched noticeably. Hartgrove was a youngish man, early thirties or so, and for the past seven years had been employed as an overseer of the Edmunstons' Haywood assets.

"He's a good man, Basil, Hartgrove is," responded Thomas to his son's message. "He's been one of my best overseers up here. Wish he could've stayed on with me, but I can't blame him one bit. Bought himself a good piece of river frontage below the Forks, and I expect him to make something out of it. He'll make a go of it, that's for sure."

Then peering caringly into his son's dark, walnut-brown eyes, Thomas offered up this sage fatherly advice. "Hartgrove will be one of those whose opinion you should seek in most matters, son. He can help straighten out some of the African vexations—attitudes and obedience difficulties, disputes, laziness, and such. He knows the tenants too—the good ones, the tolerable ones, and the bad ones. Knows the leases and the corn they should make, how much they ought to owe. Some of those farmers are contrary as the dickens—you yourself know that—and will try your patience a sight. But take care of them, son. You know we need good tenants. If you have to, then give them a little corn in the winter so they can get by. Hartgrove knows their property lines and where the fencing ought to be kept up. Knows our stock they are keeping. He has credited most of the men you will need to collect from. If you have dunning troubles, then he ought to be able to help you. Seek him out, Basil, and don't you be backwards about it. And, of course, Colonel Deaver can be of valuable assistance to you as well."

And so went the reunion that wintry night in the very same log cabin the father had constructed almost forty years before. Thomas Edmunston was turning over the Haywood farming operation to Basil. Turns out, it had all been settled just a short time before during the Christmas season.

When Hartgrove had resigned his overseer service, a new agent, one that could be completely trusted, was needed to manage the Edmunston's Haywood assets. These included more than five thousand acres of land along the East Fork River and a profusion of livestock of every variety—cattle, milk cows, horses, mules, oxen, hogs, sheep, geese, turkeys, chickens, ducks, guinea fowl, and more. A small population of thirteen slaves was quartered on the property to tend to these animals and to work the fields. The property was so expansive that eleven tenant farms were contracted out in various locations where the ground was suitable for raising grain crops and grazing stock.

Basil's two older brothers could not rightly be obliged to take over the overseer job. William had too many worries of his own. In addition to assisting his father at Fort Catawba, he had entered into speculative land deals in Alabama that required his presence in that state for months on end. And Walter had his own budding law practice that could not be forfeited or neglected. Since Colonel Deaver had been unable to recommend a local farmer from Forks of Pigeon as a suitable replacement for Hartgrove, Thomas had been left with little choice. He turned to his youngest son, who at that time was attending the state university at Chapel Hill.

Over the holidays, Thomas had sat Basil down and thoroughly explained the situation to him. Everything was at stake, he had said. Property taxes had to be made and paid, debts had to be settled, and stock and slaves had to be fed. It was Basil's familial duty, was the way his father had put it. And how could the son have refused the venerated father—one who meant so much to him and whose will and judgment were beyond question or reproach? Basil simply could not let his father down. He had no real choice in the matter.

Popular in school and a good student, Basil had been extremely distressed to return to Chapel Hill after Christmas to pick up his things and bid farewell to his professors and many friends. But he knew in his heart and mind that a return to the important academic studies was imminent—just as soon as his father could find and hire a proper overseer for Haywood. After all, that had been the promise Thomas had made to him. No rocks would be left unturned, the patriarch had allowed, in the pursuit of finding a real overseer to replace Hartgrove. But until the new overseer was found, Basil was "the man."

Thus Basil Edmunston found himself on this cold night in a foreboding cabin in the middle of nowhere. While his father patiently coached and methodically laid things out for him, Basil's mind raced to comprehend the reality of the situation. *Is this actually happening to me?* Filled with apprehension and more than a few doubts, he wondered whether he would be up to the task—this new duty of his—and could he ever hope to meet his father's expectations?

Chapter 2

Handing Over the Reins

The day after Basil's late-night arrival on the East Fork, he and his father set out on horseback and spent more than a full week inspecting the property and livestock, paying visits to the tenant farms, and searching for land boundaries and corners. Riding from daylight until dusk, they traveled to the furthest reaches of the Edmunston's vast Haywood farm and points in between.

Strictly speaking, the Haywood County farm that Basil was taking over could not rightly be called a "farm." It was so much more. The extensive land holdings belonging to Thomas Edmunston and his wife, Louisa, lay along the East Fork of the Pigeon River and amounted to more than five thousand acres. The couple had received most of the land as a wedding gift from Louisa's father, who had acquired vast acreages of Cherokee Indian land before the ink was dry on the treaties. The newlyweds had been excited to investigate their property endowment, which was secluded in the imposing dark mountains just west of Asheville. Soon after making an exploratory trip, Thomas and Louisa—along with a passel of slaves—settled there in 1807.

Their land was covered with verdant, virgin forests that climbed from both banks of the pristine river to rugged mountaintops towering thousands of feet high. For almost twenty years, Thomas and Louisa's heroic pioneering efforts toward raising livestock and corn and other grain crops on their Haywood land met with no financial gain. Yet they were successful at other pursuits, including raising a family. Louisa bore six children, including Basil, in a span of almost twenty years of seclusion on the East Fork. The frontier mother did her upmost to raise and educate the children in such a dreary, unpromising country—a land devoid of schools—where the children grew up as wild as Indians. And the pioneer Thomas became a political and militia leader in the county, who was elected several times to represent the county citizens in the State General Assembly.

But in 1826, shortly after Basil's birth, Thomas and Louisa were afforded a fortuitous opportunity to move back to Caldwell County. General William Edmunston, a Revolutionary War hero and a man with significant political influence in the state, had invited his son to return to the plantation homeplace and manage the estate's business affairs. Although Thomas had become a well-placed and respected man in Haywood County, he had proven to be a disappointing failure in producing monetary wealth from his and Louisa's valuable real estate and slave assets. So the Edmunston family happily made their escape from the mountains and fled back to Fort Catawba, leaving most of the slaves behind under the custody of overseers.

Some two decades had passed since Thomas had vacated the mountain property holdings that he and Basil were slogging across on horseback this day. For protection against the weather and road mire, both men wore frock-coats extending almost to their knees and wrapping their denim britches and heavy woolen shirts. Pants legs were stuffed into knee-high boots, and head coverings were pulled down tight against their ears. Loose strands of Basil's ebony hair fluttered in the wind as he peered under the low brim of his floppy gray felt hat. These two Edmunstons must have cut curious figures to those they encountered on the road. For the attire of many of the settlers on the East Fork, including several of the Edmunston's tenants, consisted of animal hides covering their bodies and little or nothing to protect their bare feet.

At the upriver extremity of the property, five or six miles from the Edmunstons' quarters, were established two tenants—Delaney Trull and Isaac Poston. Their lease holdings were on opposing sides of the river and comprised about two hundred acres of land each—mostly rocky, steep, and forest-covered acreage. The families were lodged in old log cabins built years before by previous tenants, and only small irregular patches cleared of trees were suitable for tilling and growing crops. Trull and Poston were contracted to raise corn in the clearings and tend Edmunston livestock grazing on their leased land. Similar contracts were in place with the remaining tenants upstream and downstream from the Edmunstons'—two Ivester brothers, a Burnette, Brookshire, Crawford, Pless, Davis, Miller, and Josiah Anderson.

On these visits to meet with the renters, the elder Edmunston made it plain to each of them that his son was the new landlord. Thomas explained that Basil would now be the man to deal with regarding any problems or issues that might arise. He gave them to understand that his son's word would carry the heavy weight of an Edmunston and thereby be final in all matters of judgment or dispute.

Josiah Anderson held the lease for what was called the "Crab Orchard farm," located on the north side of the river approximately three miles above the main Edmunston place. Deriving its name from the dense thickets of native crabapple trees that grew on the hillsides, the Crab Orchard tract was uncharacteristic of the East Fork land. It contained an expansive flood plain spreading from the river's edge to gentle slopes that rose gradually before converging with the heavily-forested crags. More than thirty acres of the farm's fertile alluvial soil had been cleared by the Edmunstons' slaves and previous tenants. Not only was this land tillable, but it was ideally suited for growing the grain crops that were so highly coveted and valued by mountaineer farmers. These valuable Crab Orchard acres held the most productive potential of any of the tenant leases. Yet Josiah Anderson and his two sons invariably produced disappointing yields.

After their cursory meeting with the Andersons, Thomas cautioned his son as they rode away from the Crab Orchard, "Keep an eye on that outfit, Basil. Anderson has given Hartgrove fits ever since he gained the lease five years ago. Hartgrove says Josiah and those rough boys of his are contrary to deal with and come up with all manner of excuses for their piddling production and excessive stock losses. He gave up on them last fall and advised me not to keep them on. Well, I guess I bucked him when I decided to give Anderson another year on his contract, though I did send word to Josiah that it would be his last chance to make something. So then, see what you can do with that bunch, son."

After taking a long moment to consider this gloomy message, Basil replied, "Of course, Father. I'll do my best, sir." While nodding to his father an affirmation of his good intentions, Basil could not help thinking to himself that if the almighty Hartgrove failed to get Josiah Anderson to fulfill his contract, then how for heaven's sake was he supposed to do it? Josiah Anderson had seemed all right to him. But those two sons of his, Jesse and Manson, who lived in separate quarters at the Crab Orchard with families of their own, seemed a surly breed. Both were a few years older than Basil. They had remained sullen and quiet during the brief meeting, and neither had looked Basil straight in the eyes when he shook their hands. As Thomas and Josiah conferred on the upcoming planting season and the plowing that would have to get started sometime soon, Basil noticed the young Andersons' smirking glances and the cruel grins formed by their tobacco-smeared mouths. Basil did his best to ignore them as he focused on the several commitments Josiah was readily making to his father. But he had a bad feeling about those two. They gave all appearances of being shiftless and irresponsible. For sure, they did not seem like the kind that could be trusted, and Basil figured he would have to be wary of any dealings with them.

"The old schoolhouse building on the Crab Orchard property, Father—is it still being used?"

The query seemingly sparked some life into Thomas, and he animatedly replied, "Oh, yes. This winter's term just finished up, and I'm told there were about fourteen or fifteen scholars. Still having preaching over there, too, almost every Sunday. About once a month, one or another of the Methodist preachers comes up from Forks of Pigeon or the church down around Pigeon River Ford and conducts a service. On the other Sabbaths, Delaney Trull reads from the Bible for those dedicated enough to stand it. He's a hard-core religious enthusiast you're going to find out, but he's not all bad, though. They have quite a crowd most Sundays, I hear."

"The building looked pretty well kept up to me," Basil noted.

"It sure as well should. Couple of years back, Columbus Hartgrove had a carpenter that lives below Osborne—Blalock is his name—put a new roof on it. Set me back twenty dollars, it did!"

"Well from the looks of the place, you got your money's worth. Who's the schoolmarm these days? Still that old Pless woman?"

"Don't know for sure, but I believe it might have been Anderson's daughter this winter. Hear tell she'll be in confinement before long and, far as I know, she's not married. Too bad."

"Hmm, that's interesting," Basil mused as he reflected on the Anderson menfolk he had just met, especially those two shifty sons. But he had not seen the daughter about anywhere.

During the evenings in the shadows of the poorly-lit cabin, both father and son sat together at the dining table and ciphered for hours. Over the hand-hewn chestnut boards, they spread all the tenant contracts and reviewed what each leaser had agreed to pay to live on their land. Because all of the lease-holders owed a share of the corn crop to the Edmunstons, Thomas instructed Basil to split the crops by using wagon loads as a metric. He told his son to always make sure the wagons are filled alike and to be sure to share proportionately the best corn and the worst frostbitten corn.

They also reviewed survey plats, poured over ledger books, and discussed future plans for the farm. Basil received specific directions on feeding the stock and was instructed to pay particular attention to the salting troughs, stable doors, gates, fences, grain and fodder stacks, corn cribs, shuck pens, blacksmith shop, and on and on. No details were left out, and nothing was left unsaid—at least twice—was Basil's impression of those intense sessions.

The cruel winter weather abated somewhat during that period Thomas Edmunston was handing over the overseer reins to his son. On the eve of the vernal equinox, sunshine spilled across the East Fork valley, rousing the sap and warming the blood of everything that lived and grew within the sprawling watershed. Although not yet making their appearance in the lowland regions, the bears, ravenous from a long sleep, were beginning to stir and exit their winter lairs. Scrubby rhododendron bushes that sprawled across the rocky ridges were unfurling their tightly clutched evergreen leaves. And the mountain laurels that huddled along the damp creek banks and dark coves were at last thawing and stretching out stiff green-leafed limbs.

Sprinkled everywhere throughout the hardwood bottoms, early wild flowers began to push their teeny heads out of the leaf-covered, earthen floor. Patches of tiny bloodroot bloomed, with its delicate white petals remindful of the traces of snow that still lingered on the north sides of the mountains and wherever the sun's radiance had not yet reached. Wild leeks, called ramps, were shoving long green leaves out of the deciduous forests' rich moist ground. The ramps' subterranean onion-like bulbs, distinguished by a pungent biting aroma, would soon be dug up and heartily consumed by the East Fork farmers seeking a nutritional tonic for the long, harsh winter without vegetables and greens.

Most of the forest canopies were still leafless, but tiny buds were beginning to appear on limbs slowly flushing with sap. The mountain dogwoods and crabapples were yet to flower, but in the orchard above the Edmunstons' log cabin the peach trees were beginning to blush with pink blossoms. Spring was erupting all over the East Fork, and planting season was not far off.

As Thomas Edmunston readied himself for departure and a hard day's ride to Asheville, he could not resist imparting more wise counsel to Basil. "Now remember, son, don't confine yourself too closely to these quarters. Get out. Go to preaching and other places. Enlarge your acquaintances, and hear the opinions and transactions of the neighbors."

"Don't worry, sir. I'll go to preaching every Sunday," Basil responded while he steadied the horse as his father struggled to mount it. He had felt guilty before the words were even out of his mouth. Although he was raised to fear God and was compelled to place an unquestioned faith in Christ and the Bible's teachings, Basil's devoutness ran shallow. At an early age, he had worked out that there surely must be a God or some other omnificent entity responsible for creating the marvelous and perplexing world he lived in. There could be no other explanation, he had reasoned. Nature, human beings, and the limitless universe were far too complex to have simply occurred randomly. And how else could he rationalize his own existence—his intellect, his thoughts and feelings, the smells and sights that continuously flooded his being, and even the breath of life and inevitability of death? Only a Supreme Creator could have produced such unexplainable intangibles he believed.

Over the years as Basil's mind matured and as he gained life experience, he began to harbor weighty doubts concerning the doctrines of Christianity. His mother and father were faithful Methodists, and Basil himself had strived to abide with Methodism as well. But the ministers he was accustomed to hearing could not reach him with their carrot-and-stick, heaven-and-hell orations. Their sermons fell woefully short of explaining or justifying the sufferings and injustices and the sadness and sorrow that existed in the world. And thus far, no amount of ranting or agitating or inciting or trembling by evangelical pastors at churches and camp meeting revivals had convinced Basil of the veracity of Biblical tales and Christian dogma. He was as lost spiritually as he was physically in the East Fork wilderness.

All but one of the slaves, who happened to be sick in bed, crowded around the father and son to wish their master a good journey. "Goodbye, Massa Thomas. You has youself a good trip now, you hears us?" said one. And another rejoined, "We's gonna be fine, Massa. Now don't you worries youself none 'bout us." Still another chimed, "You gots to come back to us real soon." All of the Edmunstons' Africans were excited and jabbering, and they crowded ever closer and closer. They respected their master because he was a good man. He treated them fairly, for the most part, and had always looked after their comforts and welfare.

As Thomas slowly rode out of the throng, he contorted his body and turned his head in an effort to see his son one last time. "Remember to write me every two weeks, Basil, and oftener in case of unexpected occurrences. Good luck, son!" Then he turned back around, spurred his horse, and began descending the hillside toward the river road.

Basil watched his father ride away and disappear around the bend in the road. As he did, a growing twang of anxiousness began to overcome him. The burdens of control and management of the immense Haywood property holdings were now his to bear and his alone. He was now the Master of the

East Fork. His family's expectations were high, he knew that for sure. *Maybe they were too high,* Basil thought. *What in hell have I gotten myself into?*

Before, there had never been a lack of self-confidence in the young Edmunston. Conversely, he was extremely comfortable within his own skin—tall, lanky, strong, and uncommonly handsome. And early on, he sensed that the girls seemed a mite partial to him. But as of yet, he had not taken a liking to anyone special of the female gender, except, that is, a cousin he had once danced with at a party. Something about her had sure been different though—her smell, the texture of her hair, those rouge-colored lips, her shapely body. He could not rightly figure it out. Whatever it was, it got him all stirred up inside. Primal feelings from deep within his body had oozed into the cells and fibers of his midsection and invaded his heart and being. Strange urges had battled to take control. He had not understood those yearning sensations or what they meant, other than there was a curiously pleasurable feeling about them. But those feelings had not lasted long. His peculiar expressions, flushed face, and odd behavior soon gave away his afflicted condition to friends. Immediately noticing something different about him, they began hooting and hollering and funning so much that the baffling urges retreated to their mysterious origins.

Basil was not self-centered by any means. On the contrary, he made great efforts to distract attention from himself and divert it elsewhere. Neither could it be said that his personality was flamboyant or arrogant. Restrained would more aptly describe his demeanor and approach to others. And he had no patience with those who dandied about or flaunted their cock feathers, so to speak. He preferred to conceal his own convictions that he was smarter or better than those around him and contrived to have them think just the opposite.

Confidence is one thing—over-confidence is quite another, and Basil would not suffer accusation of the latter. He had enough confidence in himself to believe he actually could run his father's plantation. However, believing and doing are two very singular things. Obviously Basil was no stranger to farming, having worked in the fields behind plows and horse teams for years. But that was something different. Usually his father, brothers, or one of the slaves had simply told him what to do and why, and he had complied with their orders. Now it was going to be up to Basil to determine what crops would be planted, when and how it was to be done, and who would do it. Come harvest time, it would be "the young master" who decided when to pick the corn and mow the wheat and oats. It would be his responsibility to ensure that this valuable grain production was processed as efficiently as possible and utilized to the greatest benefit and value to his father's farming enterprise.

The large population of livestock was still another matter. The animals had to be bred, fed, corralled, milked, pampered, doctored, slaughtered, and sold—all requiring timely decision-making and communications. Every single day, including Sabbaths, it would be up to Basil to issue precise and firm instructions to the slaves on what had to be done. It would be his responsibility—his alone—to impart these judgments and orders such that his father would realize a profit.

Finally, there were the tenant farms that fell under his general oversight. Basil had an inherent obligation to treat all of his father's lease-holders fairly, but they must meet their contractual obligations and provide reasonable stewardship of the Edmunstons' property. It would be up to him to see that they did just that.

Essentially, it all boiled down to the fact that Basil's management of the slaves, crops, stock, and tenants must yield an income that exceeded expenses and taxes. He would be looked to for all the decisions, and he would be giving out the orders. Those were his father's expectations, and that was his familial duty. His father had said so. Basil had the Edmunston name to uphold. He was proud of his name, and he wanted his family to be proud of him. His father believed in him. But as much as Basil believed in himself, he knew that until he got the gist of the thing—of being the Master of the East Fork—he would just have to do the best he could. After all, what else could he do?

Chapter 3

A Masterful Meeting

Basil dubiously studied the interior of his new rustic quarters and wondered whether he would ever become accustomed to the place. His father's slaves had constructed the cabin out of poplar logs way back in the early 1800's. It was a small, rustic structure, only eighteen feet by twelve feet, but it was plenty stout to resist the worst of the East Fork winter ravages. Peering through one of the window openings, he surveyed his surroundings. Just below the cabin, at the foot of the hill, he could see the spring, which was surrounded by a small log structure to keep out the livestock and other varmints. Not far removed from this springhouse were two log corn cribs and a shuck pen. On the other side of a trickling creek sprawled various other log buildings and infrastructure. These included two small cabins inhabited by the slaves, the barn and stables, smokehouse, blacksmith shop, chicken coop, hog pens and slop troughs, dog pen, and several stock corrals fenced with split-wood rails. There were also a couple of privies on the property, one of which was dedicated exclusively for the master's personal convenience.

As Basil stepped away from the window his eyes began to roam the interior space of his new habitat again. He could not fathom the time when his mother and father lived there with six children, including himself. He had been barely six months old when his parents vacated the cabin and moved back to Fort Catawba, so he harbored no recollections of the depressing place. However, now that he was going to be confined there for some time—at least until his father found another suitable overseer—Basil resolved to make it into a comfortable home for himself. And what better way to start sprucing up than to give these old dreadful quarters a proper name?

His father had always referred to the Haywood accommodations as "the poplar cabin" in his correspondence with the extended family. Just that—the poplar cabin—with seemingly no sentimental attachment whatsoever to the frontier home where he and his large family lived. Well, Basil figured he could surely come up with a better name than that. So he began to entertain several romantic and inspired notions, including "Bachelor Hall" and "Bachelor's Retreat." Finally though, after much deep consideration, he came to favor the moniker "Bachelor's Den." *That should do nicely*, Basil thought, as the slave cook, Patsy, interrupted his private deliberations. Carrying a tin plate stacked with food, the old woman placed it on the dining table.

"Here's you's brekfest, Massa Baz—it be bacon and cornbread. Can I gits you some milk to drink?"

"No thanks, Patsy. I think I'll just have some fresh water. By the way, I've thought of a new name for these here quarters. What do you think of the name Bachelor's Den?"

Looking a little befuddled, she pondered on the question for a long moment before replying, "Oh, I don't knows, Massa—I don't rightly knows. Why, what do's 'batslers' mean, anyhows?"

"That's 'bachelor's', Patsy, 'bachelor's'. It means a man that's not married. I'm a bachelor because I don't have a wife. And these quarters of mine—this cabin—is like a bear's den, it seems to me. I'm all denned up in here. So that's why I aim to call it Bachelor's Den."

Patsy looked at Basil right serious-like and then broke into a beaming smile, "Yessa, Massa. I sees now. I sees. So you's gonna holes up here in dis here cabin jus' like dem ole bears do's in da wintertime?"

"You've got it, Patsy. This will be my den where I'll hole up," Basil replied, feeling somewhat confident of Patsy's general understanding and appreciation of the new name.

"Yessa, Massa Baz. But dem bears don't eats when dey be holed up in dem dens—do's dey now? I 'spect you's gonna still want somethin' 'nother to eat. Dat 'bout right, Massa?"

Feeling somewhat baffled, Basil just looked at the slave cook and nodded to confirm that he would also be eating in the cabin.

"And whur 'bouts you's gonna lives when it ain't da wintertime, Massa?"

Basil's first independent management act as Master of the East Fork was an attempt to communicate with his Africans as a group. He wanted to explain to them how things were going to be now that he was taking over the farm, and he intended to outline a few expectations to boot. So, the anxious Basil assembled all of his slaves in front of Bachelor's Den to have a little talk with them.

"Massa Baz, you's our massa now, ain't you?"

"That's right, Jacob," the young master replied, not yet being accustomed to the title "Massa" his slaves used to address him.

"Well, Massa, dis be's all of us, 'cept my Jenny. She still be's sick and bedded."

Basil knew most of his father's Africans. Basically there were two families of them living at the Haywood farm, although from time to time, the slaves were transferred back and forth to the Fort. Jacob and Jenny, a married middle-aged couple, had three children: Lark, Rebecca, and Harry. Jacob's mother, Patsy, was now more than sixty years old and had been the cook for years. Lizzie was Jenny's younger sister who had never married, even though she had one daughter, Avaline, still living with her. The other family was headed by Jake and Caroline, who were also married—not a given with slave couples. Jake was a blacksmith, a pretty good one at that, and had a shop near the barn. The couple had three sons working with them on the East Fork: Uriah, Gabe, and Erwin. One of their daughters had relocated to the Fort, and the other had been sold to an Edmunston cousin in Burke County, whereupon she was allowed to marry another slave.

All of the slaves were dressed in shabby, worn, homespun work clothes made by their own hands. Lizzie and Avaline had spun and woven the flax and sheep's wool into a coarse linsey-woolsey cloth. Using patterns brought from the Fort, they, along with Jenny, had fashioned pants and shirts for the male slaves and simple dresses for the females. Most of the men and boys were bareheaded this time of the year. But each of the women had colorful scarfs wrapping their heads to cover their coarse, matted hair. With the exception of Harry and Erwin, who were barefoot, the slaves wore crude, low-cut brogans that Jake had crafted at the wooden last in his shop.

Basil noticed that the little dog that had tailed him from Pigeon River Ford had taken up with Harry. The boy was teasing and playing with the lively hound—picking it up to show to the others, rolling it over on its back, and rubbing its belly. The dog was growling and barking, and Harry was laughing as the others looked on with restrained amusement. One heckler spoke out, "You's bes' watch out, son. You's gonna git bit. Dat li'l dog's gonna eat you's up."

Basil raised his voice slightly to be heard over the commotion and began the meeting with a response to Jacob's attendance report, "OK, thanks, Jacob. I'll get by to check on Jenny directly. Now, I've called all of you together so that I can let you know what to expect from me as your new master. I don't know how you got along with Hartgrove, but—"

All of a sudden, the teenaged Harry let loose of the dog and broke in, "Massa Hartgrove, he wus good to us, Massa. He shore wus. Ain't nobody can speaks nothin' diff'rent 'bout him, no suh. But he don't thinks much 'bout da way we's manures da fields."

Basil quickly tried to regain control of the meeting, "Well, I don't know how you've been going about manuring the fields, Harry, but—"

"Oh, we's do's it right, now, Massa. Yessa, we's do's," Harry again interjected. "But Massa Hartgrove, he says to us dat we's don't plows in da manure good and deep. He says to us to plow it so's it never be's seen agin. But, Massa Baz, we's do plows it so's nobody sees it agin." And then Harry pointed dramatically to a freshly-plowed field below them, "Lookit yonder at dat bottom field. Can you sees da manure? Don't dat look manured good?"

And in this manner, Basil's first get-together meeting with his slaves began. Gabe, who appeared to Basil to be about his own age, allowed that they were hard up for bacon. "Massa Baz, we's all been talkin' 'bout how much bacon we's gits to eat. Three pounds don't do me no time, and dat's all I gits in a week. And deese here female folks don't gits but two pounds. Don't seem right, somehows. Whut's you thinks 'bout dat?"

Basil did not know what he thought about Gabe's grievance but remembered that the portions mentioned seemed to be in line with the ones his mother used at the Fort. "I'm sorry, Gabe, but you don't look like you've been starving to death. Father says you're the briskest rail-splitter on the river, and I don't doubt it a bit by the looks of you." Thinking that witty retort might give Gabe something to reflect upon and keep him quiet, Basil began to talk about the spring planting plans. But Gabe was hardly satisfied and would not be put off so easily. He quickly interrupted his master.

"Dat's right, Massa. I be's da bestest splitter 'round here 'bouts. Ain't no one's gonna says nothin' diff'rent, I 'spect. But you sees, I be's da strongest and works mo' harder dan da others. Dat's why I needs me mo' bacon, Massa. You sees dat?

Damn it to hell. He's not going to let that bone go, Basil thought, and he strained his intellectual capacity to formulate an answer to Gabe's challenge. The thing was, Basil believed there might possibly be some truth in Gabe's argument. But he knew he was not going to settle this dispute now in front of every African he had. What could he say to Gabe, and the others, that would be credible yet not sound patronizing? Clearing his throat first, he moved over closer to Gabe so that he could speak more directly to him.

"I see what you're saying, Gabe. You probably know, just as all of you know, that the bacon and meal portions allowed here on this farm are the same as those at Fort Catawba. I've not been on here long enough to closely monitor your affairs, but you can be sure that I will see that the food quantities given out here are the same as those used at the Fort. And, Gabe, getting to your point, I will study and judge if the Fort's portions are fair and adequate. Or let me put it this way, if I see that you are outworking everybody else consistently, day in and day out, as you say you are, then trust me—I will make an equitable adjustment to your proportion."

Basil was certainly no Solomon, and he knew that he was in perilous territory talking about changes to the slaves' food allowances. For years, his mother had meticulously measured and worked out the quantities of bacon and meal to be given to the slaves at the Fort. There would certainly be grave repercussions in the African community there if he allowed the Haywood slaves more. And if he increased Gabe's allowance and not the other Haywood slaves, then there was sure to be a revolt within his own quarters. He determined to proceed slowly and deliberately with this issue and possibly even seek Columbus Hartgrove's advice on the matter.

Gabe nodded his head and decided to drop the subject for the time being, replying simply, "Yessa, Massa Baz. I shore 'preciates it."

In Basil's unusual gathering with his slaves, the topics varied greatly and ranged from the enlightening conversation with Harry on manuring fields and the quantity of bacon allowed to the slaves to eat every week to the number of bushels of corn to be ground into meal each week, and whether or not one of the male slaves would be permitted to walk to Colonel Deaver's store on Saturdays to buy chewing tobacco, and on and on. Basil discovered that he was not comfortable speaking in front of the slaves as a group, and unfortunately he never regained his composure following the initial manure business. After about an hour of mostly listening, he finally adjourned the Africans, with the final words not being his own but those of the ever inquisitive and youthful Harry.

"Ain't no one's ever gives a meetin' with us like dis here one, Massa Baz. We's all be's mighty thankful to you. Jus' lets us know when you wants to do's it agin. And, Massa Baz, any times you wants to go down and sees how good we's manured dem fields b'low, jus' says so. I be's real proud to show you."

Chapter 4

Struck by the Belle

That afternoon after the meeting with the slaves, Basil had one of them saddle-up his horse and bring it to the cabin. "Thank you, Uriah. Tell Patsy I'll be back by dark, and she should have something prepared for me to eat about then. Oh, and remind her not to let the fire go out."

"Yessa, Massa Baz. I'll do it fo' shore. Oh, Massa Baz, Jake knows you be goin' to da store. Don't know how he knows, but he knows. And he axes me to axe you if you'll bring him a twist of tobacco. He gives me da money to give you."

Basil put out his hand for the money and at the same time boasted to Uriah about the fine horse he was about to mount. "What do you think of Fashion, Uriah? She's a beauty, isn't she. Father gave her to me last year to take to the University."

"She shore 'nough is, Massa. Fashion, huh? Must be 'bout what—fo', five year old? Dat 'bout right?"

"Almost four. Father gave her the name. He thought she was about the prettiest foal that had ever been born around the Fort. With this light chestnut color of hers and her white blaze and sock markings, he thought she was bound to be a fashion-setter around Caldwell County. Before you know it, he was calling her 'Fashion,' and the name stuck. She sits good and canters real smooth-like. Still spooks a sight around water though, but I expect there's enough water around here that she ought to get over her scariness directly."

Uriah and his family had lived at Fort Catawba years ago, and Basil had gotten to know him pretty well then. The two of them had worked alongside each other in the kitchen garden and on occasions had whiled away precious leisure time fishing at the family's millpond. Uriah was one of the few Edmunston slaves who could read and write a little bit, and over time Basil had developed a high level of trust and respect for him.

"See you later," Basil said with a tip of his slouch hat to Uriah. Then he clicked his tongue twice and gently kicked his spurs into Fashion's flanks, and the horse and rider broke for the river road leading toward Forks of Pigeon.

Basil aimed to call on Colonel Joseph Deaver and pay his respects. After all, his father and Deaver had been the closest of friends ever since Thomas Edmunston's pioneering days on the East Fork. And Basil's father had impressed heavily on him the idea that the Colonel's advice and assistance would be of extreme value. Although Joseph had had little schooling as a youth, he had managed to learn to read and cipher. And with that meager educational foundation and his keen native intellect, he became one of the most prosperous men in the region.

Colonel Deaver had two grown-up sons and a daughter who had already been married off. There was yet another daughter that Basil could remember meeting years ago. He thought she was a tad younger than he was, and his father had recently mentioned in passing that the young Deaver girl was now the belle of Forks of Pigeon. On this trip, Basil meant to see what he allowed about the girl too.

Striding into the store, Basil immediately spotted Colonel Deaver, who was busy assisting a customer. They were towards the back examining an item in the leather-goods section, where bridles, harness riggings, saddles, saddle bags, and other such items were displayed on the shelves. Electing not to interrupt the Colonel's business, Basil began browsing the premises, taking in the myriad fragrances and inspecting the merchandise.

He noted that wood logs were ablaze in the enormous fireplaces at the store's flanks. The smell of smoked meat emanated from the section where bacon hams, sides of beef, and jerky were hanging from the wall and rafters, wafting throughout the building. Hand tools of every imaginable description were scattered over display shelving. There were hatchets, axes, froes, adzes, augers, hammers, wedges, chisels, awls, hoes, spades, picks, rakes, saws, wooden helves, and many other such items. Smoking and chewing tobacco filled a wooden bin in a corner near the pickle barrel, where deer and bear skins were tacked to the wall. Still another area of the store was dedicated to the home textile industry and contained bolts of dyed and undyed fabrics, hand-woven from local sheep's wool and flax. Other imported linens, coarse denim cloths, sewing and knitting needles, scissors, thimbles, spools of thread, skeins of yarn, and iron and wooden parts for spinning wheels and looms could be found in the bins alongside the linens.

Several rows of shelves and cabinetry filled the center section of the store and were stocked with coffee beans, seeds, local food items, honey, salt, varieties of spices, herbs, a large selection of hard candy, feathers, and iron fabrications such as nails, pails, kettles, buckets, and shoe lasts. And along the back wall could be found larger implements, including plowshares, chains, hooks, single and double trees, and several wooden pulleys of varying sizes. Just about anything and everything the locals might need was carried in Colonel Deaver's inventory.

Basil had taken up a folding knife from one of the counters and was intent on prying open its blades for a look when suddenly a hushed voice from behind startled him. "Hello there, can I help you?"

He turned quickly to see who it was and to respond, but for some reason, just froze in a trance. A girl was looking straight at him, grinning with a quizzical look on her face as if she knew him. Basil did not recognize her at first and was utterly taken aback by the girl's striking appearance. Recovering his senses in a moment, he smiled back and answered almost shyly, "Oh, no! No thanks. I was just waiting for Colonel Deaver and wanted to speak to him."

Can this be the Colonel's daughter? It has to be. No more than eighteen or nineteen, he figured, and such a beauty. Her hair was the color of golden wild honey and styled in a tight bun in back of her head. She was about middling height, making her more than half a foot shorter than Basil. Although she wore a blue calico dress that concealed all but her head and shoes, he could not help but admire the wonderful shape of the dress's contours and curves—it was downright pleasing to him.

Breaking the spell he was under, the perky girl asked, "You're Basil Edmunston, aren't you?" She was still grinning, and her eyes scanned him from head to foot.

He had regained his composure somewhat and, still smiling, replied, "Yes. That would be me. And let's see, I'll venture to say you are Colonel Deaver's daughter, right?"

"Yes. Julia Deaver," she replied with a slight giggle. "I'm so very pleased to meet you, Basil. My father told me you had moved here from Caldwell County."

Chuckling himself, Basil replied, "Indeed I have. The newest resident of Forks of Pigeon, I reckon, and Master of the East Fork, they call me. God help us all."

Julia laughed with him, surprised at the witty retort and appreciative of an inner charm that the handsome boy was reluctant to reveal. Within a minute or two, Colonel Deaver came over and interrupted their banter.

"Ah, lad, how ere ye? Yer father allowed hows ye would come down to see me."

Although the storekeeper was relatively affluent compared with his highland neighbors, Basil noted his heavy dialect. The Colonel's pronunciations were not much different from the other locals', there being a strong hint of Scotch-Irish ancestry in his speech.

"Doing well, sir. Father and I were busy this past week going over things and looking in on all the tenants, and I didn't have a chance to come down sooner. I'm feeling a little overwhelmed, to tell the truth."

"No, no. Now don't ye fear none atall. We're neighbors and friends and have to look ater one another, now don't we?" Deaver reassured him. "Any troubles ye can't handle alone, ye come see me. We'll help ye, me and Columbus Hartgrove and some of the others will."

A patron strolled in and walked over to the area of the store that was dedicated to postal business. Excusing herself, Julia bid goodbye to Basil but encouraged him to come visit again soon. "Now don't be a stranger around here, Basil, you hear? Oh! Why don't you join us for church service this Sunday—the Methodist Church just on the other side of the river? There will be a dinner-on-the-ground afterwards. We'll feed you and introduce you to all of our friends."

Feeling elated at the prospect yet somewhat shaken by the tingling primal urges flowing around on his insides, Basil gushed back at Julia, "Sure, that sounds fine to me. I might just take you up on it. What time does preaching begin?"

"Ten o'clock. Reverend Smathers from the Dutch settlement will be up, and his sermons normally don't last more than a couple of hours," Julia replied as her father looked on with an amused smile.

"I'll be there, then. Thanks, Julia." As the girl turned and walked away toward the post office, Basil thought that maybe his father was right after all—about a couple of things. One, the Deaver girl was indeed something to look at. Anyone could see that. And, two, just as Thomas had advised him, Basil could appreciate now that it might not be such a bad idea to go to preaching so as to enlarge his circle of acquaintances. *This Sunday might not be a bad time to start enlarging!*

The Colonel and Basil sauntered over to the corner near the pickle barrel, where a few chairs were placed for patrons to take respite. These were situated among the whittling residue and close to a spittoon, which was surrounded by a large slick of spent tobacco coating the puncheon floor. They sat down, Basil and the Colonel did, and talked for a good long while. Only on a couple of occasions when Julia needed the Colonel's assistance with a customer was their conversation broken.

Refusing a chaw of twisted tobacco, Basil asked the Colonel's opinion of a couple of the tenants, Alfred Crawford and Josiah Anderson, and he got his ears filled. And the Colonel told Basil where to find another man who owed fifty dollars on a receipt of corn, and he even advised Basil on how best to approach the debtor. Basil had left one of the African women, Jenny, grunting, and after hearing a thorough explanation of her ailments, the Colonel pronounced a prognosis and offered recommendations for curing her. Regarding some surplus bacon hams left over in the Edmunstons' smokehouse, the Colonel allowed how he could take them. And so the unlikely pair talked about such matters for almost two hours as they sized each other up and established the foundations for a friendly, trusting relationship.

As the time wore on, Basil grew more relaxed and confident and was manifestly impressed with Deaver. The Colonel himself was surprised at the earnestness and eagerness that Basil demonstrated and the meticulous details he sought. Also, Deaver was struck by the boy's keen intellect and demeanor. Most certainly, the young man's physical bearing and handsome features were not lost on the astute merchant. *If Basil Edmunston proves to be an honest, forthright man—one who demonstrates fortitude and conviction and fairness in his dealings with the neighbors and tenants—then perhaps he might be a suitable match for Julia,* the Colonel considered. He would have to ponder on it more, but he thought it could be so.

Basil also wondered about the potential for a match, as he rode Fashion in a slow, steady walk back up the river road to Bachelor's Den. He was excited about meeting Julia and thought she was about as fair a girl as he had ever seen—at least more beautiful than any of the Caldwell County girls he was acquainted with. The lonely, faint call of a wolf high up on the mountain side roused him from the romantic musing spell, and he turned his mind to the immediate challenges ahead.

It was already early April, and the preparations for planting had hardly begun. Basil had to get the boys stirred up and working. The same could be said about the tenants, and his thoughts immediately fell on the Anderson clan, with no little amount of trepidation. First thing tomorrow morning he aimed to ride out to Crab Orchard and pay them a visit.

Chapter 5

Barefoot Beauty

Basil and Fashion had gotten off to an early start on this morning. As they approached the Crab Orchard property, he gazed toward the largest field where there was no evidence of farming activity. It was a cold morning, and as the sun peeked over the eastern mountains the frosty field glistened brilliantly. However, it lay fallow and desolate—just as it had been when Basil and his father had visited with Anderson more than a week before. Several smaller clearings lay in the same state, each spotted with corn stubble and grown over with sporadic clumps of wild green grasses and weeds. No cover crops had been planted, and the fields had obviously not been worked or touched since last fall's harvest.

Anderson's old log cabin was perched on a rise away from the river and overlooking a small tributary creek. As Basil rode up, he spied a young woman outside in the morning sunshine, busily working at a spinning wheel. It was a large walking wheel, and as the spinner stood alongside and slowly worked at it Basil easily made out that not only was she barefooted, but she was heavy with child. *This must be Anderson's daughter, the schoolmarm,* he surmised as he quickly took her measure. She was tall and well-formed. Sunlight glistened off her long, sable locks, which fell smooth and straight well below her shoulders. She was dressed plainly yet neatly in homespun, her ample breasts and extended belly stretching the coarse fabric to its limits. It was apparent to Basil that her baby was due anytime right about now.

"Hello, there!" Basil called out in a slightly raised voice as he slowly rode closer and closer, not bothering to dismount.

Apparently the lovely spinner had not noticed his approach. Startled, she looked up from her work uneasily. Then regaining her composure somewhat, she replied, "Oh! Hello—I didn't hear you ride up." One hand immediately rose to conceal her long hair that hung so suggestively free.

"Sorry to surprise you like that. I'm Basil Edmunston. Is Mr. Anderson about anywhere?"

"No. Father's down at the barn with my brothers, I'm afraid. Don't believe they're up to much good this morning," she said, knowing that the three men were hung over from a long night's drinking spree. She had heard much talk of Basil from her father and brothers. Talk about how this young rich Edmunston boy was taking over his father's farm and was going to manage the tenant properties. "Sorry I'm such a mess. I wasn't expecting visitors so early this morning," she apologized, abandoning all efforts to hide her hair.

"Altha, who's that ye're talking to?" snapped a voice from inside the cabin walls. Before Altha had a chance to reply, an older woman impatiently poked her head through the door and then shuffled out into the sunlight to see for herself. With her eyes almost squinted closed, the old woman peeked out from a deeply wrinkled face to get a look at who was in the yard. She was unkempt and dressed in ragged homespun draped with a dirty apron. The woman's gray uncombed hair and haggard worn looks made her appear far more ancient than her fifty-odd years.

"Hello, ma'am. I've come here to see Mr. Anderson," Basil said as politely as he knew how.

"Mother, this is Basil Edmunston," replied the spinner, as she turned toward Basil, "and I'm Althea, Basil, but 'most everybody in these parts calls me Altha."

Before he could mutter a nicety, the mother said in a low, slow voice as she crept ever closer toward Basil, "So ye're him, huh? It's good t' meet ye, son. My man says that ye're taking over fer Hartgrove. Well, good riddance is all I kin say. Always pushing and worrying us, he was. Hain't got nary good thing to say 'bout him. You checking up on my man this morning, are ye?"

"No, no," Basil replied hastily with a chuckle, trying to make light of the thinly veiled accusation. "I just came up to talk about some farming business and to see if Mr. Anderson needs anything."

Scowling at him, she responded, "Huh. I doubt ye're gonna git much outta him this morning, son, but ye're welcome to try. Nice meeting ye." Then she ducked back into the cabin as quickly as she had come out.

Basil and Altha just looked at each other for a brief moment without saying a word, one appraising the other. He reckoned she was not much older than he was, but she seemed so much more mature and, well, grown-up. And she had such a pleasant manner about her—or maybe it was just the kind way she acted. For Altha's part, she could not get over what a handsome figure this stranger struck, sitting on his reddish horse, hat in hand, and his dark mane blowing about in the morning breeze. *How knightly he looks*, she thought, *even with that several-days-old scraggly beard he's sporting.* But she took nothing for granted and wondered what kind of man he really was.

Altha's ears had been filled with her father's poor opinions of the Edmunstons. Josiah had told them all, "Basil Edmunston ain't gonna be no different than his father nor that no-good overseer Hartgrove they employed." He had also remarked to just about anybody who would listen to him, "It sure 'nough is a fact that Thomas Edmunston has imposed on the people of the East Fork and hain't helped nary no one get their own land fer support."

"Why, them Edmunstons," Josiah had allowed, "serve us like the boy did his master's monkey. When his master told the boy to cut off the monkey's tail, what do you think the boy did? Why, he begun at the end of the tail and proceeded to chop it off little piece by little piece. Yessir, little piece by little piece. The boy allowed that he was afeared to kill the monkey if he cut off the whole tail at once." And Josiah Anderson had likened Basil to that same boy and allowed that the young Edmunston was not going to help no one get their own land, just like Papa Edmunston had prevented them from bettering themselves.

Finally Basil broke the trance he and Altha had slipped into. "When's your baby due?"

"Two, three weeks, best I can figure. It won't be too soon either."

"Ha, I'll say," Basil responded with a chuckle. Not able to resist a temptatious curiosity, he then went on to ask, "You and your husband live about here somewhere?" He remembered his father had thought the girl was unmarried, and he meant to find out about the baby's father.

Altha paused, obviously uncomfortable with the question. Then looking straight at Basil, who remained mounted on his horse, she replied, "I'm staying here for the time being. My husband's not with us anymore." With a deep breath she turned, looked into the distance, and offered only this explanation, "He was killed in a logging accident shortly after we were married."

"Oh, I didn't know. I'm so sorry." Searching for the right words to say, Basil hurriedly jumped down off Fashion. Then leading the horse closer to Altha, whose gaze had turned toward her cold bare feet, he attempted to refocus her thoughts in another direction. "Althea—sorry, Altha, I hope everything turns out okay with your confinement. I mean, I hope it will go smoothly and all." Still stumbling for a coherent, sensitive message, he added, "Listen, if there's anything that I can do, just—"

Altha could see where this was going. Although appreciative and touched with Basil's good manners and sensitivity, she interjected to cut him off, "No. Don't worry. I'll be okay. Mother will be here to help me, and I'm sure things will turn out for the best."

It was evident that any assistance he might provide in the impending child birth was neither expected nor desired. Nevertheless Basil continued, "Okay, then. I expect you have a midwife lined up, or a doctor, don't you?"

"Only Mother. And she's been confined enough times that she says she can take care of me."

Basil was taken aback. Certainly he was no expert in these matters, but he had been close by on a couple of occasions during his own sisters' confinements and knew how difficult and chaotic things could become. One of their babies had died shortly after being born despite a doctor's efforts. Basil had been there throughout the whole grim and stressful affair, looking on and unable to provide any useful support. *What if Altha runs into some unforeseen trouble? What then?* he could not help wondering. However, he decided not to interfere in this instance. After all, what did he know? He did not really know these folks at all. Altha was comfortable with her plan, it seemed. Apparently, she thought her mother's attendance was all that was necessary. So Basil decided to let things be.

"Okay, then, Altha, good luck. If anything, anything atall comes up that I might be of some assistance to you, please don't hesitate to let me know. I'm not going to be a stranger in these here parts, and next time I see you, who knows? You'll probably be the mother of a healthy boy—or girl," he said while grinning as he mounted Fashion. "Going to try and find Mr. Anderson now. It's been nice talking to you, Altha, and I look forward to knowing you." Then he reined the horse in the direction of the barn.

"Goodbye, Basil. Thanks! It was good meeting you too," replied Altha as she looked wistfully after him. After a few moments, she turned back to her wheel and the spinning work.

"Mr. Anderson! Josiah! Josiah, are you in there?" Basil called loudly from outside the crude barn. Built of round logs, many of them badly rotten now, the walls were perilously close to collapse. Rafter poles sloping from the high side to the lower one incredulously remained in place and supported what few wooden roof shakes remained. From the one open doorway at the side of the shelter, a milk cow sauntered out and looked suspiciously toward Basil. Raising her head slightly, she let out a low, long bellow that registered her angry complaint at this man on horseback who dared intrude so. "Sorry, girl. Josiah! It's Basil Edmunston! I want to talk to you!"

Anderson had indeed had a rough night of it, as had his sons. All three had passed out on the barn's muddy floor, which was covered with manure and hay in varying degrees of decay. When Josiah at last discerned that someone was hollering out his name, he gently raised his head and pushed himself up from the bed of wet straw he was sprawled on. "Huh? What? Who's that calling out there?" he moaned.

Basil could see him moving around through the spaces between the logs. "It's Basil Edmunston, Josiah. Come on out. We need to talk."

It took a few minutes for Anderson to raise himself from the ground and shake off some of the filthiness that covered him from head to toe. Unfortunately, most of the smelly manure stuck to his clothes, and not only did it look a frightful sight, but it stunk to high heaven. His boys, Manson and Jesse, stirred and shifted a little but simply rolled over in their straw nests and went back to sleep. Josiah followed the cow's path out of the barn doorway and staggered in the direction where Basil had dismounted. Holding his hand so as to shield his eyes from the morning sunlight, the tenant farmer blurted out,

"What's this all 'bout?"

"Hello, Josiah. Looks like you put on quite a bender last night," Basil said matter-of-factly as he stared at the pitiful excuse for a human being wobbling and trying to stand in front of him. Pathetic and miserable as Anderson appeared, a sliver of sympathy lurked in Basil's heart for the man. His own father had always practiced temperance when consuming spirits, and Basil had been brought up to do likewise. However, there had been more than one occasion at the university when he had strayed from this prudent practice—the times when he and a few classmates had made nocturnal visits to the local taverns and had imbibed ardent spirits in the extreme. Once he had gotten so drunk that his friends had to help him back to the dormitory. Now, with the pitiable Anderson wobbling before him, Basil was reminded of those better-forgotten times. *Damn—how could I have ever been so stupid?* he contemplated as he studied his sorry tenant.

"Nah, me and the boys jest had a drink or two. Besides, it ain't no business of your'n that I can see, is it?" replied Josiah as he labored to deliver his words so they could be understood.

"Well, you're right there, Josiah. It's not my business that you and your sons drink and carry on like this. But those fields out there aren't going to get plowed by themselves, best that I can allow. And you promised my father that you would start breaking those grounds last week. And I reckon that is my business."

Josiah struggled to comprehend Basil's message. Stiffening himself a little straighter, he very deliberately replied, "Yeah, I 'spect I did tell you and Edmunston that. But we ain't had no rain. Them fields are too hard to break without no rain. Can't ye see that fer yerself?"

That's strange, Basil thought to himself before replying to his tenant. "Don't rightly understand that, Josiah. I left the boys down at my place this morning plowing up a storm on one of our bottom cornfields. They weren't having any problems atall that I could tell. I don't reckon that ground is any harder than your land—that is, unless you figure it might have rained down there and not up here?"

Josiah's mind was definitely not clear. He was confused and tried hard to focus his addled thoughts before carefully replying to Basil's rebuke. "Ain't saying that neither. My ground is hard as the dickens—maybe it ain't thawed out good yet—and that there wooden plow of our'n jest won't cut into h'it. We hitched it up to the ole mule Hartgrove lent us last season, and h'it jest rode atop the ground. Why, it'd take a man with a belly a sight bigger than a Justice of the Peace's to anchor down and guide that there plow. Ain't making this up nary bit, son. Jest ask them boys of mine if you don't believe what I say," Josiah concluded motioning toward the barn.

Basil paused for a moment as he glanced in that direction. "Don't aim to disturb your sons' sleep, Josiah. What do you mean wooden plow? Did you say you're using a wood plow?"

"Hartgrove know't about it. Our reg'lar iron plow got broke somer's how last year. The tip of the share got busted off, and that there blunt end of the board don't bite into the ground nary bit. We were trying to use the old wood plow we brung up with us from Burke County. But, like I said, h'it don't work nary good atall."

"That so? Let's have a look at that broken plow, Josiah."

After looking over the busted implement with Anderson, Basil told him that his slave blacksmith, Jake, might be able to fix it. Anderson avowed that he and one of his sons would haul the plow downriver to the Den that very afternoon to be repaired. And then, just as soon as it was gooder than new, he would set in to breaking his ground.

"Now, we are agreed on this—that right, Josiah?" Basil asked to ensure they had an understanding. His tenant had sobered up somewhat, but Basil wanted to make absolutely sure.

"Yes sir, son. Ye get that plow welded together agin like ye say, and then me and them boys will set in directly to busting sod. We'll git every last acre done, and it'll be ready fer planting in early May. Ye kin mark my word on that."

Of course Basil marked Anderson's word, but he marked it not with a bold stroke, but ever so lightly, and he did so with little confidence that the word would be kept. As he mounted Fashion and turned to ride away he called back, "Okay, Josiah. We'll be waiting on that plow. Better rouse those sons of yours and get them started. See you shortly."

When Basil reached the river, he looked back up toward Anderson's cabin and, sure enough, he got a glimpse of Altha still working at her wheel. Although by that time most of the frosty sparkle had melted off the leaves and grasses as the sun's rays had tilted steeper, the cool crispness of the morning still lingered. He thought of her feet and how cold they must be. *How can she stand it? Is Anderson's family so destitute that shoes could not be had by his grown girl?* He then thought of her condition and hoped that the baby would be born healthy and, most of all, that the birth would not be uncommonly difficult on Altha. There was something about Altha that he liked, liked a lot, and he was bothered by it all the way back to Bachelor's Den.

Chapter 6

Rendezvous by the Mill

A few days had elapsed since Basil's visit to Crab Orchard. Jake was able to forge and weld a new iron point onto Josiah Anderson's plow share. And Basil lent Anderson another mule so he could use a team to break the ground. The tenant farmer could not believe how easily the restored plow slid through his stiff East Fork soil. Over the coming days, even Basil was surprised by the good progress that was being made up at the Orchard.

At his own quarters, the Africans were methodically going about the farm work at a languorous pace that Basil was not yet accustomed to. The crucial fertilization of the crop land was the first step. He observed the slaves as they slowly and deliberately shoveled huge quantities of manure droppings from the barn and stable areas into an old farm wagon for transporting to the planting fields. The ancient wagon with its boxed sideboards had been around since Thomas and Louisa Edmunston's pioneering days. Jake kept the iron wheel rims tight and replaced the few other iron fittings when necessary. Jacob, crippled with one leg dramatically shorter than the other and the best carpenter of the lot, maintained the wagon's wooden assemblage in a tolerable condition and kept the axles lubricated. Although crude, the contraption was extremely utilitarian and indispensable for executing all manner of farm work

Working under various overseers over the years such as Columbus Hartgrove, the boys had worked out a fertilization process utilizing manure—or horse and cow shit—reclaimed from the stables and barn. Their process was simple—shovel the shit into the wagon, haul the shit to the field, and then shovel the shit into huge piles across the planting ground. Then after all the shit had been gathered and hauled and dumped into heaps on the field, the slaves would proceed to drag the plow thorough the smelly waste piles and try to bury the shit to the overseer's satisfaction. As Harry had first allowed to Basil, Columbus Hartgrove had been a hard man to satisfy in regards to burying the shit. And so would their new master be.

Basil watched the boys load and haul manure for most of the morning, and he could see that their methodology was badly flawed. He had his own idea how it should be done, and as the Master of the East Fork, he determined to set things straight. Boldly walking into the field and over to the manure wagon he called out, "Hold on boys! Why don't you rest a spell?" His words were received with great relief and gratitude, as the Africans put down their shovels and pitchforks and wearily huddled around the wagon. Each in turn began quenching a giant thirst from a water bucket lashed to the side of the wagon.

"We's shore 'nough needs ourselves a rest, Massa Baz—shore do's." said Erwin as he took a gourd ladle and filled it with water.

Gabe chimed in, "What you's thinks 'bout da way we's manurin', Massa Baz? We's do's it likes Massa Hartgrove tells us to do's."

"Jus' wait 'til we's plows it, Massa. You won't sees no signs of dis here manure, jus' likes I tells you's befo', 'member?" the youth, Harry, added.

Basil remembered very well how in that first meeting with his slaves, Harry had bragged about their fertilizing prowess. He had even invited Basil to walk down to take a look for himself. Well, after witnessing this morning's work, Basil was not impressed, and he meant to change things up.

"Yes, I remember, Harry," Basil said to the young boy, and as he looked around at the whole gang, he dropped this bombshell. "I appreciate that all of you are working hard to get this manure spread. You're doing it just like Columbus Hartgrove told you to. But I want to switch things up a little."

The slaves just looked dumbfounded at Basil for a few seconds, and then an incredulous Harry blurted out, "You means change da ways we's manurin', Massa?"

"That's right, Harry. Here's what I have in mind, and if anybody doesn't understand, then stop me. I'll explain it again." And so Basil laid out his new plan to the boys. He told them that he had no qualms with the manner they were loading the manure. Each one of them was doing his fair share of shoveling and pitching the smelly shit into the wagon. But he wanted the slaves to alter their method for spreading the manure, and he explained his new scheme.

Jacob would drive the wagon. Being crippled as he was, Basil figured this was the best use of the man, although he did not bother to explain his rationale. Instead of dumping the manure in large piles across the ground, Basil wanted it spread as evenly and thoroughly as possible before the plowing began. He suggested that Jacob should drive the wagon slowly across the field and stop at about ten-foot intervals. At each of these stops, Gabe and Erwin, stationed in the wagon, were to shovel out portions of the manure onto the ground. Positioned on the ground with rakes and shovels in hand were to be Uriah, Harry, and Lark. Their job was to spread the manure behind the path of the wagon as evenly as possible, making it much easier to plow under. In this manner, the men were to work as a team to broadcast the manure and return its valuable organic nutrients to the East Fork soil.

Basil did not get too many questions, and the ones that did come he handled rather easily. Erwin first asked, "You means, Massa Baz, fo' me always to be's in top of da wagon shovlin'—and stays in da wagon?"

Lark was unclear on another point. "Whut we's do's when we's spread all dis manure real good, Massa? Do's we's tell Jacob to keeps on goin'?"

Basil superintended the afternoon's work, and with the boys' help and cooperation, he fine-tuned some of the rougher areas of the process. By the end of the day, his Africans were working as a cohesive unit and were surely the best shit-spreaders as could be found in Haywood County. And Basil grew some that day too. He gained confidence that he could oversee his slaves and learned that they could in fact be instructed and led to affect productive farm work. And with that newfound confidence came a latent sensation resonating within him. It was one that suggested the real possibility that he might be cut out to be a master after all.

On Easter Sunday, Basil rode down to Forks of Pigeon to attend the morning service at the Methodist Church. It was a beautiful morning to ride, and he found himself marveling at the blossoming trees and flowers of the East Fork wilds. The flowering redbud and wild cherry trees glazed the mountainsides with their blushing pink colors, while the ubiquitous dogwoods added a generous speckling of white blooms. Along the sides of the river road, delicate flowers grew, huddling away from traffic and spurting their colors almost in defiance at the passers-by. Fashion's hooves trod dangerously close to clusters of dainty pink lady and painted trilliums, while the daffodils ducked their brilliant yellow-flowered heads away from the passing horse and rider.

When Basil arrived at the church, he was greeted with a chorus of sweet music that resonated from within the small frame building and wafted through the open windows. Realizing that the service was already underway, he proceeded to scold himself. *This is real good, Basil. Why in dammed hell can't you get yourself to a church service on time? Oh, and that's real good, too. As soon as you get to church your thoughts turn straight to hell.* He was seething mad inside and flustered at his tardiness as he tied Fashion up to a hitching post amongst a buggy, a couple of wagons, and several other horses and mules. Taking off his hat as he approached the entrance, he ran a hand through his hair a couple of times to comb it back behind his ears. Then he took hold of the handle on the heavy church door and gently pulled. If he had planned to slip into the room inconspicuously and slide into a back row seat, his strategy immediately ran afoul.

The slight tug at the wood door produced a piercing squeak as Basil budged it open. And as he continued to pull on the door handle, the squeaking developed into a loud screeching sound, much to his horror. Basil's noisy entry certainly got the attention of the congregants inside, even as they stood and sung at the tops of their lungs. All of the singers in the house—that is, every person present for that morning's worship service with the exception of small children—turned their heads to gape at the intruder. Basil paused for what seemed an eternity to him and smiled politely toward the group. Incredibly, the rhythm of the worshippers' singing did not break, but their stares remained fixed toward him.

He recognized many of the folk gathered there that morning, including the Osbornes, the Terrells, and the Moores, Columbus Hartgrove, the Catheys, and of course, the Deaver family. As was customary, the women all sat on the right side of the church, and the men folk on the left. Julia was there, standing next to her mother and pretty as ever. Her surprised look turned into a smiling beam as she caught Basil's eye. Colonel Deaver motioned for him to come over, and after shutting the creaking door, Basil made his way to the Colonel's side as graciously and quickly as possible. Taking a place in the pew next to Deaver, he stood and listened as the last verse of the hymn was sung.

Or if on joyful wing, cleaving the sky,
Sun, moon, and stars forgot, upwards I fly,
Still all my song shall be, nearer, my God, to Thee,
Nearer, my God, to Thee, Nearer, my God, to Thee!

The Reverend Horace Smathers from the Dutch community down at Pigeon River Ford had come up to preach the Easter sermon. This was a very special day for every Christian in the world, and that included this faithful audience of mountaineers. All listened as the good preacher started with a slow, deliberate delivery, and reminded each of the congregants of the sacrifice that their Lord, Jesus Christ, had made for them ages ago. The listeners were unusually attentive to these lofty matters and were anxious to be forgiven for their host of sins recently committed. The cadence of the preacher's speech grew faster and faster, and he gradually increased the volume of his voice to a near-shouting level as time wore on. Although he censured his listeners real good for their immoral thoughts and actions, he offered them a remote hope of being forgiven.

The Holy Trinity was beseeched to look favorably on His children gathered there and to forgive each and every one of them for their failings, shortcomings, and insufferable transgressions. The good reverend reminded all those poor souls that sat on hard crude benches before him of the words from one of the hymns they had sung that very morning. The words promised that the water and the blood that had poured from their Savior's wound would save them from wrath and sin. The preacher went on to qualify the message by saying that the blood of Jesus would make them pure if, and only if, they would believe in Him and live their daily lives as He would have them to and as the Bible had taught them.

With the exception of Basil, every highlander in the audience that Sunday morning was a believer, and this was the very message they had come to hear. On this day of Resurrection, the fearful worshippers were inspired to believe that when they died and rose to a world unknown, Jesus would be there waiting for them with his promised gift of forgiveness. And even Basil was moved to the point that he made a promise to himself to search harder for a niche in the Methodist canons that he could follow and hold true to.

Finally, after two hours of blessing and rejoicing and preaching and singing, the Reverend Smathers led his brethren in a final prayer and concluded his plea with a final "Amen." In turn, the congregation responded in unison with "Amen," and great breaths of relief were exhaled. As some of the impatient churchgoers broke for the door, the Colonel turned toward Basil and offered, "Good to see ye again, boy. Glad ye could make it down to pray with us."

"Thanks, Colonel Deaver," Basil replied. He noticed Julia trying to edge past her mother toward him. "Hello, Julia. It's good to see you again," he said as they squeezed each other's hand. He spoke to Julia's mother, Maggie, whom he had met the previous Sunday at the dinner-on-the-ground event following the church service. It had been a cold windy afternoon, and Basil had offered the matriarch his coat after seeing that she was shivering. "Good to see you, Mrs. Deaver."

Maggie, not having forgotten the boy's thoughtful act of kindness the week before, made a considered suggestion, "You too, Basil. I hope you can come back to the house and have dinner with us. It should be just about ready when we get there. And don't you worry none. There will be plenty of food. We had hoped you might make it down today, since it is Easter and all."

How could Basil refuse such an invitation? They were expecting him for dinner apparently. He should further his acquaintances in the community his father had told him, so he reasoned this was another such opportunity.

Not to mention he might be able to wheedle some alone time with Julia. *Now that would be nice*, he allowed to himself. Maggie's invitation was eagerly accepted, and Basil followed the Deavers' buggy back to their home.

It was a fine large house compared with the other ones in the community—but not a grandiose mansion by any means. Built of timber framing and sawn clapboard siding washed in white paint, the building rose two stories high. Along the front at both levels, covered porches extended the entire length of the house. A hallway on the main floor ran straight between the front and back doors, splitting the plan into halves. On one side were the dining and morning rooms. On the other was a large sitting room where Colonel Deaver had a desk and Maggie claimed a corner for reading and sewing. The bedrooms were located on the second floor, and a large kitchen was attached to the rear of the house. Huge river rock chimneys at each end of the structure sprouted from the ground and rose high above the roof.

The imposing home was located in close proximity to the frothy junction of the east and west forks of the Pigeon River. Also nearby were the Deaver's store and grain mill, as well as good roads leading west to the county seat town of Waynesville and north to the main turnpike at Pigeon River Ford. The turnpike, a vital link to Asheville and the commercial markets beyond the mountains, was a mere four or five miles away.

Basil reined Fashion off of the road and walked her through the Deavers' yard, which was covered with green grasses, weeds, and fragrant wild onions. Yellow dandelions were blooming in wild profusion, and several planting beds were flush with pretty little daffodils of the same color. Once again showing his gentlemanly ways, Basil hustled to tie Fashion to a fence rail and help Maggie and Julia out of their buggy. As the party made its way into the residence, the pungent wild onion smells from the outdoors were replaced by the enticing cooking aromas emanating from the kitchen.

Caroline, the Deavers' slave cook, had busied herself all morning preparing this dinner. Using the cast iron stove and a kitchen hearth, she had baked three chickens and prepared a mess of leather-britches beans. To go along with these mouthwatering fares, taters, three skillets of cornbread, spring creases, and wild onions and ramps fried in bacon grease had been prepared. Caroline had worked extremely hard to get this food ready for her mistress and master, and now she fussed to lay it out on the dining table, along with pitchers of sour milk.

There were more eaters than places to eat. All of Colonel and Maggie Deaver's children along with their families had joined them for this Easter feast. The youngsters were relegated to a makeshift area in the kitchen, leaving the grownups to crowd around the expansive main table. Everyone ate to their heart's content and forced Caroline to blush from the many praises of her culinary skills. Basil tried not to overdo it, refusing the offered second helpings, with the exception of an extra piece of cornbread that he readily smeared with butter and molasses and gobbled down.

There was polite talk on a variety of subjects, ranging from the spring planting progress to the coming county commissioners' election. Basil learned that the ginseng market in Georgia and South Carolina did not pay near as much as in Virginia the past year. In lieu of the Augusta, Georgia, marketplace, the Colonel was thinking of sending a drove up the Buncombe Turnpike through eastern Tennessee and into Virginia this coming fall. He would hire local men to drive livestock—hogs, cattle, sheep, and even turkeys—to the exchange. Wagons loaded with ginseng, apples, feathers, hides, and bacon hams would be hauled to the market as well. These essential droves to faraway places to sell their homegrown produce were annual affairs for Deaver and many of the mountain farmers. He encouraged Basil to think about joining in and partnering with him on the drive, if he had a mind to.

Basil kept his eyes on Julia during most of the eating and conversing. Twice he caught her shooting coquettish glances his way, whereupon she gave him suggestive grins and then looked away. Somewhat taken aback by her foolery, Basil initially let these incidents pass without any sort of acknowledgment on his part. However, he was ready for her the third time around. When their eyes next met, Basil stared directly at Julia and answered her flirty smile with an approving nod of his head. *That ought to do it,* he thought—signaling his intention to carry this newfound relationship to another level. And then he wondered if that was in fact what he had done. *A head nod—what kind of a signal is that?* he worried.

Eventually everyone's appetites were sated, and as the conversation ebbed, Julia's older siblings and their families began to depart for their own homes. Maggie had taken leave to superintend the kitchen cleanup work, leaving Basil alone with Julia and the Colonel. As the two men swigged hard cider, Basil plotted in his mind a way to steal Julia away to the porch or some other secluded location. *How can I get her all to myself?* he fretted. Well, he need not have worried atall, because Julia had something in mind herself.

"Father, you don't care if I walk up to the mill with Basil, do you? It's on his way home, and I need to exercise a little after eating so much."

Surprised at the suggestion the Colonel replied, "Well, dear, we don't aim to hurry Basil out of here now, do we?" and he looked first at her and then to Basil.

Basil knew it was now or never, and he jumped in, "No, no, Colonel Deaver, I have to get back on up to the Den, uh, to my place. That's what I call the old cabin, the Den—the Bachelor's Den. Patsy was grunting this morning when I left, and I should get back up and check on her."

Colonel Deaver bent to Basil's wishes. Although suspecting that a clandestine rendezvous might be the real motive for the rushed departure and Julia's sudden need for exercise, he permitted her to accompany Basil up the East Fork River as far as the mill.

"And no need to tarry neither, girl. Ye get yourself back here directly, fer yer mother and I don't need to worry 'bout ye none."

While leading Fashion behind them, Basil and Julia moseyed side by side up the road. Julia remembered something Basil had said earlier that had intrigued her. "The Bachelor's Den, huh? So that's what you've named your father's place?" she asked as they approached Deaver's grist mill situated on the bank of the river.

The mill stood idle and silent, its water source having been diverted away from the huge undershot wheel. Although the mill was shut down for Easter Sunday, Basil and Julia could hear the intermittent sound of hammering and voices seemingly coming from the interior of the mill. *How odd,* Basil thought. *The Colonel must have employed workmen to make some needed repairs or possibly change out a set of millstones, even though it's Easter Sunday.*

The couple stopped and sat down on top of a low rock wall buffering the road from the mill property. As they were taking their seats and scooting closer to one another, Basil responded to Julia's query, "Yep. That's what I'm calling the ole cabin. How do you like it?"

"It's fine, I suppose," she replied, thoughtful of its meaning and wondering just how long he would maintain his solitary status. Julia was excited to have become acquainted with Basil and was keen on broadening the relationship beyond just being friends. His good looks were obvious, but she wanted to get to know him as a person, learn his innermost thoughts, his feelings, and ambitions. She suspected the prospects of his being very special were good as she continued the conversation, "Do you think you will be staying in Haywood very long, Basil?"

"Oh, I don't know for sure. You should have heard what Patsy had to say about the name—Bachelor's Den. I had to explain to her what 'bachelor' meant. It was so funny." He paused for a moment before continuing, "I'm not certain how long I'll be staying out here, Julia. My plan is to go back and study at the university when Father finds another overseer for Haywood. That's our agreement anyway."

Although Julia had surmised that might be the Edmunstons' plan, it was not what she wanted to hear. So she instinctively attempted to divert the direction of the conversation.

"Well, hopefully you will be able to do that soon. How do you like things out here so far?"

Just as Basil began to reply, the young couple observed Colonel Deaver's miller and one of his slaves come out of the mill to get some fresh air. "I like it fairly well, I suppose. Not sure if I'm cut out to be a farmer, though. But at least I'm going to give it a try. Father said it was my duty, and I aim to do it, even if it kills me." He went on to tell Julia about his doings with the Crab Orchard tenants and some of the issues he was having with the slaves.

"The hardest thing by far is dealing with my Africans. They vex me to no end sometimes and dearly try my soul." He told Julia about the concern Gabe had raised regarding the amount of bacon allotted for them to eat. As of yet, he had not addressed this contentious dilemma but was forming a pretty firm idea that the food portions at the Den were not going to be increased.

They carried on in this way for a while until both realized that precious time was slipping by and that Julia should start back down the river soon. But before breaking off their covert rendezvous, she was desperate to exchange more intimate feelings. Placing one of her hands on his forearm, Julia looked Basil square in the eyes and stated shamelessly, "Basil, I really like you and feel that we should get to know each other better. What do you think about that?"

The touch of Julia's hand on his arm surprised him. They were leaning closer to each other now, Basil noticed. It was very close range, and he could even smell her and he lustily inhaled this wonderful scent. He was able to plainly see her beautiful complexion, the deep oceans of blueness in her eyes, the golden sheen of her hair, the few individual freckles that dotted her face, and the wonderful form of her moist pink lips as they quivered slightly at his fixed gaze. Interestingly, he felt that same uneasy queasiness in his stomach and loins that he had once experienced for his distant cousin. His heart was racing, and Julia was definitely making him feel woozy. He tried to calm himself and focus. *What was it she had asked me? What would I allow about that?*

"Me too," he clumsily muttered searching for the right response. "I like you too, Julia. So will it be okay for me to, maybe, call on you again sometime?"

A smile broke over her face as she sensed his discomfort. Then as a low laugh erupted from her, she gave Basil the answer. "Why it most certainly will be, Master Basil," and she suddenly leaned toward him and planted a kiss on the side of his clean-shaven face. "The sooner the better, as far as I'm concerned," she said still chuckling. And before Basil knew it Julia had hopped down off the rock wall and was pacing down the lane for home.

Almost in a daze, Basil gawked at her as she disappeared around a bend, and then he turned his stare in the direction of the mill and river. He was spellbound, lost in bewilderment at what had just happened. Rushing through his body was an electrifying thrill that charged his soul. Whether a result of exhilaration or fear, he was uncertain. But he was sure of one thing. Julia sure was different, all right.

Chapter 7

Feet First

In the wee hours of that Easter night, Basil sat at his dining table writing a letter to his older brother, Walter. The cabin's only light source was the hearth's low burning fire and a solitary candle positioned close to his work. Although he had sharpened and smoothed a new nib on the quill pen, it was still leaving a splattered track of brown walnut ink. But Basil was unperturbed. He reckoned his older brother could decipher his script and, besides, it had been such an eventful day he was anxious to share the news with someone.

Basil was not alone that evening. Sitting in a chair staring trance-like at the dancing flames of the fire was an elderly slave woman. She was of a lighter color than most of the Edmunston slaves, almost a light chocolate; and her nappy gray hair hung looser and longer than customary. The old woman was talking to herself and ignoring the needlework lying idle in her lap. On the floor in the middle of the cabin the slave cook, Patsy, was lying restlessly on a feather tick. Basil had found her grunting and quite sick on his return from the Deavers' that afternoon.

She had complained of a great pain in her side, her tongue was badly swollen, and her pulse was almost two hundred beats per minute. Basil's experience with these sorts of things was extremely limited, and he had been at a loss as to what ailed Patsy and how best to treat her symptoms. Nevertheless, he ordered the boys to carry her to his cabin and put her to bed. Then he proceeded to feed her a teaspoonful of French brandy to lower her pulse and a dose of calomel in hopes of purging whatever afflicted her. Uriah told him about an old slave woman at the Osbornes' who was reputed to possess extraordinary healing powers. So perturbed was Basil about Patsy's condition that he immediately sent Uriah down the river to fetch the healer woman.

I asked the healer woman a while ago how Patsy was keeping, Basil wrote to Walter, *and the healer told me she "was keeping sorta poorly and dauncy but won't get quite bad enough," whatever that means. And would you believe that she had the gumption to ask me for a teaspoonful of gunpowder? I think it's about time to decamp before the old Bachelor's Den goes up in a flash.*

Basil also wrote of his planting activities at the Den and the condition of most of his livestock. The tribulations of the Crab Orchard tenants took more than a page to set down, and two additional leaves were taken up with details of the Easter church service, his dinner with the Deavers, and the budding romantic prospects with Julia. The relationship Basil had with Walter was close, and there was not much that came to his mind that went unrecorded in the long letter. The final closing paragraphs were taken up with breaking news on the healer woman and the ailing Patsy.

That old woman has come to me again and says that she put the powder in some tea for Patsy. Did you ever! Basil wrote incredulously. *Well I have heard of gunpowder tea, but never before of tea made from the real genuine Brimstone gunpowder! Isn't it an important discovery?*

He continued to mock his new discovery and wrote, *Who knows what important bearings it may have on our commercial intercourse with the ancient Empire of China? Attend to it ye Importers! Ye Politicians! Ye Statesmen! The march of science runs onward and with a rapid pace!* Wrapping up his correspondence that night Basil penned, *I will close the subject by remarking that I have no idea of trying the gunpowder tea as a diet, believing it to be rather explosive.*

After addressing and sealing the letter, he stashed it in his shoulder bag to be carried to the office at Deaver's store in the morning. Patsy had finally dropped off into a fitful sleep, and he rearranged her blanket. The old healer woman, he noticed, had also nodded off in her chair at the fireplace. It was now far later than his usual time for turning in, and he was dead tired. It had been a long day. After stripping off his shirt and pants and hanging them from a wall peg, he jumped under the bed covers, closed his eyes, and tried to go to sleep. But his mind was still racing wildly and turning over the events of the day. Just before finally lapsing into a deep sleep, brilliant images of burning brimstone flashed through his head along with stirring reflections of Julia and their rendezvous at the mill.

Bam! Bam! Bam! The sudden thunderous hammering on the Den's heavy plank door awoke the three inhabitants inside with a start. Basil vaulted out of bed and to his feet.

Again came the loud sound–*Bam! Bam! Bam! "Edmunston!* You in there?" An agitated voice from outside boomed.

"Hold on. Who's there?" Basil shouted back as a tingle of apprehension shot through his body, and his adrenalin level surged. He could not have been asleep for more than an hour he thought as he reached for his father's old flintlock rifle scotched above the door on a set of stag horns. Not sure of the gun's condition, Basil took it down and quickly verified that it was primed and loaded and might possibly fire. At the same time, he listened anxiously as his night visitor identified himself.

"It's Manson Anderson–Josiah's son!" the man responded.

Now what in hell could he want this time of night? Basil mused as he quickly called back, "Hold on!"

The heavy wooden plank securing the door was lifted out of its brackets, and the door was cautiously swung open. Manson stood there alone and stared nervously at Basil. The tenant had his hat in hand and appeared to be in a state of panic. Not only was the man agitated and swaying badly from side to side, barely remaining upright, but he looked a frightful sight. His dirty brown hair was hanging in his face and partially covering his eyes. His clothes were ragged, with one of the pants legs partially torn off. And his toes could be seen protruding from holes in the hide shoes he was wearing. It was obvious to Basil that Anderson had been drinking. *But what is he doing here for God's sake?*

"It's Altha. The baby won't come out. It won't come out atall. Been goin' on more'n a day now. She wants ye–she sent me after ye, Edmunston."

It was all Anderson could do to speak coherently as he continued to stagger about. At first Basil could not think straight, and he struggled to gather his wits about him. *Altha's in trouble? Is that what this man said?* "Is Altha in trouble? She's having the baby?" an extremely perplexed Basil asked.

"She be in real trouble, Edmunston. The baby won't come. She asked fer ye. Don't know how much longer she kin last." These words were delivered slow and sluggishly, just as a drunkard would speak them, yet to Basil the message was plenty sobering enough.

Well, that's it then, Basil thought. *Altha's in trouble. I've got to go up and do my best to help her.* He immediately sprang into action. Grabbing hold of a cast-iron bell hanging just outside of the cabin, he rang it furiously to arouse the slaves in their quarters. In no time, the majority of them were at the Den's stoop to see about all the commotion. There was no nervousness or hesitation now as Basil addressed the group and put them into action.

"Uriah, you know where Doctor Allen lives, don't you, down about Flowery Garden?" Basil asked not knowing whether Uriah knew the place or not.

"Yessa, Massa Baz. I do," Uriah confirmed nervously, sensing there was an emergency.

"Good, I want you to take one of the work horses—never mind saddling it—and ride down to Doctor Allen's. Tell him he's needed at Anderson's up at Crab Orchard. He is to come immediately. Tell him that. Do you understand? Tell him I sent you and that it's a matter of life and death. Got it?"

"Yessa, Massa."

"And, Uriah, you come up with him. We may need you for something else."

"Yessa, Massa, we both of us wills come up dare." Uriah replied as he sprinted toward the barn to get the horse.

"Gabe, you and Erwin go saddle up Fashion and one of the Leviathans as fast as you know how. Hurry on now, we've got to get moving," Basil anxiously ordered. He had surmised that Manson had footed it down the river since there was no horse about. "Manson, you can ride back up with me. That big old Leviathan is tame enough, and she ought to be able to keep up."

Within ten minutes, Uriah was riding downstream to fetch the doctor, and Basil and Manson were trotting hard up the river. It would not be sunup for several hours. The moon was almost at full stage, so they had sufficient light to give their horses plenty of rein. But Manson was not fit to ride and had trouble sitting his horse. He fell off twice within the first mile of travel. After the second upset, Basil left him behind and in less than half an hour reached the Andersons' cabin at Crab Orchard.

The door was wide open, and Basil could hear ominous moaning and screaming sounds from inside. He vaulted off Fashion and burst into the cabin's dark interior. Taking only a few seconds to glance around in the faint light, he quickly made out the situation. By a single candle's shimmering soft light, he could see Altha sitting on the dirt floor on a wet bloody quilt with her back against one of the log walls. It was her constant cries of pain that he heard, and they were continuing as her face contorted and grimaced in agony.

He also saw Altha's mother collapsed on her stomach across a low bed with arms outstretched and her feet still touching the floor. As he tried to gather his wits about him, the older woman moved her head slightly to see who had just come in. *So she is not unconscious but apparently incapacitated, probably from exhaustion*, Basil surmised. He also noted incredulously that neither Josiah or the other brother, Jesse, nor any other Anderson family member was there helping with the birth of Altha's child. There was no one else around to provide assistance—absolutely no one.

Basil threw off his hat and fell to his knees at Altha's side. She was still crying out in anguish and did not immediately acknowledge his presence. "Altha—Altha! It's Basil. What can I do? What can I do for you?" he asked as he firmly grasped one of her arms.

"Help me!" she cried out, and then as another bolt of pain shot through her body, she screamed again, "Help me, pleasseeee!"

Basil was utterly overwhelmed and shaken by the situation. He felt powerless to intervene and offer any real assistance to the young woman. Useless or inadequate or incompetent would be other ways to express how he felt at that moment. Most certainly he did not know how to deliver a baby. What could he do? There had been numerous times at the Fort when he had looked on in fascination as his father's cows calved and the horses foaled—and likewise for the several other varieties of livestock that were raised there.

Only on a few occasions had he witnessed complications in the natal process where human intervention had been necessary. Singularly emblazoned in his mind was the time when older brother William reached with both hands up inside a struggling mother cow, grasped the forelegs of an unborn fetus, and pulled and tugged out a slimy, living calf. It was a miraculous experience that he remembered clear as day.

However tonight's circumstances were all together different. It was not a cow that was in trouble. It was Altha, a girl he barely knew—and a human being and a female to boot. He could not go poking around in her private areas to deliver a baby. Or could he? Altha was in desperate trouble, and Basil knew he had to act and act soon. He had to do something—but what? What could he possibly do?

From the bedstead where the mother lay came a barely audible message, "You've got to get it—get it out."

Still kneeling at Altha's side Basil looked over toward the woman, "What? What did you say?" he asked fretfully.

Seconds passed, an eternity in Basil's mind, before the woman again muttered, "Got to get...baby...out of her. They's both gonna...be dead soon... if'n ye don't."

Jumping up from the floor, Basil quickly moved to the woman who was struggling to raise herself. He sat on the bed next to her and pulled her in his arms, gently cradling her head. "How? How do I get the baby out?" he asked desperately.

The woman opened her eyes briefly, stared at Basil without really seeing him, and gasped to breathe her last breaths. "Pull the baby, pull—," and then her eyes slowly closed, and her body fell limp in Basil's arms. Altha's mother was dead. She had died in his arms pleading for him to pull the baby out of her daughter. This childbirth had proved to be so much more difficult than the ones the mother herself had endured. The stressful energies she had expended over almost a twenty-four hour period to assist Altha through the travails had simply been too much for her aging heart.

"Damn, is she dead?" Basil muttered to himself. *I believe she is. She's dead! Now what? What in hell do I do now?*

He was helpless and at a loss about what to do in this crisis. As he stretched out the mother's body on the bed, another scream of agony arose from Altha. The rhythmic waves of pain were obviously not ceasing just because her mother had expired. Basil turned and saw that Altha was looking at him with a hopeful, pleading look that stabbed into his heart. He thought many things at the same time. *Does she realize her mother is dead? Altha wants me to help. She believes I can help her. How can I help her? The old woman said to pull the baby, pull it out.* Suddenly Basil was aroused from this reflective state when Manson staggered into the doorway.

Basil caught Manson up quickly. As the young man stared in a stupor at his dead mother stretched out on the bed, Basil formulated the first steps of a plan. "Manson, before your mother died, she told me to pull the baby out of Altha." He was interrupted by yet another loud screech from Altha that soon tapered off to another bawling holler for help.

"We've got to try, otherwise they're both going to die. The doctor won't be here until sometime past daylight, if then. I need your help, Manson. Can you give me some help?" Basil pled with a look of expectancy toward the brother.

Turning away from his mother, Manson replied, "Yeah, I 'spect I can. What ye need me to do, Edmunston?"

"Okay, I'm going to need to examine Altha real good, and I will need some light. Get that candle. You'll need to hold it for me." Basil looked around and found a piece of linen that was tolerably clean. He quickly immersed it into the water bucket and rung out as much of the water as he could. Both he and Manson fell down on their knees in front of Altha as she looked at them warily but with an expectant, almost hopeful, expression. Between her tortured screams, Basil told her he was going to take a look down there, down there where the baby was supposed to come out, and she readily nodded her agreement. She still had her plain dress on but it was pulled way up above her huge belly.

"Okay, Manson, give me some light over here." Basil directed as he squeezed between Altha's spread legs and used the wet towel to wipe away the blood from between her thighs and pubic area. Motioning for the candle to be held closer, he crouched down and moved his face as near to Altha's birthing opening as possible in order to see better. He had never looked at such a thing, and it was as foreign to him as a Chinaman in Haywood County. Basil examined her closely and at last perceived something that seemed to be a little odd to him and out of place.

Another forbidding scream escaped from Altha as yet more instinctive muscle contractions surged through her body. The involuntary reactive spasms that pushed against the fetus to force it through the womb opening and into the birthing canal were meeting with severe resistance. The tissue surrounding the opening was not only stretching to accommodate the passage, as it should, but it was also tearing. Something was amiss in this natural biological process, and the fetus was not budging atall. These endless cycles of unrelieved excruciating pain had extended beyond twenty-four hours now, and they were not about to end, at least while Altha was alive.

"It's a foot," Basil exclaimed to no one in particular. "I think I can see a foot barely sticking out," he continued while still checking her closely. Although Basil was unaware at the time, his discovery unveiled the birthing problem that Altha was experiencing. The fetus was not ideally presented for birth with a normal headfirst orientation. Instead, a single foot was breeched through the womb opening, meaning the other leg was undoubtedly twisted such that it was blocking a normal passage out of the womb. In this position, the labor forces that usually drive the fetus out of the mother's body were woefully inadequate, making a natural birth quite impossible.

"Yes, yes, it is a foot. I can see its toes," Basil exclaimed excitedly as he rose up to see how Altha was faring.

"Ahhhhhhh—ahhhhhh, hurry—hurry!" was the response he received, as another contraction with the incumbent pain ravaged through her body.

"Altha, I can see a foot. I can see your baby's foot, but that's all. I'm going to feel around and try to find the other one," he said reflecting back on how calves were born.

Surely both feet and legs have to come out together, he reckoned. Looking at Manson, he explained, "We need to get Altha into another position, Manson. The way she's sitting now, I can't get to her to do any good."

They worked swiftly to maneuver Altha around and into an all-fours posture, where her knees and hands were resting on the dirt floor of the cabin. But she did not move into this crawling position quietly. A bout of spasms hit her at that moment, triggering an eruption of sickening screams to ease the agony. And the new position was not comfortable for her, and she told them so.

"This won't do," she said gasping. "I can't push good. Ohhhhhhh—ohhhhhh! "Please stop these awful hurting...pains," she cried out to the two men.

Basil was trying. He was doing the best he could. He ciphered quickly and came up with a solution to Altha's pushing problem. "Okay, Altha. We're going to stop them," he said as he stooped over and tried to see her face. "Manson, find some string or ribbon to tie her hair back away from her face," he barked. Then speaking as calmly and confidently as he could muster, "Altha, let's move you over here against the wall. You can put your head against the wall and push against it to help the baby come out." Altha was too weak and fearful of another excruciating attack to offer much resistance. Intuiting that she must reserve what little strength remained, she crawled submissively, yet ever so slowly, over to the log wall.

Getting up and finding a coverlet, Basil folded it and placed it between her head and the logs as a cushion to push against. Manson returned with a piece of rawhide and they fixed Altha's hair back and out of her face.

"Okay, Manson, get your candle. You're going to have to hold it down here where I can see the baby," he said pointing out the location where he wanted the candle. Manson was sobering up in a hurry, and he moved quickly and dutifully to Basil's directions. The death of his mother and the realization that his sister might soon follow her had hastened the recovery process. As Basil helped Altha spread her legs wider so that he could get in between them he thought of something else. "Manson, how about bringing the water bucket over here. I'm going to need to wash and lubricate my hands."

In just a few moments, Basil had rinsed his hands and was laying on his side on the floor with his right hand inside Altha feeling around for the other foot. Her painful contractions were continuing. As he slipped his fingers and then hand by the breeched foot and then deeper inside her, a terrible burning sensation erupted through Altha's body. She welcomed the entrance of his hand with an ear-shattering scream and a healthy dose of cursing directed square at Basil. It hurt him to hurt Altha so, but he had no other choice.

He could feel wetness and sliminess as his fingers slid along the leg of the breeched foot and felt around for the second foot. A *foot should feel hard*, he reckoned, as he nervously and desperately probed for it in the womb. And finally, with his hand inserted well past the wrist and the cabin interior resonating with a cacophony of Altha's screams and oaths, he felt the other foot. But finding the foot was the easy part he soon discovered. He wiggled and worked his thumb and fingers in myriad ways to grasp the tiny appendage with enough force and traction to pull it through the womb opening. But there was not enough friction. His hand was too slick. The foot was too slick. He just could not grab hold of the foot.

For several minutes, Basil grimaced and mumbled and cursed to himself as he worked to secure a grip on the second foot. In the meantime, Altha's painful contractions went on unabated, and he could feel the pressure of each one squeezing his hand.

Finally, Manson had to ask, "Kin ye ketch it, Edmunston?"

"Damn it all to hell, no! I can't hold on to—wait, wait a second. I may have it. I believe I do. I've got it!" At long last, Basil had been able to secure two toes between his fingers with enough traction and force to pull the foot. He slowly started working the foot downward and out as the excruciating, burning pain from the stretching and tearing of tissue tore through Altha. Basil lost his grip twice during the extraction process but was now able to reach and secure the toes easier as the tiny foot approached Altha's opening. The final few inches of the foot's passage were the tightest, as it had to slip out of the womb alongside of the other foot. Basil readied Altha with a warning, "Just a little further, Altha. Hold on." And then he tugged stoutly at the toes as the foot surged out of the mother, pulling free and clear.

"Ahhhhhhh—ahhhhhh!" Altha screeched loudly to announce the passage, not knowing the status of her baby's birth or that both of the child's feet were now breeched. But she could feel some slight sense of relief as the baby moved slightly with her next contraction.

Basil glanced with satisfaction at Manson and then caught Altha's eye, "Both feet are out now, Altha," he delicately and calmly reported. "It should get easier from here on. You try and push, and I'll pull the baby's feet at the same time."

Over the next several minutes, a miracle occurred in front of Basil's and Manson's eyes. In concert with Altha's contractions and bawling and screeching shouts, Basil tugged slightly on the two little feet until, to their wonderment, the baby's umbilical connection was exposed. Now able to grab the fetal hips, Basil timed his pulls to coincide with Altha's pushing until first one and then the other shoulder had cleared. Almost, Basil thought. It was almost out. Just one more push and pull and the head should pop out, he reasoned. A gratifying sensation began to come over him until he peeked at Altha. And then his heart sank.

She gave the impression of a limp rag doll and did not appear to be able to finish this thing off. *Can she go on?* Basil worried. *Surely she can make one more push.* But he feared the worst—that Altha was ready to give up on her child and herself. She was listless, and her head was drooping limply almost to the dirt floor. But she remained on all fours. That was good. How she stayed in this awkward birthing position for so long Basil could not fathom.

It was vital that he stimulate her for one more big push. "Altha, one more push and the baby is out—just one more push. Can you do it?" he asked as he glanced worriedly toward Manson. Altha did not answer. She remained unresponsive and quiet.

Then Manson moved over close to Altha and whispered softly in her ear, "Ye kin do it, girl. It's a boy. I done seen it's a boy. Ye've got to finish it up so's ye kin raise him proper."

The brother's encouraging words aroused something deep inside Altha—deep within her soul—and rekindled her maternal flame. She breathed a few deep breaths and spoke out to the men in a low, almost defiant tone, "Okay, one more push—one more. Get ready!"

Basil got ready, and as Altha pushed and screamed and finally collapsed, he pulled the baby as hard as he thought prudent. At last the tiny head swept out of Altha's birthing opening and into Basil's cushioning hand. The umbilical cord hung loose and pulsated with the last life-giving fluids. It was a boy, just as Manson had said it was, and it was a bloody, slimy mess. But it was breathing and crying and appeared to be perfectly healthy.

Immediately Basil held the baby out for Altha to see. But poor Altha, she was barely alive, it seemed to him. The worn-out mother strained mightily to raise her head up and contort her ravaged body so she could get a glimpse of her newborn son. Basil watched with a restrained joy as Altha's weary eyes focused on the child, and a look of relief and sweet motherly love spilled over her face.

Chapter 8

Knight in Shining Armor

Uriah and Doctor Allen slogged through a nasty rain to reach the Crab Orchard farm sometime around seven o'clock that morning. Upon their arrival, they found things fairly calm and settled. Basil and Manson were still very busy cleaning and pampering both the mother and child. Altha was still hemorrhaging lots of blood, and the two inexperienced midwives were keeping rags packed into her birthing opening in an effort to stop the bleeding.

Doctor Allen could see that the umbilical cord was still dangling from the baby, but he did not readily spot the corpse lying on the other bed concealed under a coverlet. After shedding his hat and wet overcoat and placing the heavy black satchel carefully on the floor, he hastily went to work. Basil reported all of the details of the delivery, while the doc gave his undivided attention to Altha and the baby. Not looking away from his patients the doctor declared aloud that he was astonished at what the mother and son had gone through, let alone that both of them had survived the child birth.

He immediately tied off the umbilical cord close to the baby's belly and got rid of the excess. Altha's bleeding had to be stopped, and for more than an hour he worked, with Basil's steady assistance, to suture the tears that he could reach around the birthing opening. More than once during the ordeal Altha cried out in pain as the doctor's needle penetrated her sensitive genital area. When Doctor Allen was finished, he pronounced the baby healthy but could not say with confidence whether Altha would make it or not.

She had lost an extreme amount of blood during and after the birth of her child. Moreover, there was a good chance the wounds he had stitched and dressed, as well as those he could not get to, would become infected. If that did indeed transpire, Altha would likely as not succumb to the compounding effects of blood loss and infection.

When the physician had wrapped up his doctoring work, he approached Basil who was standing in the doorway. Giving the young man an appreciative look, Doctor Allen proceeded to commend him for his efforts that morning. "Basil, it is beyond my comprehension what you and Manson did for this young woman. The fact of the matter is I myself could not have done a better job of delivering this breeched baby. You should feel awfully proud of yourself, son."

Although surely satisfied with the outcome and somewhat content that he might have been useful in the matter, Basil attempted to deflect the attention and praise. "Thanks, Doctor Allen. I guess you can just credit it to blind luck. I didn't really know what to do. And to tell the truth, I didn't know I was delivering the baby backwards. If I had known, I would have been scared stiff for sure."

"Wasn't entirely luck, my boy. Took some real thinking and courage and that's all I'm going to say about it. Now let me take a look at the body over here," the doctor said as he moved toward the bed where the mother lay. He pulled down the coverlet and looked closely at the face and the hands and feet. Then after sniffing around her face he pulled the cover back over the corpse and announced that the woman had likely died from a stroke or heart attack. Rigor mortis was already setting in, and he advised that the body be interred as soon as possible.

Doctor Allen left things under Basil's watch, promising to come back the next morning. But he asked to be sent for if Altha's condition began to deteriorate. Before letting the doctor get away, however, Basil requested that he stop by the Den on the way down river and check on Patsy, his old slave cook. Peering anxiously out the door at the rain falling in torrents, the doc said he would be happy to. He allowed as how he could not wait on the weather, for there was a patient over on the West Fork who was in a dire state and needed attending to. With that said, he strode resolutely out into the miserable elements, medical bag in hand, mounted his horse, and rode off through the mud with no little anxiety about crossing the river fords.

Earlier that morning before the doctor had arrived, Basil learned from Manson and Altha the whereabouts of the rest of the family. Altha's father, as it turned out, had gone to Waynesville in search of his other son, Jesse. The elder Anderson had ridden off on the back of a plow mule just before Altha had gone into labor. He had been unaware of the dangerous difficulties that lay ahead for his daughter, or so Basil was told. At the time, Josiah had been more concerned for his wayward son who had set out a day or two before to sell a beef cow and had seemingly disappeared. And of course, Jesse's wife had been worried sick for him too, and she had tagged along with Josiah on foot.

Manson had explained to Basil how his wife had been kept busy attending to Jesse's infant son and daughter along with their own two small toddlers. He had argued that there was no way his wife could have assisted Altha during her labors. Besides, no one had anticipated such a trial as Altha had endured. They had naturally assumed it would be a routine birth—one where the woman just bends over, grunts a few times, wiggles her behind, and out plops the baby. Upon hearing all this and remembering the attention his sisters' confinements had drawn, Basil thought these excuses or justifications for the absentee family members to be beyond ludicrous.

Stepping over to the still open doorway of the cabin, Basil called for Uriah. In just moments, the trusted slave was standing in front of his master while shaking the rainwater from his head and wiping his face with both hands. Basil had another mission for him.

"It's a poor day out there, isn't it, Uriah?"

"Yessa, Massa Baz. Shore 'nough is," Uriah replied as he continued trying to dry himself off.

"You did good getting the doctor up here so quick. I've been so busy I didn't get to say that to you before. I knew I could count on you though."

"Yessa, Massa. Wusn't easy to find his place in da dark. I stopped by Massa Hartgrove's on da way down and woke him up. He 'splained how to find da doctor's house, and I finds it finally."

"Good for you, Uriah. Now I need you to do something else that is important, real important."

"Yessa, Massa. Whut's it?"

"The woman who lived in this cabin died this morning, and her body is lying on that bed," Basil explained as he motioned in the direction of the bed. "We need to get a coffin—a box—we need to get a wood box made to put the body in so we can bury it. Understand?"

"Yessa, Massa. 'Spects you want Jacob to build one. Dat 'bout right?"

"That's exactly right, Uriah," Basil replied as he realized Uriah was way out ahead of him on this, and he was taking more pains to explain things to Uriah than was necessary.

"Take a measure of the body and ride down and have Jacob make the box right away. Try and have it finished and back here by nightfall. And have one of the others ride back in the wagon with you."

"Yessa, Massa, I'll do it. And don't worry none. We'll be back 'fore you know it."

The slave then moved quickly over to the bed, kneeled down and spread his arms to gauge the dead woman's height and then took off toward his horse. Basil called after him,

"Be careful crossing the river, Uriah, and put on some dry clothes when you get there, you hear?"

Uriah turned back toward Basil and obediently responded, "I will, Massa. I will."

He watched Uriah trot off on the horse into the stormy weather. *Hopefully,* Basil brooded to himself, *Uriah will not encounter any mishaps on the flooded roadway, especially on the way back.* He was very much aware that the crossings of the rain-swollen East Fork River in a coffin-laden wagon would be perilous at best.

Josiah and his daughter-in-law finally wandered in just before dark, and Jesse was not with them. The tenant farmer noticed quickly that the baby had come, and he could see that Altha was a sight poorly. Before he could ask after her and his wife, who was nowhere to be seen, or take notice of the covered body on his bed, Basil broke the shocking news to him. Josiah was dumbstruck, and he walked directly over to the bed and pulled back the cover to reveal his wife's frozen, ashen face. He stared at it for a while and then suddenly fell on his knees as he broke down and wept for his faithful partner. Basil just let him be and allowed the tenant farmer all the grieving time he needed.

Later that night, Josiah shared the troublesome news regarding Jesse. They had found him locked up in the county jail, charged with disorderly conduct and destruction of private property. Seems as though he took the money he got from selling the cow and headed straight away for one of the local taverns. After a drink or two, he got himself crosswise with a couple of Garrett brothers from down around Jonathan Creek. One accusation led to another, slanderous curses were shared and so forth until a barroom brawl could not be avoided. Jesse got hit in the head with a broken chair leg during the row and woke up to find himself incarcerated and in the custody of the high sheriff of Haywood. The Garretts were long gone when the sheriff arrived at the scene, and all witnesses including the tavern owner placed the blame for the fracas squarely on Jesse.

"That there no-good sheriff weren't 'bout to release Jesse unless I come up with fifty dollars fer bail," Josiah angrily explained. "He knows gooder and well I ain't got that kind of money. But he allowed if'n I provide a note that is secured by some'ns with money or property, sech as yerself, he'll free Jesse till the next court in two months."

Basil was as vexed with this legal dilemma his tenants had gotten themselves into as he was with their abandonment of Altha during her confinement. With so much evidence stacked against Jesse, he was surely going to be locked away in jail for a few months, unless the Andersons came up with a way to pay for the damages to the bar property. There was no telling what that bill might amount to. Basil surmised that he would probably have to secure that note as well as the one for the bail money, and he had little confidence that these Crab Orchard tenants would ever be able to pay him back. Why had his own father not listened to Hartgrove and evicted this bunch last fall?

After mulling things over for a few minutes, Basil made an offer to Josiah, "Things don't look good for Jesse, Josiah. He's probably going to be jailed for a while unless you can get that barkeeper to take your and Jesse's note for the damages caused by the fight. Now here's what—"

The cantankerous farmer interrupted him, "Don't need nary none of yer preaching or dealing, Edmunston. No sir, nary none atall. Me an' them boys and Altha and that there new grandson will be jest fine. Don't ye go to fretting none 'bout us."

"I'm not trying to preach to you or swindle you, Josiah. Now hear me out. You still have them fields to finish plowing and planting, don't you?"

Josiah nodded his affirmation.

Basil continued, "You've made a mighty good start on that work, I have to admit. If you and your sons will give me your solemn promise to finish that planting and another ten acres to boot and do everything in your powers to double your last year's yield, I'll secure those notes to get Jesse out of jail. Plus, I'll give Jesse work at the Den from time to time so he can earn money to pay off the note. Now how's that?" Basil asked as he finished up his proposal and looked expectantly at his tenant.

Josiah frowned and fretted as he considered the offer. He could not stand the thought of his boy sitting over in Waynesville in the jailhouse with a bunch of lowly criminals. The boy's wife and children had to be considered in all these doings, too. They needed Jesse worse than he did. Nobody else but Edmunston would venture to secure their notes, he was sure of that. His and his boys' reputations were not the shiniest in Haywood County neither. He had no other choice, the way he saw it, and so he put this to Basil.

"I 'spect we kin grow ten more acres of corn with yer help. If you continue the lend of that there mule ye giv us and giv us the corn seed, why then we'ns can try and double the yield."

Basil was pleased but not satisfied, "Okay, Josiah. But it's only a deal when you get both your sons together and the three of you make that promise to me. And all three of you have to be sober when you do. Deal?"

Still grimacing and mumbling to himself, Josiah searched for the loopholes or catches in the deal that the upstart Edmunston boy was offering. He could not readily find one and finally consented to make the pledge once they got Jesse out of jail and back home.

Realizing that Josiah had probably not given much thought to Altha's situation, Basil strongly advised him to make arrangements with his daughters-in-law to look after Altha and the baby for the next few days on an around-the-clock basis. Her life was still in the balance, and the baby certainly needed caring after. Basil also informed Josiah that a coffin box was being made for his wife, and he offered to let Josiah bury her in a wooded plot near the schoolhouse. Not knowing whether his tenant would want to have a pious burial service, Basil had demurred from making any arrangements. But he prompted Josiah with the idea of sending up the river for Trull so that the lay preacher could hold a respectful service for his wife.

Josiah had understandably been rattled with the events unfolding around him and had truthfully not considered these painful things that Basil was bringing to his attention. So, surprisingly perhaps, he put aside his old grievances and feelings toward the Edmunstons and reacted with a reluctant appreciation for his young landlord's suggestions and actions. The crusty old tenant was able to utter up a genuine thanks for the thoughtfulness and allowed that he would take care of the matters just as Basil had recommended.

Only twenty years old and new to this sort of thing, Basil was making it up as he went along. The deal and guidance he gave to Josiah Anderson seemed fair and logical to his way of thinking. And Anderson needed the help for sure. Whether he was a good tenant or bad one mattered little at a time like this. The man had just lost his wife, his only daughter was barely alive after giving him a new grandson, and one of his sons had just been pitched into the jailhouse. In a span of a couple of days, these events were certainly a huge shock and burden for Josiah to bear. Basil had the means and wit to help his tenant, and he meant to do so. He also meant to give Altha and her new baby all the support in his power.

After concluding his conversations and dealings with Anderson, Basil moved over to the bed where Altha and the baby were resting. She was awake and had been able to change out of the bloody soiled dress into a clean one. An obvious effort had been made to comb out the tangles in her hair, which was now pulled back and fixed neatly behind her head. Altha reported that not only had she suckled the baby but had even eaten a few morsels of food herself. Although noticeably appreciative for the attention Basil had given her throughout the day, she appeared to be anxious toward him.

"Oh, Basil, I'm so sorry about all the terrible things I said to you when I was having those awful pains. I couldn't help it. Please don't think bad about me."

Basil just laughed big and said, "Girl, that's the last thing you need to be worrying about right now. Are you feeling any stronger?"

"Maybe a little bit. But I sure don't feel any worse. I'm still having quite a bit of pain down there," she said nodding shyly and casting her eyes down in the general direction. "But I believe the bleeding has finally stopped."

"Doctor Allen said that as long as there is no infection, you should be fine. Let's keep our fingers crossed," Basil encouraged her.

Altha looked at him and then hesitantly asked, "Basil, I've got to come up with a name for my son and I was thinking, if you're okay with it, that I might name him after you—after all that you have done for me and him. What do you think?"

Whhooaaa, Basil thought. *What do I think?* He did not think he liked it atall, that is what he thought. "I don't know, Altha. Don't you think one Basil on the East Fork is enough?"

"Why, I don't see a problem with it atall," she quickly replied while looking at him and trying to surmise some logic in his reluctance.

But there was none. He just knew he did not want that baby named Basil. *It would not look good for one of his tenants to be naming a baby after him. And besides—besides what would Julia think?*

"I really appreciate your thoughts, Altha. I really do. It's a very kind consideration, but I believe it would be best not to name him Basil. I would be most grateful if you didn't."

She was puzzled that he rejected the idea so offhandedly. Why had he not reacted with joyful pride at the notion as she suspected he would? Altha could not comprehend the reason, but graciously, yet with obvious disappointment, she conceded to Basil's wish, "Okay, I'll think of another name. Do you have any good ideas?"

He thought for a brief spell and was able, surprisingly, to come up with an inspired suggestion, "How about Rufus? That was the name of my younger brother. He died a few years ago, but I believe he would have liked for your fine young son to sport his name. And I would appreciate it too. So ponder that one with due consideration."

Altha grinned toward him and replied, "Okay. I'll put Rufus in the hat, and we'll see what shakes out." Then a more serious look came across her face, and she confided to him, "Basil, I can't thank you enough for what you did for us. If you hadn't come when you did, we would be—well, you saved us both, and I will be forever grateful and beholden to you for it." As Altha concluded her heartfelt expressions, she looked away from him, her eyes tearing up.

Basil looked at Altha and thought that she was simply beautiful. It was not the first time he had recognized her natural beauty. He had perceived it the first time he laid eyes on her. Even in these circumstances where she was unwell and unbathed, there was an inexplicable aura about her. It was something strange, something that he could not quite get over. It was a presence or a mysterious seductive allure that drew him to her. Maybe it was just those high cheekbones or her long, straight, black hair. *How could she possibly be Anderson's daughter,* he wondered. *Surely she has some Indian blood running through her veins, at least what little blood she still has left in her.*

"I'm just glad that you didn't forget me and that you remembered to call for me," Basil replied with his customary defensive diversion.

"What? Forget you! Basil Edmunston, you're not very forgettable, believe me. In the back of my mind, I knew if there was any trouble atall, you would be my knight in shining armor. You were so kind that first day we met, and you offered your help so generously. No, I wasn't about to forget you, Basil."

He did not know what to say to that. And he felt himself falling for this girl too. He could feel it. He had the same kinds of feelings for Altha that he had for Julia Deaver. *Damn, how can I be falling for two girls at once?* he fretted. *It's not natural. It's impossible, surely.* As these wild thoughts bounced around in his mind, he struggled internally and externally to get it together.

"Too bad then, Altha. Now you're going to have to put up with my frequent visits to Crab Orchard to see how you and Rufus are doing. Ooops, did I say Rufus? Sorry. I'll be looking in on you and your son, no matter what name you decide to give him."

About that time, Basil heard a wagon and team splattering through the mud outside the cabin. "Must be Uriah with the coffin," he said looking toward the doorway. "Okay, Altha, you get yourself some rest now. I've got to give your father some help," and as he looked into her deep green eyes, he reached over and took her son's little foot in his big hand and gently squeezed it. It was the same foot that he had been able to catch inside Altha.

Doctor Allen was true to his word and showed up early the next morning as a brilliant sunshine spread over the mountains and across the East Fork valley. After a brief examination of Altha, he announced that she might just make it after all. That afternoon, Anderson's wife was buried with a simple graveside service led by Delaney Trull. On the day following the funeral, Basil accompanied Josiah on a ride over to Waynesville to bail Jesse out of jail. Josiah had to give his note for fifty dollars, which the sheriff only took after Basil countersigned it for security. And finally, upon Jesse's return to Crab Orchard, all three of the Anderson menfolk stood in front of Basil and gave him their sober solemn oaths to increase the farm's planted acreage and attempt to double their last year's corn yield.

As things became settled at the Crab Orchard farm and Altha showed encouraging signs of improvement, Basil resumed his lonely life at Bachelor's Den with his slaves. Altha's emergency and Jesse Anderson's stupidity had diverted his attention from farming business for the past few days. He now had to regain a focus on his father's enterprise. But there were other distracting things weighing heavily on his mind—less tangible things and far more complicated. For instance, there was this business of his falling for two girls at once. He had to somehow get to the bottom of that conundrum and sort it out. And there was Rufus, or whatever name Altha was going to bestow on her son. Basil had actually delivered the boy into this world, forcibly pulling him from his mother's womb. That peculiar sensation he had felt when he last took hold and squeezed the baby's foot could not be extinguished. It smoldered in him, and he did not know what to allow about that.

Chapter 9

Smack Dab in the Middle

By early May, the wilderness setting surrounding Bachelor's Den was awash with vernal aromas and colors. Withering blooms of the dogwood and redbud trees were now being outshone by the pinks and whites of the resilient crabapple and wild cherry trees' flowers. Azalea bushes were setting whole hillsides ablaze in a fiery hue, and mountain laurel blossoms were beginning to brighten the dark coves. Underneath these blooming canopies, the forest floors writhed with a host of wild flowers. Not amiss amongst them were the dainty violets and trilliums, with their pretty purple and white blooms. Nature's tinted spectacular spoke loudly to the highlanders—the message being that winter had blown its last cold blast, and it was high time that the planting get done. And Basil received the message loud and clear.

Things were looking up on his homefront. He and the boys rounded up the stock of all varieties and found the herds to be in tolerable shape coming out of the winter. The cattle losses appeared to be within acceptable limits, and not only did the sheep appear to be in better shape than common, but the flock had grown with the addition of twenty-seven large lambs that had survived the frigid weather.

Fortunately, an optimal mix of April showers and sunshine had made the ground finely suited for cultivating. Basil and the boys prepared and planted corn in three large bottom fields. In another poorer patch—one the slaves told him had never made anything—they planted clover. In the upper fields, crops of oats and winter wheat, badly bitten from a late cold snap, stood ready for harvesting. And when not working the fields or tending the stock, the Africans were kept busy cleaning out the drainage ditches and repairing the fences that surrounded and protected the planting grounds.

During one particular rainy day's work lull, Basil's attention turned to his fruit orchard. He had noticed soon after taking over at the Den that many of the old apple trees had died from the ravages of the long cold winters. His parents had planted the trees decades ago, and he was determined to resurrect the orchard. Because the day seemed too soggy for outside work, the slaves occupied themselves with piddling chores that could be performed in the dry. Spotting Harry loafing nearby, Basil called for his help at the shed where the cider press was housed. The youth came running over with his four-legged friend, Frank—the same dog that had followed Basil from the settlement at Pigeon River Ford. Harry had adopted the mutt and given it the name 'Frank' for no practical reason that Basil could determine. Arriving out of breath, the young man huffed and puffed and asked, "Yessa, Massa Baz? You's gots a job fo' me and Frank, do's you?"

"Yep, sure do Harry. Need your help here. See all that dried-up pommace in the bottom of the press vat?" he asked pointing at the thick layer of caked sediment.

"Yessa, I do's. What you's needs me to do's wif it?"

"That dry apple pulp still has a good amount of seed left in it, and we aim to find the seeds, Harry—me and you. But we have to wash the pulp to extract the seeds," Basil slowly explained trying to make it clear to Harry what he wanted him to do.

"Yessa, Massa. Dem seeds—you wants me to find dem seeds. Is dem apple seeds, Massa, in dat pu'p?"

Easy now, Basil, he told himself as he continued to describe the job so Harry could understand. "That's right, Harry. They're apple seeds, and I want to collect them and then plant them over in the orchard yonder," Basil explained as he waved toward the hill behind the den.

Completely understanding the job now, Harry perked up and allowed, "I sees now, Massa Baz. You wants me to find dem seeds, den collects dem seeds, den plants dem seeds. Dat 'bout right, Massa?"

Fearing that this little task might actually take longer to explain than do, an idea popped into Basil's head. He would demonstrate to Harry how to do the job and that should speed things up, and it did.

"That's right. You've got it now, Harry. Now watch how I do it. Fetch me a bucket of water." And he and Harry proceeded to grab handfuls of the dried-up pommace and wash and sluice it in water until the seeds were uncovered. They then picked them out, one by one, and within a couple of hours had collected about five pints of clean apple seeds.

Satisfied with their work so far, Basil stood back and boasted to his work partner, "Now just look at all those seeds, Harry. That should be more than enough. Good job!"

"Wusn't nuthin', Massa. You's do's most of da work anyhows."

Basil simply chuckled and disregarded the comment as he looked toward the orchard and then upward to the sky. The heavy downpour had slowed to a steady rain, yet he was undaunted. There was a job he wanted done, and the sogginess could not stand in the way. "Harry, go get Gabe and Erwin. Tell them to bring the crosscut saw and meet me in the orchard." In scant minutes, Basil, Harry, Gabe, Erwin, and Frank were in the orchard field cutting down the worst of the old dead apple trees and planting the newly collected seeds near the base of the stumps.

More than twenty dead trees were cut out, and Basil ordered the trunks and debris to be dragged and piled in a nearby pasture to be burned later. Around each stump, Basil planted at least three seeds, increasing the odds that a tree might actually sprout in that particular spot. If the seeds were good and more than one sprung up, the bonus trees could always be transplanted somewhere else.

By dusk, the party of apple tree planters, all drenched and dirty and thoroughly done in, had completed the job. As they picked up their tools and started back for the slave quarters, Basil thanked each of them for their hard work. But he stayed back while watching Frank bark and yelp at his Africans' heels as they traipsed home through the greening orchard grass in the pelting rain.

Finding a rock to sit on, Basil fixed his gaze upward to survey the day's work and to just contemplate things. *Will Father appreciate these labors to rejuvenate the old orchard? He should! Those new trees are going to grow up and bear fruit for at least another generation or two of Edmunstons. Won't be me though,* he assured himself. *But someone is going to enjoy those apples and cider. Wonder who.*

Then suddenly he thought of Rufus, or whatever name the baby was going to take, and Altha. He wondered how they were doing tonight and resolved to get up there to the Crab Orchard soon to check on them. And out of nowhere Julia's pretty face popped into his mind, and he began conniving various reasons or excuses to call on her. When at last it dawned on Basil that he was fantasizing about the two girls again, he exploded. *Damn it all, things are getting way too complicated around here! Hell fire I'm tired,* he concluded at once, after recognizing the heavy weariness that overwhelmed his body. *Wonder what Patsy's got cooked up.* And with the thought of her tasty delights, he rose up from the hard seat and trudged toward the Den, with heavy 'master' problems echoing through his mind.

Overnight the rain moved out of the valley, and the morning dawned clear and breezy, with just a few puffy white clouds skating across the blue sky and hiding the sun from time to time. Basil had finally gotten the boys busy cutting the winter wheat. He had found the mowing scythes to be in such poor condition that precious early morning hours were lost fixing the helves and tightening and honing the blades. As he stood by watching Gabe and Erwin's smooth mowing strokes, he was surprised to hear someone calling from the distance—down below toward the Den. He could see a tiny buggy and team with three passengers—two ladies and a man, from the looks of it.

"Stay at it, boys. I'm going to see who's come to see us," he called out to the slaves and then bounded down the side of the hill to see who his visitors might be.

"Hello, Basil, my boy," called Colonel Deaver as the young master slowed to a halt in front of the buggy, where the Colonel, his wife, and Julia were still lodged.

While Basil caught his breath, he was hardly able to greet them. "Hello! This is a great surprise! What brings the Deaver clan to my humble Bachelor's Den?" he said as he paused intermittently to catch his breath.

"Got somethin' here to give ye, lad. Then we aim to go on uppers towards Josiah Anderson's place. Been meaning to get up there to pay our respects 'bout his wife."

Impressed with this kind act of thoughtfulness toward his tenants Basil commented, "That's mighty neighborly of you, sir. Josiah's getting over his loss about as good as could be expected, I believe. Altha and Rufus, that's the baby boy's name, or might be his name—don't know yet—seem to be getting along quite well too."

Maggie Deaver could not hold back any longer. "Dear boy, we all heard about the miracle baby. Joseph says that Doctor Allen came by the store and told him it was nigh a miracle how you saved that baby's life—and the mother's. The word's all about the area what you did. We're so proud of you, Basil," the matriarch finished and looked over expectantly at Julia.

Then the pretty belle, radiant as ever with a blue ribbon and bow in her hair and wearing a matching blue and white calico dress, spoke up, "Basil, do you think you could spare the time from your work to accompany us up to the Andersons'? I see you're busy mowing. But we would love to have you come along. And there's plenty of room for you in the buggy," Julia finished while patting her hand on the wooden seat at her side.

He thought for a few seconds about leaving the boys alone to mow the wheat and decided they could manage without him. Then a potential difficulty popped into his mind. He would be in the presence of both girls whom he believed he held romantic feelings for. *Might not that be a troublesome encounter?* Instantly he weighed the goods and bads and finally figured it might not be such a bad thing atall. With both girls together at the same time, he should be able to cipher out his problem once and for all—pick one of them over the other. Or at least he thought so.

"Sure, I would be happy to—if it's okay with you, Colonel?" Basil asked.

"Sure it is, lad. Julia's done asked us, and we ain't got nary problem with it. Here, Basil. Here's some money fer ye. It's what I owe Thomas fer the cattle I sold at market last fall. Got some right fair prices down at Augusta.

This here be nigh to one hundred and five dollars of hard species money, son," the Colonel said as he handed Basil a bag of gold and silver coins.

"Thank you, Colonel Deaver. When we return, I'll find your note for the cattle and give it back to you," said a wide-eyed Basil as he hefted the heavy bag of money.

"Right ye ere, lad."

Basil quickly ducked into the Den and slid the money under his bedstead. Patsy was poking about, and he told her where he was going and that he might be gone for several hours. As he splashed water over his face and toweled off, he directed the slave cook to get word up to the boys that he expected the entire upper field of wheat to be cut by nightfall, and there were to be no excuses. Masking the excitement he felt, Basil stepped out of the cabin, hopped into the buggy, and squeezed into the rear seat next to Julia. It was a tight fit, and their arms and shoulders and hips were pressed together and touching. *Not bad,* thought Basil, *and a sight better than mowing wheat.*

As the Colonel drove the team away from the Den, the young couple was bumped and jostled against each other, provoking giggles and laughs from both. It was a bone-jarring ride that required two fords of the East Fork River. There was plenty of small talk along the way until just before the Crab Orchard property came into sight. The subject had turned to Altha's ordeal and plight.

"Althea came into the store a few times last winter to buy supplies for her school. What a beautiful girl she is. Don't you think so, Joseph?" Maggie queried looking over at the Colonel as he guided the team.

"That she is, dear. She be mighty fetching fer a daughter of Anderson."

Julia added, "I've seen her in the store but have not met her yet. It's so terrible what happened to her. How can a man do such an awful thing?" It was an innocent comment that instantly aroused Basil's curiosity and caused the Colonel and Maggie to glance at one another.

"How's that again, Julia?" Basil asked looking directly at the belle. "What awful thing do you mean?"

A surprised Julia responded, "You don't know, do you? Well, last summer at the camp meeting, an awful man had his way with her and—and left her with child."

Basil just looked at her incredulously. Finally he got these words out of his mouth, "What? What do you mean?" and then stared dumbfoundedly at Julia and then toward the Colonel.

Deaver had stopped the buggy, and both he and Maggie had twisted around to see Basil.

"Sure 'nough, lad. T'was a Beck, Sam Beck, from the West Fork. He follered the girl off in a woods where she went to sprinkle and jumped her. Folks were making so much infernal shouting noise with the preacher that no'ens heared her scream. When Anderson and them sons of his and a couple more men caught up with Beck a few days later, they put a bad whuppin' on him, real bad. Pert' near kilt him," Colonel Deaver explained.

Basil could not believe his ears. "When I met Altha for the first time she told me that her husband—her son's father—had been killed. What about that?"

The Colonel looked first to his wife, then his daughter, and lastly to Basil. "Don't know 'bout that," he responded and then went on. "That man Beck is nuthin' but a drunkard, a no'count trifling scamp. There were sure 'nough a shotgun wedding, but he weren't no husband to speak of atall. In less'n two months, I believe it was, Beck abandoned the girl and hightailed it out of this here country. Some folks believe he's laid up some'rs in the hills of South Carolina. Others say he's gold digging out fer to the west of here—out 'bout in Macon or Cherokee County. He knows better than to show his face 'round here again."

Basil was in a state of shock. He had heard enough and simply hushed, not being able to readily reconcile Altha's story with what the Deavers were telling him. *Why did Altha tell me that yarn about her husband being killed? Surely there's something else to this tale.* He would have to find out. The Colonel cracked the whip across the lead horse's hide to get the buggy moving again, and before long, they were pulling up to Josiah Anderson's cabin.

"Hello, Anderson! You in there?" hailed Colonel Deaver from the buggy.

Right short-like, Josiah Anderson appeared in the cabin doorway, shielding his eyes while they adjusted to the sunlight. He had obviously been into the hard cider barrel but was not too out of sorts yet. Recognizing the visitors right away, he offered a polite greeting, "Hello, Deaver, ma'am, missus," and lastly he growled, "Edmunston." Then demonstrating his finest social skills, he immediately asked, "What brings ye folks round here 'bouts?"

After the entire crew in the buggy had greeted Josiah, the Colonel responded to Anderson's question. "Came to pay our respects to you and your daughter, is all. Mind if we come in?"

"No, no, not atall. Please." Josiah was not happy about the intrusion, but he did not let on none as he led the party inside.

Basil had been delighted to spot Manson and Jesse toiling in one of the fields. Their planting was almost done and, so far, the Andersons had steadfastly labored to keep their end of the bargain they had made with him. Upon entering the cabin the visitors, and especially Basil, were surprised to see Altha on her feet and walking toward the door to meet them. She looked so much better than she had just a week ago when Basil last visited. He took the initiative to present her to the Deavers, and then everyone had a turn gushing over the baby and asking after Altha. The seating arrangements were difficult but eventually sorted out. The Colonel and Maggie chose the only two chairs, Altha and Josiah sat on Altha's bed where the baby was lying, and Basil and Julia rested themselves close together on Josiah's bed.

"We were very sorry to hear 'bout yer loss and wanted to come up and tell ye personal-like. Wanted to do it earlier, but we jest couldn't get headed this way fer one reason or t'uther," the Colonel explained.

"Thank ye, Deaver. We 'preciate it, we really do," replied Josiah, who was battling the effects of the cider and trying valiantly to put forward his best civil front.

Of course, Altha's miracle delivery quickly became the topic of interest, and the new mother was not bashful in lauding the efforts of her savior knight from the Bachelor's Den. "Neither of us would be alive today if it hadn't been for Basil. He came straight away after I sent for him. It must have been God who guided Basil to us and to do what he did. If there ever was an intervention by Him, then this was certainly it."

Altha was expressing her true, sincere sentiments. But as she continued to describe Basil's deeds with even more glowing accolades, the impossible thought crossed Julia's mind that this new mother was enamored with him.

She began to feel a bit of jealous anger as Basil blushed noticeably with embarrassment.

Julia abruptly entered the conversation, "Oh, Altha, I do like the name Rufus. How did you come to give that name to your son?"

Great, Basil thought as he turned redder. *This should be real good.*

A surprised Altha responded, "So Basil told you about the baby's name, did he? Why, I don't believe I've even mentioned to him that I finally decided to name the baby Rufus," and she chuckled and paused for a moment. "Well, it took a while for the name to grow on me. I first fancied the name Basil, but for some reason," she teased, looking at him, "Basil would have nothing to do with that proposal."

Basil just grinned sheepishly as he looked from person to person in the cabin.

Altha continued, "But he did suggest the name Rufus. That was his younger brother's name, who died. So after pondering over it for a few days, that's what I finally settled on—Rufus Josiah Anderson."

"Oh, how very nice—and pretty," chimed Maggie as Julia cut a glance toward Basil whose red glow and anemic smile persisted.

Josiah was surprisingly adept and talkative, too, given his slightly inebriated state, and offered to the Colonel some news about Jesse's recent incarceration. Maggie had brought a basket of baked goods and a side of bacon, which she gave to the Andersons, and the visit ran on and on, running its course in an hour or so. For Basil, the conclusion of the social call came none too soon. The ride back to the Den was just as jarring as it had been before. But it seemed to Basil the buggy seat was a bit more expansive this time around, and the bumping contact between Julia and him was much diminished. He also sensed a frostiness in her demeanor and noticed that she had lost her chatty disposition. Needless to say, this joint encounter with the two girls failed to meet the high expectations he had imagined.

Basil had not been able to conclude who he yearned for most. Julia's immaturity bared its ugly self as she manifestly grew jealous of Altha's obvious affections for Basil. That little fact would have to be weighed in the balance against her. But even he had been caught off guard with Altha's glowing tributes and praises in his favor. To tell the truth, he was a little disconcerted to be caught smack dab in the middle of a romantic triangle. Or 'scared' would probably be closer to the truth. It was the pace of things that disturbed him most. He needed to be more in control of the whole process, able to sort things out and make reasoned decisions one step at a time. He had to slow things down a little, he figured. And then there was that distressing business regarding Altha's husband. *What the hell was that all about?*

Chapter 10

An Old Hog Thief

That afternoon, after the awkward social visit to the Crab Orchard, Basil glanced up at the wheat field and saw that the boys had not finished their work. Less than half of the field had been cut, and his two mowers looked none too lively. He was vexed for sure at their lack of progress and vowed to himself to have it out with Gabe and Erwin. This was a serious matter that had to be dealt with strongly, and he aimed to do it. Maybe a severe disciplining was in order. So far, Basil had not resorted to the extreme measure of whipping slaves at the Den. He was not easy with the idea but knew the day would come when it would be necessary. A keen sense of dread hinted that this just might be that day. Maybe there was a legitimate reason for the holdup in today's work. At least he hoped that was the case.

Patsy was in, and Basil asked her to make him a hoe cake and fry some bacon. All the worrying and stress he had suffered so far that day had left him famished. As he was gulping down a cup of milk and waiting for the food to be pulled from the fire, he could hear a loud commotion over at the Africans' quarters. Jumping up from the table, he ran outside and looked over at a great frolic taking place. The Negroes were extremely agitated and were screaming and hollering and pointing at a large bear pacing down the hill through the barnyard. The animal had its head down and was apparently hot on the trail of a young hog running before it. Basil could not believe his eyes.

He had not bothered to pen the shoats, so his first thought was that the bear must have followed the young Berkshire pig from the range on the high mountain rising above the Den. The bear was moving steadily between the shop and the main barn, still tailing the frightened pig and appearing to take no notice of the excited male slaves running to surround him. Harry was among the gawkers, and so was his new four-legged friend, Frank. The adrenalin surge from the sight of the bear resurrected Basil from his doldrums. Flushed with excitement, he quickly removed his father's flintlock rifle from above the doorway, grabbed the powder horn and ammunition pouch, and ran as fast as he could toward the action.

The boys had snatched up whatever weapons they could quickly lay their hands on—an ax, hand spike, smith irons, shovel, and knife. Luckily all four of the hunting hounds were in the barnyard area, and they immediately pounced on the track, chasing the bear and easily outracing the Africans. Soon the dogs turned the bear away from its quarry, with the monster changing course and splashing across the creek and running toward the corncribs and the Den in the distance. The dogs caught up with it quickly, as Frank joined the fracas as well. They fought the bear past the cribs and into the garden patch, crashing through the rail fencing. All across the garden the dogs and bear battled. The hounds could not be shaken, and as the bear tried to climb over the split rails and up a tree, they latched on with their teeth and pulled it back. This prize was not to be denied them, and with an innate persistence, the pack fought and worried the critter down.

But the old bear had plenty of fight left in him. It turned quickly on one of the canine pursuers and slashed it fiercely across the neck with its fearful claws. The wounded dog fell heavily to the earth, whimpering and yelping and dying a slow death. Somehow the bear was able to get free of the dogs' clutches and climbed a tall poplar tree near the creek to escape and rest. The baying hounds surrounded the tree, and Basil saw his chance to strike a lethal blow. Carefully clutching the loaded musket, he warily approached the base of the huge poplar, searching for a clear shot. Around and around he circled, until at last the bear was in his sights. Quickly hefting the heavy firearm into position, he took dead aim and fired. *Bang!!*

At first, Basil thought he had missed the bear, and with his ears still ringing from the loud shot, he hurriedly starting reloading. The thing had not flinched a bit and had not immediately fallen out of the tree. Although his aim had been directed at the bear's head, the lead shot had actually penetrated its shoulder and passed through the back. Letting out a tremendous growl of pain and anger, the wounded animal slowly descended the tree toward the dogs. At a level of about ten feet above the ground, it let loose of its tree hug and fell crashing down onto the hounds. Frantically the dogs pounced on the critter and sunk their teeth into its hide, while the ferocious beast in turn took up in its mouth the nearest antagonist. It was Frank. The feisty dog had showed no fear throughout the chase and had not backed away from the bloody action. Seizing on Frank's head, the bear bit it cruelly time and time again. The little dog had no chance, and its end came quickly.

Suddenly the bear released its dead victim and lunged directly into the remaining hounds. Then it broke free from them again and loped by the springhouse and up the hill toward the Den, with the dogs in close pursuit. As Basil hurriedly worked to reload the old rifle, he glanced up to spot where the bear had run to. The door of the Den was ajar and, of all things, there was Patsy standing in it. The old slave cook, an innocent spectator to the action below, was only trying to see what all the noisy fuss was about. Basil screamed at her to retreat inside and bolt the door, but she did not budge. The dogs at last caught up with the bear when it was within mere yards of the cabin. Patsy, apparently oblivious to the approaching peril, remained steadfast in the doorway. She took no heed of Basil's screaming warnings and did not move a step to protect herself.

Basil ran to a vantage point where he could draw a bead on the bear. Again he raised the old flintlock, aimed, and fired. *Bang!!* Time seemed to stand still for him as the pan flashed, the powder charge exploded, and the lead ball was propelled at extreme velocity directly toward the wild animal. And almost instantly he lost all sight of the target as the smoke from the black powder blast enveloped him. Quickly he moved away from the smelly cloud and saw that the bear was down but still moving. He had hit it again for sure but had not killed it. However Uriah, who had out-footed all the others and caught up to the battle, fell upon the bear with an ax and in short order put an end to its life. At last the beast was dead.

Upon a closer examination of the bear, Basil could see that it was a skinny old male, almost too poor to pork. But it was as long a bear as he had ever seen and undoubtedly a real old hog thief. He looked over at the Den, and there Patsy still stood in the doorway, unimpressed and impatient for her master to come and eat the food she had dutifully prepared for him. Casting his gaze back down the hill toward the creek, he spotted the distraught Harry kneeling over Frank and crying like a baby. And then Basil's eyes were drawn to the partially mown wheat field in plain view on the hillside. With all the turmoil surrounding the bear chase, he had forgotten about the mowing work. *Better not delay in addressing that issue,* he told himself as he walked by Patsy and through the doorway to see what she had cooked up.

Late that evening, after an unusually exasperating and eventful day, Basil sat at the table penning a letter to Brother Walter by candlelight. He was catching his brother up on most of the farming news around Bachelor's Den—crops, wheat harvest, condition of his stock, and such. Previously he had communicated Altha's story and his role in the birth of her baby. Tonight he proudly revealed the news that the baby boy had been named Rufus after their dearly departed brother. He gave few details regarding his and the Deavers' visit to the Crab Orchard earlier that day, but he described in depth and with vivid details the bear tale and how he and the boys had managed to slay an old East Fork hog thief. Finally, and with a pained and heavy heart, he wrote of his vexations with his slaves, Gabe and Erwin in particular, and how he had been tried beyond his limit that very afternoon.

Basil sadly allowed to Walter that just after the bear frolic, he confronted the two men on their lack of progress cutting the wheat. When asked why the job was not completed, he got his ears filled with excuses. It was too hot, Erwin was stung by bees, and one of the scythes had broken. As Basil pressed and questioned them, Gabe became extremely agitated and said some things he should not have. Gabe had been unhappy ever since Basil had ruled the weekly bacon allowance would remain the same as that given out at the Fort, and that an exception would not be granted to him. From time to time, Basil had discerned the slave's smirking looks and obedience lapses and suspected Gabe might be contriving behind his back some means of a general protest. On this evening, Gabe had gone too far. He had become insolent with Basil and made some crude disparaging remarks that essentially implied his master did not know what in the hell he was doing.

Gabe immediately realized that he had transgressed over a forbidden threshold, and he regretted it. He was not unlike the rest of the Africans at the Den. All had come to appreciate and like their new master. Although Basil lacked the experience of other overseers and might indeed not know what he was doing, the young man was energetic and respectful of them. In this instance, Gabe had strayed way out of line, and Basil could not let it pass. Otherwise, the rest of his Africans would see it as a weakness on his part and would surely intrigue to exploit it.

It was with extreme difficulty that Basil described to Walter his disciplinary actions earlier that evening, scripting the letter in this manner:

> *I called up Gabe this evening and told him that it was necessary to give him a sound thrashing and I was ready to attend to him. I tied him fast to the horse rack and commenced pretty sharply upon him and he tried to stout it out. Soon, however he humbled himself a bit and promised his obedience. I stopped sooner than I expected, talked to him a while, and untied him. He said he was glad it was over, and he felt better satisfied.*

Basil certainly did not relish this slave-discipline business. Given a choice, he would not take a slave's weight in gold to go through it again. But circumstances had made him a slave owner, or master, of his father's slaves, and as the master, he did not always have a reasonable alternative to harsh physical discipline. In order to establish and maintain control over his slaves—to keep them polite and obliging and industrious—he had no doubts that the lash would be used again at the Bachelor's Den, but only as a last resort.

The next day, after Basil had started Gabe and Erwin cutting wheat, another slave vexation rose up to challenge the Master of the East Fork's managerial capacity. Badly needing to talk to his master, Lark approached Basil in the barnyard with a disturbing proposition. "Massa Baz, I needs to talks wif you 'bout somethin'."

"Hello there, Lark. What is it?" Basil asked with as much patience as he could muster at the time. He knew Lark to be a good slave.

"I finds me a girl and wants to marry her, Massa. She lives at Osbornes' and is real sweet."

Surprised, Basil thought about it for a moment and then said, "Don't rightly see how that's going to work, Lark. We don't need another girl around here and you understand, I hope, that I can't let you have a wife away from home. Just can't allow that," Basil replied realizing that if he let one take a wife away from home, the others would also want to find themselves a spouse elsewhere. Before long, no one would be around to do the farm work. They would all be off with their consorts doing what husbands and wives do—consorting. That just would not do atall.

"Yessa, Massa. I figger you's gonna say dat. But I done talks to two men who'll go security for Colonel Blalock. You sees, Colonel Blalock can buys us both, and we's can git married. Whut's you thinks 'bout dat, Massa? You b'lieve dat might do?" Lark finished looking expectantly at Basil, who frankly was mystified.

"Lark, does Colonel Blalock know anything about this?"

"I 'spects not, Massa. But he needs hisself a girl, I b'lieve, and I 'spects he could use me. I wus hoping, Massa Baz, dat you might talk wif Colonel Blalock fo' me."

Basil was simply astounded by the slave's proposal. Lark was one of his first-rate boys, about Basil's age, and he did not really want to lose him. But he wanted to do right by Lark, and if this was Lark's chance to have a wife and family and be happy, then perhaps he should consider helping his slave.

"Okay, I'll look into it, Lark. I'll talk to Colonel Blalock and see if he's interested. But you do realize, don't you, that I won't take less than nine hundred dollars for you, and the payment will have to be made entirely secure? And I won't sell you to Blalock unless he is willing to buy the girl from Osborne, and Osborne is willing to let the girl go. Do you understand?"

"Yessa, Massa Baz. I's unnerstands and I 'preciates it. You do's me a big favor. Yessa, you do's, Massa," a thankful Lark replied.

Basil had no confidence what-so-ever that a deal like this would ever be consummated and tried to ground Lark with some realism.

"I'll see what Blalock allows about it, Lark, but don't set your hopes too high. There are a lot of 'ifs' in these goings on. I'm not sure how Blalock can secure his payment to me, let alone to Osborne. And I will be very surprised if Osborne sells your girl. I hear he's not one keen on selling his Negroes if they're any good atall. But we'll see."

"Yessa, Massa. We's sees. Thanks you, Massa." And the excited Lark returned to his work in the stables, knowing that his fate was in good hands and genuinely believing he would have a wife sooner than later.

Basil was highly doubtful that anything would come of this marriage business, but he would give it a try for Lark's sake. He guessed he would have to ride down to the Forks in a day or two and have a little talk with Blalock. And it would be best not to rouse Osborne before feeling out Blalock and determining his interest and ability to offer a secure payment for the slaves. Anyway, he had a hankering to call on Julia and needed an excuse to get down the river.

Ever since their trip up to the Orchard and Julia's cool treatment toward him, Basil had been infected with a poor feeling. He felt an urgent need to work out exactly what had dampened her affections. If it was jealousy, as he suspected, he would try to assuage it as best he could. He meant to snuff out those hateful embers before they raged any hotter. And he had not stopped thinking about Altha either. Just as soon as possible, he meant to get up to the Orchard and ferret out the truth about Altha's no-good husband, Sam Beck.

Chapter 11

Hurtful Truth

Basil did not get down the river right away as he had hoped. Important tenant business kept him busy for a day or two, as he rode from one end of the Edmunston property to the other—that is, from the lower end of the East Fork to the upper. Below Bachelor's Den, a property dispute between Ivester and Burnette required his attention and mediation. Ivester wanted to clear more land and build a fence, as he had been contracted to do, but Burnette figured the neighbor was encroaching onto his lease. Thomas Edmunston's old survey plats were not definitive in regard to splitting up his huge tracts of land into distinct tenant plots. So Basil got the two men together, heard them out, and told them where he wanted the fence built. Burnette grumbled and allowed it weren't right, but he finally agreed to the delineation.

Another tenant reported that a fair number of sheep had been lost from his flock over the winter. Since the man's contract included the turnover of one-half of the sheep and wool to the Edmunstons after three years, Basil visited the farm to investigate. Another, who had been contracted to build a new cabin, wanted clarification on where to cut the timber and what size log structure to build. Along the river and up the creeks, Basil rode and talked and learned, settling one dispute or issue after another and sorely testing the limits of his patience and wisdom.

On his return from a tenant call at the head of the Edmunston property, Basil stopped by the Crab Orchard to check on the Andersons. All the planting, including the additional ten acres, had been completed, and the fields looked to be in proper order, with some of the crops beginning to sprout. He met with Josiah and his sons and received a reasonably warm reception. Jesse supplied more information about his impending court appearance at Waynesville and made plans to come down to the Den and work a few days with the boys. Rufus was almost two months old now and seemed to be growing faster than the weeds in his grandfather's cornfields. And Altha was looking much better too, Basil thought, and getting around spritely. But he noticed that she was still walking around without any shoes on her feet, so he made a mental note to remedy that situation soon.

When the right opportunity arose, Basil availed himself of a chance to talk to Altha in private. Catching her by the arm with a light grasp and looking directly into her eyes he spoke lowly, "Altha, let's sit down. There's something I've been meaning to talk to you about."

"Sure, let's sit over here," and she guided him to a wobbly chair at the small dining table. Altha was plenty intelligent and had a good notion what the coming discussion might be about. She had never felt completely at ease around Basil, knowing that she had lied to him from the beginning about her marital status. "Been hoping you would get up to check on us. We've been missing you. You look tired, Basil," she said looking at him tenderly.

"It's been a tough day. Rode by here early this morning and went all the way up to Poston's to see that bunch. Been doing a great deal of riding and skirmishing with my good tenants lately," he said with a grin on his face, trying to relieve the tension somewhat.

"Least you don't have to skirmish with Father today—I hope. I've been proud of the way he and my brothers have been working so hard."

Basil nodded and replied with no little satisfaction, "They're doing real good, Altha. You keep those spurs of yours dug into them, and I'll keep my fingers crossed."

Altha reared her head back and laughed, "Okay, I will."

He then got down to the business he wanted to discuss. "Altha, something's been bothering me for a while now. I want you—"

But she interrupted him, "Wait. Wait just a minute, Basil. I have something to say to you first, if you'll let me," and Altha paused to gather herself.

"Ever since we first met—that day you came by and I was spinning—I've felt just awful about telling you what I did about Rufus' father. I'm sure you've heard by now that he's not dead. At least I don't believe he is. I lied to you, Basil. I outright lied to you. And I'm so ashamed of it," Altha covered her face with her hands as she came to the end of her hurtful confession.

Basil moved over closer to Altha and took one of her hands, "That's okay, Altha. Don't worry about it, please. I don't mean to upset you. All I want is to find out the truth, that's all. If you say it's none of my business, then I'll drop it."

She hesitated and then, after sniffing a couple times and taking a huge breath, relieved her conscience. "He left me high and dry a few months after we were married, knowing I was carrying his child. When he left, he said he couldn't be cooped up with a woman and baby. He said he had living to do, and there was no future in being married to me and farming a piece of hard scrabble West Fork land."

Basil listened intently and let Altha go on.

"He didn't want to be tied down. He was no good, Basil. He was a monster, and I had to live with him those awful, awful months. It was such a dreadful time, and I'll never be able to forget it. Why did they make me marry him?" she asked pitifully, breaking down into crying heaves, as Basil moved to her and took her up in his arms. He squeezed Altha tightly and attempted to console her, saying that everything was going to be all right.

Eventually Altha was able to pull herself together and reveal the hurtful truth that tortured her so. She told Basil how her husband—Sam Beck was his name—had overpowered her in the woods at the summer religious revival and had had his way with her. The report that Beck received a severe beating at the hands of the Anderson men folk was confirmed. And Altha related how everybody told her she was a ruined woman, and how she was forced into marrying the man. Pain erupted within Basil's heart to hear what this young woman had endured. *How had the poor girl managed through it?* he wondered.

Altha described in alarming detail what it was like being housed over on the West Fork in an old log stock shed without a hearth or mud chinking. She divulged how Beck forced her to have intimate relations whenever he bothered to show up at the crude shelter, usually after drunken benders with his clan. If she withheld, he beat her until she submitted. It had been a Godsend when Beck suddenly up and left her. But ever since that day he disappeared, she had lived with terrible memories and the constant worry that one day he would return.

"Basil, you were a stranger, and I was too ashamed to tell you the truth. So when you asked me about my husband, it was easier to simply say that he had died," Altha rationalized.

"I understand, Altha. There's no need to worry about it anymore."

"You do understand, don't you? You mean it? I didn't know you. I didn't know if I would ever even see you again."

"Yes. Yes, I understand. Now don't you worry your pretty little head anymore, you hear?" he said while rising out of his chair. "We won't talk about this again. Now, I expect I've got to be on my way. Let me just hold this little boy over here one more time," and he reached over on the bed and picked up the wiggling Rufus.

"Hello there, little fellow. Growing up like a weed, you are. Yes you are."

Basil tried hard to remind himself that this was not his baby. It was Altha's, hers and some other man's. Although he adored and loved holding Rufus, Basil forced himself to put the baby down after a few brief moments of cuddling. He was afraid of becoming too attached to this baby. It didn't belong to him.

He left the Orchard feeling better about things, knowing why Altha had spun the yarn about her husband. It all made perfect sense to him now, and he could not blame the young woman atall. Almost two months had passed since she had given birth—since he had delivered her baby—and she was looking much better these days. For those long acquainted with Altha, she had simply regained her God-given good looks. But Basil's acquaintance with her was a relatively brief one, and with each visit to the Orchard, he was witness to a phenomenal metamorphosis. As the girl's health returned, her captivating beauty blossomed before his eyes. And there was that inner radiance and mystique about Altha that utterly captivated him. In her, Basil began to appreciate a woman's wholesome beauty and goodness and realize that Altha was not just another pretty girl.

But the Sam Beck business was worrisome though. A man like that—there was no telling what he might do if he ever came back and learned that he has a new son. Basil figured he would cross that bridge when he came to it.

Just as Basil had suspected, Colonel Blalock knew nothing about the wife business of Lark's. The elderly farmer, a respected pioneer of Forks of Pigeon, was as surprised as Basil had been when he heard of the matter; and he did not have any thoughts on how Lark might have come to entertain such a notion. Upon departing Blalock's place for Colonel Deaver's to see Julia, Basil mulled over exactly how he was going to break this news to Lark.

As he rode up to the Deaver's home, Basil could see that he was not the only one calling that day. Several horses were tied off near the house, and he suspected one of them might be Columbus Hartgrove's. The Colonel welcomed Basil into his home and into the crowded sitting room, where he was greeted not only by Maggie and Julia Deaver but also by Hartgrove and two unfamiliar gentlemen. The two youngish men, not much older than himself, if that, were dressed in stylish riding attire, and their aristocratic bearing was not lost on Basil. Hartgrove made the introductions.

"Basil, allow me to introduce these here fine gentlemen. This here one is Mister Wade Hampton."

Hampton reached out and sturdily shook Basil's large hand. "How do you do, sir? Wade Hampton from Columbia, South Carolina, at your service."

Basil nodded politely to Hampton, and then Hartgrove introduced the other man. "And this here is Mister Frederick Rutledge."

"Fred Rutledge, sir, from Charleston, South Carolina. Pleasure to make your acquaintance," he said and offered Basil a firm handshake.

Basil spoke to both of them, looking from one to the other, "Pleased to meet you gentlemen. I'm Basil Edmunston from up the East Fork River a ways."

Hartgrove interjected and explained, "Basil, these gentlemen looked me up to see about doing a little hunting and fishing on your place. I was just going to escort them up the river to see you, but I first wanted the Colonel and his family to have the pleasure of their acquaintance."

"That's right, sir," Wade Hampton broke in and hastened to explain further for Basil's benefit. "We've come up to the North Carolina highlands early this year—even before, I'm afraid to say, our parents have opened their summer houses over at Flat Rock. So until they arrive in a couple of weeks, we've taken rooms at the Sulphur Springs Hotel near Asheville and are enjoying the healthful waters at that quaint establishment." Hampton paused a brief moment to study the good-looking East Fork farmer, wondering why in the hell he had chosen to live in such a dark forbidding place. He quickly continued, "A fine gentleman whom we bumped into over dinner a couple of nights back extolled the pleasures of a fruitful hunting and fishing excursion he had once experienced under the guidance of Squire Hartgrove here. This man raved so much about the beautiful East Fork wilderness that we decided to try an adventure ourselves—that is, if you are amendable to the idea. Squire Hartgrove tells us that you, sir, are the land owner, and he suspects you might be favorably inclined to host us."

Basil felt every eye in the room bear down on him. Was he amenable to the idea? He was familiar with men such as Hampton and Rutledge and had gone to school with many of their ilk. Born to wealthy, genteel families on expansive cotton or rice-growing plantations worked by hundreds of slaves, they were not yet burdened with immense responsibility as that he had so recently taken on. Most were expected only to develop themselves into educated and refined southern gentlemen and to bide their time until the great landed estates and family fortunes were given over to them. These two young adventurers in front of him appeared to be such men and were seeking further development of their psyches, their physiques, and their sporting skills on Basil's very own East Fork plantation. *Farmwork be damned,* he thought, as he savored this unique opportunity to socialize and take a break from the daily routine.

"Yes sir, I expect I can change my plans to guide you two gentlemen into the darkest reaches of East Fork Valley," Basil wryly replied. "How many days do you expect to stay on here?"

"Thank you, sir. That's mighty gracious of you," a delighted Hampton replied. "Our immediate plans are to stay for two nights, including this evening. Would that be acceptable to you, Mr. Edmunston?"

"Please, you should call me Basil—or maybe Master of the East Fork will do. Right, Julia?" Basil looked toward Julia, hoping his witty query might reveal some slight emotion or sign indicating that the lovely girl's previous tinge of frostiness had thawed with time. But no such luck. Julia evaded his glance and instead seemed to be entranced with this new visitor Basil was addressing. He could not help but notice that her smiles and attentions were directed toward Wade Hampton, who in turn simply beamed toward the beautiful hostess. Hampton was a handsome man, no doubt about it—average height, shorter than Basil by several inches, long wavy brown hair covering his ears, and eyes of azure. Admittedly, Hampton was very distinguished looking, and Julia was definitely captivated.

"Oh, please, I think Basil might be much less cumbersome, don't you, Mr. Hampton?" Julia replied without taking her eyes off the gentleman.

Hampton broke from his trance-like gape at Julia and answered with a chuckle, "Most certainly it would be, Miss Deaver. How right you are," he said as he bowed politely toward her. Addressing all of his hosts, he added, "And to all my good Haywood friends, we are Wade and Fred, at your service. In your presence, please let us be known by these simple, unencumbered titles." There were hearty laughs, a "hear, hear," and head-nodding all around. And then the small group proceeded to visit for a brief spell.

It was painfully obvious to Basil that Julia's courtesies were undivided and converged not on him but on the handsome South Carolinian, Wade Hampton. The enraptured gentleman, for his part, reciprocated as he pondered how such an exquisite belle could be found in a backwoods country like Haywood. He thought Julia to be finer and more charming than any of the young husband-seekers that travelled in the aristocratic social circles he was accustomed. Why, he was so captivated by the girl that he eagerly asked both her and her parents if he might call again at the conclusion of his East Fork diversion. They readily agreed.

That night, Basil's humble Bachelor's Den was livelier than it had been in years, perhaps since his father and mother and their brood had vacated it some two decades earlier. He and his South Carolina guests got along famously. They were the same age, approximately, and shared common interests including politics, science, nature, and world affairs. As darkness fell around the cabin, the famished boys devoured Patsy's hoecakes, bacon, and left-over potatoes dug up from the winter stash. Washing the food down with generous doses of sour milk, Wade and Fred launched into a feverish dialog about the heightened tensions between the Free and Slave States.

Their hatred of northern abolitionists was unmistakable. Fred stated, "All Yankees be damned if they think they are going to take away southerners' rights to own slaves. My family has been using bonded Negro labor on our Santee River rice plantations for generations." Speaking primarily to Basil, he asked how they could possibly continue their profitable enterprise without the Africans. And Fred was quick to point out that the Rutledge's slaves were well-fed, content, and much better off than the so-called freed slaves in the North.

Basil, for the most part, kept his beliefs about slavery to himself. He did not suppose that these men would appreciate his opinions on the matter. Certainly they would challenge him with heated debate, or maybe even to a duel, if he revealed his wishes that the whole race be sent back to Africa.

Wade Hampton espoused the sympathies of many southern fire-brand citizens and politicians and believed that sooner, rather than later, the Slave States would be forced to break away from the Union. No matter how peculiar the institution might be to Yankees, and even other foreign countries of the world, slavery was the foundation of the South's economy and society. Wade explained to Basil, as if the Master of the East Fork did not already know, how the cultivation of huge cash crops such as cotton, rice, and sugar cane was possible only through the availability and leverage of slave labor. Wade thought it undeniable, as did Fred, that the anti-slavery wedge being driven between the North and South by the abolition movement would inevitably cleave apart their country, entirely and forever. Basil was not so sure, but the guests considered his silence to indicate acquiescence with their sentiments.

The two gentlemen also brought Basil up to date on the impending war with Mexico. He had already heard the thrilling news at Colonel Deaver's store that President James Polk had declared war with the neighboring country over disputed territorial claims. But Wade informed Basil that militia groups were already being mustered in South Carolina's capitol city, Columbia, to bolster the standing army. Also, at the Sulfur Springs Hotel, he had heard that a militia company was being got up in Asheville. Basil had not heard of a movement to do so in Haywood, but he informed his guests that he thought it likely and that it would probably happen sometime soon.

Late into the night, the men visited and talked and joked by candlelight, enjoying each other's company. Basil liked the two men. There were no pretensions about them, and each spoke his mind as he sincerely believed things to be. He could see they were extremely prideful and confident with their stations in life. They, in turn, had been astonished to discover that Basil, an obviously intelligent person with a relative lofty status in society, lived such a hard and lonely existence in these mountain hinterlands. With keen interest, they had listened to their host's story about suspending his scholastic studies at his father's behest and moving to Haywood County. But Basil had assured them that it was by choice and that he was becoming somewhat partial to his new life on the East Fork.

Wade finally got around to inquiring about the beautiful young Deaver girl. He asked Basil what she was like, how well he knew her, and those kinds of things. Without giving evidence of his own romantic inclinations towards Julia, Basil responded to the inquiries as best he knew how. Deep down, though, he was somewhat dismayed and a little jealous to hear how infatuated Wade was with Julia, and that the gentleman intended to call on her again on his way out of Haywood.

As the night wore on, Basil had Uriah fetch a couple of cornshuck ticks for the two guests to sleep on. The gentlemen from South Carolina collapsed on these rustic beds on the puncheon floor, harboring notions that they were truly roughing it, much like the early pioneers had. Basil doused the candle and slid into his own comfortable bed, and in the darkness of the cabin, the three men talked expectantly about the coming day's activities. One by one, their low voices died away, and finally only the howls of wolves, the cries of a panther, and an occasional snore invaded the quiet serenity of Bachelor's Den.

Chapter 12

Gentlemen's Excursion

Wade Hampton and Fred Rutledge, Basil's guests from South Carolina, awoke before sunrise the next morning, excited with their primitive East Fork lodgings and anxious to hunt large wild game. Patsy had come over early to scare up some breakfast for the three inhabitants, including sufficient leftovers to stow away in their saddlebags for nourishment throughout the day. And Uriah and Lark had saddled the horses and led them over to the cabin for their master and his highfalutin' guests to ride. Lark was the best woodsman in the county, some said. He walked in front, leading the group away from the river and steeply upward toward the thickly forested ridges of Cold Mountain, which loomed high above the Den. It was the highest mountain in a region that hosted many lofty peaks, rising to an altitude of more than six thousand feet above sea level.

Daylight had not broken yet, and through the last vestiges of darkness, Wade and Fred could not possibly see the imposing range where Lark was taking them. That was probably for the best. Had they been able to study the towering destination, their spirits would have dampened with dread and their mood turned instantly sober. Instead the unsuspecting gentlemen were cheery and jovial as they poked fun at Basil and the old long rifle he was carrying.

"Basil, you're going to have to retire that old flintlock if you aim to fight the Mexicans," Fred advised. "These percussion locks that we have are the way to go now," he said referring to the weapons the South Carolinians were toting. "They are surefire and much easier to carry and reload. You can probably find a smith in Asheville to convert yours, don't you think? Hey, why don't you let us check around over there? Besides, it will give us something to do until the summer places are opened up at Flat Rock."

"Well this here gun worked pretty well on that old hog thief whose skin you saw nailed to my barn wall," Basil replied proudly with a chuckle. "But I guess you're probably right, Fred. See what you can find out for me." In addition to their cap and ball rifles, Basil noticed that the gentlemen were each packing smaller side arms. "Where did you come by those fancy pistols?"

Wade was the first to respond, "My father gave me this one a few years ago. It's a dueling pistol, and he said that a man has to prepare himself to defend his honor. I've practiced enough with it now that I feel prepared to fight a duel if it ever comes to that, though God help us it doesn't."

"Same goes here," Fred added. "Father once told me about a challenge he accepted when he was not much older than we are. It was over a girl he had danced with at a ball, of all things. There was an older gentleman in attendance whose intentions for this special young lady were strong, very strong as it turned out. This man got his feathers all ruffled when Father invited the girl to dance. Thinking that Father had mocked his manhood, one thing led to another, and they wound up facing off with pistols. Both fired shots simultaneously from twenty paces and were wounded, but not severely. Afterward, the man said he was satisfied that his honor and manhood were intact, and they were able to shake hands and walk away from the field. That was it. She's my mother—the girl Father dueled over." Fred tried to conceal a prideful expression as he glanced toward his host for some reaction to the story he had just shared. But the Master of the East Fork was lost in deep cogitation.

Basil had listened with heightened interest to Fred's tale and had recalled hearing whiffs and spits of an affair involving his own father and the southern dueling code. It had occurred soon after Thomas Edmunston had arrived on his East Fork land. Seems as though Thomas had received information second or third hand that a man had defamed his father, a Revolutionary War hero. During the Buncombe County Superior Court week in Asheville, this man had allegedly asserted that William Edmunston had refused to declare himself for King or Country, in the latter phase of the

Revolution. Thomas's bosom had burned with indignation upon hearing such a slanderous charge, and he had sought to remedy his damaged sense of honor with dueling pistols. However, the man in question publicly refuted claims that he had made the inflammatory remarks, and the whole thing blew over without loss of honor or life.

These were all the details that Basil could recall hearing, and his father had always declined discussion of the matter. However, there was sufficient information to instill in Basil a great deal of pride for his father and even a sense of foreboding that one day he himself might become embroiled in a duel over some minor slight or misunderstanding. *It's high time to get one of those pistols,* he concluded to himself as Fashion stumbled slightly and jolted him to respond kiddingly to Fred, "Glory be! Good thing for you and your mother, Fred, their aims were off."

Lark led the men higher and higher, following first the stock paths and then the game trails. Finally even those ran out, so they hobbled the horses and proceeded on foot, breaking their own paths where only Indians had tread before them. They crawled through dense laurel and rhododendron thickets and passed under verdant hardwood trees that were fully leaved, blocking out the sun's early morning light. Wade and Fred were reminded of accounts of explorers penetrating deep into the dangerous, dark jungles of Africa and never being heard from again. They nervously trusted that Lark knew where he was taking them and, more importantly, prayed that he would be able to extract them from the gloomy wilderness of Cold Mountain.

The slave urged caution as they crossed over slippery creeks and passed along rock precipices some hundreds of feet high. A man could fall off the cliffs and his body would never be recovered, one of them commented as they carefully peeked down over the edge of a rocky ledge. Gradually, as the men ascended to the higher altitudes, the climate became noticeably cooler, and the lush-leaved hardwood trees grew perceptively smaller and less plentiful. Rhododendrons, azaleas, and other dense shrubs abounded across the mountainside, filling the intervening spaces between the diminishing hardwoods and towering black balsam trees. These magnificent evergreens grew more and more prolifically as the party scaled upward, higher and higher.

Finally, after more than three hours of horse riding and climbing on foot, they topped out on a ridge just under the peak. At that lofty spot, they encountered balds, or clearings, where a man might get off a clear shot at a deer or bear or some other unsuspecting wild animal wandering into the open areas. Grasses, low shrubs, and brambleberry bushes predominated through these bald heights, and the men reckoned this nourishing vegetation might attract an unwitting creature into their sights.

Lark suggested that the gentlemen separate, and he selected two vantage points where the hunters could conceal themselves in silent vigilance behind trees and rocks. Basil and Fred took one of these hideaways, and Wade and the two Negroes occupied the other. Then they sat quietly without so much as a whisper, as the late morning and mid-day sun passed overhead. Wade and Fred found these hours of silence to be extremely peaceful and soothing. And with each passing moment, they tingled with anticipation that a wild beast was going to emerge from the dense forest thickets into their waiting ambush.

The weather was optimal, and the breezes across the ridge top kept the hunters cool and their scents wafting away from the kill areas. So far, the only wildlife venturing into the open balds were of the feathered variety—an eagle, several blue jays, and a few crows. But the huntsmen waited patiently and quietly while they nibbled on the refreshments Patsy had fixed for them.

The hours drifted by, and before long, late afternoon was upon them. To the hunters' chagrin, nothing worth shooting had been sighted. Once the solitary howl of a wolf increased the hunters' blood flow for a few brief moments, but their pulses soon returned to normal, with the quiet solitude again pervading the mountain top. Then, as the thought of a wild-goose chase began to enter Wade Hampton's mind and the sun edged ever closer to the western horizon, he felt a slight tap on his arm. It was Lark signaling for him to look to one side of the clearing under their observation. Wade directed his attention to the spot and immediately perceived a slight movement, something out of the ordinary. Then, after a second or two, he saw a large bush jerk about unnaturally. His pulse rate climbed. His nerves were on high alert, and then he saw the movement again.

Wade could not make out what it was, but something was stirring in a dense rhododendron thicket just fifty yards or so away. Slowly he began to make out a form—no, forms! One, two, three deer Wade counted as they crept out into the open where he could easily observe them. One was small and obviously immature, but the other two were large animals. He nervously pulled back the hammer cock into firing position and slowly raised his long rifle to take aim at the easier of the targets. Almost at the same time, one of the deer raised its head in alarm. It looked in the direction of the hunter, with its nose held high in the air sniffing furiously for a whiff of danger. Wade could tell the animal was on the verge of fleeing in terror. *Better fire quick*, he worried. *It's going to be my last chance.* And then—*Bang!!*

Upon the report of the shot, the three deer bounded into the woods in flight, trying to get far away from that awful noise and the hostile creatures that had made it. As the gunshot echoed across the north side of Cold Mountain, one of the fleeing deer found itself suffering a horrific pain and discovered that it could not keep up with the others. Its ability to run was steadily and quickly wasting away. The pain was relentless, as blood gushed out of an awful hole made by the lead ball, draining the deer's life along with it. Finally the wounded animal could run no further, and it staggered to a halt near a small spring gurgling out of the mountainside. There the creature wobbled for a few seconds in place and then slumped and toppled over into the wetness.

Wade was not sure that he had hit the deer, but he had a good feeling about the shot. Gathering quickly at the location where the deer were last seen, the five men fanned out and began searching excitedly for blood signs in the direction the animals had high-tailed it. Uriah soon discovered a large patch of blood, and before many more minutes had passed, he and Lark found the dead doe sprawled in a damp thicket. It was a good-sized deer, and the three white men and two slaves congratulated each other profusely for their success and hunting prowess. Wade was understandably proudest of all. His shot had been sure and deadly, and he could not resist the urge to boast his great hunting prowess and superiority over his two companions.

Patsy was waiting for the weary hunting party when they finally found their way out of the forest and arrived at the Den several hours past dark.

She had cooked their supper and was anxious that they eat it before it got any colder. Wade had expressed an interest in taking the deer hide back with him, not having any idea what he was going to do with it. So Basil gave orders to Lark and Uriah to take the dead deer to the slaves' quarters and skin it. The meat, he told them, was theirs to divide amongst the rest.

Although the supper was slightly on the cold side, the hunters inhaled the delicious fare. Wade and Fred were highly pleased with their day's recreational pursuits. Between swigs of sour milk and mouthfuls of delightful country cooking, they talked eagerly about hooking some wild trout from the waters of the East Fork before heading back to Asheville the following afternoon. That night in the cozy den, there was far less banter and talk than on the previous evening, and the three young men easily nodded off into a deep and restful slumber.

Lark and Uriah rose early the next morning to finish cleaning Massa Wade's deerhide. Jacob was also an early riser, and finished refitting three of the slaves' old cane poles for his master and the gentlemen to use that day on their fishing outing. The cane had been cut from the riverbank, and the rigging consisted of stout cotton thread for the line, hooks purchased at Deaver's store, and tiny pieces of slag iron for weights. Jacob was highly confident of this simple fishing gear. Using earthworms or kernels of corn for bait, he and the other Africans seldom returned from the river without a mess of trout.

The fishing diversion that Basil envisioned was relatively straightforward compared with the previous day's arduous trek to the pinnacle of Cold Mountain. His thoughts were that he and his guests would simply ride over to the river, about a half mile from the Den, and bob their bait in any ole spot to catch a fish. However, Uriah encouraged his master to try another venue that he and the boys were partial to.

"Massa Baz, dat spot I spoke to you 'bout is the best fo' you and da other massas. I know you's gonna catch some fish in dat spot 'cause we do's all da time. And, Massa Baz, we shore want dem to catch some fish, now don't we?" Uriah asked as he looked at his master intently. He knew that Basil was unfamiliar with the fishing holes up and down the river. As a matter of fact, Basil had not even wet a hook since his arrival on the East Fork three months previous.

"But, Uriah, one spot is just as good as another. Let's go down there by that lower cornfield above the ford and plop our lines in the water. I'll bet we can catch some fish there," Basil countered as he pointed to the spot he had in mind.

Uriah was unrelenting and responded, "I be's tellin' you, Massa, dat spot I know is mo' better dan here. And 'nother thing, it's mo' beautiful dan da ford spot over yonder." Uriah was insistent because he wanted the men to catch some fish and not go off skunked without anything to show for their efforts. Besides, the spot Basil had in mind was too close to the ford and pastures. He and the boys had never had any luck there and consequently never fished in close proximity to the Den.

Basil looked at Wade and Fred. His guests were maintaining a polite silence and looked toward him with expressions that translated to *we don't care—we just want to go fishing.*

He gave in. "Okay, Uriah, you and Lark lead the way. We're going to catch some monsters this morning, aren't we, gentlemen?"

"Right you are, sir," Wade answered.

"Lead us to the aquatic monsters, Uriah! We knights of Bachelor's Den are about to slay those East Fork whales—not with harpoons mind you, no sir, but with these flimsy yet wondrous cane fishing poles. Lead on!" Fred enjoined raising his pole high above his head. The levity of his charge was infectious and infused both of his companions and even Uriah and Lark with a spirit of joviality. The happy fishermen rode toward the river behind the slaves, who were footing it at a fast pace to Uriah's favorite fishing hole.

After twenty minutes or so of brisk travel, the fishermen halted and tied up the horses as close to the fishing spot as possible. Uriah then led them down through a tight cluster of laurel bushes until suddenly they broke out at the water's edge. The view was breathtaking, and Basil's guests fell silent and stunned. Even Basil gawked in awe at the gorgeous natural wonder that he gazed upon.

Before them was a long pool of water so clear that the trout could easily be seen swimming along its bottom. Upstream, the brawling East Fork waters cascaded through and around and over rock boulders and outcroppings to spill heavily into the pool. The waterfall that Nature had created there was twice as high as Basil was tall, and its crashing water boiled with white froth. The three young men excitedly shed their boots and bounded over the boulders, admiring the surroundings and amazed at God's splendid natural wonder. They felt the cool fresh breezes blowing across their faces, heard the thundering and roaring sounds of the stream pouring into Uriah's fishing hole, and felt the cold, cold waters with their bare feet. This was an amazing place, they all agreed. Uriah had chosen well.

Animated and filled with content for the delightful setting, the men splashed and carried on a sight in the very same hole where they intended to fish. The freezing cold water did not deter them atall. They took off their pants and shirts and waded over the rock-bottomed shallows, too busy talking and laughing to notice Lark and Uriah's exchange of dubious glances and subtle head shaking. *Deese here white men never gonna catch no fish makin' such a fuss*, the slaves thought. Eventually Basil and his guests settled down to do some fishing. They took up the cane poles, baited their hooks with wiggling earthworms, and plunked the slimy critters into the water. Of course, the fish had been so spooked by then that they took no notice of this new source of nourishment, having fled to the protection of deep hiding places on the rocky bottom. So Basil and Wade and Fred sat on their stone perches and waited for the fish to bite—and waited and waited.

They passed the time by continuing to share tales and bantering about a whole myriad of topics. One subject especially caught Basil's interest.

"You say these Devonshire cattle from England your father is raising might be hardy enough for Haywood?" Basil inquired of Wade. He had already come to the conclusion after discussions with his father, Colonel Deaver, and a few of the tenants that raising beef cattle in the highlands was not a terribly lucrative business. Year after year disease, predators, and the harsh winters decimated the herds and nearly nullified the increase in heads due to natural reproduction. Wade was touting the English breed so highly that Basil thought it might be worth his while to investigate the matter.

"I wouldn't bet a king's fortune they could survive the hard winters up here. But I believe it might be worth the venture, Basil," Wade replied.

"Let me cipher on it then. If things about the farm are settled after the harvest season, I may head down to Columbia and pay you and your father a visit. That is, if the drovers and stock herds will let me share the turnpike with them," he jested. "What do you say about that?"

"Be glad to have you," Wade replied. "Besides, it will be a good chance for you to vacate these lonely environs. There's another world out there waiting for you, Basil. I'll introduce you to some of the loveliest South Carolina belles you would ever want to meet. Although I don't know if you could ever convince one to come way up here to live at Bachelor's Den," he said with a chuckle. "But I'll tell you one thing. You won't find any as cute as that Deaver girl. You can bet your last dollar on that. Can't wait to see her on the way out this afternoon."

"I got one!" yelled Fred as he raised his pole to reveal the catch to his companions. Flopping and fighting, the small brook trout almost escaped his clutches before he was able to secure the slippery fish in his hands and have a good look at it. It was barely ten inches long, if that, and not the whale they had hoped to land. But its colors were absolutely brilliant. As the fish struggled to breathe and regain the water, the men closed around to study it. The entire body of the fish was covered in brilliant orange and green, with rich red spots splattered across each side. Wade and Fred had never seen such a beautiful fish and were raring to catch more of them, only bigger ones.

Over the next couple of hours, they did catch more trout, several more as a matter of fact, with the largest being almost sixteen inches in length. Although the fish were not as sizable as the men had imagined, Basil's guests were highly satisfied with the East Fork River fishing experience. However, before rolling up their lines and calling it a day, Wade decided to try one last promising spot.

Initially, they had thought the little secluded corner tucked under some overhanging laurel branches was out of their reach. Getting to it would require a long leap from one boulder to another across a sizable chasm. But for some unknown reason, Wade had concluded independently that his prospects for making a safe jump and accessing the enticing location were good. Or at least he figured them to be within his tolerance for risk taking. So after taking a running start, he launched himself into the air and soared over the rushing water below. But unfortunately, Wade had not adequately judged the span or his athleticism, and the descent came far too quickly. His leading foot landed short and awkwardly on the steeply sloped, wet side of the target boulder. Instantly, faster than a trout snatching an insect from the water's surface, the foot slipped completely off the slippery face of the rock. There was no time for Wade to react to this unexpected and unfortunate occurrence—not even enough time to cut loose of the fishing pole or cushion his fall from the impact. The cracking of his head was audible, as he fell terribly hard against the immovable boulder.

As this fateful event was transpiring, Fred's attention was directed elsewhere, as he pulled in another brookie. But Basil happened to look up in time to see his new friend's limp body tumbling down the side of the rock and splashing into the water. It was at the deep end of the pool, and as Basil sprung to action and jumped in to save Wade, he saw his friend disappear under the water. Basil was not a good swimmer atall. But somehow he was able to sink down and reach Wade, who was lying motionless on the river bottom where the trout cringed in fear under the rocks. He grabbed hold of the young gentleman's arm and, using his feet and legs, pushed forcefully off the rocky bottom to propel the two of them upward. In frantic fury, Basil flailed with his powerful legs and free arm to regain the water's surface and, eventually, paddled himself and the motionless Wade into the shallows.

Half-submerged and sitting on a rock, Basil cradled Wade's bloody head in his arms above the water. Fred had rushed to his side by then, and he and Basil looked anxiously for any signs of life. A knot as big as a hen's egg puffed out of Wade's brow, and a slight stream of blood trickled from the wound. Panicked minutes passed as they fretted over Wade. Finally, his eyelids began to twitch and then bat slowly. He was alive, thank goodness, and Basil and Fred began trying to communicate with him.

After rousing Wade back into semi-consciousness and determining he might live, the party loaded up and started downriver to Colonel Deaver's. There Wade could receive the proper care he needed until a doctor could be found. It took more than an hour to ease the patient down the river road to Forks of Pigeon, and when they at last arrived, the Colonel was not in. But Julia and her mother were and, although greatly distressed with the situation, they took Wade in and immediately began tending to him. In the meantime, Basil rode frantically down the Pigeon River, pushing Fashion hard, and returned with Doctor Allen within an hour.

While the doctor was working Basil tried his best to talk with Julia but to no avail. She barely left Wade's side. At last, after a seemingly interminable length of time, the doctor pronounced that Wade had suffered a severe concussion and likely had cracked his skull. However, as bad as that sounded, the prognosis was encouraging. The patient would likely suffer severe headaches for at least a few months, but these should cease in due time, and the swelling would vanish as well. The doctor informed everyone that he saw no reason the young man should not make a full recovery, but he cautioned Wade against strenuous activities in the interim. It was great news, and a giant sigh of relief echoed around the room. However, Doctor Allen advised Wade to stay in bed for the next couple of days and, by all means, not to travel.

Maggie insisted that Wade stay with them so that they could look after him properly. Of course, he consented to this kind gesture, and Basil could hardly blame him. The East Fork master, having grown quite close to both Wade and Fred over the past couple of days, was awfully grateful that his guest would make a complete recovery. He believed—with good reason—that the friendships they had started would endure for years to come. But Basil was more than a little uneasy with the turn of certain events and, justifiably, felt some uncomfortable tugs of jealousy. It surely appeared to him that Wade and Julia shared an infatuation for one another. So he naturally fretted about where that left him.

Before Basil took off for Bachelor's Den, Wade called him over to his bedside. "Basil, I haven't rightly thanked you for pulling me out of the water and saving my life. Damned if I know why I tried that fool leap. But if it hadn't been for you, I would have drowned for sure. Fred can't swim, you know." Although Wade was speaking with a great deal of pain, his message was devoutly sincere. "I asked him to give you fifty dollars for your hospitality and time and trouble. If that's not enough, just tell him how much. You sure earned it."

"No, Wade, it's all on me. You don't owe–," Basil was interrupted before he could finish.

"Stop! Don't want to hear such foolishness. You take our money–you hear that, Fred?" Wade said in a raised voice as he cast his eyes toward his companion, who was standing nearby with Julia. "I want you to give that money to Basil."

"Don't you worry. I'll give it to him, Wade," Fred replied as he nodded in affirmation.

Wade then turned back to Basil, "You take our money and go buy a pistol in Asheville, and get that old flintlock fixed too. You hear?"

It was obvious to Basil that Wade was not to be denied. "Okay, Wade. If I don't see you before you go back to the hotel, I'll write to you. And you can look for me this winter at Columbia. I want to take a gander at those Devonshire cattle you're so high on. Take care now, and get better. I'll expect another visit from you two deer slayers this summer, you hear me good? We'll get us a bear next time–another big ole hog thief." Basil took Wade's right hand and squeezed it with both of his strong hands. He was a little emotional, and it showed to both Julia and Fred, who were looking on.

The ride after dark back up the river to the Den was one of thoughtful deliberation. Basil could feel that he was losing Julia–not that he ever really had her, mind you. But the sentiments that she and he had once shared for each other at the mill on Easter Sunday apparently had evaporated, at least as far as she was concerned. Other weighty circumstances had drifted into their lives, including the business with Altha and Rufus. And neither had it helped for the handsome Wade Hampton to just drop in for an adventure on the East Fork and innocently and unknowingly wedge himself between Basil and Julia. It was obvious to Basil that things were working against Julia and him for some reason or other. But he was not about to give her up. And he certainly was not giving up on Altha either. Altha's allure had snagged him when they first met and continued to tighten its relentless hold. Finally, however, Basil tired of these vexatious ruminations, and his mind wandered back to more substantive things–like all the farming work he had to catch up on.

Chapter 13

Mountain Justice

Basil bumped into Julia at the store a few days after Wade Hampton had returned to the Sulfur Springs Hotel. She acted as friendly as ever toward him and could not wait to spill some great news. Wade had invited Julia and her parents to a party at Flat Rock. It was to be a combined celebration of the Fourth of July holiday and the opening of his family's house for the summer.

"Can you imagine, Basil, who's going to be there? Father says it will be the crème de la crème of the state of South Carolina, and he is not looking forward to going atall," she said, laughing.

"Should be a great time, Julia. I don't blame your father though. I would be a mite uncomfortable myself partying with a bunch like that."

"Oh, Basil! You're going too! I almost forgot to tell you! Wade told me to be sure to let you know about the party and that he expected you to show up with us." Julia was excited, and it showed. "He said he wanted you to escort me over there and to keep us safe from all the wolves and bears along the way. And, oh yes, he said that there weren't to be any more head knockings either. That's exactly what he told us," and she laughed, hoping to lighten Basil's spirits and possibly mend the rift of her own creation that had opened between them.

Basil did not have to think about the invitation very long. There was no way he was going to a party at Flat Rock. For one thing, he did not have the proper clothes to wear. Such fine attire might be found in Asheville, but probably not. And Basil was not about to lose a couple of days going over there to buy a fancy outfit. In addition, it would be at least a three-day event—two days of travel and the day of the party. When you added that to the clothes-buying spree, then five full days would be lost to the highfalutin' frolic. And the crops were not even laid by yet! No, he could not see his way clear to join the Deavers in this lark.

"I don't know, Julia. I'm not too keen on the idea, to tell the truth. But I'll cipher some on it," the hesitant Basil finally responded, with a noticeable lack of enthusiasm that disappointed Julia.

They talked a bit more while he roamed the store selecting and purchasing a few items for the slaves. Then after exchanging pleasant goodbyes with Julia, the Master of the East Fork headed back up to Bachelor's Den, still dead set against the Flat Rock party business.

"Hello, Jacob. What's on your mind this morning?" Basil said as he greeted his slave in front of the Den. Jacob had come over and was all excited with distressing news about his son, Lark.

"It be 'bout Lark, Massa. He done gone and runs away with Delia. He shore 'nough has. Be's two nights now dat we's don't sees him. I be's 'fraid he done gone and runs away," the worried Jacob reported.

Delia must be Osborne's girl, the one Lark's sweet on and wants to marry, Basil surmised. He knew Lark had not been content with the news that Colonel Blalock refused to buy him and the girl. How Lark had got that idea in his head in the first place Basil still could not figure out.

"Okay now, Jacob. Take it easy," Basil said as he tried to calm the father and gather his thoughts. "Did Lark say anything to you or Jenny or any of the other boys that leads you to think he has run away?"

"No suh, Massa. But he done gone and packs his clothes and takes 'em in his bag wif him. And I 'spects he takes da big kitchen knife too. No ones can finds it. And he takes his ole hat too, Massa."

Basil had heard enough to believe Jacob's suspicions were credible. He was inclined not to concern himself too much over Lark, but the slave was his father's property, so he would have to report the runaway and make a search.

"Sounds like he might have done it, the damn fool. This isn't good, isn't good atall, Jacob. I'll go down to Osborne's and check to see if the girl's gone. If she's disappeared, then we can be pretty certain the two of them have run away, and I'll have to go looking for them. Try to keep the rest of the Negroes here simmered down, Jacob. It's not going to go down easy for your son when we find him. I'll have to deal harshly with him for this, if he has truly run away."

There was no end to Basil's vexations with the slaves, it seemed. *Lark could not have picked a worse time to pull this stunt,* he thought as he spied Josiah and Jesse Anderson making their way on foot across the river and toward the Den. Jesse's court appearance was set for early that afternoon, and Basil had promised to testify on Jesse's behalf regarding his character. The runaway business would have to wait a day or two.

On the ride over to Waynesville, Basil probed Jesse about the details of the fight with the Garrett brothers. By this time, Jesse had grown comfortable talking to his landlord. As a matter of fact, the entire Anderson clan had finally accepted Basil for what he was—a young, rich landlord who was not a bad person atall. They would always be beholden to him for saving Altha and Rufus. But that was not all. Basil had treated them fairly so far. He had given them the support they needed to get their crops in the ground, and he had provided Jesse with an opportunity to earn some money to pay off his legal obligations. And now here was Basil going out of his way to try and get Jesse out of this scrape.

"They were the ones who started the fight," Jesse began to explain. "I shouldn't ought to been in that there bar spendin' that money I got fer the beef cow, but I couldn't help it none, I reckon. Them boys a'started picking at me soon's I walked in—them and another man."

"What did they say to you?" an intrigued Basil asked.

"Them twins got themselves over close to me and starts to sniffing 'round at me. One of 'em smarted, 'Boy, ye smell a sight. Do ye live in a barn or a hog pen?' And then the short-haired 'un pokes in and says, 'Nah, he ain't good 'nough to live with the stock. He's done gone and stole them manure-smelling clothes of his'n to come to town.' Well, after that, they kept on hooting and hollering and making insults 'bout me. They weren't nuthin' but bullies, and I tolt them rascals a piece of mind. Just taking up fer myself, mind ye. And them bullies wouldn't never let go of it. After a while, we started in to settle it, and that's when I got my head busted."

Basil had heard enough. "Sounds like you got the raw end of the stick and the law, Jesse. Can't figure out why the sheriff couldn't round up any witnesses to vouch for your story. It doesn't smell right to me."

County court week in Waynesville meant big business for the town's people—citizens, storekeepers, lawyers, and such. Farmers brought in goods, stock, and produce to sell. Debtors skulked around the streets and fled from their creditors when they appeared. The creditors, men who were owed money, were usually the more substantial farmers and businessmen. They relentlessly pursued the debtors in their hiding places and dunned them for the money owed. But with cash almost always being scarce during court week, the creditors usually returned to their homes with near-empty pockets and little else to show for their time and efforts. However, the tavern keepers' pockets were not empty. Their supply of ardent spirits usually disappeared long before the last legal proceeding at the courthouse, keeping the sheriff busy rounding up the drunkards off the streets.

That afternoon, Jesse was called in front of the Court of Pleas and Quarter Sessions, during which three justices of the peace presided. One of them, Basil noticed, was obviously under the influence of too much hard cider and could barely sit upright in his designated chair. It had previously been determined that His Worshipful Justice Jeremiah Love would take the lead and administrate all cases on this day's docket. Love was an old-time jurist from Waynesville and infamous for his swift judgments and harsh justice for law breakers.

The sheriff opened the proceeding by stating the case against Jesse and giving the particulars of the fight as he knew them. The proprietor of the Bear Wallow Tavern, Latham Ferguson, insisted that Jesse had instigated the fracas. He professed to having seen the entire affair play out from his vantage point behind the bar. Ferguson presented the judge with a detailed account of the damages sustained at his establishment, which totaled almost thirty-five dollars. The Garrett brothers were conspicuously absent from the proceedings, and when the judge asked where they were, the sheriff was taken off balance.

"Well, Judge, I didn't see a need to hear their story. Mr. Ferguson said he saw the whole thing, and Anderson sure had the look of a shiftless trouble-maker. So I just figured with the one good witness against him that he was guilty enough and that we wouldn't need the Garrett boys' testimony here today."

"You did, did you?" asked Judge Love as he frowned and squinted at the sheriff. "I always heared that it takes two to make a fight. You ever heared that old saw, Sheriff?"

"Yes sir, Judge. I believe I have," the sheriff responded while looking around nervously.

"Mr. Ferguson, them Garrett twin boys. Are they regulars in the Bear Wallow?" the judge asked.

Ferguson rose out of his chair and replied, "Wouldn't say they're regulars, Your Worshipful. They come in ever' now and again."

"You happen to know what the fighting was all about, do you?" Judge Love continued his queries of Latham Ferguson.

"No, Your Worshipful, I can't rightly say what got them crosswise. But all was at peace until Anderson drug in. He riled them boys up a sight though," Ferguson replied.

"That a fact? Sheriff, them Garrett brothers–they from down around Jonathan Creek, are they?" asked the judge, referring to a remote community in the county. "I've heared of some Garretts from down that way."

The sheriff replied, "Yes sir, Judge. They be from down that direction some'rs."

"I see–hummmm, figured as much." The judge paused a moment and pondered. "Mr. Ferguson, you got any relations over on the Jonathan Creek?" asked the judge, whose natural instincts and suspicions had been inexplicably aroused. He wanted to know more about those Garrett twins.

"Uhh, uh, well, Your Worshipful, as a matter of fact I have a cousin–no, she's a niece. She's from over that way," Ferguson reluctantly answered.

Judge Love had a hunch, and he was playing it out. "You do, do yuh? What would that girl's name be, sir?"

Ferguson hesitated and then responded, "Her name is Samantha, Your Worshipful. Samantha."

"I see, sir. Tell me now, Mr. Ferguson, does this niece of yours, Samantha, have a last name?"

"Yes sir, she does," replied the nervous barkeeper, and then he clammed up, hopeful the judge was not going to persist down this road any further.

"She does, does she? Well then, what might her last name be, Mr. Ferguson?" The judge had had enough of Ferguson's coy answers, and his temper was aroused ever so slightly.

"Garrett, Your Worshipful. Her name is Samantha Garrett."

"I see. Now would your niece, Samantha Garrett, be any kin to those Garrett twins who busted Anderson's head in your tavern?"

Reluctantly, ever so reluctantly, an embarrassed and scared Ferguson confessed, "She's married to one of them Garrett twins, Your Worshipful."

"She is, huh?" Then turning toward the sheriff His Worshipful continued. "She's married to one of those Garrett boys. What do you think about that, Sheriff?" Judge Love pointedly asked his chief county law-enforcement officer. It was obvious he was not overly impressed with the Sheriff's investigation of the incident.

"That's news to me, Judge. Didn't know nuthin' 'bout that kin business."

The Judge had almost heard enough, but he wanted to hear testimony to Jesse's character.

"Let's see, where is Mr. Basil Edmunston? You in here somewhere?" the Judge asked, as he looked around the small but packed courtroom.

Basil stood up tall and replied, "Yes sir, I'm Basil Edmunston."

"Sheriff reports that you want to speak for Anderson. Let's hear what you allow about him."

"Yes sir. Jesse and his father lease a piece of land from me over on the East Fork River. They've been tenants now going on six years. Already this year, they've planted more than twenty acres of corn and another fifteen acres of wheat. I've been highly impressed with their industry this season, Judge." As Basil finished up, he did not notice Jesse cutting his eyes toward his father. Jesse realized that Basil was going way out on a limb to stick up for him. Nobody had taken up for him like this before.

The Judge stared at the impressive young man speaking before him and wondered first to himself and then aloud, "Edmunston, huh? You wouldn't be Thomas Edmunston's son, would you now, boy?"

"That's right, Judge Love. He's my father. I'm working as his Haywood overseer. Been here since mid-March, more than three months now," Basil confirmed for the Judge.

"I thunk as much," Judge Love said. "Son, your father and I go way back, longer than I can remember, I'm afraid. We go back to the days of this county's founding, and I reckon we served together at least twice in the State Assembly as Haywood's representatives. Thomas was a good man, was indeed—and still is for that matter, I reckon, unless he's not with us any longer. I haven't laid eyes on him since he went back east. What's it been now, about twenty years ago?

"Yes sir, about twenty years ago, right after I was born, when they—we—moved back to Caldwell County. He and my mother are getting along just fine, sir," Basil answered the judge.

"Well, Basil, you give him my regards when you next write or see him. Will you?"

"I will, Judge Love, I surely will." Basil assured him.

"Now, Mr. Edmunston, do you have anything else to say for Anderson?" asked Judge Love.

"Only one thing, Judge, and so far today, a lot of the questions I had about this case have been answered. Jesse tells me that he didn't start the fight, and I have no reason not to believe him. He said that those Garrett brothers began bullying him and mocking him for the poor clothes he had on and because he smelled high of the farm. He says he was only fending for himself against their bullying ways. That's all I have, Judge, and if need be, I will secure Jesse's note for whatever the award will be in this case. Thank you, sir." Basil finished and again took his seat, satisfied that he had done what he could to help Jesse.

The Judge took only a few minutes to consult with the other justices, or rather the one that was still awake. After breaking out of the huddle, he took a few minutes to scribble some notes on a piece of paper. And then the Worshipful Jeremiah Love looked up, gazed at those gathered in his front, and pronounced the court's decision. "Mr. Anderson, please stand, sir! Jesse Anderson, I dismiss all charges this County has brought against you, and I am entirely embarrassed about the way the whole affair was handled. That will be for me and the sheriff to take up later," and he looked sternly toward the sheriff, who for some reason was intently studying the shine on his boots.

And then Judge Love favored the tavern owner with a scowl and shaking of his head. "As for your damages, Mr. Ferguson, I suggest you take that up with Mrs. Samantha Garrett's husband," the judge said as he waved the bill of damages in the air for Ferguson to see. But he was not finished with Ferguson. "And believe me, sir, your deception in this case was absolutely abhorrent. I'll be giving your performance here today much consideration, and don't be surprised if charges should be brought against you for your dishonest conduct. Case dismissed! Next!"

The sheriff gave back Jesse's note for the fifty dollars bail money and made a feeble attempt at an apology for the way the East Forker had been treated. On the way back home, the talk was sparse, but the men's spirits were definitely heightened. Jesse and Josiah let Basil know how obliged they were for everything he was doing for them. They aimed to make it up to him, the Anderson men said, with the crops they were going to produce. And Basil was fine with that. He was pleased things had turned out so well for Jesse. It could have been so much worse.

And speaking of worse, he had other problems preoccupying his mind as he bobbed up and down in the saddle to Fashion's canter. It was that infernal business with Lark. Basil had to deal with a runaway slave, of all things, when he got back to the Den.

Chapter 14

Brightest Star of the Night

Ephriam Osborne was none too happy about his slave girl running off with Lark. He confirmed to Basil that Delia had gone missing at about the same time Lark had disappeared from the slaves' quarters at the Den. Both Osborne and Basil understood that this was bad business—this runaway business. But the chances of Lark and Delia making it very far were slim.

Negroes traveling alone on the roads in the South were treated with natural suspicion by the white farmers and village citizens. They were immediately challenged as to their business or the whereabouts of their masters. Without clarifying documents in their possession or other credible explanation, the slaves would usually be bound immediately and taken to jail. And it was not uncommon for runaway slaves to be mistreated and even whipped by their captors. Eventually, the slaveowners would hear through the post or by messenger of the capture of their runaways. Of course, there would be expectations for handsome rewards—anywhere from twenty-five to two hundred dollars to be paid out by the slave masters to those responsible for the recovery of their valuable property.

Basil and two of Osborne's grown sons packed their horses for the anticipated long days ahead, and rode off from Forks of Pigeon in search of the escaped slaves. They first checked in with the sheriff of Haywood County at Waynesville and filled him in on the situation, giving the names and physical descriptions of the two runaways. The slave hunters had no idea which direction Lark and Delia might have taken, so they decided to ride to distant Asheville and check around over there. It took more than a day to travel to the largest town in North Carolina's mountains, some thirty-five miles east of Waynesville. They passed Patton's stagecoach stop just shy of Pigeon River Ford and another way station—Smathers' Inn—at the Buncombe County line. Inquiries at both of these busy places were fruitless.

Arriving in Asheville, the three slaveowners immediately called on the Buncombe sheriff. No suspicious slaves had been brought in or reported, they unhappily learned. From this growing commercial hub and county seat, the Buncombe Turnpike led northward to Tennessee and stretched southward all the way to South Carolina. The men could not imagine that Lark would flee anywhere but northward, where he and his girl might possibly find sympathizers that could guide them along the secretive path to freedom, otherwise known as the Underground Railroad.

Although neither Lark nor Delia was educated, there was an abundance of information available to them through the slaves' subtle networking channels. By word-of-mouth mostly from other plantation slaves, they routinely received news tidbits of slave doings, escapes, beatings, and such. And their ears were never deaf to the white folks' talk of the Yankee sympathies for Africans and the growing northern demands to abolish slavery. Of course, the Forks of Pigeon posse was well aware of all this and thus determined a northern vector for their search, lighting out on the turnpike toward Tennessee.

The slave hunters stopped at every stock station along the turnpike, which usually were spaced six to eight miles apart. These commercial hotspots, so vitally important in the fall and winter for sheltering drovers and for corralling and feeding their vast herds of livestock, were community gathering and information centers. Basil and his companions notified each proprietor about their runaways and made queries regarding news of any strange Negroes on the road. At Alexander's Inn, Vance's, Barnard's, Candler's, and several others, they stopped. And because every little farm house and log cabin along the route might harbor potential clues of the Africans' whereabouts, the riders called at each of the residences they encountered.

It was a grueling, tiresome slog for Basil and the Osborne brothers, and after more than a week of constant riding and searching, there was nothing to show for their efforts. Like two African ghosts, Lark and Delia had apparently become transparent, and no one claimed to have seen hide nor hair of them. So their pursuers called off the hunt. The authorities had been notified, and a good many innkeepers and farmers were alerted to be vigilant for the escaped Negroes. Undoubtedly, they would eventually be discovered slinking about the countryside somewhere and captured. But Basil was still disheartened that the slaves had not been recovered by now, and not simply because he wanted them back. He was more afraid of how they might be treated when found, or that they might become subjects of hateful foul play.

Ruthless slave hunters, lured by the certainty of monetary rewards, would doubtlessly be on the prowl by now. And there were no assurances that Lark and Delia would survive the manhunt. If one or both were killed by dogs or human pursuers, not a court in the state would prosecute their murderers. This runaway business had a sobering effect on Basil. He worried not only about the welfare of the two slaves, but he knew that a severe lashing would have to be inflicted on Lark's hide. And he dreaded the mere thought of it.

It would be daylight soon, and Lark and Delia were exhausted. After meeting at their rendezvous point near Osborne's farm, the pair of darkies had traveled at night down the familiar road to Pigeon River Ford. Their passage had been relatively uneventful, since no other travelers had been encountered. As they passed cabins located close by the road, the slaves dodged stealthily around them and maintained enough distance to not set the dogs to barking. With the approach of dawn, they had left the road and found a thick woods set back a ways from the Pigeon River. It was in this cover and hiding place that Lark chose to lay up for the day.

"We's be's safe here, Delia. We's gonna stays here all day and gits off again when it gits dark," Lark said trying to comfort Delia.

"Oh, Lark, I be's so tired. You think we's gonna be's safe here?"

"I b'lieve so, Delia. We's be's good here," Lark replied confidently.

For their hiding place, they had chosen a densely wooded area away from the planted fields, pastures, and obvious trails. Burrowing under some thorny bramble bushes, they lay down together on the ground and clutched each other closely. Their hugging embraces became ever tighter, and they both felt the pleasing comfort and warmth of the other's body. As their faces met in a grinding crunch, their lips inevitably began tasting and sucking and sensing the passion flowing through them. It was the first time for both to become so intimate with another person, and they relished the pleasurable effects it produced.

Lark could feel Delia's youthful firm breasts pressing against his chest, and it felt so extraordinarily good. He felt her legs and bare feet wrapping around him and squeezing ever harder. Their thick lips remained locked in furious wet kissing, only breaking the passionate embraces to catch their breaths. Delia was only sixteen years old, but she was a mature woman physically and fully capable of pleasing the twenty-one-year-old mate she had chosen. And, importantly, she too could enjoy the pleasures of sexual intimacy.

The young slave woman pressed her loins firmly against Lark's midsection and felt the stiff manly organ that was stabbing so firmly into her. Innately she reached for his penis and tried to grasp it with her hand. Through the coarse material of Lark's pants, she felt it and anxiously gripped it tightly. Its throbbing largeness inexplicably filled her with an exhilarating satisfaction. Lark broke from Delia's clutches just long enough to shuck off his pants as Delia excitedly and nervously waited. These feelings she felt on her insides were so strange. She wore no underclothes and could not comprehend the extreme wetness down there in the place where she normally makes water and where babies come from.

In a matter of seconds, they were back in each other's embrace, hugging and kissing and frantically pushing against each other. Lark and Delia knew about sexual relations or, as they thought of it, the act of making a baby. In the dark close confines of the slave quarters both had seen others, including their parents, lying close together and had heard the emotional grunts and screams of gratification. Now it was their own time to make a baby, and they were on the verge of enjoying the indescribable joy and fulfillment derived from the process.

As Lark pushed and thrust against Delia, she reciprocated and was overcome by the gratifying and sensual feelings that she was experiencing. Lark felt similar pleasures as he pressed himself harder and harder against her beautiful, lithe body, devouring her face and neck with his mouth and lips.

The two slaves pushed and pressed and groped as they struggled feverishly to satisfy their hot primal urges.

Finally, Delia found Lark with her hand again and guided his engorged appendage between her thighs and into her warm, wet cavity. At first, the penetration met with resistance inside Delia. But after a bolt of pain racked through her body, Lark plunged himself deep within the girl. Their erotic cravings and sensual desires had never before been tapped to this extent. The more they thrust against each other, the more aroused and the more desirous of continuing forever this newly discovered behavior they became.

Very soon the euphoric couple reached the climax of their first sexual experience, and Delia screamed loudly to release the extreme orgasmic pressures within her. So loud was her screaming that Lark was genuinely concerned their presence might have been revealed to the locals. But he was not so alarmed to prevent the eruption of his own pent-up juices inside his amazing Delia. Both of them were extremely fulfilled and satisfied, and they believed that surely they must be in love with each other. Such blissful happiness they had not known existed but were certainly pleased to have discovered it now. And over and over again, for the rest of the day, they kept on discovering it.

During one brief interlude between intimate sessions, Delia whispered to her chosen partner, "Lark, we's makes a baby, don't we's?"

"'Spects we's did, Delia. You feeled real good, girl, real good."

"Do's it means we's married now, you think?"

Lark thought for a moment and then replied, "No, I don't b'lieve so. Gots to has somebody like a massa o' a preacher to says words fo' us befo' we's married. Deese words gots to has God's name in dem. And His Son's name, Jesus, gots to be's spoke too. Don't you worry none, Delia. We's can still loves one 'nother and keeps on making babies. We's can do's dat in da daytime when we's not runnin' fo' it."

"Dat's good, Lark. I like dat a sight," a beaming Delia replied as she planted a kiss on her man's lips.

The runaways were exhausted when the daylight gave out and darkness began to descend on them in their hideout. Catnapping between their several sexual encounters did little to restore their energies. But the fugitive slaves realized they had to keep moving and get out of the Carolina highlands, where they would be known to be on the run. Their masters would surely be searching for them. Strange men would be putting mean dogs on their trail and seeking them out. They had to keep going.

It was a warm night. Upon rising out of their briar patch, the couple began brushing the grasses out of their hair and off their clothes. Delia wore only a light summer dress of dark-blue material that closed under her neck and reached almost to her ankles. Underneath the homespun garment, the fresh night air felt cool to her bare skin, unencumbered by underclothes. Lark had stowed the bright red scarf that Delia usually wore wrapped around her head in an old sack bag he carried over his shoulder. Her tight curly hair barely concealed her ears and fell just half way down the nape of her neck. Although bare, the girl's feet were tough, and the walking and running that lay ahead of them should not be of concern, she assured Lark with youthful confidence and excitement.

Lark stripped off the light-brown shirt he was wearing and stuffed it in the bag with a few other items he had brought along, including a large double-edged kitchen knife. Besides the obvious utilitarian uses of this dangerous-looking weapon, he had no doubt it would be needed for protection against both critters and white men disposed to meanness. His black skin was much darker than Delia's and would help to mask his stealthy movements at night. In traveling mode, he wore only a coarse pair of linsey-woolsey pants and some stout brogan footwear that Jake had fashioned. Thankfully, just a day or so before his escape, his mother had cut his hair extra short such that the battered felt hat he used rested on top of his ears.

This slave couple was traveling light for sure, and Lark reckoned there was only one way for them to head. "We's wants to go to da North, Delia. Dat's 'bout alls I knows. Dat's where dem Yankees lives dat wants to makes all us slaves free slaves."

Lark had heard talk about the Yankee northland from some of the other Edmunston slaves in Caldwell County. Also, around Deaver's store and mill, he had picked up morsels of information from overheard conversations about the slaves being free in the northern states, just like the white persons were. He was not real sure what it all meant. But he had suspicions that made him believe there was a real possibility he and Delia could be free slaves and get married somewhere north of the Carolina mountains. And that's exactly where he aimed to go.

"Do's you know how to goes north?" Delia innocently asked.

"I do's," Lark answered and to make her feel a little more at ease with this assurance and his dead-reckoning capability he continued. "You sees dat star way up in da sky? Da brightsest one up dare?" he asked while pointing and trying to help Delia find the star.

Lark was an excellent woodsman for his young age. He had worked the mountain stock ranges around the East Fork farm enough to be uncommonly comfortable in the woods. And he and the other slaves spent a great deal of time tracking and hunting during the winter months to supplement the portions of meat given to them from the Edmunston's smokehouse. At an early age, he had learned from the older slaves about the constellation of stars that formed the shape of a drinking gourd with its brightest star being the North Star. The concept that the bright North Star stays up there in the night sky in one place, night after night, had always intrigued him. Other than this one star, he knew little to nothing else about the regulated movements of the sun, moon, and earth, or about the other constellations that filled the night sky.

"B'lieves I do's see it," Delia answered as she looked hard for the bright star Lark was pointing towards.

"Dat star be's da North Star, Delia. It stays dare all da night and all da time, and we's always gonna goes towards dat star. Dat be's north, Delia. And dat be's whur we's goin'. Lookit good now. Dat be's whur our freedom is and whur we's gonna gits us married."

He and Delia did not rightly know what freedom would entail. The abstract idea of not being owned by somebody, told what to do, how to live, what to eat, what to say, what to wear, or how to act was a truly perplexing one. They worried whether they would know how to act or what to do if a master was not there to tell them. Although they were unsure about all this, the sweet thoughts of getting married and living together, making babies whenever they wanted to, and raising a family was mighty enticing. Enough so that the two slaves were convinced it was worth running away for and worth taking the inherent risks associated with that desperate act—even the risk of losing their lives.

Lark did not need the North Star for direction as long as he was in familiar country and knew the roads. His intentions were to find the French Broad River over in Buncombe County and then follow the turnpike road that more or less paralleled the river northward. He had used this road before, the Buncombe Turnpike, but it had been many years ago, when he was just a boy. He knew that the traffic along this road was heavy and that he and Delia would have to stay well to the sides and out of sight as they travelled, even at night. But it was the only tactical idea that he had been able to concoct, and he thought it might work out. When unfamiliar territory was reached, it would be necessary for Lark to find a route, preferably a path along a watercourse or another road, which headed in the direction of the drinking gourd and its bright star.

All night long, they travelled very carefully, working their way beyond the settlement at the Pigeon River fording place and northward up the small Beaverdam Creek. Before the sun broke above the horizon, they crossed over a mountain range and moved into the Sandy Mush area of Buncombe County, a distance of almost fifteen miles. Daylight drove them to cover, and they piled up in a secluded woody spot near the creek named by an unfortunate pioneer who had discovered sand in his breakfast mush. From this hidden vantage point, a small farm comprising only a log cabin and stock shelters could be monitored.

The runaways were hungry but not starving. They had been able to see well enough during the night to gather some blackberries and raspberries to eat. Delia waded into one especially dense bramble thicket beside the road and, to her horror, was startled by the loud buzzing of a rattlesnake lurking nearby in the dark. She froze in horror, too terrified to move, as Lark pushed his way between her and the warning sound of the rattler. He started jabbing a walking stick toward the furious rattling while Delia moved hurriedly back out of the thicket. The perturbed serpent had struck at Lark once, but its venomous fangs glanced off his brogans. Never having seen the snake and not realizing his good fortune, Lark nervously backed out of the briar bushes after Delia. It had been a close warning call, and, for sure, any future berry scavenging would be done with much more caution and no little trepidation.

Lark figured they could not live on berries alone, though. For that reason, he chose a daytime resting spot where he could stake out the little farm and weigh their chances of stealing some food. During the wakeful interims when he and Delia were not busy enjoying each other intimately, he surveyed his target. His confidence level rose some after discovering where the chickens were cooped and learning that the farmers, strangely enough, kept no dogs around. Although there were certainly risks involved, he believed a careful nighttime raid might yield some real nourishing results and keep them going.

During a steady rain in the middle of the night, the runaways sneaked out of the woods and down a steep hill into the barnyard. Delia stayed back a ways while Lark moved in closer to the coop. Encountering no difficulty at first, he gained entry into the henhouse and began stealthily robbing the eggs and stuffing them one by one into his hat. But the hens were not fooled for long by his sly, thieving measures. In little time, they began attacking Lark and creating such a loud ruckus that he cut short his filching and fled away from the farm in terror. Delia fell in behind him, and they ran for their lives, both of them scared to death and sure they were done for. Behind them, the farmer could be heard crashing out the cabin door and hollering and cussing to the mountain tops. Delia was sure she heard a gunshot fired, but they kept on running anyway.

When the runaways reckoned they had raced far enough, they hid in some bushes for cover and to catch their breaths. As Lark carefully opened his crumpled hat, Delia eyed its contents. Her mouth gaped open upon seeing that her man had been able to snatch more than a dozen hen eggs. Although a few had broken and spilled their golden contents, the two hungry slaves were grateful for those precious ones that remained intact, and they hurriedly devoured them raw. First Lark broke an egg in Delia's cupped hands, and she sucked the nectar down. Then Delia broke one for Lark to slurp up. And in scant minutes, the sumptuous fare was gobbled up, and they were on their way again. Hand in hand and with lifted spirits, the two fugitives stole down Sandy Mush Creek in the rainy darkness toward the distant French Broad River.

Chapter 15

First Kiss

Basil parted ways with the two Osborne brothers below Forks of Pigeon. The three men had been on a futile runaway-slave hunt for eight days and were road-weary and longing to sleep in their own beds that evening. July the fourth was only two days away, and Basil suspected that the Deavers would be heading over to the party at Flat Rock early the next morning. At least, he hoped they had not already left, because he owed it to Julia to let her know his intention not to go. Basil had no idea how she would take the news, but he prepared himself for the worst.

"Hello, Colonel Deaver, good to see you," Basil said as he was greeted at the door by the patriarch. "I've come to see Julia for a few minutes, if she's in."

"Hello, there my boy. It's high time we laid eyes on ye down here. We've heared all 'bout the slave business—Lark and Osborne's girl running away and all. Did ye ketch 'em?" replied the Colonel as he showed Basil in.

"No, we didn't find them. Rode all the way into Tennessee and didn't run into anybody who had seen or knew of any suspicious Africans about. Can you believe that?"

"Don't ye worry yerself none 'bout it. They'll be found, they will. Let's jest hope they don't git themselves kilt. That there slave boy and girl sure 'nough ere high-value property. A man can't much afford to lose such valuable assets. Your father won't be none too happy 'bout it, neither. 'Spect you've done wrote to Thomas 'bout it. Now let me go fetch Julia, boy."

"Thank you, Colonel," Basil responded, as he damned himself for not having communicated the news to his father already. He had been so busy with Jesse's trial and then the search for the slaves that the notion to write to his father about the incident had completely eluded him. After a good self-censuring, he made a vow to himself that the letter would be written that night without fail.

"Well, hello there, Master Basil. It's good to see you down this way," the smiling Julia greeted him as she entered the Deavers' sitting room. Maggie must have been in the kitchen or upstairs, and the Colonel considerately elected to give the couple some time to themselves and begged his leave.

"Hello, Julia. You're looking mighty sprite and pretty on this fine day," Basil replied, and he meant what he said. Julia was glowing and just as beautiful as ever.

"Oh, thank you, sir. You're spreading it on pretty thick, aren't you?" she mocked while cocking her head playfully and looking intently at her handsome neighbor. And then Julia could not help herself, as her face formed a grin of sorts and her mouth spewed a cutting query, "Do you butter up that Anderson girl at Crab Orchard too?"

It might have seemed like a cruel jab to Basil, but Julia had not meant to issue a hateful accusation. She just wanted to prod and tease him and to study his reaction so she could better assess his feelings for her rival. When Julia had been with Altha and Basil—the day her parents had visited Josiah Anderson at Crab Orchard—she had been sure that Altha harbored strong feelings for Basil, even though the young mother had tried to hide them. Julia had seen through the sheer façade—or at least thought she had. And it had been those suspicions that had provoked her subsequent immature cool treatment toward Basil.

Basil did not appreciate one bit the insinuation nor the nature of Julia's prickly inquiry, and it showed. His intuition had been correct. Julia was jealous of Altha. Well, he aimed to expose the ugly envy she concealed right here and now, and he sounded out, "Julia, now why would you ask something like that? What are you trying to say?"

Realizing instantly that she had poked a hornet's nest, Julia attempted to change the tone of the conversation. "Oh, I don't know. I just thought you might have become partial to Altha after you helped with the baby's birth, is all. I certainly didn't mean to hurt your feelings or anything, you sensitive boy."

"Yeah, well, we're friends, and that's it. And I think a lot of Rufus, but that's all. I wouldn't say I'm partial to her, though, whatever you mean by that." Basil was riled and ready to change the topic and spill the news that he was not going to Flat Rock.

"I didn't mean anything atall by it, Master Basil. Please forgive me for saying it, and I'm so sorry. Okay? Now then, you haven't forgotten the Flat Rock party, have you?" Julia asked, ready herself to change the subject.

"That's why I stopped by—to tell you that I won't be going," he spurted out and then waited expectantly to see what response he got.

"Oh no, Basil! You're not serious, I hope? What will I tell Wade?" The disappointment was obvious, but Julia tried not to be cross with him.

"Julia, for more than a week now I've been on the road chasing after runaway slaves. And I don't have any suitable clothes here in Haywood to wear to the ball. Just give that message to Wade for me, and tell him that I'm sorry I couldn't make it. He'll understand. I'm sure of it." Although confident of Wade's understanding, Basil was not so sure Julia understood.

"You do look worn and weary, Basil, and I believe you could use a bath," she said as a sympathetic smile grew across her face. "I was very much looking forward to your company for the next three days. Guess Father will have to keep the wolves and bears beat off of us along the road, now that you're not going. And Wade will have to keep me entertained as best he can. Now, if you are a real nice boy while I'm gone, I promise to show you my dance card when we get back. I dare say it's going to be filled with the names of handsome southern gentlemen like Wade and Fred. Too bad, though, your name won't be on it. Isn't it?" she finished, realizing that her prospects for having a good time over in Flat Rock were greatly diminished with the news that her East Fork feller was not going to be in attendance.

Yeah, too bad, Basil thought as he wondered how many times Mr. Wade Hampton's name would be scratched across that card of Julia's. And then he thought of something else he wanted Julia to convey to Wade and Fred.

"Oh, Julia, there's another message I want you to give Wade and Fred for me. On the Fourth over at Waynesville, there's going to be a mustering-in ceremony for a Haywood cavalry unit. They're getting one up in response to the war with Mexico, and I'm going over to sign up. So while you're partying and whooping it up, Fashion and I will be doing our duty for our country and drilling with a bunch of farmers."

"Oh no, Basil! Does that mean you'll be going off to the war?" Julia was visibly concerned, and the anxiousness in her voice was genuine.

"Probably not. They say there are plenty of volunteers already signed up and ready to go, plenty enough to whip the Mexicans anyway. But you never can tell. I guess we Haywood men will be ready if they need us. Say, I hear your brother, Burton, is going to sign up. At least that's what the Osbornes allowed."

"No one's told me, if that's the case. But now I'm going to be worried a sight about you the whole time I'm away at that party."

Basil thought Julia to be serious. At least he did not think she was feigning concern just to make him feel good. Maybe there was some hope left for him and Julia after all. He would have to wait and see if the romance with Wade was going to flower or simply wither away. Feeling guilty for wishing the latter, Basil determined to have a good look at that dance card of Julia's once she got back.

Damn this infernal pen, Basil thought as he labored to write an overdue letter to his father. He tried to keep the message brief while informing Thomas of the status of the planting, growth of the crops, bushels of wheat harvested, condition of the stock, and the welfare of the tenants and slaves. The Jesse Anderson affair took up several paragraphs, and Basil passed along Judge Love's compliments to the elder Edmunston. In conclusion, he wrote of the runaways and his efforts to recover them. Basil was confident his father would not blame him for Lark's actions. However, there was sure to be some second-guessing as to the son's judgment and how the wife business might have been handled differently.

Actually Basil was much harder on himself than his father had ever been. He condemned himself for causing Lark to run away, feeling that somehow he should have negotiated with Blalock and Osborne and worked out an agreement so Lark could take a wife. Lark was a first-rate slave, and now the Edmunstons were in jeopardy of losing this valuable chattel.

Penning the letter was not soothing Basil's conscience or reviving his spirits atall. The retroflection had an opposite effect on him it seemed. He was beginning to doubt himself and his ability to handle the immense responsibility his father had given him, and these doubts flowed over into the last lines of the epistle to his father:

> *I feel that I may be guilty of driving Lark away, and it is likely strong evidence of bad management and a poor recommendation for an overseer. I think you ought to consider dismissing yours as an unprofitable servant. I almost wish myself clear of Haywood and that my lot be cast elsewhere for the benefit of your fortune and my peace of mind. How are you coming with the search for a Haywood overseer?*
>
> *Love to all,*
> *your affectionate son,*
> *Basil*

Basil was busting with pride as he rode into Waynesville on the country's Independence Day. Uriah and Harry had spent the entire previous afternoon bathing, trimming, and currying Fashion as well as shining the horse's tack so that it literally gleamed. Such rippling and handsome horseflesh as Basil straddled was uncommon, and he and Fashion struck an impressive figure indeed.

The temperature was in the eighties that morning and sure to pass the ninety-degree mark by early afternoon. Main Street, one of only two streets in Haywood's county seat, had been dragged with a log pulled behind a mule team to smooth out the ruts and dried-up mud holes. Efforts were being made to sprinkle water over the road surface in an attempt to smother the dust during the parade procession, which was scheduled to begin at noon time. Store buildings and offices lining both sides of the avenue were decked out in red, white, and blue bunting and other patriotic décor. The nation's stars and bars flew over the tops of the courthouse and jail, and a large banner was draped high across Main Street with a pronouncement of the country's seventieth birthday.

All of the town's citizens and a host of farmers and their families from across the county were already beginning to line the street in anticipation of the parade. As Basil rode down the festive avenue, with his silver spurs glimmering in the sunlight, he received catcalls and whistles from onlooking spectators as well as enthralled glances from the ladies—young and old alike. Wearing a bright red shirt and indigo blue pants with the bottoms stuffed into the tops of his knee-high black boots, Basil was embarrassed by the extraordinary attention cast his way. His first instinct was to just ride along and ignore the gawkers, but then he thought better of such aloof behavior. So instead, Basil leaned back and rode high in the saddle, while touching a hand to his hat and offering a smile along with a slight tip of his head to the onlookers.

In front of the courthouse, a large crowd of men had gathered. Hitching Fashion to a nearby post, he waded in amongst them. Trying desperately to be heard in the noisy throng, someone at the top of the steps was yelling out, "All those desiring to join up with the Mountain Guards, please step forward and move inside. Ye can sign up in there, and we'll have the swearing in directly." The man cried out these instructions over and over again.

The turnout was impressive, in Basil's estimation. There were plenty of young men ganging around who were obviously ready to serve their country and many older ones who just wanted to jabber and look-on. The enlistees came from all ends of the county and for the most part were farmers' sons. Before their names were added to the roll, they had to attest to either ownership of or access to a horse and saddle. Basil and thirty-seven other Haywood men were sworn in that morning to serve with the Mountain Guards Cavalry Unit attached to the Nineteenth Brigade of the North Carolina State Militia. Burton Deaver was elected captain of the unit, and he immediately informed his recruits that drills would be held every two weeks at Waynesville until further notice.

Deaver and his raw troops formed up near the head of the parade that day, just behind a few musicians tooting brass instruments and tapping drum heads. Astute onlookers and listeners might have been able to discern the tunes of *Yankee Doodle*, *Hail Columbia*, and *The Banner of the Free* blaring forth. Trailing the cavalry troopers were mule-drawn buggies carrying local politicians, the sheriff, the County judges, a couple of surviving Revolutionary War veterans, and many elderly soldiers who had served in the Haywood militia unit during the second war with Great Britain. This was the same company that Thomas Edmunston had commanded, a fact that Basil was surely keen to.

Rolling along behind the veterans were wagons loaded with storekeepers advertising their wares and pretty young ladies wearing long dresses and bonnets. And finally prize heads of stock—oxen, cattle, bulls, horses, sheep, and mules—brought up the rear, nervous and jumpy from the fireworks that were exploding across the parade route and in the air. It was Haywood's largest celebration of the year, and Basil thoroughly enjoyed it from his vantage point on Fashion in the middle of the cavalry pack.

Several days had passed since Basil's return from the mission to find his runaway slave. The farming business at the Den was progressing about as well as could be expected. Between terrific summer thunderstorms, the Africans were kept busy in the cornfields pulling and hoeing out the weeds. The wheat and oats crops were doing tolerable well. Basil figured that in two or three weeks, the oats would be ready to cut. But he was bothered by all the fine beef stock grazing in the pastures and figured he would soon not be able to pay their board. They were eating up all the grasses he meant for the calves to feed on. So he figured he would try to sell a few head right soon.

It had been quite a spell since Basil had been up to Crab Orchard, and he had a hankering to visit with Altha and Rufus. So he called for Jake to bring the shoe last and leather, and the two of them rode up to the Orchard on a cloudy afternoon. As they drew near to the tenant property, the Anderson men could be seen hunched over with hoes in hands attacking the weeds that were infesting their precious corn rows. Basil hailed to them as he rode by, and they stopped long enough to throw up their hands in reply.

Altha was pleasantly surprised when she looked up from her loom and weaving work to spot Basil riding into the yard. She was working outside where her brothers had assembled the loom under a simple lean-to shelter off the cabin wall. Almost fully recovered now from her childbirth nightmare, she tossed the shuttle one last time before standing up and walking in her bare feet to greet Basil.

"Basil, it's so good to see you. We've been missing you dearly," the beaming Altha greeted.

"Hello there, young lady. I trust you've been well," he said as he resisted an inherent urge to hug the beautiful woman whose eyes were locked on his. Taking Altha's hand awkwardly and squeezing it, he continued, "By 'we' you must mean you and Rufus and not the Anderson menfolk," he joked with a quizzical look.

"Yep, me and Rufus. Come on over and see him," she said, leading Basil to a crude crib sitting next to the loom.

"Oh, he's sleeping. Better not wake him, I guess," said Basil as he looked down at the slumbering child.

"No, it's all right. He's been asleep long enough now and will have to be fed soon." Altha reached down, gently picked the baby up, and handed him over to Basil.

"Hello there, big boy. How's my Rufus doing?" Basil crooned in a low tone as the baby awakened and stared back at the face of the strange man holding him. But Rufus did not look strange to Basil. He looked like someone who was a part of his life now, a big part. Basil did not ponder on it too long but did wonder why it felt so good to hold Rufus in his strong arms and why it seemed so natural.

"Oh, I almost forgot, Altha. The reason I brought Jake up is that we're going to get you some shoes made. What do you say? While you and Jake get to that, I can hold this here pretty little baby boy all to myself."

"No, Basil, I couldn't," Altha quickly retorted.

But the Master of the East Fork was insistent. He had nurtured this plan to get some shoes on the girl since the first time he saw her. Basil called Jake over, and after the slave took a good gander at the baby, he sat Altha down and proceeded to trace the outline of her dirty feet onto the sole leather. Throughout the entire shoemaking process, Basil held on to Rufus while having a good heart-to-heart with Altha. He told her about the runaway slaves and the party at Flat Rock that he was skipping. It made him proud to tell her he had enlisted in the Mountain Guards cavalry unit, and he bragged about riding Fashion in the parade at Waynesville. For her part, Altha did not have much news to relate. She had been just taking care of Rufus and her father. That was all.

"Oh, Basil, Father told me how you spoke up for Jesse at his trial. He said you told the judge about us being good tenants and all. Father says he can't understand why you did it. He allowed that Columbus Hartgrove would never have done it. Don't know why he carries on so about Mr. Hartgrove. That man's been nothing but good to me. He helped me get the teacher's job for the winter term at the schoolhouse, knowing that I was with child and the circumstances. When Father and my brothers were going through one of those awful binges of theirs and couldn't lend a hand getting in firewood for the school, Mr. Hartgrove came up the river with Uriah and worked all day in the snow cutting and splitting wood."

As Altha paused and reflected, Basil spoke up. "Figured it was the least I could do for my tenants and your family. Besides, I only spoke the truth," he said sporting a kind of a foolish grin on his face. Then on a serious note he continued, "They've done right smart work getting those fields plowed and planted, and I let the judge know about it, that's all." Then he remembered her comments about Hartgrove and added. "What you say about Hartgrove is consistent with what I hear from others. I've not gotten to know him hardly atall since I've been here, but Father and Colonel Deaver sure speak highly of the man."

"Father says he aims to do you right, Basil. He says he's going to bring in a good crop even if it kills him. You don't realize what a positive influence you've had on him and my brothers, do you? They're not drinking near as much as they used to, at least I don't believe so. And they're working every day in the fields or repairing fencing or tending to your stock. Seems they're always looking for things to do, and that's a sight different, I tell you. Did you realize what a change you've brought to this place?" Altha's comments were heartfelt, and she purposely left out the part Basil had played in her own life.

"Nah, I hadn't really thought about it that way. I'm just pleased they've become farmers again. We, you and me, we can't let them slip back to their old ways either, Altha."

Jake was still hammering away at the shoe last, and Altha decided to broach a far more tender subject. "Do you mind if I get serious with you a little, sir?"

"Well, I mind if you're going to address me as 'sir'," Basil came back quickly. Still holding Rufus in his arms, he walked over to the crib and placed the baby in it. "Let's see how he likes that," said Basil as he took Altha by the arm and stepped out of earshot of the slave. It was fine with him if Altha wanted to get serious. He didn't mind atall.

"Okay, no more 'sirs.' I was just wondering—well, I just want you to know that I think you are very special, Basil." As Basil looked at her with wide-open eyes and began to reply, Altha continued. "No—no, let me finish please. I don't mean special as a friend. Sure, we are friends now, but I feel more than that for you, Basil. But I'm afraid of ruining things between us. I don't want you to feel obligated toward me—that is, feel that you owe me the same feelings I have for you." She had said enough for the time being, although stumbling badly. But she needed to stop and gather her thoughts before trying again to communicate the entire message she very much was of a mind to convey.

Basil hesitated as Altha searched for the right words to continue. He did not know what to think or say, and he was not completely sure where Altha was headed. But he hoped she was trying to tell him that she felt more than a friendship for him, that she had deeper sensual feelings similar to the ones he had harbored for her ever since that first crispy spring day he had found her spinning in her bare feet. He hoped that was where she was headed, because, if so, he wanted to go there too. And it was about time. He had been too cowardly to state his own true sentiments before. *Now is the time to take a risk,* he thought. *Now it's your turn—so tell her!*

"No, Altha, I don't feel obligated to have any kind of feelings for you," Basil began as he told himself, *Take it easy, don't get ahead of yourself, this is important.* "But the truth is I do have special feelings for you—and for Rufus, too, for that matter. And as you say, not like a friend. I feel a stronger pull than that—one that's been pulling hard at me ever since that first day we met. I think—I think I might really be in love with you, Altha. I mean—I don't think—I believe I am." There, now he had got it all out there—spilled his heart to her. He had been led to the edge of the cliff, and sure enough, he had plunged off into the void. Had he misjudged Altha? He hoped the hell not and waited apprehensively to see what the repercussions were going to be.

They were standing near to each other but moved closer with their faces separated by only mere inches. As they grasped each other's hands, Altha blurted out in surprise, "Do you mean it, Basil? I was so afraid you didn't feel like I do. Our backgrounds and stations are so vastly different. And the lie I told you about my husband—I didn't know if you could ever forgive me for that. I didn't think it was possible for you to ever love me, Basil, as I so dearly love you. Ever since that first day I saw you, I think I have been in love with you. No, I know I have been in love with you all this time."

Altha finished her emotional confession with tears of joy running down her face. As Jake, who was still at work making the shoes, cast a curious glance their way, Basil pulled Altha to him, wrapped her tightly in his arms, and gave her the most passionate kiss that he knew how to give. It was his first kiss, and he did tolerably well.

Chapter 16

Drowning in Happiness

Altha and Basil were beset by myriad emotions when their lips finally parted. They remained in each other's arms hugging and feeling the exchange of passion flow between them as the complexity of the unlikely romance slowly began to infiltrate their beings with prickly thoughts. Basil had hoped to be clear of Haywood before year's end, or as soon as his father found another overseer to take his place. During the long embrace, he considered among other things whether this love affair with Altha would squash his chances of completing a university education. *And what about Julia?* he worried. He still had emotional ties to her as well, or at least he thought he still harbored special feelings for her.

Altha could not purge the wicked specter of Sam Beck from her mind or the fact that she was still a married woman. Almost simultaneously during this hugging and kissing episode, both Basil and Altha came to independent conclusions that these complicated issues and many more would have to sorted out in due time. The important thing now was they had each other to love and care for. And they had Rufus.

"Gots da shoes all ready, Massa," Jake called out as he held Altha's new footwear up in the air. He had interrupted the loving couple as they poured out their crazed affections for each other and mentally groped to understand what it all meant. It was probably for the best. The troublesome issues that lay ahead vanished from their minds as Altha broke out of Basil's arms and strolled over to admire the shoes. They fit her feet perfectly—and comfortably—and she was awfully proud and thankful to have them.

About that same time, Josiah came wandering in from the fields and Rufus started to bawl out for his mother. With their heart-to-heart conference definitely at an end, the excited young couple tidied up a few things between themselves and said their goodbyes. Basil picked up the crying baby one last time, and then handed him over to Altha to nurse. He promised to call on her as often as possible, depending on his work and the situation with Lark. Finally, he asked Altha to accompany him to the camp meetings that were scheduled to start the coming Sunday. Although the mention of the religious revival brought back horrible memories, Altha was much obliged to Basil for inviting her and readily agreed to attend with him.

"Good morning, Julia," Basil greeted as he walked into Deaver's store. It was the morning after he and Altha had confessed their love for each other. Basil had decided to break the difficult news to Julia sooner than later, and he had no idea how he would do it, or how she would react.

"Hello, Basil. I've been expecting you down. Can't wait to tell you all about the Hamptons' party," replied the radiant belle.

"That's why I came down. Well, that and to post this letter."

Colonel Deaver put up his hand to acknowledge Basil's presence as the young man escorted his daughter towards the back of the store for a quiet chat. The Colonel appeared to be busy attending to his customers, and consequently Julia and Basil were able to seclude themselves for a few minutes of somewhat private conversation about the Flat Rock ball. They found a spot well away from the whittling debris and nasty spittoon, and Julia commenced to regale Basil with all the exciting details of the party.

Her enthusiasm was bubbling over, and as Basil politely listened, he tried to work out in his mind exactly how he wanted to broach the subject of Altha with her. He was also anxious to learn if the pending romance with Wade Hampton had matured during the festive Fourth of July party over at Flat Rock. Well, Julia was fixing to fill his ears with news on that front.

"Oh, Basil, it was the most sumptuous affair you ever wanted to see. Their house—oh, it was so magnificent. I could never describe how beautiful it was. It looked like a fairytale mansion," Julia raved as she began to verbally illustrate for Basil the foreign setting the Deavers had been thrust into.

She went on and on describing the stately residence, beginning with the huge white-pillared columns that fronted the two-storied manse. The exterior walls, Julia allowed, were clapboarded and freshly painted a brilliant white, and the interior plastered walls were covered over with the finest imported decorative paper that could be found. Guests entering the house from the portico through large double doors accessed the ballroom through a splendid entry gallery. On each side of this entrance foyer, glorious curving staircases wound their way up to the second-floor balcony, and Julia told how she and Wade had traipsed up and down these very steps numerous times. Plunging down from the highest ceiling, two and a half stories overhead, was the most breathtaking chandelier Julia could ever imagine or describe. Fully eight feet in diameter, she thought it was, and its crystal and mirrored glass ornamentation shined and glimmered as the candle flames reflected from their surfaces.

Basil had heard enough by this time but resisted changing the subject for fear he would hurt the pretty girl's feelings. Carrying on, Julia described the ballroom as being approximately the size of their store, and she waved an arm around to indicate to Basil the size of their surroundings. Candelabras, wall sconces, and more modest chandeliers garnished the room and cast their dazzling glows across the dance floor into the early morning hours.

"You should have seen the gowns all the ladies were wearing. And the materials they were made from—why, I never! Mother and I felt so poorly dressed, but beforehand we had already agreed to pay it no nevermind." Julia was a proud girl, and she had a lot to be proud of. She was beautiful, and she knew it. She came from good stock, and she had the best life ever at Forks of Pigeon. But, truthfully, Julia had been flushed with envy as she looked on in astonishment at the incredible dresses adorning the stylish women surrounding her. Unlike her own rather plain one made from the best linen and lace that the Colonel carried in his store, theirs were fashioned from the finest muslins, tulles, and other imported materials, the likes of which she had never seen.

And Julia had taken notice of the quizzical glances and poorly concealed smirks directed her way from a few of the lowland belles and matrons. Although unperturbed at the time, she had since experienced misgivings about such superficial airs and doubted that she could ever fit into such a lofty setting and lifestyle as Wade Hampton enjoyed.

"Look, Basil. Wade and I danced together six times. See!" Julia said excitedly as she pulled her dance card from a dress pocket to show him. She pointed to the names as Basil carefully perused it. "Oh, Basil, you should have seen how worried Mother was for me. She thought that someone might take exception to Wade's behaving a little too forward or familiar with me, southern etiquette and all. She warned me how men are not supposed to monopolize a lady's time at balls and such," Julia finished while laughing out loud.

"Yep, was exposed to all that etiquette stuff at the Fort and boarding schools. Looks like you danced with Fred a couple of times, and another Rutledge or two. Let's see, a Blake, Baring, and a sight of others. Looks to me like you danced the entire program, Julia," Basil confirmed as he handed the card back to her. And then he teased, "I expect you were the most popular—and the tiredest—girl at the party. That's not bad for a country girl from Forks of Pigeon." They both shared a laugh, and Basil added, "Seriously though, I hope you and your folks had a pleasing diversion."

"We all did, Basil. Wade's parents were such good hosts and treated us so well. They opened up their entire house to us. And our fathers struck if off exceedingly well, I believe. Father says that Mr. Hampton is going to introduce him to a few of the large merchant-house owners in Columbia. Oh! By the way, Wade's head is looking so much better."

Basil perked up a little. "Good! What about the headaches? Is he clear of those yet?"

"No, he's still suffering them, a great deal it seems. But he says they are easing a bit." Julia went on to share some rather intimate details in regards to Wade, surprising Basil with her openness and making him feel a little uneasy and defensive. Wade had confided to Julia that he had not been able to stop thinking about her. He believed she was the most remarkable and beautiful girl he had ever known, and he wanted to dedicate himself entirely to her. And he had asked Julia if she entertained similar feelings for him and whether she would commit herself to a romantic courtship so they could explore the depths of their feelings for each other. When Julia explained to him her plans to attend the Davenport Females College at Lenoir, Wade had been undaunted. He promised to come up to visit her at least once a month—under the strictest chaperoning arrangements, of course. And so, after he had spilled his heart out to her, Julia had been beguiled and persuaded to commit herself to Wade.

As she finished relating all of this to Basil, she fingered a necklace around her neck and deftly opened up its tiny silver locket. Reluctantly, almost bashfully, Julia held the keepsake up for Basil to see the contents—a few curled strands of shiny brown hair.

"It's Wade's. Can you believe it? Please don't have hard feelings towards me, Basil. I know that I may have encouraged you to call on me, but I couldn't help it. Please believe me," pleaded Julia as she stared intently at the astounded Basil. Julia still had strong feelings for him, and this fling with Wade had exploded way beyond her control. She was in a real predicament and unsure of what she should do or say to Basil.

The first thing that crossed Basil's mind was that Wade Hampton didn't dilly-dally around like somebody else he knew. *They're courting now? Already! Isn't that way too fast? Whoaaa, Basil. Simmer down now*, he thought. *This is not all bad. It's actually good news.* He had been afraid of what Julia's reaction might be when he got around to spilling his guts about Altha. Now it appeared that she would not mind atall. *Julia seems to be happy now. Wade's certainly happy.* He believed Altha was happy. *So, why can't I be happy*, Basil wondered. *I am happy*, he realized, *and now everybody is happy. We're all drowning in happiness.* When he finally assimilated all this happiness in his mind, his belief in God swelled. It seemed that He was looking out for the Master of the East Fork, as well He should.

Basil congratulated Julia and wished her much happiness and success on her forthcoming romantic escapades with Wade. He assured her that there were no hard feelings. As a matter of fact, he had important news of a like and intimate nature for her, and then he proceeded to recant the whole affair with Altha.

"Don't say anything yet to your parents," Basil requested of the stupefied Julia when he was done. "I aim to talk to the Colonel concerning it and see what he thinks I ought to do about this marriage business of hers and that no-good husband, Sam Beck. Colonel Deaver can put me straight about the legal considerations. Expect I will need to get a lawyer before it's over, though."

"Do you aim to marry her, Basil?" asked the incredulous Julia.

"Aim to? Yeah. Don't know when, but I expect we will get married, if she will have me, that is. Aim to give that boy a father, too, Julia. That's what I aim to do."

Fingering the pendant at her throat, Julia just stared at Basil as a queasiness inexplicably rose in her stomach and dissolved all traces of giddiness and smug thoughts of Wade Hampton.

The runaways, Lark and Delia, were soaking wet when they found the deserted turnpike on the east side of the French Broad River. In the wee hours of the morning, they had crossed the wide stream just below the mouth of Sandy Mush Creek. At that spot, the water current was slow and weak and even Delia, who was a good half foot shorter than Lark's six-foot stature, was able to simply wade across. At the deepest pools, which reached about to her shoulders, Lark had secured her by the arm and tugged the girl along behind him.

They had chosen the busiest road in western North Carolina to lead them northward out of the mountains and possibly to freedom. In the fall and winter, it was always jammed full with cattle, hogs, and sheep being driven to market. However, during this early summer period, the traffic was much lighter, and farmers doing business at the way stations, stagecoaches filled with tourists, and local pedestrian traffic had the run of the road. Although these travelers normally used the turnpike during the daylight hours only, Lark and Delia stayed well back from the road as they followed its track northward during the relative safety of darkness. They could not chance stumbling upon the odd nocturnal traveler, who would certainly sound the alert about the two runaways. In that case, it would be only a matter of hours before the slave catchers' dogs would be sniffing up their trail.

Twenty miles or so north of Asheville, near the small hamlet of Lapland, Lark and Delia finally halted their night's advance. Finding a lair in the bramble bushes well away from the nearest house, they lay down in the heat of day to rest. It was during a wakeful moment that Delia fortuitously spotted three guinea fowls that had apparently strayed from a farm. The animals were oblivious to the presence of the slaves as they pecked along the ground and fed on every insect within their reach.

"Lark! Wakes up, Lark. Lookit dare. Sees da guineas? You think we's can kills us one?" Delia whispered as Lark looked for the chicken-like creatures.

At last locating the stray fowl, Lark's empty belly growled as he replied, "Oh me, Delia, lookit those fat guineas! 'Spects we's can gits us one, but we's gots to do's it real quiet. I believe I can gits us one if I can find me's a rock."

Wide awake now, Lark found a good throwing rock and took a position where he could ambush the oncoming fowl. And just as he planned it out in his head one soon came within range. Delia watched anxiously as Lark slowly cocked his left throwing arm and in a blinding fury hurled the stone at the guinea. The unsuspecting animal was slow in reacting to the sudden ruckus, and the impact of the well-aimed projectile knocked it to the ground, momentarily stunning it. As the other two guineas cackled loudly and fled wildly away, Lark pounced upon the floundering prey and broke its neck.

Amazed at their good fortune, the two nervous slaves grabbed their kill and fled deeper into the woods to seek another hideout farther removed from the settlement. There Lark struggled to kindle a fire, and by the time he finally got it going, Delia had the dead guinea stripped of its grey plumage and run through with a spit. She placed it over the low flames, and the two waited nervously for the meat to cook, afraid that someone might see the smoke and come to investigate its source. After only five to ten minutes of roasting time, they doused the fire and ate heartily of the partially-cooked guinea fowl. It was truly a feast for the young slaves, and they savored each and every bite. *Life is good,* they thought as they reclined in the bushes to enjoy their good life.

Just as the gloaming light was about to give out and while they were delighting in making a baby, the sound of voices pierced the quietness of the forest. Lark and Delia, still in each other's clutches, froze in horror in their thorny refuge as a young boy and girl excitedly approached. These youths were calling out and whistling in the forest as loud as they could while bearing straight in the direction of the concealed slaves. The runaways were terrified and convinced they were about to be discovered for sure. Closer and closer the children came until finally they stopped scant feet from where Lark and Delia were lying in fear, hiding and afraid to even breathe.

The runaways could clearly hear the frustrated young girl gripe to her companion, "It's getting dark, Zach. We've got to get started back. That ole mean guinea will show back up. Wait and see."

"It's your fault. You didn't latch the coop, did you?"

The brother and sister knew they were in big trouble for losing one of the guinea fowls. Scared of the consequences of their carelessness, they abruptly turned in the direction they had come from and took off running and arguing. Lark and Delia, who were still clinging tightly together, just waited nervously and stared at each other until finally breathing a great sigh of relief. It had been such a close call, and they had been lucky. In order to make it all the way to the Yankee land where freedom beckoned, the slaves knew they would need much more good fortune like this.

It was nearly time for them to set out after the North Star again. But it was not quite dark enough yet, so the two slaves determined to finish the business that the young guinea hunters had interrupted so inopportunely.

Chapter 17

Camp Meeting Shivers

When Basil and Altha arrived at the camp meeting at Forks of Pigeon, it was already in progress. The mother and Rufus had been conveyed in the Edmunston's old buggy, driven by Uriah, and Basil had escorted them on his fashionable mount. The ancient buggy was one that had been used at Fort Catawba for many years, but its dilapidated state had forced its banishment to Haywood, where it was thought some utilization might still be made of it. Basil had now found a good use and had employed Jacob and Jake to refurbish the buggy and make it East-Fork–worthy for his lady friend and her baby.

It was a sunshiny Sunday morning, and quite a crowd was gathered for the start of the religious events, which were to take place over the entire coming week. This particular camp meeting week was scheduled earlier than usual so that full advantage could be taken of a noted itinerant preacher who was making his way through western North Carolina. Normally the gatherings, which lasted for two to three weeks, occurred in August after the wheat was harvested and the corn was laid by. But this session was shortened in recognition of the farmers, who had to hurry back to tend to their crops. The worship hours were always exceptionally long, with religious services planned for morning, afternoon, and night. And, of course, the camp meeting was being held in the hottest season of the year when afternoon thunderstorms were likely.

Most of the families from outside of the Forks of Pigeon area actually stayed and camped in their covered wagons or in crude, makeshift shelters on the actual meeting grounds. Basil and Altha, however, had decided on a commuting arrangement from the Den. The mother and her baby son were to sleep inside the cabin, and the master was relegated to the outdoors under the stars—barring inclement weather, that is.

"Looks like things are rolling already," Basil said as he dismounted and helped Altha out of the buggy. "There's some crowd here today! Let's hope there will be room for us out of the sun," he continued while looking at all of the wagons and buggies lined up in rows and the saddled horses tied alongside. He gazed across the field toward the preaching building and could hear the minister trying to outdo the loud shouting of the Lord's flock herded under a large, rustic shelter. It had not taken the preacher long to stir the congregation to a fervor, Basil thought, and he could not help but believe this camp meeting was going to be interesting.

Leaving Uriah to babysit Rufus in a shady spot near the river, Basil and Altha walked shoulder to shoulder toward the entrance doorway and the agitated worshippers. Before entering, Basil whispered lowly with a grin, "Don't forget we can't sit together."

"I know that. This is not my first time, silly. Hope you enjoy it, and don't get too worked up," Altha replied with a grin.

Upon the fine-looking couple's entrance, heads turned and eyes stared until Basil and Altha separated to take their seats on the hard slab benches. Basil found a vacant place near the back, settling between a couple of strangers. As he looked around at the animated audience, he spotted several familiar faces. But there were many, many more that were not recognizable. He figured the large assembly might comprise two hundred people or more from all reaches of the county. It was an enormous crowd of faithful and unfaithful Methodists, Baptists, and Presbyterians that had gathered to participate in the exhilarating religious and social aspects of this camp meeting.

These people had endured a long cold winter and toiled endless springtime hours in the fields to plant their life-sustaining crops. And now they were hungry for some interaction with their neighbors and, most of all, their Savior above. Of manifest importance to them was that they leave this week-long revival—after all of the shouting, praying, singing, and preaching was done—with a keen sense of personal salvation and the knowledge that their sinful thoughts and actions had been forgiven.

Basil was not looking for personal salvation atall. He mostly wanted to socialize with his neighbors and spend some quality time with Altha. As the service wore on, he wondered what possessed these good, intelligent people, to reach such high stages of passionate agitation. To him, it almost seemed that his neighbors were being hypnotized by the preachers' overpowering zeal and the ambiance surrounding them. They were purposely allowing themselves to become excited and emotionally charged into a state of delusional fanaticism, Basil firmly believed.

At least every few minutes, he cast a glance over toward Altha to make sure she was not getting seduced by the magic of the place. *Such a beauty,* he thought to himself as he studied her. Her gleaming coal-black hair was pulled back across her ears and coiffured neatly in a bun behind her head. Those deep green eyes and high cheek bones along with the pleasing proportions of her other facial features—not to mention the rest of her shapely form—worked together to cause Basil to think she was the most beautiful person in the world. He was amazed at how much had transpired since that frosty morning some three and a half months ago when he first met her. *It was such a short time ago,* he thought. Then Altha caught Basil staring at her, and both their faces erupted into playful grins. When she turned her attention back to the preacher's sermon, Basil reluctantly did likewise.

He soon, however, found himself gazing about again, as many around him were jumping and dancing and screaming fanatical exhortations to the religious cants of the minister. Basil himself was excited by the excitement, but one thing was for certain—he was not about to be saved. His perusal sharpened to study the architecture and construction details of the expansive preaching venue surrounding him. Upright locust poles were set in the ground and sided all around with split logs as high as the roof. Openings were left near the top of the east and south walls to allow the outside light to enter and to provide some needed ventilation. An entrance doorway was hacked into one end of the rustic shelter and the roof was covered with long rived oak boards. That was it, all there was to it. The preaching building was simple and crude, but it was not half bad for Haywood, Basil mused.

Shortly after twelve noon, the preacher gave out, and the sermon wound down. Altha joined Basil as they made their way back to the buggy. She was concerned about Rufus and wondered how he and Uriah had done.

"No, mistress, Rufus don't cry one time while you and the massa were 'way. We has us a good time, me and Rufus do," Uriah said to a relieved Altha.

"Oh thank you, Uriah, for being so good with him. I was worried sick that he might be pitching a great fit with you."

"No, mistress, he don't pitch no fits. He's a fine li'l baby, Rufus is."

Basil chimed in, "Okay, Uriah, if you need to go take care of some business in the woods, better go ahead now. We'll be here for a while."

As Uriah went off to relieve himself, Altha fed Rufus, and then she and Basil enjoyed some of Patsy's homely victuals and some very warm buttermilk. Before they were finished eating, however, visitors started coming over to the buggy to greet them. Julia was the first, and the perky beauty was as nice as she could be to Altha. They chatted about the baby, Altha's quick rebound from her travails, and her noticeable good health. When Basil excused himself and moved off to look after the three horses, Julia took full advantage of his absence to introduce a more intimate topic.

"Altha, I don't mean to be forward, and please tell me, won't you, if you think I should mind my own business?" Altha had no clue where Julia was leading the conversation and simply nodded her confirmation. Then Julia continued, "Basil confided to me—I hope that's okay with you, Altha—that he has very deep feelings for you. He told me that he was very much in love with you. And he said you felt the same way toward him. Well, I just want you to know how very happy I am for both of you."

Julia's remarks, albeit candid, were not necessarily sincere. Ever since Basil had confessed to her his true intentions for Altha, she had become a lost and desperate soul. It had become abundantly clear to her that the interest and attentions she had directed toward Wade Hampton were almost entirely superficial. She had channeled her youthful jealousy into a game of sorts intended solely to cause Basil some trifling hurt and to bring him back to her. However, Julia had terribly miscalculated the situation and feelings all around, and she now found herself caught up in a ruinous dilemma. She was entailed romantically with someone she did not love while her one true love was apparently lost to her forever—all by her own doing.

Oblivious of this intrigue, the more mature and grounded Altha considered Julia's comments for a few moments and then surprisingly confided some deepfelt sentiments and reservations, "Thank you, Julia. I do feel that way about Basil too. I couldn't believe it. I mean, I couldn't believe he could feel that way about me. I had been in love with him from the start, the first day he came to the farm. It was just beyond all my hopes that someone like him could love me. I'm still afraid that it's all a big fantasy and that one day it will blow up in a huge puff of smoke."

About this time, Colonel Deaver and Maggie came over to visit a spell, interrupting Julia and Altha's delicate exchange. Later on, Columbus Hartgrove brought over his family and introduced his wife, Nannie, and their eighteen-month-old son, William. The Osbornes and Catheys paid their respects, as did others. Few who lived around Forks of Pigeon were unaware of Altha's story or had not heard of Basil's heroic efforts to deliver her baby. Certainly all of these neighbors thought well of the partnership and knew if it panned out, there was a glimmer of hope that an Edmunston might again actually reside on the East Fork. Basil and Altha discerned no inferences or slights regarding their complicated situation or the absentee husband. Surely there were a few who entertained more than a little surprise that the Master of the East Fork was courting a girl of such low status—his tenant's daughter, for heaven's sake. But these folk were good enough to hold their qualms about the matter, it being a camp meeting after all.

After the ten-o'clock service, there was an afternoon sermon at two o'clock and then a later candlelight preaching, each lasting about two hours. It took several preachers to maintain such a demanding agenda throughout the week and keep the assembly in a perfect sense of agitation and expectation. Between the formal programs, Basil and Altha visited, entertained, and dined with friends and made new acquaintances. They relished this society with their neighbors and endured the nerve-racking sermons as best they could. For the entire week, they followed this rigorous and tiring camp meeting schedule, and each night they returned to the Den well after dark had set in. And then early the next morning, they arose again and were on the road to the campground by nine o'clock.

The Saturday candlelight session that concluded the camp meeting ended in an amazing spectacle. Men, women, and children who were taken up with the spirit of the Lord were moved to chant and jump and dance with each other until such time as they felt the enveloping presence of their Savior. When that point was reached, several of the campgoers began to tremble and shiver and mutter gibberish that could not be understood. One man who was under such a feverish stupor just happened to be carrying on right beside Basil. Suddenly, before Basil knew what was taking place, the man grabbed him by his shoulders and began to shake him and scream nonsense in his face. Basil was so startled that he utterly froze for a moment as the man held on to him and began trembling furiously. Then, unexpectedly, this fervent lay man just up and passed out and collapsed right into Basil's arms.

A few others followed suit in these extraordinary acts to ensure their salvation. All of them seemingly fainted but were quickly revived and brought to their senses just as the meeting came to its conclusion. Basil actually had kept the man next to him from falling and carefully laid him down on the straw-covered ground. This man's wife and children rushed to his side and in less than a minute were hugging their loved one, who had miraculously come to his senses. Basil was flabbergasted by the incident, figuring that the man must be crazy. So he begged his leave and hurried off to find Altha.

Altha's view had been blocked, and she had not noticed Basil's unwitting act of assistance. As he was relating the story to her on the way to the buggy, they noticed Uriah appeared overly nervous and excited. Suspecting that something was amiss, they rushed on to see what was the matter.

"A man jus' comes up to me and axes me whose baby is it. I never sees da man befor'," said the worried Uriah, obviously nervous and upset. "I be real careful and don't say nothing 'bout Rufus. He axes me again if it's da mistress's baby. But I don't tell him whose baby is it, and I tell da man he best leave da baby alone, or I wills holler fo' Massa Baz."

The agitated Uriah immediately got Basil and Altha's full and undivided attention, and now they were alarmed. Basil asked for more information. "Uriah, what did this man look like? Describe him to us."

"He be's here jus' fo' a minute. I b'lieve he be's 'bout tall as you, Massa—real tall. And his hair be da same color as fresh straw."

Basil noticed the grimace that racked Altha. "Sound like anybody you know?" he asked as he hid his worst fears.

Altha held her hands to her cheeks and answered, "It must be him. Why has he come back? I knew it! I just knew it!" She then broke into sobs and tears, knowing the man surely was that low-life husband of hers. Taking Altha into his arms and trying his best to console the sobbing girl, Basil felt apprehensive shivers run through his body. He had an idea what this was all about and could only mutter to himself that it must be that damned Sam Beck.

Chapter 18

Ferry Snatchers

With their hunger pains eased by the guinea feast and other physical cravings satisfied, Lark and Delia resumed their northward trek with the onset of darkness. It was becoming a practiced routine for them—traveling at night and laying up during the day. They became expert food scavengers, primarily living off of the various types of berries along their path. Another easy source of nutrition was found in the grain fields associated with almost every farm they passed. Under the cover of darkness, Lark and Delia waded out into the peripheries of the fields and gathered the oats and wheat in their hands. Cleaning as much of the chaff and stems away as possible they crushed the remaining particles between rocks and consumed the residue—seeds, chaff, hulls, and all. It was only on rare occasions that they were able to eat a more substantial fare, like the guinea fowl still digesting in their stomachs.

The couple kept mostly to the bushes and woods bordering the turnpike and followed that track toward the Tennessee–North Carolina border. Anytime a traveler approached or a settler's cabin was encountered, they kept well out of sight. So far so good, though. No dogs had been loosed on them, and they were making good progress up the road. As they approached Warm Springs, near the Tennessee border and the furthest point north that either of them had ever been, they proceeded slowly. From a good distance away, Lark and Delia could see the grand hotel that was located on the far side of the river. It was a popular destination for tourists, who valued the therapeutic qualities of the natural warm spring waters located on the grounds. For Lark, the sight brought back recollections of the time he spent with Basil's father and several other Edmunstons who gathered there for a reunion. He had served as Thomas Edmunston's young valet on the trip and harbored distinct memories of the few days spent at these very same springs.

The midnight hour had long passed, but from their position at the edge of the woods, the slaves could see movement on the spacious upper porch of the hotel. It appeared to be a light from a single burning candle. And they could also detect faint flickering lights in a few of the numerous hotel windows. Lark and Delia gazed in silence toward the huge structure and tried to imagine what the people staying over there in all those rooms were doing at this late hour. *Might deys be making babies in dem rooms?* they pondered. *O' meybe dat person over dare walking 'round on da porch jus' can't sleep. Meybe dat person done steps outside to cool off in da nightstime air o' to smoke one o' dem big ol' tabacky cigars.*

It occurred to them how different their own plight was as compared with those other persons lodging over there in the big hotel across the river. The guests were free persons who could do whatever they wanted, whenever they wanted to. Those persons had the freedom to marry a loved one and had money to buy food and drink and whatever struck their fancy. Lark and Delia pondered for only a minute or two on the freedoms and privileges and rights of those persons in the hotel and their own lack of the same. But then it suddenly dawned on them that those strange persons may possibly represent danger and an obstacle to their flight to freedom. So they hurriedly decided to move on under the cover of darkness toward the drinking gourd beckoning in the black moonless sky.

Just beyond Warm Springs, they stole past the Paint Rock without noticing the ancient Indian pictographs that were made ages ago high on the rocky cliff face. As they moved along the turnpike beyond the Paint Rock, Lark began to worry. He had been monitoring their direction, which was very noticeably veering farther and farther westward and, importantly, away from the North Star and their path to freedom. Then just before he was about to cut away from the turnpike and take a proper heading, the hand of Providence intervened.

"Sees dat road dare, Delia? Da one dat goes dat ways?" Lark asked Delia as he pointed to a fork in the road and the trail that led northward.

"Yes, I sees it. Dat da road we's wants to goes on, Lark?"

"It's gots to be's. Yeah, dat's da road we's gonna take. It goes fo' da North Star. Sees?" Lark responded as he directed her eyes skyward toward the Pole Star. It was beginning to fade, and it would not be long before the sun began to peek over the brim of the eastern horizon.

"Oh, yeah, Lark, I sees it. We's gonna keeps on goin', o' we's gonna finds us a place to hide?"

"We needs to keep goin' up dat new road, den we's can stop."

Lark wanted to get away from the road junction, soon to be active again with the normal daytime traffic, and climb back into the mountains where the new road seemed to lead. It aimed northward directly into Tennessee's Paint Mountains, and very soon, the runaways were contently on their way again along this corrected path to freedom. They walked for less than an hour up the new road and across a gap in the mountain range. These slopes were not nearly as steep or as high as those in Haywood, and the slaves found them to be an easy climb.

The day was already dawning when Lark and Delia finally decided to call a halt to the night's trek. Finding a spot near a tiny log cabin, Delia flopped down exhausted and closed her eyes to nap. Lark immediately began reconnoitering the little farm's infrastructure and activities. He and his girl needed something to eat, and he hoped there might be an opportunity to snitch some food at the place.

Between napping spells throughout the day, they observed the movements around the cabin and outbuildings, and things did not look atall promising. Mostly there was a couple of good-sized, mean-looking dogs prowling around the premises, and Lark meant to stay way clear of them. Eventually he judged a bacon raid on the smokehouse or a plundering dash into the chicken coop was not worth the risk of setting the hounds off, although these acts of thievery were certainly enticing. They had eaten some berries the previous night, and this little nourishment, along with memories of the delicious guinea fowl, would have to suffice until they could hopefully find something later that evening.

At the onset of dusky dark, the runaways were again in flight. The traffic on the crude road they were following was busier than expected that night. Lark and Delia first had to hide from a herder driving sheep to the south. And then there were several stragglers, who were staggering and singing as they plodded along after the shepherd and his flock. These men came up on them so quickly that the slaves barely had time to find concealment in a thicket along a creek branch. At about two o'clock in the morning, after they had trudged down the rough trace for a good length of time and levelled out, the runaways' passage to the north came suddenly and unexpectedly to a raring halt.

Through the heavy brush along the edge of a bluff, Lark and Delia peered out at a wide and meandering river. It was the Nollichucky, and the road they were following simply ran up to the river's bank and abruptly ended, blocking their passage northward. They were frightened by this sight and trembled at the prospects of having to cross the expansive body of water. Neither of the slaves could swim, and it was obvious that the river could not be waded at this site. Disconcerted and pressed with making a decision on how to proceed, Lark fought back disturbing thoughts that they were done for. Although both he and Delia were terrified of the river's deep water and strong current, he felt there had to be a way for them to make it over to the other side. There just had to be. But he needed more time to cipher it out and more time to weigh their options.

Frantically Lark racked his brain to come up with a crossing plan. But he came up with nothing. He could not see well enough to determine if there were shallows or if there was another road or path they could follow. Fighting off nervous excitement, he finally concluded that it would be best to wait until it was daylight before determining a feasible crossing option. He would need the light of day to see, and he had to see good what he was up against. So Lark and Delia scrooched into a thicket on the river bank amongst the groundhogs, beavers, and otters and waited for daylight.

The rising sun brought things into a much clearer perspective for the runaways. They could easily see their road on the other side of the river, where it ascended a low bluff and continued northward through the river valley farmland. To accommodate turnpike travelers in the valley, a rope ferry operation had been established to carry wagons, stagecoaches, horses, stock, and people from one side of the river to the other. Lark noticed that the proprietor of the thriving business lived in a timber hut on the near bluff overlooking the Nollichucky and the boarding area. And he watched closely as horse-drawn wagons lined up one after another on both sides of the water, waiting their turns to be ferried across.

There were certainly no ferry contraptions akin to this in Haywood, but Lark had seen a similar set-up on the French Broad. However, he was only accustomed to fording the rivers over the shallow bottoms and had never actually ridden on a ferry boat himself. Pretty little Delia had never witnessed such a thing in her entire short life. She could not have been more impressed if it had been a great sailing ship plying the ocean waters. Neither slave slept much that day. Burrowed away in their sticky nest on the riverbank, downstream from the ferry, they carefully studied the operation and brainstormed other ideas for reaching the far bank alive and undiscovered.

Lark figured that the ferry boat was located in this spot for one reason only—there were no other shallow fording possibilities close by, upstream or downstream. He was still determined and convinced that the road to freedom lie just beyond them on the other side of the river. And high water or not, he meant to discover a way to get across to it. They talked about collecting some driftwood along the river bank and lashing the pieces together to construct a float or crude raft. It was a viable option, they thought, but where could they find rope or vines to fix the logs and limbs together? The real drawback with this plan, however, was that they were simply too frightened of the treacherous river to try it. Both were doubtful they could summon up the courage to fling themselves across such a flimsy craft and launch out into water that was undoubtedly over their heads.

Maybe they could steal a small boat somewhere, if there was one around to steal. They had not seen one, but that would certainly be a creditable option to consider if one could be found. However Lark could not stop thinking about the ferry. He marveled at the simplicity and ease with which it moved from bank to bank. There was not much to the craft itself. It was just a rudimentary, long, flat boat fashioned from logs and rough sawn boards and built plenty strong to float. Even with the heavy burdens of loaded wagons, cattle, and horses, the buoyant vessel rode high in the water.

Lark pondered the operation and wondered how in the world it worked. A strong rope as thick as a man's arm was strung overhead between the river banks—that was obvious enough to him. The ferry boat was secured to this overhead guide rope with attachment lines at both ends of the craft. Each of these attachment lines was fixed to the overhead guide rope so as to slide along it as the boat traveled from bank to bank. What was so intriguing to Lark, however, was the fact that the boat seemed to propel itself across the water. No evidence of winches or horses or even people pulling or poling or paddling the ferry could be seen. The boat just mysteriously moved by itself, or so it seemed to Lark.

"You sees dat, Delia? Dat ferry boat jus' moves along da water wif no one's pullin' it. I dunno hows it do's it."

Lark was an intelligent man. But this self-propelled ferry was something else indeed, and he was genuinely perplexed. All day long, they watched the boat working back and forth, from one side of the river to the other. Lark observed and studied and contemplated the operation until at last he perceived a repetitive routine that might possibly explain the secret of the ferry's movement.

It dawned on the astute slave that just after the operator pushed off from shore he always took up the slack in the attachment line at the front of the boat—the end pointed toward the opposite shore. Conversely, the man would slacken the rear attachment rope to let the back end of the boat swing farther downstream than the front end. This operation was always reversed on the return trip. Lark realized that this must be the way it moves itself—the back end of the boat always had to be further downstream than the front end so it can inexplicably move across the water on its own. Although uncertain how this simple maneuver drove the boat, he figured he could do it. Cleverly, logically, unknowingly, the slave from Haywood's East Fork backwoods had worked out how river rope ferries used the stream's current to push them across the water. He excitedly explained his suspicions to Delia and tried to win her confidence that he could operate the strange boat.

"You shore 'bout dis, Lark? I still don't sees how you's gonna gits us to da udder side in dat boat. You's shore you's shore 'bout dis, is you?"

"B'lieve me, Delia. I knows I knows how to drive dat boat. I can gits us to da udder side, b'lieves me. Don't you b'lieves me?" Lark badly wanted his girl to believe in him.

"I b'lieves you, I do's. But I dunno how you's gonna do's it. You shore you knows how?"

After much further conversation, Lark finally convinced Delia to go along with him. There were no longer any weighty doubts in her mind, and she truly believed in her man. She believed that if Lark said so, then he must certainly know how to drive that big boat. At least she hoped he did, because she was still clueless herself about how that ferry boat worked. So with Delia back in the boat, so to speak, the slave couple began strategizing and plotting the night's crossing in earnest.

Just after sunset, the operator secured the ferry boat after the last wagon and horse team had been ferried. Then Lark and Delia watched as he worked at various chores around the little cabin of his. A woman, probably his wife, was busy coming and going with regularity and a slew of children were running about. Thankfully, there were no dogs. Darkness set in, and candlelight gleamed through the windows. The slaves imagined a spread of food on the table as their shrunken bellies growled in pain. Finally, the light in the cabin was extinguished, and the riverine environment surrounding the ferry spot grew relatively quiet. The trickling and gurgling sounds of the river flowing by were constant and natural. Songs of the crickets and tree frogs and the occasional croaking of amorous toads filled the air with nature's din of pleasing, though sometimes cacophonous, music. Lark and Delia listened in silence to all these sounds and nervously waited.

At last, around midnight, they arose from their hiding place and moved quickly and stealthily to the ferry boat. The night was overcast and black dark, with the waning quarter moon hidden under some clouds. *Thank goodness fo' dat,* the runaways thought as they sneaked through the darkness up to the ferry boat.

"Delia, you do's jus' like we's say. Gits in and lay down," Lark whispered.

"Okay, Lark," she replied and obediently hopped on the boat's platform and fell down on her stomach.

The ferry boat was tied off to a heavy post, and Lark quickly undid the rope and tossed it onto the craft with Delia. Then he reached down and began pushing against the near end of the boat with all his might to move it out into the river's current. Quickly jumping onto the platform, he noted that both ends of the ferry boat were tethered snuggly to the thick overhead guide line. Instantly realizing that he would only have to adjust one end of the boat, he began playing out slack in the rope attachment nearest to shore. The rear of the ferry boat swung further downstream, and as it did, Lark could actually feel the motion he had anticipated. Slowly, ever so slowly, he could feel and sense the boat beginning to move across the water. The attachment tethers at each end were sliding smoothly along the overhead line just as they should be. It was working! They were moving! He had correctly figured the thing out after all.

Then Lark lay down next to Delia, and they both remained still and quiet so their senses could survey for danger. So far no sounds of alarm had been detected. The only unusual or unfamiliar sound was the noise made by the boat's attachment ropes as they slid along the thick overhead line. A unique squeaking or rubbing sound was produced as the boat's greased wood attachment collars slid along the overhead guide rope. Lark feared the noise might arouse the attention of the sleeping operator or his family, so his gaze remained firmly fixed on the cabin.

The ferry kept moving toward the far shore, ever so slowly and steadily. It took several long minutes for it to travel approximately fifty yards and reach the center of the stream's span. But then, just as the ferry boat reached the mid-point of the passage, the cabin door burst open with a loud crash and the operator rushed out in a fury carrying a long rifle. The unusual rubbing sound of the rope sliding through the greased wooden collars was a familiar one to the hysterical man running down to the river's edge. His ears were attuned to the sound. It was the sound of money to him—the sound of his livelihood. But this familiar sound of the squeaking and squealing of his ferry's attachment ropes was never heard during the night. Consequently, the familiar daytime sound was so unusual and unfamiliar at night that it actually awakened the man from a fitful sleep.

The ferryboat snatchers were horror-stricken at the sudden turn of events. Lark knew that they had to get across the river as quickly as possible before the man began shooting. They were again in the hands of Providence it seemed. The operator rushed down the sloping ramp to the river and began screaming out as loud as he could holler.

"Come back, damn you to hell! Get back over here! You owe me money!"

The night was too dark for the operator to possibly see that it was two runaway slaves who were cheating him out of his toll. If he had been able to distinguish them as such, his calls for the return of the vessel would have been a sight coarser with the word 'nigger' interjected occasionally for hateful effect. Black or white, the man did not mean for these infernal ferry snatchers to get away. He raised his primed gun, took aim at the two forms lying down on the deck, whoever those ferry snatchers were, and fired. *Bang!!*

Lark and Delia could see the flash of the gun and hear and feel the lead ball ripping into the ferry's wood timbers before they actually heard the gunshot. Both of the runaways winced at the crash of the bullet and hurriedly crawled back and cowered as close to the edge of the boat as they could get. They were sure they were done for now. The sound of dogs barking in the distance could now be heard. Lark realized that the gunshot would undoubtedly wake up some of the valley farmers, and he feared one or other of them might make a quick response to the scene of the shooting. As the operator worked feverishly to reload the gun, Lark came up with an idea.

"We's can't stay here. We's gots to gits in da water behind da boat. He's gonna kills us if we's don't. Do's like me, Delia," and the extremely agitated and scared Lark slipped into the water while continuing to hold onto the side of the boat. Delia, watching Lark closely, immediately understood what to do and splashed in beside her man. Although terrified by the water, they preferred to brave that peril as opposed to the lead ball that was about to roar at them again and soon. Both of the runaways hung on for dear life and ducked their heads.

The ferryboat, being driven by the river's current, continued to slowly plow through the water. Its bulk and wooden structure provided the slaves an excellent defensive cover against the rifle shots. Although they were too frightened to realize it, the ferry operator could not have hit them if he fired all night long. As it was, he got off two more shots at the elusive targets before the boat reached the far shore. Feeling their feet dragging the bottom, Lark and Delia turned loose of the ferry and splashed out of the water like two frightened animals. As the lead balls continued to fly and the barking of the valley farmers' dogs resonated louder, the scared slaves hustled to the top of the riverbank and found the road on the other side. Then they ran and ran along it as fast as their legs and dreams of freedom would allow.

Chapter 19

A Human Being Right

During camp meeting week, Basil had received a letter from his father. Unlike his customary practice of immediately devouring the contents and fretting over the words and meaning of what his father had written—or had not written—he had only perused the epistle very quickly and put it aside for further study and a response later. On the Monday following the busy religious festival, after things had settled down somewhat, Basil took up the long letter again and read it more carefully. In addition to briefing his son on the state of farming labors at Fort Catawba and news of his mother, brothers, and sisters, Thomas offered an answer to his son's last communication.

The father had been somewhat surprised by the negative nature of Basil's letter. In that previous correspondence, Basil had inferred that it was his own fault that Lark had run away. And he had confessed to his father to be an "unprofitable servant" and that he thought his father should replace him. In reply, Thomas wrote that he was very pleased with the way his son was handling the Haywood affairs, at least what he understood from Basil's letters. His father told him to put any thoughts of a new Haywood overseer out of his mind for the time being. Thomas reaffirmed that Basil had a duty to perform and that he should not endeavor to find fault with his own actions and results so hastily. *Learn from your experiences and those of your neighbors,* his father encouraged, *and strive to demonstrate some persistence and confidence so as to better business relations with the slaves and tenants.*

Basil read with deep emotion his father's sincere and earnest sentiments as well as the following wise advice he gave:

> *As you have arrived to an age that you ought to be capable of judging and deciding for yourself on a matter of so much importance, you should duly consider the whys and wherefores a change should be made, and the prospects of being benefited thereby. One of my most ardent wishes is for your prosperity and happiness, both of which may be materially affected by some conclusion you make in undue haste. And should you be permitted to live to an old age and be denied the pleasure of looking back on a long life spent in as profitable a manner to yourself and the world as it might have been, I fondly cherish the consoling hope that you will have the great consolation of knowing that you have generally, if not always, endeavored to do what your judgment dictates as the best.*

Basil's heart lightened when he read those final thoughtful words. By happenstance, he and Altha were professing their love for one another at about the same time Thomas was penning this letter. Consequently, Basil's attitude had changed, and he now wanted to stay in Haywood for as long as it might take to make a family with Altha and Rufus. However, the Sam Beck business—his turning up at the camp meeting—had presented a snag in Basil and Altha's relationship and future prospects. Basil had known he was going to have to settle the matter of Altha's marital situation one way or another. He just did not know it was going to be so soon.

It was late afternoon at Deaver's store when Basil strolled in to post a letter. After almost a week of deliberations and procrastination, he had finally composed a reply to his father's last correspondence. It was an important communication in which he gave the necessary assurances that all was well at the Bachelor's Den and that there was no need to replace the current overseer after all. Basil promised to be a profitable servant and assured his father that he had things completely under control. And, finally, he summoned up the courage and confidence to break the news to his father about the romance with Altha.

Basil was not sure how much information his father had received from old Haywood friends. However, he had a suspicion that Thomas might have heard something about the midwife service provided to the Edmunston's Crab Orchard tenant. He only wrote that Altha was Josiah Anderson's daughter but left out the details that she was married and had recently given birth to a son. Those piddling facts he reckoned could be delivered at a more convenient time when the future allowed.

Another reason that Basil came down to the store was to soak up a little of the Colonel's wisdom as it applied to divorce and Sam Beck and all. But it did not appear that the Colonel was around anywhere, or at least, Basil could not readily spot him. Julia, who had waved to him when he came in, was with a customer, and Columbus Hartgrove was at the post office drafting a document of some sort. Basil walked over to speak to Hartgrove.

"Hello, Columbus." Basil had become well enough acquainted with the former Edmunston overseer to feel comfortable calling him by his given name. Hartgrove was several years older than Basil but appeared even older because he was balding prematurely. Although still relatively young in years, Columbus was an old soul whose keen mind and upstanding character had earned him the respect of the good folk living in the Forks of Pigeon community. Not only was he respected, but he was well-liked—so much so that he had recently been appointed Entry Taker for the county. And there was talk going around that he might even pursue one of the county commissioner chairs the next term.

Distracted and flustered, Columbus looked up from his work to see who had interrupted him. He had been so focused on his writing that he appeared perturbed at the inconvenience. But he settled down immediately when he recognized Basil and responded, "Hello, Basil. Good to see you down this way. Suppose the boys kept things tidied up round the farm while we were doing all that singing and stomping?" he queried with a slight smile on his face.

Basil grinned. "I wouldn't use 'tidy' to describe what they did, but I suppose they did get a bit of work done. Got most of the wheat cut and bundled anyway. Now we've got to see about the threshing."

"Same here. Don't know 'bout yers, but my wheat was a mite rusty. Say, did ye hear that the Colonel and Osborne ere starting up a threshing business?"

Puzzled, Basil replied, "Haven't heard a thing about it. What do you mean, starting up a business?"

"They's purchased a newfangled threshing machine. Arrived jest yestidy in wagons from Charleston. Ain't seen it yet, but the Colonel says horses ere used to power it. He and Osborne aim to haul the machine 'round to all the farms in these parts and charge folks to thresh their wheat."

"Well, I'll say. Things are looking up for Haywood," Basil said with a bit of mockery as well as amusement in his voice. "I'll have to see what kind of debts a man might incur to contract some threshing work from Deaver and Osborne Company, or Osborne and Deaver, or whatever name they choose to give the business."

"Ain't seen the Colonel 'bout anywhurs. He kin learn you all 'bout the machine and what he'll take to do yer threshing."

"Okay. Uhh, Columbus, can I speak to you in confidence about something very personal?" Basil asked as he looked around to see just how privately they could talk.

"Anything ye have to say to me will be safe, Basil. Ye have my promise," Columbus replied nodding his head to confirm he meant exactly what he said.

Basil believed him. He had heard too many good things about this man to think otherwise. "I trust you a lot, Columbus. You and the Colonel are the only ones I would choose to confide in, to tell you plainly. Well, you know that I'm with Altha now. At least we're courting. I'm sure you figured that out when you saw me with her every day at the camp meeting."

"Yep, I knowed you two ere together now, Basil. Ciphered that out right quick-like. She's a good girl, and I can't say that I blame ye atall. She did a fine job at the Orchard school too. Everybody knows so."

"Altha told me all about Sam Beck and what he did to her. They're still married and I need to know from you—well, I don't know what to do about it. What are the chances she might be able to win a divorce against him?"

Hartgrove thought for a few seconds and looked away toward where Julia was still working with her customer. He at last brought his gaze back to Basil and stated his considered opinion on the matter. "Fer as I know, the County Court of Pleas has jurisdiction over divorces now. Yep, the State Legislature had to give it up—taking too much of their precious ruling time is how it was tolt. Ha! Ain't that a hoot? Still, a divorce is something can't be got easy, Basil. Even with a man like Sam Beck and what all he's done to Altha—cruelty, abandonment, and sech. Don't much believe ye could win it though. Best ye see a good lawyer and confirm what I've tolt ye. But I believe it to be pert near true."

Basil nodded his agreement and thought for a long moment and then asked, "So, Columbus, if Altha can't divorce him then, well, don't me and her still have a right to take up with each other and live as man and wife—and son?"

Again Columbus pondered over what Basil had put to him before responding, "Basil, yer family's got a good name and reputation in these here parts. Altha, for those that know her, can't be beat. But Sam Beck is a devil if ever there were one, and people round 'bout here know it. Fer as I can cipher there's nuthin' other than a divorce or Beck goes and gits himself kilt somehow that would make it legal fer ye and Altha to live together as a man and wife. How-some-ever, if not legal, then I think you'ns have a human-being right to do it—yes sir, a human-being right. That's to say, I do believe God would favor it. I indeed do. And ain't nary none of them Haywood County Your Worshipful Justices of the Peace going to say contrary neither. Nary none of them."

Basil hung on every word his neighbor spilled forth. *Hmmm*, he thought, *a human-being right. That's about what I figured.* However, he felt more comfortable now after hearing this validation of his own unqualified views on domestic justice. But he was bothered about something else. "That's good to hear, Columbus. Sounds reasonable anyway, but what about Rufus? What would happen if Sam Beck shows up all of a sudden and lays claim to the boy?"

Hartgrove began shaking his head slightly back and forth. "I feared ye would get 'round to asking that directly. If that sure 'nough happened, then legally Sam Beck would have as much right to the boy as Altha does. The court wouldn't have no grounds to deny it, in my own opinion. Don't know if they would consider holding a custody plea or not. Anyhows, it would get complicated a sight."

That was what Basil feared. It was what had kept him awake the last few nights, ever since Beck had showed up at the camp meeting. This talk with Hartgrove confirmed his worst suspicion that he and Altha could lose Rufus if that no-good, trifling scamp came back to claim him. *And that would not do atall,* Basil thought.

"I was afraid you might say that, Columbus. But I believe you've got it about right. Listen, I appreciate your time. Your advice and opinions mean a great deal to me. I can see why my father always speaks so highly of you. And please, Columbus, don't say anything about this. I'm going to take your advice and look up a lawyer over at Waynesville to get another opinion. Although I'd probably put more stock in what you say."

"No, best to hear it from the horse's mouth. Ye go and do that, Basil."

Sensing that the conversation had reached its fruitful end, Basil bid a thankful goodbye to Hartgrove, who returned to his paperwork at the desk. Basil slipped his letter into the appropriate box at the post office and turned around to look for Julia. He saw that she was finishing up with her customer and stepped over to talk with her.

Julia was as stunningly beautiful as ever but not her usual animated self, Basil noted. Something was bothering her for sure. "Hello, Julia. Looks like you're staying busy."

"Well, hello to you, Mr. Master of the East Fork. Good to see you down. And yes, it is fairly busy for some reason. I'm filling in for Father this afternoon. He and the boys are fretting with that new threshing contraption. It seems they've got some learning to do, figuring out how to put it together and operate it properly."

"I've got to have a look at that thing," Basil replied and as a look of faux seriousness and pomposity grew over his face he broke into his best stump-orator rant, "Hear ye, hear ye, ladies and gentlemen! Be ye fairly warned of the threat that is at our threshold. I now hear that the latest mechanized farming machinery has found its way through the outlying mountain redoubts and threatens our lonely, simple farmsteads. Hark! We Haywood farmers must rise up against despots of the likes of Osborne and Deaver who dare try to relieve us of our toiling drudgery and what little money we so carefully conceal in our pockets. Why, what might next loom ahead? Dare someone introduce fire and vapor to drive our mills and pull iron wagons laden with our crops and stock to the markets far beyond these hills? Surely no, never let that befall our fair county of Haywood. We must rise up, I say, and resist the drumbeat of modernity. Who here stands with me? You, madam? Do you stand with me?" As Basil finished his foolish oratorical tirade, he looked with feigned importance at Julia, and then the two of them broke into loud laughter.

"Oh, Basil, you can be so silly sometimes. You know that father is not a despot."

"Okay, Julia, I'll concede that to you. But I'm not so sure about Osborne," Basil replied somewhat seriously, and they again had a good laugh.

Then Basil made inquiries about Wade and was surprised by Julia's reticence to share any news on that front. After awkwardly dodging several of his questions, she finally burst forth with a bombshell revelation. "It's over, Basil. Wade and I are finished."

Taken aback and never more surprised, Basil could only stare at Julia in bewilderment. Finally he was able to utter, "Finished? What happened, Julia?"

"Oh, Basil, it's all my doing. Wade couldn't have been better to me. He is such a fine person and gentleman. But I couldn't keep up the deception any longer. At first I thought I could love him, but it wasn't love of a true nature. I'm sure of that now. And I was not only deceiving Wade, but I was deceiving Mother and Father and even myself. Couldn't you tell, Basil? Don't you realize it yet? I could never stop thinking about—"

"Basil! Over here! Two postings jest got here fer ye!" Columbus Hartgrove blared out from across the store. At the very moment Julia was about to reveal the reason for her break-up with Wade Hampton, she was interrupted by the untimely message from Hartgrove. So distracting was the disruption that the flustered girl immediately shuffled a half-step back from Basil. He did not look away from Julia and maintained his intent gaze toward her. She took a few deep breaths as the sorrowful look on her face transformed into one of sheer frustration.

"Oh, Basil, you can tell I'm still upset. Please allow me to gather myself and my thoughts, and we can talk about this on another day, soon, okay? Would you mind very much, please?"

He surely would consent to her wishes. Basil was as much of a gentleman as Wade Hampton was or anybody else. But what was Julia about to disclose to him? *Realize? Realize what? Never stop thinking about what–who?* Although greatly perplexed, he refrained from querying her further and considerately offered his reassurance, "Of course, Julia. I can see that you are upset. Please forgive me if I have caused you this distress."

"Not atall your doings, Master Basil," she said while forcing a smile and levity. "We'll carry on with this conversation some other time soon, I hope. Now go on over and pick up your mail." Julia's best efforts to tidy up and conclude their short chat failed to allay Basil's uneasiness. He was still baffled as to the reason she had broken off the romantic fling with Wade, but he reluctantly took his leave and turned toward the office. Julia wistfully watched him walk away while mentally berating herself for not spilling out her heart to Basil. She had been put off balance, and the courage to speak her mind and reveal her love had been shaken. Until the time when that weighty burden could be lifted, she would suffer the lonely pangs of unrequited love.

Seeing the letter carrier reminded Basil of the message he had just posted to his father. In three to five days from now, Thomas would learn that his Haywood overseer had fallen in love. The patriarch would read it from the horse's mouth, as Hartgrove would say. Basil wondered what repercussions would come of it and what thoughtful sentiments his father's prose might next bring.

Hartgrove handed the letters over, and Basil quickly glanced at the envelopes to see where they had been posted. One was from the Fort, and the handwriting was unmistakably Walter's. *It's about time,* Basil thought. The other letter had been mailed from New Market, Virginia, and addressed to Mr. Bazel Edmunstung at Forks of Pigeon. *Hmmm, letter from Virginia, and misspelled my name–that's a little odd,* he thought as he proceeded to break open the wax seal to see what interesting news the strange letter might hold.

Chapter 20

HIGH PRICE FOR BACON

It had been slightly more than three weeks since Lark and Delia stole their way across the Nollichucky River on the rope ferry. For those many days, they had been on the run, and as a result of their fugitive circumstances and primitive lifestyle, they were starved and beat. The slave couple did not know how much longer they could last. Their path, always directed toward the North Star, had led them through some of the most beautiful farming land they had ever seen. Passing across wide bottoms hemmed between low mountain ranges on either side, the pathway just seemed to go on forever. Inexplicably, and thankfully, these natural corridors were channeling their flight on a northward bearing toward the drinking gourd's Pole Star and the land where freedom could be found.

Bountiful grain fields and lush green corn crops nearly head high were their lifeblood. These cereal grains along with whatever variety of bramble-berries could be found along their pathways remained the slaves' primary food sources, barely keeping the fires burning in their diminished and poorly nourished bodies. Of the two slaves, Lark was holding up better. His bruised black frame appeared much bonier now, having suffered the loss of almost twenty pounds of muscle and the little fat he had once carried. Wounds and cuts in various stages of infection covered his arms and legs. His pants legs had been torn and frayed so badly by the briar brambles and brush thickets that he had cut them off. But the shreds of torn cloth were put to good use. Lark wrapped and tied the scrap pieces around his shoes to hold the soles and uppers together. But even so, the tedious battle of maintaining his footwear was nearly lost.

And poor Delia—she was suffering so. Lark was in prime condition compared with her. Thin to begin with, she was now a walking skeleton. The diet of berries and grains, which were rarely supplemented with hens' eggs or some sort of scavenged or wild meat, had not been enough to keep the girl in traveling form. And her nappy hair was hopelessly clogged and entangled with bits and pieces of grasses, insects, and other debris. She had become so disheartened with it that all grooming efforts had ceased. To make matters even worse, the weeks of trudging barefooted through woods and along the roads had nearly crippled her. Cuts, blisters, bruises, and infections covered both of her feet, and it was truly a testament to her fortitude and love for Lark that she had kept on trekking. Lark routinely bathed her foot wounds during the day and occasionally wrapped them with scraps of clothes from his sack. When especially difficult terrains were encountered, he carried Delia across his shoulders until the going got easier. But eventually even Lark became too weak to carry the pitiful girl.

Their tramp beyond the Nollichucky had been a grueling adventure. The road to freedom had taken them through several eastern Tennessee frontier settlements. Of course, the runaways did not parade up the town streets. They gave these little villages and towns wide berth as they surreptitiously moved by in the darkness. Always cautious, always stealthy, they were ever vigilant of the road traffic and remained extremely cautious of dogs.

They kept at it night after night until, unbeknown to them, they penetrated into the state of Virginia while pursuing a primary turnpike leading northward. Skirting around the town of Abington they trudged and limped onward through great valleys bordered by imposing mountain ranges. For more than two hundred miles, the runaways plodded, first passing between the Clinch and Iron Mountains and later traversing amid the Allegany and Blue Ridge ranges. Their pathways climbed and descended the lesser mounts, crossed large and small tributary creeks, and hugged formidable rivers straight into the heart of the Shenandoah Valley.

It was in the beautiful Virginia countryside that they found themselves on this hot and humid day. Nervously secured in a patch of woods where, as usual, a thorny thicket provided them cover amongst the rabbits and coons, they lay together and assessed their situation.

"How's da feets, Delia?" a sympathetic Lark inquired.

"Dey hurts a sight. Sees da new sore here?" Delia replied as she pointed out a new festering cut on her foot.

"Yes, I sees. It looks bad, real bad." Although Lark was hurting for Delia, he was also terribly hungry. "Delia, we's gots to git somethin' to eats. Come dark time, I goes back dare to da farmhouse we passes and sees if I finds us some food. Don't you think dat be a good thing to do's?"

"But, Lark, what if you gits caught? Don't you thinks it be dang'rous to do's dat?"

"I b'lieves it be's dang'rous, I shore do. But we's gots to do's it or we's not gonna makes it. We's gonna die if we's don't git somethin' to eat."

It should have been plain to Delia that Lark was real scared they were close to the end of their run. He was especially fearful that Delia was going to die on him any day now. If they did not eat something besides raw grains or berries soon, he figured, then his girl was surely done for, and he suspected he would not live much longer either. When it got good and dark, Lark left Delia in the hiding spot and began backtracking to a farm they had passed a short ways back. In very little time, he found a surveillance spot where he could clearly see an impressive, white-painted farmhouse and the faint outlines of several much smaller outbuildings. He made out what appeared to be the family's smokehouse on the far side of a barn, and he imagined it to be similarly stocked as the one at Bachelor's Den, with bacon hams and sides of beef judiciously salted and hung to cure. The rumblings in his empty belly quickly persuaded Lark that this smokehouse was an opportune target, and he began ciphering hard on how to go about plundering its contents.

Moving in the darkness of night deliberately and stealthily like a black panther stalking its prey, Lark approached the target while keeping the farmhouse screened from his movements. There were dogs somewhere. He had heard them barking but had not yet seen where they were kept. If all went well, there was a slim hope the hounds would not catch his scent. But his first concern now was getting a good look at the smokehouse. As it came into clearer view, he discerned that it was built of logs, just like the one at the Den. The Edmunstons' overseers had always kept the smokehouse padlocked, and he expected no less here. Earlier he had spotted three small cabins far removed from the main house that were most likely slaves' quarters. If there were indeed slaves living and working at this place, and he believed there were, then the smokehouse was guaranteed to be locked. Lark knew that white folks never trusted Africans like himself. None of them did. And they all locked their smokehouse doors for this good reason—just like his Massa Baz did at the Den.

As Lark lay behind the barn peering nervously at the small timber structure, he tried to work out a method for breaking into it. There could be no burrowing under the bottom sill logs to get inside, because the heavy puncheon flooring would be too difficult to penetrate. The chinks between the logs were too narrow to squeeze through. There were no windows. The door was too heavy to break open without creating such a racket that the white folks and their dogs would be on him in an instant. But the low-pitched roof—it looked vulnerable enough to offer an entrance opportunity. Only long poles and rocks held down the split-wood shakes, it appeared to Lark. There was a possibility the individual shakes might be nailed down, but he doubted any sane farmer would go to such extravagant lengths. It seemed to Lark that he could just break through that weak roof. No obstacles immediately came to mind that would prevent his doing that. After just a few more minutes of study, he decided he would give it a try. He was going to break through that flimsy shake roof.

Finding an axe carelessly propped against a pile of wood, Lark took it, thinking it might come in handy. As he crept slowly toward the barn, he spied the chained dogs sleeping a short distance away. Instantly he became more nervous and hushed. In a very short time, he worked his way into the barn and slipped around in the darkness until he found a good length of rope. The slave threw it over his shoulder, exited the barn, and began moving silently toward the smokehouse. The panther had its prey in sight.

It was just as he had expected. The meat storage structure had a thick timber door secured with a heavy padlock. *Dem white folks never trusts us,*

Lark thought to himself. Then he made his way to a corner of the building, where the logs were lapped and joined. The ends of the log timbers stuck out several inches beyond the walls, providing sturdy foot and hand holds for climbing. It would be a relatively simple matter, he reasoned, to scale up this providential ladder to the roof. Thinking that the axe might possibly be needed on top, he tied one end of the rope to it and looped the other end around his waist. He also figured, with good reason, that the sack bag still strapped around his neck would severely hamper his movements, so he discarded it on the ground before attempting the climb.

Even in his weakened condition, Lark was surprised at how easy the ascent up the corner of the building was. He just stepped up the logs one by one as if he was simply climbing a ladder. Then upon reaching the eve of the roof, he carefully shinnied out over the shingles on his belly. As easy and straightforward as that, he was on top of the roof.

But it had been a noisy climb, and now the shingles were creaking and cracking under the slave's weight. Breathing heavily, Lark lay still as could be and listened anxiously for danger. Only the low yipping of one of the dogs could be heard. That was all. He remained frozen and quiet on the roof for another good ten minutes to make sure he had not been found out. Eventually the lone barking dog hushed, and nothing else could be heard or seen. His luck had not run out, thank goodness.

Trying first to dislodge the shingles by hand he discovered, much to his distress, that they were nailed to poles underneath. Undaunted however, he took hold of the rope tied to his waist and carefully tugged the axe up the side of the log wall and onto the roof where he could grab it. Slowly, very slowly, he used the heavy tool to pry the shingles loose, one by one, from the support poles. Fortunately the iron nails broke loose easily, and he was able at last to make an opening large enough to shove an arm through.

All Lark could see as he peeked inside was blackness. However, the aroma wafting through the breach was absolutely overwhelming—and good! Stimulated almost beyond control, he reached an arm through the hole and felt around underneath for ropes or hooks that the hunks of meat must surely be suspended to. Nothing! But Lark did not give up. He could not give up. Delia was counting on him. Doggedly he struggled to remove more shingles and make the hole even larger. And then he again reached into the void, deeper this time and thrusting his entire arm through the breech. Blindly feeling in all directions with his hand, he reached as far into the darkness as he possibly could. He stretched and moved and waved his arm until at last—at last his hand bumped something. He could feel a dangling tether of sorts with something or other attached to it—something very heavy he reckoned. Lark strained to pull the rope up, desperately hoping that a slab of meat hung on the other end. Delia needed it badly. Both their lives were probably at stake, he knew that. When he was finally able to haul the weighty object up high enough to see what it was, he could hardly believe his eyes.

It was a good-sized bacon ham! And the sight of real meat thrilled Lark as he was instantly infused with a sudden shot of adrenalin and extra energy. He wrestled the treasure through the small hole and into his arms. Then taking extra care and aim he heaved it to the ground as deftly and quietly as possible. To extract himself from the lofty heights, he simply lunged down to earth, thinking the ten-foot jump would be the quickest way of making his escape. While it may have made the quickest descent, it proved not to be the quietest—nor smartest. Lark landed on one of the loose shingles he had removed, and the dry wooden shake split and broke with a loud cracking noise. Indeed it was loud enough to wake the sleeping dogs!

All of them, ever how many dogs there were, began barking furiously. If they had not been restrained with chains, Lark's lot would have been up then and there. As it was, he picked up his bacon and ran for Delia as quick as his legs would carry him, having forgotten his sack bag with the kitchen knife and personal belongings inside.

Delia heard Lark come busting through the brush and was dreadfully frightened to see the nervous state he was in as he collapsed next to her. Yes, he was exhausted and scared, Lark was, but he was also proud. He had done it. Righting himself on his knees and with a terrified look on his face, Lark held out the bacon for his girl to see.

"Whut's it, Lark? Is dare trouble?" an alarmed Delia quietly asked.

"We's gots to eats and git goin'. I wakes up da dogs, and dey's gonna be's loosed on us soon." And just then he realized that he had forgotten his bag at the smokehouse. "No! No! I done forgets da sack and da knife." The confounded look that Delia gave him did nothing to abate the instant fury and disappointment that he felt. He readily grasped the significance of his foolish act of carelessness—that his most prized possessions, the kitchen knife and shreds of fabric, were now lost forever. He could not risk going back to get them. He would be caught for sure. But he had managed to hold onto the stolen meat.

Using his hands and teeth, Lark tore a large hunk out of the ham and gave it to Delia to eat. He then ripped off a sizable chunk for himself. They stayed hidden there and gorged themselves for almost half an hour before bursting out of the lair and starting on a frantic dash along the side of the road. They ran and ran until the light of day forced them into hiding again. And there they waited in absolute fear and terror that the slave hunters and their dogs would pick up the scent and trail.

Back at the farm, most of the inhabitants had been awakened by the unceasing noise of the barking dogs. A quick investigation revealed a hole in the smokehouse roof, a missing bacon ham, and the tools—the rope and axe. Also a battered and torn sack containing some clothes and a large kitchen knife were discovered, undoubtedly the belongings of the thief. At first light, a search was organized to apprehend the intruder. The slaveowner and the overseer of the place used the clothes rags they had found to give the dogs a scent to track. Carrying their long rifles in one arm, the slave trackers followed on horseback close behind the dogs, while three male slaves tried to keep up on foot. In less than fifteen minutes, one of the dogs picked up the trail and then the hunt was on.

It did not take long for the hunting party to make up the distance that Lark and Delia had put between themselves and the farm. By mid-morning, the runaways could hear the dogs barking close by. They were frightened and utterly at a loss about what to do.

"Whut's we's gonna do, Lark?"

"I dunno. We's can stay here and sees if dey's gonna finds us. O' we's can run fo' it and try to outrun dem mean dogs. Dem dogs is mean, Delia.

We's in big trouble now, shore 'nough in trouble—I loves you, Delia!" And then the flustered Lark drew Delia close into his arms.

"Oh, Lark, I loves you, too. I always gonna loves you," Delia said back to him, and they embraced and hugged each other until the dogs came dangerously close.

The barking and baying sounds of the ferocious hounds kept getting nearer and nearer until the terrified slaves sprung from their hideaway and fled like two scared rabbits along the river. It was not the first slave hunt their pursuers had been on. These experienced runaway hunters could sense their prey was in reach, and they urged and pushed the dogs on. Once the overseer finally got a good glimpse of the fugitives, he quickly pulled up his horse, took sure aim, and fired at the running black blur. *Bang!!*

The lead ball found its target, and Lark fell to the ground in a writhing heap, with blood spewing everywhere. Delia collapsed on top of him and cried in desperation for her man. "Oh, Lark! Please don't dies. I loves you, Lark! I loves you!"

The excited snarling canines were on top of the runaways in no time, their razor-sharp teeth slashing and biting into the arms and legs of the slaves. Before the men could pull the hounds away, both Lark and Delia suffered horrible wounds from the frenzied animals.

Sporting a genuine sense of exhilaration from the chase, the overseer looked down at the pathetic slaves and said with a degree of smugness reserved for men of his sort, "Betcha they's going to be a nice reward for these two blackies—if'n that there male nigger don't die."

The smirking slaveowner agreed and replied with an ingrained aloofness, "I'd say so. Should pay for a bacon ham or two, I expect."

Chapter 21

Unbroken Shackles

Basil was intrigued with the curious letter that had just arrived for him at Deaver's store. It held a postmark from New Market, Virginia, a place he had never heard of before. Noting that the spelling of his name was badly butchered, he eagerly broke open the wax seal, unfolded the short missive, and studied its contents.

"Well, I'll be damned. They've been caught!" Basil exclaimed aloud to everyone who happened to be in the store but to no one in particular. He shoved the letter toward Columbus Hartgrove, who was still busy talking to the postman nearby. "If that don't beat all! Here, Columbus, take a look at this."

Hartgrove took the letter from Basil and studied the message carefully.

New Market, Virginia
July 23, 1846

Dear Mr. Bazel Edmunstung,

Yesterday two niggers were taken up near this place. They were a male and female, and the male one give his name as Lark. He states he belongs to you. The female one give us her name as Delia and says she belongs to a Mr. Osburne who is a neighbor of yours, as I understand. The male nigger is about a score old and suffered a gunshot wound when he was taken up. The doctor has a right good feeling he will live.

Please, sir, could you send us a prompt reply if you indeed have a runaway slave by the above name and whether you intend to claim your property. Also please be so good as to allow Osburne to read this letter and let him communicate his intentions for the girl.

As I am sure you are aware, sir, the taker-uppers are expecting to be adequately compensated for their troubles in capturing the slave property, as is customary in these parts.

Your obedient Servant,
Wendell Funk
Sheriff of Shenandoah County, Virginia

When Hartgrove finished reading the letter, he just shook his head back and forth. As he handed the communication back to Basil, he said, "I declare them two slaves sure must have wanted each other bad to go to all the trouble they did. They run a fer piece to get all the way up yonder to that Shenandoah country. I 'spect, Basil, ye'll want to get up there pretty quick-like to fetch 'em. There be no telling how bad Lark might be hurt and suffering."

"Yep, Lark wanted to get married real bad all right. I figure I drove them to do it. What's the best route to take from here, Columbus, to get up to New Market?"

"Well, a few years back, when I was about yer age I reckon, I drove a herd of cattle through Tennessee for the Colonel up about there. Let's take a look at the map over here, and I'll show ye how I'd figure on going."

And the two started studying a large map that Colonel Deaver had tacked to the wall and discussing the various road options for the quickest journey to the Shenandoah Valley. Before they parted for a second time, Hartgrove gave Basil some more sage advice.

"Basil, don't make the trip alone. Ye're going to need some company and backing in case of trouble on the road. Believe me, it's a sure 'nough long ride, and ye're going to pass through country a sight more back'ards than Haywood, if'n you can believe that," Hartgrove said grinning and nodding his head for emphasis. "And ye're going to want to take ye a gun. Never know but you might need it."

Within only a couple of days of receiving the letter from the Shenandoah County sheriff, Basil was headed out of Asheville toward Virginia to retrieve the runaway slaves. At his side riding on a borrowed horse from the Den was his tenant, Jesse Anderson. Basil had immediately replied to Sheriff Funk's note and confirmed his intent to travel to New Market and claim the two slaves. Hartgrove had declined Basil's request to accompany him, citing an ailing wife and the pressing harvest-time chores around his farm. However, Columbus did offer to look in on the Edmunstons' slaves and make sure the corn got harvested, shucked, and put away in the cribs. It was now the second week of August, and Basil figured to be gone for more than a month. Lark was wounded, no telling how badly, and Basil wanted to get to his slave as quickly as possible. This business could not have come at a more inconvenient time, Basil fretted, other than maybe spring planting. His worries were somewhat eased though by the realization that the former overseer, Hartgrove, was going to look after the Africans while he was gone.

Osborne had begged out of the long, grueling trip claiming that it was Lark who had taken Delia, and Basil ought to go get her and bring her back. The old codger allowed that his sons could not go either, seeing as how they were still busy threshing wheat in the neighborhood with his and Deaver's new machine. Besides that, they had corn crops to tend to. Basil failed to appreciate Osborne's position on the matter, but he did not want to buck him neither. The elderly man was respected in the area and was his father's old friend and compatriot. But when the prosperous farmer suggested that Basil ought to be libel for all of the reward money, the Master of the East Fork took a firm stand.

He had said to Osborne in no uncertain terms that Delia had not been abducted. She was a willful, aiding, and conspiring runaway and was entirely Osborne's responsibility. However, since the trip up there had to made anyway to get Lark, Basil told Osborne he would be willing to bring Delia back—providing, that is, Osborne paid his share of the reward money and any other associated fees. After an interminable time of hemming and hawing and jawing, Osborne eventually relented and handed over to Basil a sum of one hundred and twenty-five dollars to get his slave girl back.

So without the backing of Hartgrove or the Osbornes, Basil had resorted to Altha's brother, Jesse Anderson, as a companion on the long journey. At one dollar per day compensation, Jesse had been disposed to go along. But his father, Josiah, had pitched a fit about needing his son for the corn harvest. It took all of Basil's persuasive powers and additional promises to lend slave labor to the Orchard before Josiah could abide with the idea. And Altha had not been overly enthused with the thought of Basil's extended absence. Theirs had been a tender parting, and Basil had pledged to be extraordinarily careful and not to tarry along the way.

Riding north on the Buncombe Turnpike, the two sojourners led a third horse packed with supplies for the trip. Not knowing Lark's condition, Basil thought his slave might require this mount to get back home. His father's old flintlock rifle was strapped to the extra horse and a new pistol, purchased in Asheville for the occasion, was hidden away in his saddlebag. It was similar to the dueling guns that Wade and Fred had toted on the hunting excursion. In order to become proficient with the pistol Basil stocked up with plenty of powder, percussion caps, and lead balls so he could practice shooting every day on the way up to Virginia. In addition to the two firearms, both he and Jesse had large hunting knives tucked under their belts. Hartgrove said there could be trouble, and Basil prepared for the worst.

They had estimated the distance to New Market from Asheville to be almost four hundred miles. At a pace of twenty-five to thirty miles a day, Basil reckoned to reach his destination in a couple of weeks. They rode hard and long each day, stopping at inns, if convenient, or sleeping along the roadside under light blankets. At the Nollichucky River, the men paid a toll of one dollar to board a rope ferry and cross the expansive stream. Instead of stealing through the woods at night along the sides of the roads, they traveled in broad daylight down the middle of the turnpikes. They rode through the same villages the two slaves had avoided and ate wholesome food from the inns or markets along the way. The bountiful valleys of southern Virginia were flush with fine corn crops that were made and ready to be harvested, and the hills and mountain slopes were covered with apple trees bent under the heavy burden of ripe fruit. Through nature's veritable breadbasket they wandered—on and on and into the Shenandoah Valley.

It took Basil and Jesse exactly fourteen days to ride to New Market from Asheville. Upon their arrival there, they had no trouble finding Sheriff Funk, who gave them a friendly greeting as they tromped through the door of his little jailhouse. The lawman—who was almost twice Basil's age and heavyset with a head-full of graying hair—asked if he could be of any assistance to the dirty and weary-looking sojourners.

"Hello, Sheriff. I'm Basil Edmunston. Came to claim my runaway slave," spoke up Basil almost forcefully, but politely, as he extended his hand to Sheriff Funk.

"Well, you made fine time, you sure did, sir," the surprised sheriff replied as he gave Basil a hearty handshake. "Sheriff Wendell Funk at your service. Got them two blackies out back in the slave pen. Let's go out right now and have a gander at them," he said as he led Basil and Jesse through a back door to the outside.

Behind the jailhouse, Basil looked into a heavy wooden stockade and saw Lark and Delia reclined on the ground talking to each other. They were huddled together under a small shed roof out of the sun. Neither of them seemed to be too out of sorts. Basil could discern that Lark must have a shoulder wound. It was wrapped heavily, and the dressing appeared to be in dire need of changing.

"There they be, Mr. Edmunston. Both are in one piece, with the exception of the dog bites and a gunshot. That male nigger of yours almost didn't make it. For nearly a week, we feared he was a goner, but he pulled through somehow. We penned that female up with him to help liven his spirits, and I do believe it was cause of her he stayed alive. I sure do. No sir, the taker-uppers sure didn't want him to die. They figure he's worth a purty piece and expect that you're going to give them a nice fat reward for taking up them runaway blackies."

When Lark saw Basil, he slowly got up off the ground and moved over closer to where the three men were standing. Basil saw no defiance or animosity atall in Lark's reactions or the expression on his face. On the contrary, he could tell Lark was elated to see him. "Good to sees you, Massa Baz. It be's real good to sees you. I 'spected you'd comes to git me. I shore is sorry fo' all da trouble I makes fo' you, Massa Baz." Lark hung his head in embarrassment as he apologized to his master.

"Confound it, Lark!" Basil could not help himself as he almost let his pent-up temper overcome the emotional relief he felt upon realizing Lark was going to be okay. He started to lash out at his runaway, but somehow found the will to hold back his anger and frustrations. There would be plenty of time for that. When they got back to Bachelor's Den and the slave was healed properly, he could then mete out the punishment Lark had coming. Now he needed to make sure that gunshot wound was healing. He needed to get Lark to a doctor. In a less irate tone, he continued, "Sorry, I didn't mean—it's good to see you too, Lark. How are you feeling?"

"I do's good now, Massa. Dis gunhole in da shou'der hurts terrible befor'. But it be gittin' mo' better now," Lark replied holding his hand to his shoulder. "It gonna be's like new soon."

By this time, Delia had made her way over and Basil could see why Lark thought so much of the girl. She had gained some weight back, and with Lark's help they had picked and cleaned and combed out the severest tangles in her hair. Her feet had healed for the most part, and she was now able to walk without pain. For a slave girl, Basil thought her to be a fine specimen, a fine specimen indeed.

"And how are you doing?" Basil asked in an easy polite manner.

"I be's good, Massa. We's be's good now dat you's comes to gits us," Delia replied with a happy look as she held Lark's hand.

The master thought better of telling Delia that her real master—Osborne—did not think enough of her to come get her himself. He simply allowed, "Good. We're going to get you and Lark home."

Basil then went back inside with Sheriff Funk to settle the accounts. He produced a note from Osborne authorizing the sheriff to release Delia into his custody. There being no established reward sum, Basil offered the sheriff one hundred and fifty dollars to compensate the captors of the two runaways. The sheriff thought this to be a right good sum to satisfy the taker-uppers for their pains. An additional fee for holding the slaves, including the doctor's care and taxes, amounted to about thirty-five dollars apiece. Basil paid the sheriff, thanked him for his trouble, and walked out of the jailhouse with his pockets considerably lightened.

After a local doctor had cleaned and re-dressed Lark's gunshot wound and treated the several festering dog gashes on the slaves' bodies, the East Forkers began backtracking south to Haywood. New clothes were purchased for the Africans, but their feet were left bare. Basil reasoned they could survive the walk home as easy as they had endured the failed run to freedom. That quest—the run to freedom—having gone awry, Lark's and Delia's shackles remained unbroken. However, the two slaves appeared delighted with the exchange of the jailer's hard shackles for the familiar ones of slavery.

A good pace comfortable for the horses and not too brisk for the slaves to keep up was established. On a good day over a decent road and level terrain, they were able to easily put eighteen to twenty miles behind them. Buying provisions in the various villages they passed through or at remote farm houses located conveniently near the road, the sojourners were able to eat enough to squelch the hunger pains.

At night, the group routinely laid up near the roads, where there were trees to sleep under, water to drink, and grass for the horses. After the animals were hobbled, a small fire was usually built and the four travelers made themselves comfortable nests to sleep in. The late summer evenings were cool enough so that the East Forkers were obliged to use light blankets to keep comfortable at night.

Jesse Anderson surprised Basil on the demanding trip. Altha's brother was not accustomed to complaining and was always ready to do his share of the work, whether it be tending to the horses, unloading and loading supplies, building the fire at night, or fetching water. Both of the men grew on each other as the days wore on. They became friendly enough to converse steadily, thus helping to lighten the stress and boredom of the journey. Interestingly, Jesse had brought with him an old mandolin that he had learned to play as a young boy.

Each night, he took it up and strummed and sang a few old English and Scotch-Irish ballads that had been passed down through the generations. Jesse's ancestors and those of his Haywood neighbors had brought most of the lyrics and tunes with them on their migration from Ireland's Ulster region to Pennsylvania, and subsequently down through the beautiful valleys of Virginia into North Carolina. Those old songs were ingrained into Jesse's being, and he kept them alive around the fire at night entertaining Basil and the slaves.

Every evening, Basil watched with a keen interest as the two slaves scooted and wiggled and worked themselves close to each other—close enough so they could touch one another. They were not foolish enough to try and make a baby or anything like that, but the love they shared could not be resisted. Strangely, the feel of the other slave's foot or hand seemed to satisfy their immediate urges for intimate affection. As Basil lay awake each night looking up at the moon and stars or into the tree canopies, he randomly contemplated his fate, God's creation, his corn crops, and a host of other things. But always, his mind soon reverted to Altha and Rufus. Just as the slaves needed an outlet for their feelings, Basil desperately wanted to be close to the woman he loved and the child he had pulled into this world. He wanted to touch their hands and feet and be a part of their lives. One day he hoped they would be a real family.

Chapter 22

A Rude Awakening

Basil had a good, long, heart-to-heart talk with Lark soon after taking to the road back to North Carolina. He made certain the slave comprehended the magnitude of the trouble and expense caused by the irrational escape attempt. Also, Basil pointed out to Lark that the two fugitive slaves were not placed in chains for the return trip because he felt Lark could be trusted not to run away again. But it was also well understood by both men that a harsh physical punishment was due and that Basil would attend to it once back in Haywood, when Lark regained his full strength. During this open and frank discussion, Basil's heart got the best of him. He was moved to give assurances to his slave that greater pains would be taken to try and keep the couple together. That magnanimous gesture was well received, and a grateful Lark assured Basil that he would be a good slave from now on. He was going to be a slave his master could be proud of.

The East Fork party made good time moving out of the Virginia valleys. Within two weeks, they had passed through Abington and crossed into Tennessee. It was the first week of September, and as they skirted by the western edges of the Appalachian Mountains, they observed the busy farmers in the cornfields collecting the season's production. Basil was reminded of his own fields and hoped that Hartgrove was keeping the slaves busy picking and hauling and shucking. And, interestingly, Jesse wondered how Josiah and Manson were getting along without him. The Andersons had guaranteed Basil a bumper harvest, and Jesse meant to keep that promise.

In just a couple more days, Basil and his weary band trekked all the way past Blountsville and crossed over the Holston River near where the Watauga River pours into it. About a day's ride short of Jonesboro, they pulled off the road into a wooded area and began settling down for the night.

Darkness closed around them quickly. Huddling around the small fire, they ate their bacon and cornbread and talked about the possibility of making it all the way to Jonesboro the next day. The dancing firelight gleamed off their black and white faces as Lark fell into a talkative mood. He began to regale the men with the story of his and Delia's Nollichucky River crossing.

"Yessa, Massa Baz. Dem lead balls wus comin' ats us like bees do's when you robs dere honey," Lark explained with animation and to the hysterical laughter of his master and Jesse.

"So you two just hopped onto the ferry and rode it across the river?" Basil asked in amazement.

"Yessa, Massa. We's do's it. It wus easy, tho'. Tells him how easy it wus, Delia?"

Delia was shaking her head back and forth. "I dunno 'bout dat. I has me's eyes closed most da times."

Basil chuckled with amusement at the incredible story as Jesse took up his mandolin and began to play lowly. He still could not get over how far the two runaways had made it and what an extraordinary effort it must have been. He wondered how many other such fantastic adventures Lark and Delia shared. *Yep,* he thought, *I will have to find a way to keep those two together. They should be a good mating pair too,* he reckoned, *and they will likely bear more strong slaves to replace the aging ones at the Den and Fort.* After mulling this over for a short spell, Basil turned his mind to the strange captivating music Jesse was making.

His tenant was singing the lyrics of some ballad in a low, chanting style that was mesmerizing to the listeners sitting around the fire that night.

Shady Grove, my little love,

Shady Grove, I say,

Shady Grove, my little love,

I'm bound to go away.

Jesse prepared his captive audience with this intriguing chorus and then continued with the first verse,

I wish I had a big fine horse
And corn to feed him on
And Shady Grove to stay at home
And feed him while I'm gone.

Lark and Delia listened closely to these notes and words, mulling them over good in their heads. Neither of them could ever have their own big fine horse to feed. They knew that could never be. Slaves were not allowed to possess such valuable property. But they allowed that their own private thoughts and dreams were theirs and nobody else's. And although these precious treasures of the mind were not a fine horse or anything like that, they were something that could be held close and dear to their hearts, and all to themselves. As Jesse sung the melodious verses one after another, they dreamed dreams of their love for each other, their own home, and the children they hoped to have one day.

After repeating the intervening chorus, Jesse continued his chant,

Went to see my Shady Grove,
She was standing in the door,
Her shoes and stockin's in her hand
And her little bare feet on the floor.

Basil was listening closely to the lyrics as well and especially reflected on this last verse. It reminded him of that first time he laid eyes on Altha, when she stood barefooted by her spinning wheel in the freezing cold. At first sight, he was captivated by the beautiful girl whose dark ebony tresses were whisked by the breezes and whose motherly way was so evident. He would never lose that first impression of the woman he so quickly grew to love. And tonight, with Jesse's help, he could picture Altha—his own Shady Grove—standing barefooted in the doorway at Bachelor's Den looking longingly at him.

Jesse was not through. He continued to sing more captivating verses to charm and tease Basil and the enthralled slaves. The melodic notes from the mandolin and whispered words from the singer's mouth invaded their senses and accentuated the eerie silence of the dark woods.

When I was a little boy,

I wanted a Barlow knife.

And now I want little Shady Grove

to say she'll be my wife.

There could be no sweeter thought for Basil than of hearing Altha say she would be his wife. This tender fantasy evaporated instantly as he reflected on the unsettled Sam Beck business. Could he and Altha and Rufus ever find true happiness while the specter of Sam Beck still haunted them? His mind was racing and fretting over this disturbing dilemma as Jesse chanted the final lyrics.

A kiss from pretty little Shady Grove

Is sweet as brandy wine.

And there ain't no girl in this old world

That's prettier than mine.

Lark became somewhat aroused by the thought of kissing, except he envisioned the recipient of his kisses to be Delia and not that Shady Grove lady in the song. Basil was stirred to savor Altha's beautiful sweet lips. As he conjured the taste and smell of the woman he adored, the extreme fatigue and weariness that filled his body and soul finally overcame him. Gradually he drifted off into a deep sleep by the glowing embers of the campfire.

"Git up off the ground, God damn you!"

Basil awoke with a start as he tried to make out whose belligerent, profane words these were barking down at him. *Is this a dream?* As his eyes were adjusting to the darkness and before he could see who the impudent speaker was, his head launched backward from a crushing blow under his chin. Not until his upper torso and head snapped backward and crashed hard against the ground did he feel the staggering pain. Thinking his jaw must surely be broken, he fought to regain his senses as the adrenalin began rushing through his body. *Where did this unexpected, threatening force come from?* He struggled to understand as his eyes opened and began gradually locking onto a man standing over him. The demon—for he certainly appeared devil-like—stared down at him with a fiendish scowl. Instinctively, Basil sensed a sinister danger all around him. *This must be the man who almost kicked my head off*, he instantly realized.

"You make a move or give us trouble, then I'll be obliged to put a lead ball inside yer gut," the evil-looking man said as he pointed a pistol directly at Basil.

The man was built stocky and strong, appeared to be about mid-thirty-ish, and had an ugly scar across the left side of his face. He wore an old long-sleeved shirt and a pair of deerskin britches. One pants leg fell loosely almost to the ground, while the other was partially stuffed inside his thigh-high boot. A pitiful black hat covered his head, and a knife hung dangerously at his side. And this wicked man had an accomplice, too.

The other man trained a pistol on Jesse, who had been awakened by all the fuss and now stood with a flabbergasted look on his face. The partner-in-crime was about the same age as the other, though tall and lanky instead, and had a black patch over his right eye. His long red hair was tied back and hung in a ponytail to the nape of his neck. He wore fairly new denim clothes and a pair of badly worn brogans. In addition to the pistol that he kept pointed at Jesse, he was also armed with a hunting knife.

"You two darkies over there, stay where you are, you understand?" the man with the scarred face ordered, barely able to see the slaves in the firelight.

Lark and Delia were lying close together and had been aroused from their deep slumber by the man speaking mean words at their master. They were terribly frightened by these two thieves or highway men or whatever they were and only nodded their heads up and down to confirm their intention not to move a muscle.

Basil's brain worked furiously to contrive a strategy to get out of this fix he was in, but nothing readily came to mind. He could only blurt out, "What's the meaning of this?"

Scarface—the impostor who had the ugly scar on his face—just reared his head back and laughed. "I'll tell you what the meaning is, son. We mean to take yer money and horses, ain't that right, Red?" Red did not look away from Jesse and said nothing. Scarface went on. "We see'd you two strangers pass through Blountsville with them darkies and figured you to be a long ways from home, wherever that might be. Where you'ns be from anyhow?" the sneering scar-faced man asked.

Basil was not frightened. But he was about as mad as he had ever been in his entire life. This was a hell of a fix he was in, and he could not cipher a way to get himself and his companions out of it. "We're from Haywood County," he replied without emotion and without disguising his hatred of the interrogator.

"Ain't never heared of that county. Whur might that be?" Scarface went on.

"It's in North Carolina, west of Asheville," Basil explained figuring the men wanted to be sure their prey were a long way from home. The further away they lived the less likely they would hang around and make trouble for the bandits by pursuing or setting the law on them.

"Okay, Red, give me your gun and take a look in them saddlebags and see what's in 'em." Scarface backed up a couple of steps from Basil and took Red's gun. Holding a pistol in each hand, he pointed them at both travelers. "Best not move a muscle there, men, lessen you want to get gutshot."

Red ravaged and searched through every pocket, nook, and cranny in the saddle bags and then felt around on the persons of the two white men to see what else might be concealed. He produced for Scarface's scrutiny fifty-five dollars that Basil still had remaining, a memorandum book, two pocket knives, two hunting knives, a pistol, and the old flintlock rifle. Red looked at Scarface and said, "Ain't bad plunder, I reckon. There be some bacon left in a bag yonder. What ye say we eat it 'fore we head out? I'm a sight hungry."

"Yeah, okay, git you some while I keep these two in my sights," Scarface answered as he continued to glare at the two white men. Every now and again, he cast a quick glance over at the slaves to make sure they were minding well. And he could not help but notice the young female girl. Within just a few minutes, his quick glances at the darkies evolved into long, hungry leers directed toward Delia.

After giving Red time to scarf down his fill of ham, Scarface yelled out impatiently, "Hurry up, Red! There's some more plunder here I aim to have me."

Red finished feeding his face and, while cleaning it with his shirtsleeves, walked over to Scarface.

"Here, take these. If ary one of 'em moves, shoot 'em," Scarface ordered as he grimaced and smirked toward first Basil and then Jesse. "I'm goin' to check out this female darkie over here. That be what I'm about to do—do me some plundering," Scarface muttered as he strode to where Delia and Lark were still cowering together on the ground.

"Git up, damn ye," Scarface ordered to Delia.

Quickly seeing what his partner had in mind, Red hollered over to Scarface, "Come on, Jack. Let's git. Ain't got no time fer that foolishness."

"Take that dress off, darkie. Let's have a good look-see at ye," Scarface demanded as Delia stood. "No, Red, we've got 'nough time. Don't mean to be long with this here plundering I aim to do."

Basil and Jesse looked at each other, knowing what was about to happen. Neither of them had any tolerance atall for this kind of rude behavior, but they were seemingly powerless to prevent it. Red was keenly attentive and alert and had positioned himself only a few feet away from the captives. He had them dead in front of his guns' muzzles.

"Let's go, Jack. We got to put this place and a lot of miles behind us. Let's git goin," Red urged his partner.

Scarface paid him no nevermind. "Yeaaah—well, don't you look nice now. Yeaaah—you sure look good 'nough to be bedded," Scarface drooled aloud as he grabbed Delia by her hair, drug her further away from Lark, and threw her down to the ground.

Delia had never been handled like this before. It was so different than the gentle, loving way that Lark touched her and held her. This man was not only mean, but he was ugly, and he stank. Delia thought he must have disemboweled a skunk and eaten it that very night, he smelled so bad.

Scarface quickly loosened his belt and dropped his pants. "Spread them pretty legs, darkie!" he ordered as he penned down Delia's shoulders with his strong hands and arms and moved in between her kicking legs. "Yeaaah—I bet ye're goin' to be ripe for the plucking, ain't ye now, darkie?"

Basil could not abide with such despicable carrying-on, and he desperately looked for an opportunity to overpower the thieving rascals and stop them from defiling Delia. Something had to be done to stop them, but what?

What could he do? He watched Red closely as the man turned to urge his partner to hurry up.

"Come on, Jack, we got to—" Red did not get a chance to finish his admonition.

Basil had seen Red's attention diverted for only a split second, but that was all that was needed. He reacted instantly and pounced like a wildcat on Red, as both guns exploded with a noise and violence that stunned Basil. The two men crashed to the ground and began rolling and struggling for their lives. Although Basil did not yet feel the pain in his left leg, it was conspicuously limp and did not react to his mind's signals. One of Red's pistols had discharged into his thigh, missing the main arteries and bone but blowing a hole in a large muscle. Nor could Basil see his tenant writhing on the ground in agony. He had no idea that Jesse had been hit by a lead ball fired from the other gun.

Scarface was up off of Delia in scant seconds, his efforts to enter the slave girl having been thwarted by her intense resistance and the two gunshots. He hurriedly pulled his pants on, and as he did so, he unsheathed the large hunting knife from his belt. By that time, Basil was getting the best of Red. He was on top of the man who was as tall but not as powerful as Basil. Red had a wad of hair in the clutch of one hand and with the other was attempting to jab Basil's eye out. For his part, Basil was landing one hard punch after another into Red's face, and he began to feel the man's resistance failing.

Scarface could see Red was in trouble and that Jesse was down. Paying no attention to the male darkie, he moved quickly behind Basil to get the best angle of assault with his long, two-edged knife—a fearsome weapon indeed. Red was done for, as Basil continued pounding his face to pulp without recognizing the oncoming danger behind him. Scarface raised his right arm high into the air and prepared to plunge the knife hard and straight into Basil's back. Suddenly, just as the downward thrust was initiated, the evil man's mind and sight went absolutely blank. Without ever knowing what hit him, the weapon dropped harmlessly from his hand, and his lifeless body fell limp onto the ground.

"You's all right, Massa?" Lark asked excitedly as he let drop the massive stone he had used to crush Scarface's head.

"Yeah. I'm all right, Lark," Basil replied, slowly realizing that his slave had just saved his life. "Thanks for taking care of that one," Basil said nodding toward the body of the lowest, most loathsome person he had ever encountered.

Then they both looked over toward Jesse, who they could hear suffering and moaning in anguish. Just as Scarface had threatened, Jesse had been gutshot, and his life was steadily and gradually bleeding away.

"Ba...Basil, please take...care of my...family," Jesse hoarsely whispered. Although the words were uttered low and were very difficult to hear, Basil clearly understood their meaning.

"Jesse, can you hear me? I'll take care of them—your family—I promise. Can you understand me, Jesse?" Jesse might have heard, and he might have understood, but he did not reply. As Basil tried to communicate his assurances, Jesse's eyes slowly fell closed, and his heart, emptying of blood, gradually stopped beating. He was dead, and Basil was never to know if Jesse heard the reassurances that the tenant's family would be looked after. He could only hope Jesse had understood him.

Chapter 23

Another Planting at the Orchard

After binding the one-eyed thief's hands and legs, Basil looked over at Jesse's dead body and fell on his knees trembling. Tears flooded down his face as the blood continued to gush from his severe leg wound. Lark, taking notice of the grim scene, jumped to his master's aid again. He found a dirty piece of extra clothing and began pressing and holding it against the wound with as much pressure as the patient could bear.

"Gots to stop dat blood from comin' out, Massa. Now tells me if it hurts too bad," said the slave as he frantically labored to staunch the leakage of blood. Lark was mimicking the succoring technique that the runaway captors used during his own gunshot ordeal.

"It hurts awful, Lark. Keep the pressure on. Got to. Ahiiii–Ahiiii!" Basil cried out in complaint as Lark applied even more tortuous pressure.

While Basil was writhing in pain on the ground, he was suddenly overcome with a fearful thought for the slave who was working to save him. He struggled to raise himself slightly so he could give Lark a message. Seeing that the bandit, Red, was out of earshot and still under Delia's watchful guard, Basil spoke in a hushed voice to Lark.

"Lark, it's real important that we tell the sheriff–ahhh–damn that hurts, Lark!" The pain was insufferable, but he had to make sure Lark understood. "Nobody, but nobody, Lark, can know that you killed that man. I killed him. Do you understand? I killed him."

"Yessa, Massa. I gots it. You kills him. But why we's gonna say dat?"

"'Cause it could get real nasty if they suspected you killed a white man. Makes no matter how nasty a person he was or what he did to us. They'd lynch you for sure if they found out you smashed his head in. So I killed him. You got that?"

"I sees, Massa. I gots it now. Fo' shore I gonna says dat you kills him with dat rock," Lark said as he looked wide-eyed over at Red.

"That man was almost out cold when it happened. He won't know any better," Basil whispered as he glanced over toward Red too.

Delia helped Lark doctor Basil's leg until the bleeding was stopped and a tight wrapping was secured around the wound. At the first hint of daylight, the slaves prepared to move out, heaving Basil onto Fashion with an extreme amount of care and difficulty. Jesse's corpse was hoisted and wrestled over the other horse's saddle and lashed down tightly. Leaving Scarface's dead body exactly where it had fallen, they finally got moving. Basil tried his best to stay in the saddle while Delia led the horse carrying Jesse, and Lark held the reins of the packhorse, to which Red was tethered. The hobbled thief scooted along with quick short steps as Lark held a large hunting knife on him. They were a pathetic band of travelers who looked the worse for wear as they took to the road.

The pace of travel was exceedingly slow, but the East Forkers were able to make Jonesboro just after dark. The sheriff was not in and had to be sent for. When he at last showed up and ascertained that Basil was in a bad way, he summoned someone from the street to go and fetch the doctor at once. After locking Red away in a jail cell, the sheriff listened with keen interest to Basil's story and took down all of the details of the dual killings. Lark's eyes shone white and big as saucer plates as he eavesdropped on Basil's testimony, especially the part where Basil took up a rock and defended himself against the knife-wielding, scar-faced man. Not looking up, the sheriff just scratched out the statement exactly as Basil reported it.

"Them two ain't no good for sure," the sheriff said. "I've had 'em in my jail before for thieving, fighting, and drunkenness and such. I believe they's from up about Hilton's on the Holston River, but can't say for sure. It's jest unfortunate for you they hitched onto your tail and kilt your friend—not to mention the pain theys caused you, sir. The doctor should've been here 'fore now. Don't know what might be keeping him."

No sooner than these words were out of the sheriff's mouth than, sure enough, the doctor walked through the door. Although slightly inebriated, he gave Basil a brief examination and announced that the lead ball would doubtless have to be removed from the leg without delay. So the sheriff, Lark, and the physician carried Basil to the doc's house nearby, where a proper surgery could be performed. And even in his compromised condition, the doctor's surgical skills and performance were laudable. He extracted the lead ball without major complications or further damage, cleaned the raw gaping opening, and finally tried to suture the ragged hole closed. Although the doctor told his patient to stay off the leg for a good fortnight to give it a chance to start healing, Basil had already determined to be back on the road at first light.

The next morning, after having slept on the hard operating table, Basil looked on as the doctor and two slaves wrapped Jesse's decomposing corpse in a couple of thick blankets. He fretted over the deteriorating condition of the body, knowing that he must get Jesse back home and in the ground as quickly as possible. So while suffering the doctor's protested warnings, Basil was helped up on Fashion, and he and the two slaves and Jesse's corpse resumed the long trip back to Haywood.

Interestingly, on the trip home, the trio of East Forkers had occasion to cross back over the Nollichucky River. As they and their horses boarded the rope ferry, the dubious operator suspiciously eyed the pair of slaves and the smelly dead corpse. Basil cast a glance at Lark and caught his attention. The slave and his master grinned at one another as they both recollected the tale of Lark's and Delia's previous narrow escape. Both of them wondered what this man might allow if he knew these two African passengers, paying customers on today's passage, were the audacious ferry snatchers from earlier that summer.

After five more days of punishing and tiring travel, Basil and the entourage rode up the Pigeon River toward Forks of Pigeon. It was the eleventh day of September, a full month and four days since he had started out for Virginia. As he ciphered things out now, all there was to show for his dedication of time, energy, and expense was the dead body of his tenant, a gunshot wound in his leg, and the custody of two runaway slaves. Some Master of the East Fork he had turned out to be, Basil cogitated, as he rode past Osborne's. The last thing he wanted was to deal with the ornery Osborne today. He figured Delia could go on up the river with them to Bachelor's Den. Then in a day or so, after the burying, he would deliver her to Osborne and have a talk about keeping the two slaves together.

Although it was almost dark, Basil stopped by Colonel Deaver's house and stayed just long enough to give the Colonel a brief report of the journey. Deaver could tell the boy was upset about Jesse's death, and he tried his hardest to comfort him. Julia listened with amazement and horror at the story and of Basil's travails. When he finished, she rushed to him without saying a word and gave him a big hug as she wept in sympathy for her Basil.

It was almost midnight that same night when Basil and Uriah rolled to a stop in front of Josiah Anderson's cabin at Crab Orchard. They had ridden up in the farm wagon carrying Jesse's remains in a wood box that Jacob had hurriedly crafted. Basil's leg was hurting so bad that he had chosen to ride on a bed of corn husks in back of the wagon with the coffin. For the past week, since Jesse had been killed, he had anticipated this moment with intense dread. And he still had not decided on the best way to break the news to the family.

Uriah helped his master out of the wagon and over to the cabin. Then Basil knocked loudly on the door.

Bam, bam, bam. "Josiah, it's Basil Edmunston! I need to talk to you."

Bam, bam, bam. "It's Basil Edmunston, Josiah! I've come to see you."

Finally from inside came Josiah's voice, "Holt on! Holt on out there, Edmunston. I'm comin'. Gimme a minute."

Josiah had no idea what this interruption in the middle of the night could be about and quickly threw on some clothes and opened the door. He stood there in the open doorway with a puzzled look as Altha filed in behind him. Rufus was apparently still asleep.

"What's this all about, boy? You've skeered the girl and baby half to death."

"I'm sorry, Josiah. Hello, Altha. I'm afraid—I'm afraid I have some bad news for you about Jesse. He's—he's dead. I've brought his body back to you. I'm so sorry." There, he had gotten it out. It had not been a very polished speech and could have been much better, but he had broken the bad news to Jesse's father and sister. Jesse's wife would be next.

"What—what are you talking about?" a startled Josiah asked as he moved to look behind Basil at the wagon with the coffin box in the back. "Dead? What do you mean, dead?"

The explanation was not near as hard for Basil. "We were ambushed at night near Jonesboro, Tennessee, and Jesse got shot. He died right away, and nothing could be done for him, Josiah. I'm terribly sorry."

Josiah just stared at Basil with a stunned expression on his face. Altha began to sob and moved into Basil's arms as she broke down crying. It was truly a sad homecoming for Basil and an even worse one for the Andersons. That afternoon, late in the day after a thunderstorm had passed through the East Fork valley, they buried Jesse's body next to his mother in the woods near the Crab Orchard schoolhouse. Delaney Trull came down the river to lead the service, just as he had done for the mother five months earlier.

It was a somber event, this second planting at the Orchard, with only a few East Fork residents outside of the family in attendance. Basil was there, of course, and he stood next to Altha on the bad leg, as best he could, and tried to help her through the sad rite. The air was cool and fresh and smelled of wet dirt. Basil squinted to see through the low sun rays burning through the remaining storm clouds and watched Jesse's wife as she suffered through the burying. He had not spoken with the wife about his pledge to Jesse, but he aimed to do it directly.

Colonel Deaver and Julia rode up a day or two after Basil's return to visit with the convalescing patient. They delivered several letters that had accumulated for him during his extended absence. Julia, apprehensive and obviously worried about Basil's condition, desperately wished for some alone time with her wounded beau. She had still not revealed to Basil her true reasons for breaking up with Wade Hampton. And it was clear to her that it was this ill-advised fling with Wade that had driven Basil away from her and into Altha's arms. She had blundered badly—no two ways about it. But she still thought that there was absolutely no way Altha's love and affections for Basil ran as deep as those she held for him. And for the life of her, she could not believe that Basil would actually choose someone else over her. No one loved Basil as much as she did—no one.

But sadly, on this brief visit, time and timing were not Julia's allies. She could not wrangle the personal time that was so desperately needed to mend the rift. And the very next day, as it turned out, her father would be escorting her to a far-away women's boarding college in Lenoir, North Carolina. So it likely was going to be months before Julia saw Basil again, and she would have to continue carrying her weighty burden that whole time.

A few days after Jesse's burial, Uriah carried Basil and Delia down to Osborne's. The news about the tragic trip to Virginia had spread like wildfire from Deaver's store throughout the Forks of Pigeon community. Osborne had heard of the trouble and gave outward appearances of being concerned about Basil's leg. He even acted appreciative to get his slave girl back. However, the old man was not interested atall in selling Delia to the Edmunstons and said he would hear no more about it. Lying on his back in the wagon, Basil knew better than to vigorously confront the man at that moment. So he let the thing drop. He would just have to discover another way to reason with the obstinate Osborne.

While laid up in bed, the Master of the East Fork came to a considered conclusion not to punish Lark for his runaway act and all the associated heartache and expense that entailed. The slave had saved Basil's life after all, and no amount of fretting and rationalizing could clear Basil's conscience and convince him that the African should be thrashed. Of course, Lark was ecstatic and sincerely grateful for the reprieve. So much so that he repeated his promise to Basil that he would henceforth be a good slave and a good worker for his master.

Hartgrove had been as good as his word. The slaves had been kept busy with the wheat and corn harvests during Basil's extended absence. More than two hundred and seventy bushels of wheat had been cut, gathered, flailed, and stored. One of the Den's log cribs was partially full of corn, and there were still more piles ready to be shucked and stowed away. However, the Master of the East Fork put this busy work on hold for a few days while he engaged the boys up at Crab Orchard helping the Andersons get in their harvest. But just as soon as the slaves were done at the Orchard, Basil intended to put them to work picking apples. The orchard trees above the Den were bursting with ripe fruit.

In the weeks following their return, Basil's wounded leg mended tolerably well, albeit slowly. During his convalescence, Altha came down the river almost every day to be with him. The first time, he had been stunned when she suddenly appeared in the Den's doorway with Rufus in her arms. The woman had walked the entire distance—three miles—carrying her baby and had unfortunately been caught in a drenching rainstorm. Basil would have no more such foolishness. Afterwards, he routinely had Uriah drive up to the Orchard in the buggy to fetch the mother and son for their daily visits.

The lovely young mother strived to do all she could to make Basil comfortable and herself useful. She attended to the patient's needs, assisted Patsy with the cooking and other assorted mundane tasks around the cabin, and scribed letters for Basil as he attempted to catch up on his correspondence, which was so badly in arrears. The two of them talked at length about their future and committed themselves to each other and to Rufus. Realizing that marriage was out of the question, at least for the time being, they discussed living together as man and wife and son and weighed all the positives and negatives associated with that arrangement. Basil speculated that his father was not likely to condone such an act. Nevertheless, he and Altha decided they would do it. That is, Altha and Rufus would move into Bachelor's Den with him as soon as he conveyed the decision and circumstances to his father.

One of the letters that had arrived at Forks of Pigeon while Basil was away contained news that his father was coming out to Haywood soon—mid-October or so. It had been more than six months since Thomas turned over the Haywood farming affairs to Basil, and he wanted to check on things—the runaway slave business, the harvest, tenant affairs, the special girl mentioned in Basil's last letter, and other such things. Thomas also mentioned in his letter that he wanted to talk to Basil about possibly making a drove to the market at Augusta, Georgia. The father thought there might be a good opportunity to make a tidy profit by selling some livestock, apples, and maybe a small quantity of corn. Basil was anxious to see his father and actually looked forward to receiving some paternal counsel and support. However, he could not help being nervous about the pending reunion, sensing there was more to the visit than strictly farm business.

No doubt Thomas would want to become acquainted with Altha and see what kind of girl his son had picked out. Basil had written to him about her and the new romantic relationship they shared. The father, who of course had the highest hopes for his son's happiness and welfare, was probably somewhat perplexed that Basil had been tempted and ensnared by one of the tenant's daughters. Basil also worried what the senior Edmunston would think upon learning that Altha was not only his son's girlfriend but also a mother and the wife of another man. And furthermore, how would Thomas react when he learned of Basil's domestic plans to live with Altha as man and wife? Basil suspected it would not go down very well, and he began mentally preparing for the worst.

Chapter 24

Sinful Dreams

The previous evening, Thomas Edmunston had arrived at Bachelor's Den in a buggy driven by one of his slaves. Exhausted from the long and difficult trip, he had gone straight to bed soon after Basil welcomed him into the cabin. On this fall morning, it was unusually cold outside. The hazy mist was beginning to burn away, revealing hints of a brilliant blue sky and a clear day. Blanketing the East Fork mountains, the hardwood trees were ablaze in astounding autumn hues of red and orange and yellow. The setting was perfect for a congenial father-and-son reunion.

Both men easily satisfied their early morning hunger pains by ingesting Patsy's standard breakfast fixings with generous helpings of apple butter. Afterwards they eased up in front of the cozy fire and warmed themselves as Basil related the details of his trip to Virginia. It was the same warm setting at the old poplar cabin where Thomas had received Basil exactly seven months before and had turned over the Haywood farming operation to the son. So much had transpired since then, yet the father did not know the half of it. But he was fixing to get caught up real quick.

After listening patiently and with great interest to his son's eventful story, Thomas queried Basil for better understanding on one sensitive point, "So Osborne doesn't want to sell the girl to us, huh?"

"Said he wouldn't talk about it atall," Basil answered.

"Well, we'll just have to see about that. I still hold two old notes of Osborne's worth more than a thousand dollars. I'd given up on dunning him. He's been such a good neighbor over the years that I couldn't see clear to law him for the money. I'll pay him a visit, and we'll see just how bad he wants her. Besides," an annoyed Thomas continued, "that Anderson boy gave his life and you took a lead ball in the leg to bring the girl back. We'll just see about this—we'll see," Thomas finished as he looked intently and determinedly into the fire.

The senior Edmunston was visibly moved when Basil shared the details of the run-in with thieves at Jonesboro. Learning that the tenant, Jesse Anderson, had been killed in a gunfight and that Basil had barely escaped with his life was unthinkable—almost unbearable. And he listened closely as Basil recounted Jesse's last dying words and the pledge that was made to the tenant.

"Nothing else you could do, son. You did the right thing. I'm proud of you. We'll just have to make sure that his wife and little boy and girl don't go hungry or wanting for shelter and warmth. That's the only thing we can do. You look after them, you hear?"

"I plan to, Father. Don't worry."

"Now, Basil, tell me about this girl. Altha, isn't that her name? I want to hear all about her and hope we can get up there to the Orchard today and meet her. We have to go up anyway, don't we, so I can pay my proper respects to the Andersons? Say, didn't you, or somebody, write—I think—that Josiah's wife had died earlier this year too?"

"That's right, Father. Her name is Altha, and her mother died of a failed heart this past April—at the same time Altha was giving birth to her child." And with the elder Edmunston's encouragement, Basil launched into a full account of his relationship with Altha, leaving out nothing in the process. Despite his expressed desire to hear all about the girl, perhaps Thomas was not quite ready to hear everything Basil had to say about her.

"Married! The girl is still married?" an incredulous Thomas queried. There was the remote chance he had not heard his son correctly.

"Yes, Father, that's right. She's still married. Her husband—he's a low-life scamp from over on the West Fork—abandoned her, long before the baby was born."

Thomas had thought the part about Basil's midwifing exploits unbelievable and had briefly entertained fleeting sentiments of pride for this amazing and fine young son of his. *Who else could have done what Basil did?* he asked himself. Thomas knew for a fact that he would not have been up to the task. But when he came to understand the whole picture, the Sam Beck business and the part about Altha's still being married, the prideful feeling was replaced by one of almost embarrassment and even betrayal.

"What are you thinking, Basil? You can't have that woman and her baby. She's married to that Beck fellow, and they're his. He's liable to walk right back into their lives at any time. You ought not entertain such an idea. It's just a crazy notion—crazy." Thomas was convinced his son was making a huge blunder, and he was not happy atall about Basil's meddlings into the marital affair.

"But he's not coming back, I don't believe. And besides, she won't have him back," a defensive Basil countered.

"She can't get away from him, son. Don't you understand that?" Thomas was getting riled and showing an uncustomary flare in temper. "The chances of her getting a divorce from the man, especially in this state, are slim to nil. It would take years of legal wrangling, and not only that, no justice in these parts is about to rule in favor of a woman in a divorce proceeding—unless she can prove he's harmed her in some way. It's unheard of. That's just the way I see it. I'm sorry, but I can't condone this relationship with the girl." The patriarch paused for a second or two to simmer down and get hold of himself before continuing in a slightly less exasperated tone, "What are your plans? Do you plan on living with her without marrying her?" Before allowing Basil to answer, he got up from his comfy seat in front of the fireplace and stormed out the door to cool off.

Basil was disappointed certainly, but he remained undaunted. He followed his father outside. Finding him in a huff glaring over at the river, Basil resumed the uncomfortable conversation in a determined yet courteous manner. "I'm sorry you feel that way, Father, but that's what I aim to do.

If I could locate that Beck fellow, I'd have it out with him. Nobody has got the right to keep us apart, especially Beck. That's the way I see it."

His father did not bother to reply. He wanted to cool off a bit more, but after a minute or so of reflection turned to look his son dead in the eyes, "Basil, you and that girl will be living in sin in front of the Lord and all your neighbors. Your mother will be devastated."

Basil was not prepared to confide his personal religious misgivings to his father. He was also surprised by the comment about hurting his mother. It was a delicate point that he had not given much thought—not enough anyway. The last thing he ever wanted to do was to hurt his mother. But he had made up his mind, and so had Altha. He would never give her up or go back on his word with her. "I've given that a lot of thought too, Father, the sinning I mean. It just seems to me, when I think hard on it like I have for the past two or three months, that Beck is the one that has sinned. He sinned when he raped and spoiled Altha. He sinned when he beat the daylights out of her, over and over again, every day. And he sinned when he abandoned Altha and Rufus. Nobody can say any different, no matter what their religious beliefs.

"I just don't see how we would be living in sin if we love each other, respect each other, are good to each other, treat each other as God's creatures, and live a life as God would have us live. Or live a life that He would condone. I've ciphered on it a good bit, Father, and don't believe anybody is going to change my mind. I'm sorry—I'm really sorry if you disapprove." Upon finishing the rather lengthy outpouring of feelings, Basil simply looked squarely into his father's eyes and awaited a response. It was a look of sadness as well as determination, and Thomas did not mistake it.

"I'm sorry too, Basil," and his father simply turned, hung his head in disappointment, and walked back into the cabin.

After their heated and awkward confrontation, it took a day or two for the anger, disappointment, and coolness that resided in Thomas to dissipate, but it finally did. During the afternoon following the unfortunate disagreement, Basil and Thomas rode up to the Crab Orchard, and Thomas delivered his personal condolences to the Andersons. They were very appreciative of the attention and considerate gesture. The elder Edmunston took the opportunity to confirm to Jesse's wife that he was aware of the pledge Basil had made to her deceased husband, and he assured her that both he and Basil would live up to it.

Altha was all prepared for the visit and presented herself in fine form indeed. Thomas Edumunston was absolutely stunned by her beauty and thought Altha to be the most strikingly beautiful woman that he had seen in quite some time. Everything about her—her pure complexion, shining dark hair, high cheekbones, deep emerald-green eyes—was utterly captivating, as were her sweet and personable manners. It came as a pleasing surprise to Thomas to learn that Altha's baby was named after his own son who had died tragically a few years before.

When Thomas Edmunston made an offhanded comment to Josiah that it looked like a considerably better corn crop had been produced at the Orchard this year, even Basil was taken aback by Anderson's response.

"Ye kin credit that there son of yer'n fer that, sir. Yes sir, 'twas Basil's 'sistance that done it."

Anderson went on to elaborate how Basil had supported him and his sons, including getting Jesse out of the scrape with the law. Thomas once again felt the darts of fatherly pride pricking his soul. Even Basil had not stopped to consider the constructive consequences of his helpful actions in favor of this tenant family. His logic in this regard had been unduly dampened and influenced by the deaths of the Anderson matriarch and her son. Actually, Basil did not really blame himself for the mother's death. It was clear to him that his deeds had no determination over her fate atall. But he viewed Jesse's death differently.

He had hired Jesse to travel to Virginia with him to retrieve the slaves. But in a desperate attempt to protect a slave's honor and virtue, his lunge at the armed robber had triggered the gunshot that killed Jesse. If he had only allowed the man to despoil Delia without a fight, then Jesse would likely still be among the living today. Ever since that terrible tragedy, Basil had entertained a great internal moral struggle trying to balance the death of a good man against the honor of a slave. *Was the one worth the other? Were my own actions justified?* Unfortunately, these were questions that Basil would wrestle with—and never fully resolve—for the rest of his life.

During his stay at the Den, Thomas spent a considerable amount of time discussing with Basil the financial aspects and possible rewards of selling some of their livestock at the southern markets. Instead of feeding so many head of stock through the winter, it made more since to the father to sell them this fall in Greenville, South Carolina, or Augusta, Georgia. In that lowland country, the numerous plantations created a strong market for significant quantities of meat and fruit to feed the large slave populations. But many years had passed since Thomas had attempted a drive from Haywood. The month-long roundtrip required an enormous expenditure of time and manpower. Also, there was an inherent degree of danger in making these extended drives through remote countries with large herds of animals, as Basil could testify to.

These droves required someone young, energetic, and strong to lead them. On his visit to Haywood, Thomas had heard plenty enough about his son's East Fork contributions and exploits. He had come to form a high opinion of the young man's capacity and had no doubts Basil could lead a successful drive to the faraway market places. Although it meant another lengthy separation from Altha and Rufus and yet another trip that was likely to be filled with depravation, exhaustion, and even danger, Basil could not refuse the encouragement of his father.

While on the East Fork, Thomas did not pass up the opportunity to call on all of his tenants. Other than a few trivial matters, it appeared to the elder Edmunston that Basil had performed his landlord duties reasonably well, considering his lack of experience and the distraction of the runaway slave business. Thomas also found time to get down to Osborne's farm and see his old neighbor. Osborne spoke highly of Edmunston's son and his endeavors in the runaway slave affair. When the subject of finding an arrangement whereby Lark and Delia could be married came up Osborne repeated what he had told Basil—he did not want to talk about it. But the elderly friend became more conversational when Thomas brought up the matter of Osborne's notes of debt that he still held. After a lengthy round of arguing and discussing, the two men were able to come to a reasonable solution for all. Thomas would forgive the old debts, and Osborne would give Delia over to Edmunston. It was as simple as that.

There could have been no happier slaves in Haywood—or the entire South for that matter—than were Delia and Lark when Thomas and Basil Edmunston walked the slave girl over to the African quarters at Bachelor's Den, pronouncing that Delia was now Edmunston property.

After visiting with Basil for the whole of two weeks, Thomas Edmunston returned to Fort Catawba. On his departure, he confided to Basil that Altha appeared to be a fine and remarkable young woman. He told his son that he held nothing against the girl for the circumstances she found herself in, but he simply could not condone an arrangement where Basil and Altha lived together as man and wife while she was still married to Beck. However, Thomas avowed that Basil was old enough to make up his own mind and make his own decisions, and he was not going to dictate to his son how to live his life.

Overall, Basil guessed that it had been a useful visit. Although the decision to make an Augusta market trip did not come as a complete surprise to him, it left little time to get ready. There was a tremendous amount of work to be done in preparation for the drove, and he would have to start the boys on it promptly. Basil could tell that his father was very favorably impressed with Altha. Too bad, though, that his father took such a hard stance against his dream of living with Altha and Rufus. He had suspected there might be a protest from the religious viewpoint, and the argument he had put forth was not convincing. His father remained determinedly fixed against the idea. But Basil was still set on fulfilling his dream, and as long as Altha shared that same dream, then nothing else really mattered to the young Master of the East Fork.

Chapter 25

Toll Paid in Full

The activity around the Den during the first two weeks of November was hectic and fast-paced. Basil had established a target date of November sixteenth, a Monday, to start the herds on the long trek to market. It was essential to take to the turnpikes before the winter rains, snow, and ice turned the rutted dirt paths into virtual muddy or frozen quagmires. Thomas Edmunston had departed for the Fort on the last day of October, leaving very little time to find and select the stock that was to be sold. The boys were split up and sent to the woods to catch mature hogs and to the several tenant farms up and down the East Fork to round up sheep and beef cattle. And the female slaves were put to work gathering apples and corn to fill up the old farm wagon.

Basil had become familiar enough with his tenant farmer families to know which young men might make good steady hands to take along on the trip. They would primarily be charged with the duty of driving the herds—keeping the animals together and moving down the turnpikes as quickly as possible. He recruited five youths in their late teen years that fit the mold he had in mind—strong, energetic, and full of themselves. And the boys relished this opportunity for an adventure, not to mention the one dollar per day wages that went along with the job. Also making the trip but, of course, working for no wages were Basil's male slaves Uriah, Lark, Gabe, and Harry. They would toil alongside of the youthful white boys performing the same duties, eating the same food, and essentially being equal members of Basil's East Fork drover team.

On Sunday, the day before the train of animals was scheduled to begin moving out from Bachelor's Den, Uriah was sent to the Crab Orchard to fetch Altha and Rufus. Final preparations for the drove were still underway, even on this Sabbath day, but Basil took breaks from the grinding labors to engage Altha in highly personal and intimate conversation in the warm confines of the Den. They chatted about their future, and both of them expressed an extreme anxiousness to be together and all that might entail. Basil had never been intimate with a woman before, and he was understandably apprehensive. But he dreamed of lying with Altha and holding her close to him and feeling her bare skin and body against his. It seemed that he could not look at this sweet alluring woman without experiencing an overpowering surge of emotion and an instinctive desire to take her in his arms and ravish her with kisses and fondle her captivating body. He wanted to become one with Altha and release into her the full measure of love and emotion that he held for her. But alas, all that would have to wait until after the trip to Augusta.

The couple agreed that once Basil was back from the southern markets, Altha and Rufus would move in with him at the Den. They would start out anew as man, woman, and child, and together they could take on the challenges of the world and the East Fork valley. It was all decided. It was a done deal.

"Oh, Basil, this will be the longest month of my life. I don't know what I'm going to do while you're away," said an excited Altha.

"It's going to be a great Christmas with you and Rufus. I can't wait either and am really looking forward to it. We can deck out the Den with ornaments and put up a tree. It'll be just the three of us waiting on old Saint Nicolas and enjoying Patsy's big ol' turkey. And I'll be sure to bring some nice ripe oranges back home with me."

"Please be careful, won't you?" Altha urged as she gently caressed Basil's right leg, which had healed, for the most part, by this time.

"Now Altha, don't you worry your pretty little head none. I'll have a pistol under my belt and will sleep with one eye open," Basil reassured her, alluding to the recent tragic encounter with the highway men in Virginia. Then he pulled back from Altha and picked up the seven-month-old Rufus, who was wrapped in a warm shawl. "Hey there, big boy. I do declare your mom's going to have to give you a good shearing soon. Yes sir. Look at those pretty gold locks," Basil said affectionately as he played and messed about with the boy. Running his hand through Rufus' longish blonde hair, he hopefully teased, "Are you going to miss Daddy too?"

By this time, the East Fork drovers had passed through Asheville and were headed south on the Buncombe Turnpike. It had taken them all of three days to get to this point. Basil, riding on Fashion and leading the way, looked back at his drawn-out train of stock, which stretched for at least a hundred yards behind him. He could see that his team of white and black drovers was doing its best to keep the herds tightened up, as difficult and exasperating as that job was.

Forty hogs had been chosen to sell at the market, and these nervous critters that scared so easily were at the head of the pack. Behind them was a flock of fifty sheep, and bringing up the rear were some forty-two beef cattle. The herds followed the large farm wagon, which was being pulled with a four-mule team. A cargo of thirty bushels of shelled corn and ten barrels of apples was a weighty burden, and it took all of the mules' pulling power to haul this heavy load to the tops of the steep mountain grades.

Harry was assigned the important job of stimulating the hogs to follow closely behind the wagon. Every now and again, he scooped out a small portion of corn and sprinkled it out on the road in front of the pigs. This tended to incite the animals' foraging instincts and kept them sniffing up to the rear wheels.

"Dat 'bout da right 'mount, Massa Baz?" Harry hollered at Basil.

Basil glanced backward at the young slave and coached, "Looks about right, Harry. Go easy on that corn now. Only use it when the hogs start to lag back."

"Okay, Massa, I wills. We's don't wants to use up all dat corn befo' we's gits to 'Gusta, do's we?"

"No, don't want to use it all up, Harry. That's right."

"And it be's a long ways dare to 'Gusta, I hear tell. Ain't dat right, Massa?"

"That's right. It's about two hundred miles from the Forks to Augusta. That's a fair piece, Harry," the patient master answered.

"It shore 'nough is, Massa. Two hunnert miles—shoooooeee! We's never ever gonna git dare, Massa?"

"Yeah, we'll get there all right. I expect we will make it in twenty days or so if we can cover a good ten miles per day. We're going to have to pick up the pace though. Traveling a mite slow so far."

"Goin' too slow, huh? Do's you think I needs to feeds deese hogs mo' faster, Massa Baz? I can if you wants me to."

"No, you're doing fine. Can't get them hogs to go faster than the wagon, Harry." And with that little bit of shared intelligence Basil reined Fashion around and rode toward the rear to prod the animals and his drovers.

Gradually their pace increased as they traveled from dawn until dark, hardly ever stopping or slowing unless a creek or river was encountered. From time to time, the drovers would have to move their animals to the side of the road to let faster travelers and droves move on ahead. Animals and men alike became covered from head to toe with the dust from the road. The East Fork drovers, forced to wrap kerchiefs over their noses and faces, resembled white apparitions plodding along beside the stock and scaring the poor animals up the turnpike. As darkness and exhaustion ran the animals and drovers off the road, they retreated into the stockyards of the inns and way stations. There, the animals were fed and watered first, and then the men scarfed down what food the master was able to buy or come by. For twenty or more long, grueling, and boring days, this would be the East Forkers' schedule and lot.

On the sixth day of the trek, they reached Flat Rock, and Basil could not help but think about Wade Hampton and Freddie Rutledge, whose families' fine summer residences were somewhere nearby. He also thought of Julia Deaver away at school in Lenoir and wondered why, exactly, she had called off the romance with Wade. *What could have caused the rift?* he pondered as he thought of the beautiful belle. Beyond Flat Rock, the road became considerably more treacherous as it wound its way through mountain gorges down into South Carolina. Just before reaching the state line, the Haywood group came upon a flimsy, crude bridge spanning a deep gorge through which the Green River flowed. In the absence of other practical options to get to the other side of the river, they queued up the animals and prepared to cross over the toll bridge.

"What's the charge for this drove?" Basil inquired of the toll keeper as Harry sidled up next to him, curious as ever and wanting to listen to what was being said.

The man was slightly taller than Basil, a little older, and thin as a rail. His tousled blondish-yellow hair spilled over his forehead so low that one eye was partially concealed. A weeks-old scruffy beard covered his face, but Basil could make out that the visible eye was shifty and blue. Tobacco juice and residue covered the facial hair, and the man smelled near as bad as he looked.

"Ought to be 'bout ten dollars' worth, I reckon," the man sneered as he eyed the procession. "Whur ye boys be from, anyhows, drover?"

"Out at Haywood, from up on the East Fork of the Pigeon River," Basil offered as he moved over to his horse to retrieve the money from his saddlebags. "We're taking this herd to the Georgia market."

"Haywood County, huh? Ain't much good country in Haywood. I was born and raised on the West Fork fer a long spell—too long of a spell. Can't say much good 'bout that country."

Basil did not recognize the man and was a bit perturbed at the disparaging tone of the Haywood talk. Before he could give the toll keeper the money, however, the man reached out his hand and introduced himself. "Sam Beck. What be yer name, drover?"

What was that? What did he say? Basil asked himself as he clinched the man's hand. *Did he say his name was Sam Beck?* Before Basil could react and retrieve his hand or say anything, the tall man bent slightly in Harry's direction and spat a huge glob of tobacco and saliva directly into the boy's face.

"Now how's that there taste, blackie?" the sneering man said as he turned to Basil and continued, "Didn't ketch the name, drover."

Basil jerked his hand back and pulled away from the keeper. He looked toward Harry who was attempting to wipe the spit from his face with a shirt sleeve and then toward the toll keeper. "That was uncalled for, Beck. Why in hell did you do that?"

"What ye mean, uncalled fer?" the man laughed. "He's a nigger, ain't he?"

"Doesn't matter what he is. Nothing gives you the right to do that," the enraged Basil said. After reflecting for a second or two, he continued with a fury. "Is that about the way you treated your wife—Altha?" Basil asked defiantly.

The astonished Beck looked at the Haywood stranger and stumbled to get his words out. "Altha? Say, how do ye know 'bout her? What did ye say yer name wus?"

"Didn't say. Don't you worry about who I am, Beck! I know all about you, though. Know how you spoiled Altha. Know how you beat her. Know how you just up and abandoned her. You're a low-life scamp, Beck! That's what you are."

By this time, Lark and a couple of the tenant drovers had worked themselves closer to the heated discussion. They looked on wide-eyed and filled with both excitement and concern.

"I'll be God damned! I betcha ye're that Edmunston feller—ere ye? I do declare! Heared tell ye had taken an interest in that bitch and my son. Well, ye listen up good, Edmunston. Ye kin have that woman if ye want her, but I aim to have the boy. Ye ain't got nary legal right to him, and I do. Ye hear me?" Beck blustered as he looked mean and threatening-like at Basil. He had moved over toward the tollgate and had picked up a stout stick that he began waving about in a menacing manner.

Basil was not to be intimidated atall. Although his blood was boiling and he was in a fighting temper, he gave Beck a confident and determined stare and replied, "You come back to Haywood again, Beck, and I aim to finish up what the Anderson menfolk didn't. Every one of my Africans you see here is a better man than you are. You don't deserve to live, and if you're foolish enough to venture back to Haywood, I'll see to it that you find your proper place in hell." Basil sneered back at Beck and then suddenly turned away toward Lark and the rest of the East Fork drovers and directed them in a loud voice, "Let's get those animals across the river."

But it was a mistake to turn his back on Beck. Basil had misjudged the degree of evilness that lurked within the man. Beck hauled back his weapon and delivered a crushing blow to the distracted Basil. The East Fork master was lucky though. The stick only struck the rear of his head with a glancing blow. Most of the force of impact had been absorbed by his broad shoulders and back. Nevertheless, Basil was slammed to the ground and temporarily stunned. He rolled over just in time to see the next blow coming down on him and somehow managed to shield himself, taking most of the stick's energy in his arms. Although addled and hurting terribly, Basil bounced up from the ground before Beck could launch his next attack.

Dazed and sluggish as he was, Basil was still able to bring his eyes into focus on the heavy stick hurling rapidly toward him again. His reflexes were considerably slowed, and he barely managed to dodge the force of the blow. Then almost instantly he thrust himself toward Beck. It was a desperate, mostly reflexive, effort to render the club useless. Basil crashed hard into the shiftless toll keeper and they both went flying downward through the air, toppling right over the edge of the river embankment.

They tumbled down the precipitous rocky slope, rolling over and over and never loosening the death grips that held them together. For more than forty feet, the combatants fell until finally crashing abruptly and hard into the shallow rocky edge of the Green River. Both of the men were shaken badly but were again quickly locked up in each other's clutches trying frantically to hurt and wound the other. After a minute or so, their movements began to slow as they quickly grew tireder and tireder. Each man struggled valiantly to get an advantageous hold or land a punishing blow. Like two wild animals locked in a life and death struggle, they rolled over and over, each trying desperately to keep his head out of the water in order to gasp for air.

Basil was the stronger of the two men, but not by much. The lanky Beck was not only mean, but he was tough and had managed to wrap Basil up in his long tentacles and was attempting to squeeze the life from his fierce opponent. But the East Fork drover was at last able to twist and writhe and forcibly shake loose from the ever-tightening choke hold around his neck. Holding Beck off of him with a stiff arm, Basil let fly a crushing punch into the man's face and nose. He could feel Beck's nose break, and he quickly cocked back his arm again and landed another blow to the same spot, and then another, and another. He could feel Beck's muscles grow limper with each crushing punch until at last the man collapsed lifeless into the water.

Sam Beck was out cold. Instead of leaving the evil toll keeper in the river to drown, as he surely would have, Basil pulled him onto the bank and simply left the motionless form there. It would be up to God whether Beck lived or died and, frankly, Basil preferred He would choose the latter.

Chapter 26

Silence of the Loom

The band of East Fork drovers trudged down the steep turnpike path that twisted its way out of North Carolina's mountains past the hamlet of Traveler's Rest and into Greenville. It had taken them most of eleven days to reach this upstate South Carolina trading village, which doubled as a summer getaway for wealthy lowlanders. Theirs had been an abysmal pace of only seven to eight miles per day. Basil was terribly sore from the stick beating he had received and was barely able to sit his horse and ride along at the tortoise-like rate of travel his drive was maintaining. Nevertheless he kept pushing his boys, urging them to move faster. The wagon was a good deal lighter now. Half of the corn had been fed to the hogs, and many of the apples had been eaten up by the ever-hungry young drovers. On the flatter and wider southern roads, the mules were able to pull their lightened wagon load much easier and faster. And Harry kept the pigs' noses to the ground and hustling right up to the wagon's rolling back wheels.

The slave boy was genuinely concerned about his master's condition. As he walked along beside the wagon periodically scooping corn feed out to the hogs, he kept his eagle eyes peeled toward Massa Baz. Being afraid that his master might even topple off of Fashion, Harry kept up a cheerful banter to keep Basil awake and his mind active.

"We's be speedin' up some now, Massa. How much longer you figger befo' we's reaches 'Gusta?"

"Hard to tell, Harry," Basil replied in a low tone, as it hurt him even to talk. "We've got a little more than a hundred miles left to go. If we can keep up this faster pace and the roads stay dry, I'd say we might be able to reach Augusta in ten or eleven days."

"We's a sight long ways from home now, ain't we's, Massa Baz?"

"Sure are."

"Massa Baz, dis here country we's be's passing true—dis alls be cotton-growing country? Do's dey grow lotsa cotton down here?"

"Yep. They grow a whole lot of cotton down in these parts. It's been picked already so doubt that you will see many Africans out in the fields. The Africans down here have a hard life, Harry. You East Fork boys don't know how good you've got it compared with them."

Harry reflected for a moment on what his master had just said and then replied. "Yessa, Massa. I done knows 'bout dat. We's hears things 'bout deese cotton pickers down heres and da mean massas dat works dem. We's hears mighty bad things 'bout deese cotton pickers." After pausing for a few seconds, Harry felt inclined to add, "We's be's mighty glad we's not cotton pickers. And, Massa, we's be's mighty proud dat you's our massa. You's duh bestest massa we's ever has, Massa Baz."

Basil heard Harry but did not reply. Staring off toward the southern horizon, he gave Fashion a light kick with his spurs and pondered his slave's words. *Was the boy simply patronizing him, or did he speak with true sincerity?* Basil thought it over for a time until his weariness and the pain from the bruises distracted him elsewhere.

They kept plodding and moving along the fine lowland roads until at last, twelve days out of Greenville, the East Fork stock drive reached the busy markets of Augusta, Georgia. Actually the band of highlanders found buyers for their herds at Hamburg, South Carolina, the riverfront trading center located on the near bank of the Savannah River, opposite of Augusta. Buyers that catered the Georgia and South Carolina plantations and shipped goods by steamboat to Savannah paid out handsomely for the fine mountain-raised herds.

Basil's steers brought from fifty to seventy-five dollars apiece, depending on size and condition. The sheep averaged almost twenty dollars a head. Hog meat was currently demanding an unheard-of price of six cents per pound gross weight. In addition, the two poorest mules and the remaining barrels of uneaten apples fetched an extra three hundred dollars. All totaled, the Master of the East Fork pocketed nearly forty-five hundred dollars in Georgia and South Carolina bank notes as well as gold and silver species.

Seldom had Basil seen or handled such a vast sum of money. He was so giddy in fact that his aches and pains were almost forgotten for a time. There were so many dollars, thousands of them in fact, that he was exceptionally nervous about their safekeeping. So as Basil and his little band of drovers moved through the busy town's streets buying supplies for home, he kept a gaggle of boys and slaves surrounding him for protection against thieves.

The tenants were given twenty-five dollars each for wages so they could purchase the items their parents had requested—such things as coffee, salt, and sugar. Basil bought the same supplies but in larger quantities for his Bachelor's Den and to fill an order given to him by Colonel Deaver for store stock. The teenage white boys were not immune to their personal desires either and discovered pocketknives, candy, tobacco, and boots in bountiful supply and theirs for the taking in exchange for the hard-earned dollars. And by no means were the slaves forgotten. Basil helped each of them procure candy and other needed items for themselves and the rest of the Africans who had stayed back in Haywood.

Lastly, but most importantly, Basil remembered Rufus and Altha. The baby boy was almost eight months old and crawling already, and Basil fussed a sight over what to get him. He finally settled for some soft candy that Altha might see fit to let the boy eat, and picked out a little wooden toy horse on rollers that could be easily pulled with a rawhide string. Although he was not too sure about these choices, it was something at least, and he reckoned he had tried. And for the mother, he found the promised oranges, and he bargained for some beautiful fabrics that caught his eye. One in particular—a blonde satin material—he thought would make an extraordinarily elegant dress for Altha. And he could envisage her wearing it to Sunday church meetings along with a new pair of shoes and perhaps a bright shawl draped around her neck. *How proud I'm going to be to escort her*, Basil mused, *and the neighbors down at Forks of Pigeon were bound to be impressed.*

It took only two days for these various market transactions to be completed. On the third day following their arrival at Hamburg, Basil and his East Forkers were hurrying home at a blistering rate of travel, more than twice as fast as they had come. The boys, whites and blacks, took turns riding in the wagon, but they were particularly careful not to overload and slow down the two-mule team. Greenville was reached in less than seven days, and one day later, the Haywood highlanders stood on the south bank of the Green River waiting for the toll keeper to walk across the bridge and open the gate. Interestingly, it was not Sam Beck.

"That'll be 'bout three dollars, boys," said the keeper as he pushed down on the counterweight to open the gate.

Basil, both curious and wary, glanced around and scanned the surrounding area but could see no other persons lurking about. "Don't see Sam Beck about anywhere. Where is he?" Basil bluntly queried as he handed over the toll money.

The keeper, an older man of almost fifty years, looked at Basil and then turned his head sideways and spat a juicy load of spent tobacco several feet off to the side. Looking back at Basil with an indifferent expression and a brown drool coating his mouth the stranger responded, "He ain't 'round here no more. Got himself in an altercation with a drover they says—got whipped pretty bad. I hear tolt he's went over the mountain to Haywood whur he hails from."

"That so," Basil responded as his heart began to beat to a quicker rhythm. He stiffened a little and turned to the boys and snapped, "Okay, let's get going. We want to get home, don't we?"

Sam Beck skulked stealthily through the thickest patches of woods and rough terrain on the East Fork toward the Crab Orchard tenant farm. Leading an old worn-out horse behind him, he was being very careful not to be observed by the locals—especially those Anderson in-laws of his. The last thing he needed was a confrontation with them and another thrashing.

Barely three weeks had elapsed since Beck was severely beaten and left to die on the banks of the Green River, and he very nearly did die. Only in the past few days had he been able to squint and see through swollen blackened tissue surrounding his eyes. A broken and deformed nose hindered his breathing, and a cracked rib along with a badly bruised and battered body made it generally difficult and painful to move about. But those trifling bothers were not going to prevent him from claiming what he deemed rightfully his. Besides, he had a scheme simmering in his aching head that might just allow a profit to be made from that bitch wife of his and her new highfaluting benefactor—the same man that recently pummeled the hell out of him in the next county over.

Stopping well away from Josiah Anderson's cabin, Beck sought concealment in a copse of hardwood trees. Under some low overhanging limbs of a hickory, where a precious few golden-tinged leaves still tenaciously clung, he snuggled into a small bramble thicket to hide and observe. There he laid up, waiting and watching for the right opportunity to execute his plot. Presently he spied Altha coming out of the cabin and beginning her outdoor work at the loom, even on this bitter cold day. She was in plain view and had brought Rufus out with her, placing the swaddled baby in a cradle near her work. Beck reckoned this must be his son, and he strained for a better view.

From his vantage point he watched patiently for more than an hour as Altha sat and wove. The soothing melodious sounds of the songs she sang to the child could be discerned in the relative quietness of the forest around him. Even the faint clacking of the loom's moving pieces was detectable from Beck's lair. Some sporadic chirping of birds pierced the silence. Squirrels cried out their warnings. And once from far off across the river, a jack donkey brayed a long love call for a jenny. But even over this low din, he could still hear the echoes of Altha's beautiful soft voice wafting through the crisp air. The infernal voice of hers haunted him and unreconciled memories of the troubled marriage with the songstress flooded through his mind. *Damn that bitch,* he thought as he cringed in his hiding spot and watched and listened at the familial scene unfolding. *We'll just see how happy she's going to be to see me.*

Suddenly Beck spotted one of the Anderson brothers making his way toward the cabin. Manson, he thought it was. *Now where's that other one?* he nervously wondered. The Anderson sibling was toting a rifle over his shoulder and could be seen halting at Altha's side and stooping down to tease the baby. Directly though, the old man came out of the house, and before Beck knew it, the two Anderson men were hoofing off side-by-side in the direction of the river with shooting irons in hand. Correctly guessing that they were going off hunting, he settled back down and continued the surveillance as his confidence level grew. Of course, Beck had no knowledge of the demise of Altha's mother and brother, Jesse. So he worried that one or both of them might still be inside, and he nervously searched the landscape for the other family members. But after a long spell of sitting, seething, and stressing, his patience wore thin, and Beck finally decided to make his move. Even in his current poor condition, he felt certain that he could deal with the other missing Andersons if they happened to show up.

"Well now, don't ye look something," Beck said in a low, deliberate, taunting tone.

Altha was so startled that she gave a slight jump. Turning quickly from her weaving work, she sought the culprit who had sneaked up from behind and given her such a fright. As soon as her eyes landed on the wretched creature smiling so demonically at her, a convulsion rushed through her body, and she sprung up from her hard seat. Instantly a blood-curdling scream to greet her wayward husband, Sam Beck, issued from her quivering mouth. Even he was stunned into panic. Then after recovering his wits about him, the hideous stalker took a hunting knife from under his belt and set upon Altha with cat-like quickness. He was riled up good now, and the increased flow of blood and adrenalin helped overcome the debilitating physical effects of his injuries.

"One more sech outburst, and ye're done fer, ye hear me bitch!" he yelled in her face as he held the point of the knife threateningly close to her chest. A nervous glance toward the cabin door reassured him that there was no threat from those quarters—yet.

Altha tried to back away from Beck. But he grabbed the terrified girl roughly by the hair and pulled her back to him with a violent yank.

"Ahhh! Ahhh!" she cried out loudly, reacting instinctively to the sudden shot of intense pain emanating from her scalp.

"I said, shet up, God damn ye! Ye never would take yer orders from me, would ye, bitch? Nary time would ye obey what I tolt ye!" He still held the long-bladed weapon mere inches from her bosom as he seized her around the neck in a choke hold with the other hand. The haunting stare that burned into her frightened innocent eyes began to scan across her face and down her body, taking in the woman's delightful features. Beck moved the glistening blade up to her trembling lips and began running its fine point slowly around her mouth, brushing it against the delicate skin. "Plumb fergot jest how tasty ye ere, Altha. Might go as fer to allow I missed ye ever now and again. Reckon ye longed fer me too, ain't that so, girl?" Unexpectedly, the blood gushing through his loins had aroused a pent-up desire to have this beautiful woman again. Beck had to admit to himself that the bitch was beautiful. He had forgotten just how pleasurable she could be and how good she could make him feel.

Altha was terrified and knew what evil lurked deep inside her scamp husband, such a miserable specimen of a human being if ever there was one. "No! Leave us alone, Sam. You had your chance, and you abandoned us. I've got myself another man now." As soon as the words were out of her mouth, she regretted the mention of another man in her life.

While still clutching the lethal weapon Beck loosed the other hand from Altha's neck and slapped her hard across the face. He then snatched the addled girl again by the top of her dress where it closed snuggly around the neck and pulled her sharply back to him. "Says ye gotcha 'nuther man, do ye? Well, where be he now, bitch?" Beck had already ciphered out that Basil would not have returned from Georgia yet. Still, he glanced around nervously for any threatening signs. "Don't see him 'bout no whurs. He be off to the Georgia country, ye reckon?" Then he rared back and smacked Altha again for good measure.

Altha's vision was blurred, and her blood curdled from the sheer fear of this man and his hateful purpose that day. Somehow he had learned that

Basil was out of the country. *But how? How could he have known?* Altha wondered. She was agonizing over her dilemma when Beck suddenly and literally jerked her out of her musing spell and over to the cradle, where Rufus was happily jabbering and dribbling.

"So I reckon this be my son," he said as he looked down upon the child, so content and so naïve. "Well, I'll be. He's got my shock of gold hair, he sure 'nough does. Why I do declare, look at them purty blue eyes of his'n. He's got his father's eyes, Altha, now don't ye reckon?" Beck turned from Rufus and peered directly at Altha to see what she had to allow about his perceptive observations.

Altha did not rightly know what she ought to allow to Beck. But she knew she allowed one thing, and that was Beck was not going to have this baby—only over her cold dead body would he take Rufus from her. Then a rage of defiance arose within Altha, and she summoned the courage to confront this wicked man who had fathered her son.

"He's not your son, Sam. You forsook us and left, remember. He's mine, my son, and that's just the way it's going to be." Altha paused for a few seconds trying to understand the words that had formed in her mind and that she had spoken so hastily. Undaunted and satisfied and growing more feisty as the seconds ticked by, she continued. "Rufus' natural father does not exist. Hear me? That man deserted him before he was born. He's got another father now that cares for him and that cares for me. When Basil gets back, he'll show you what's what. He's a real man, Sam. He's not the likes of you, the likes of the devil himself."

And that was all it took to push this devil off the edge. The fanatical Beck lost complete control of his emotions and mental processes. He was a sick, flawed man, and he had been pushed beyond his ability to understand and to reason and to cope. Altha had not changed one damned bit, he had discovered. She still resisted his every wish and his every command. The bitch would not listen, would not obey him atall. But not only that, now she was literally defying him. He would not tolerate it. He would not allow her to take his son from him. How dare she flaunt another man in his face. He would have no more of it, no more atall.

So with a furious, wild look on his face and a primal guttural grunt, Beck thrust the lethal blade straight into Altha's heart with all the strength he could muster. The mother's eyes bulged wide open with terror. Blood spewed forth from her wound as if from a fount, raining down on sweet little Rufus. Brutally and crazily, Sam Beck pushed the weapon deeper and deeper and twisted it until the lovely young woman slumped to the ground at his feet and gasped desperately for her final breaths.

Then the loom fell forever silent at the Crab Orchard. And the bucolic quietness of the countryside returned, broken only by a blood-drenched baby's hysterical cries and the lonesome bray of a jackass.

Chapter 27

Snatched

On December eighteenth, the team of East Fork drovers pulled up to Deaver's store at Forks of Pigeon to deliver the Colonel's supplies. It had taken them more than a month to make the round trip, and every highlander in the bunch was tired, foot worn, and mighty grateful to be back in their mountain homeland. Basil discovered that the Colonel was out and Columbus Hartgrove had apparently been left in charge of the businesses. Come to find out, Deaver had gone off to the Lenoir boarding school to fetch Julia home for the Christmas holidays.

Hartgrove's nervous demeanor immediately revealed that something was wrong. Basil spotted it easily. Usually the mountaineer was laid back and exhibited an air of casual assurance that had an easing effect on those around him. But on this occasion, Hartgrove appeared to be an entirely different man. When Basil began to offer a few details about the prices he had received at the Augusta market, Columbus abruptly stopped him.

"Holt up, Basil. We can talk 'bout them things later. I'm afeared I've got some awful bad news fer ye. Let's move over here where it's a mite quieter," Hartgrove said as he stepped with Basil away from the noisy store's entrance where the exhausted drovers were congregated, all of them hooting and hollering and carrying on a sight.

"What's the matter, Columbus?"

The two of them stood alone near one of the crackling fireplaces. Hartgrove's look was solemn and his speech sober. He reached up and placed a hand on Basil's broad shoulder and began with an unusual hesitancy, "It's 'bout Altha and the boy—Rufus." Then Columbus paused for a moment racking his brain for the right words, the best way to deliver the dreadful message. But nothing soothing or clever easily came to mind and he blundered on, "Altha's dead, Basil. She got herself killed."

Dumbfounded for a second Basil straightened his body up tall. He was unsure he had heard correctly and needed further clarification. Glaring directly back at Hartgrove, Basil asked, "What? Altha's dead? What are you saying, Columbus?"

Removing his one hand from Basil's shoulder, Hartgrove then tucked it and his other deep into his britches' pockets. He was sorry that this unpleasant task was his to carry out and that he was such an incompetent bearer of the distressing news. Had to be done though, and Hartgrove felt compelled to put it all out there at once for Basil to hear. "Altha was kilt a week or so back, Basil. 'Twas by Sam Beck, we 'spect. He ketched her alone at the Orchard cabin and stabbed a knife into her." Hartgrove took a pause and waited to get Basil's reaction. The Master of the East Fork just stared incredulously at him with his mouth gaping open. Hartgrove decided to continue. "She's done been buried, Basil. Had to! Couldn't wait no longer fer ye, as her body was deteriating bad. Josiah placed the body with her mother and Jesse at the schoolhouse site. We all figgered that would be yer desire. Ye don't have nary objection, do ye?"

Basil's mind raced to divine some sense out of Hartgrove's confusing words. Emotions raged within him as huge tear globules welled in his eyes. Thoughts of revenge against that God-damned Sam Beck began to formulate and drown out his sanity. *Beck is going to pay for this*, he thought to himself as an intense fury began to burn hotter and hotter inside. Basil was confounded and shocked and consequently did not have ready questions for Hartgrove. But as he wiped away the tears streaming down his face, he was able to murmur, "No, Columbus. No objection atall. That's fine."

"That ain't all, I'm afeared, Basil," the reluctant bearer of bad tidings continued. "The boy's gone missing too. Beck snatched him up, we 'spect, and ain't nobody seen 'im."

Basil was tired and hurting and seething mad, and it took a second or two for this latest bombshell to register. Instant rage inflated every cell of his body and Hartgrove could see it in his eyes. Basil thought of the warning he had given to Beck at Green River. Obviously it had gone unheeded. The man had gone too far and was going to pay dearly for it now. With fury boiling from within and rage glaring out of his eyes, Basil stared fiercely at Hartgrove and simply replied, "Well then, we'll just have to go get him back, now won't we?"

Hartgrove could certainly appreciate Basil's reaction. However, the look and the tone—the way Basil pronounced his intention—concerned Hartgrove who quickly interjected, "The sheriff's been involved, and a posse rode up to the heads of both forks, but ain't nobody seen 'em. Listen here, Basil, go talk with Josiah and cipher on what ye aim to do. Ye don't need to go off half-cocked on yer own to find him. The Colonel will be back tomorrow. Come git me, and I'll ride with ye to search fer the boy—Christmas or no Christmas."

Basil was not up to more debate on the matter. He knew his neighbor was trying to be helpful, and for that he was thankful. But he had to get up to the Orchard and check things out for himself. The manner in which he replied to Hartgrove demonstrated a finality to the conversation, "Thanks, Columbus. I'll ponder on it." Then he turned away from Hartgrove but almost immediately spun back around. "Listen, Columbus, I can appreciate how difficult this must have been for you. I'm truly grateful for what you did—and more grateful for having you as a friend. Thanks for the advice. I'll cipher on it."

Basil took his leave from Hartgrove and stalked over to where the drovers were still cavorting. Gathering the team around him he thanked them all—slaves and tenant boys—for their loyal hard service and paid each of the white boys the balance of their wages plus a bonus of three dollars for their efforts. After hastily settling things up, he hurried outside, mounted Fashion, and rode off at a brisk gallop up the East Fork.

By the time Basil reached the Crab Orchard farm, it was almost dark and getting colder by the minute. He rode directly over to the schoolhouse, and upon finding Altha's fresh gravesite, he fell to his knees on the frozen ground and erupted into a crying hysteria. "Why? Why, God, have you done this? She was so good!" For several minutes, he shouted and vented into the dusky night with the howling East Fork wind vying to muffle his irate cries out to God. Angry challenges and admonitions eventually gave way to pleaful prayers for guidance and direction. For more than half an hour, Basil emptied his heart of the loving, tender feelings it held for the young woman he had dreamed of marrying and sharing his life with. Only the onset of darkness and freezing temperature drove him away from Altha's grave. Reluctantly rising and casting a final sad look back at the mound of earth where his true love was interred, he left the spot a broken and bitter young man.

Upon approaching the Anderson cabin, Basil could see firelight bleeding through gaps in the window shutters and barely make out the whisks of whitish-gray smoke rising from the chimney. He noticed Altha's still and silent loom outside in the weather as he gave the shut door a heavy knock. *Bam, bam, bam!* "Josiah—it's Basil! It's me, Basil!"

It only took a few seconds for the door to swing open. There in the doorway the pitiful Josiah Anderson stood, all stooped over with a pathetic forlorn look on his face. And it was obvious to Basil that his tenant had resorted to the cider barrel for comfort.

"Come in, Edmunston," Josiah invited. "Guess ye heared by now about Altha and Rufus," he muttered as they took seats by the fire.

Basil sat with his tenant in the dimly-lit cabin, and they exchanged sorrowful condolences and grieved as one. This essential mourning process took some time, but after a while Basil felt himself prepared and ready to hear more sordid details of the affair. He asked Josiah to tell him everything that had happened. The old man hesitated for a moment and instead of recounting the terrible story, he stepped over to the dining table and took up a small piece of ragged paper lying on it. It was just a small scrap that was badly creased with a crude note scribbled over the wrinkles and tears.

"I found this under the door yestidy morning," Josiah allowed.

Basil held it up to the firelight and was barely able to decipher the writing and make out the message:

edmonton –
you pay me $1,500 and you can have the boy.
be at the top of devil's face rock on henderson line at noon dec. 23.
if there be a posse or more than one man with you the boy will be kiled.
no law!

Completely blown away, the astonished Basil wondered aloud, "How low can this man get? Kill him? Beck says he aims to kill his own son. Unbelievable!" With his mouth gaping open and his head shaking from side to side, Basil looked toward Josiah.

Anderson responded, "It's not nary a threat neither. He'll do it, son. Mark my word. He'll do it."

Basil had no doubts about it either. He sat with Josiah and reviewed the details of the murder and kidnapping. Josiah allowed that the sheriff had questioned all the folk living on the East and West Forks, including Beck's people, and no one offered a clue to the wife-murdering kidnapper's whereabouts. But now, Basil had the extortion note. It provided the information he needed to find Beck and get Rufus back. And there were clear instructions not to involve the law. He was not about to. He was resolved to do this alone. It was now a personal matter between himself and Beck—and Rufus.

Luckily, the market trip had infused Basil with sufficient cash to afford the fifteen hundred dollars ransom Beck was asking for. Of course, it was his father's money, but in this situation he had no doubts that Thomas would take his note for the money. There were serious doubts running through Basil's head that Beck actually meant to return Rufus. The boy was just a little innocent pawn caught in the middle, and there was no telling what moves Beck would make with him. Basil had a strong notion that it was all a sinister plan to ambush him in the remoteness surrounding the Devil's Face Mountain.

Beck was an evil, wicked man—of that Basil was assured. He was not going to underestimate the man again. In Basil's way of thinking, there were only two ways about the thing. Either Beck was going to kill him, or he was going to kill that low-life miserable scamp.

Basil and Columbus Hartgrove were in agreement that it was going to be a risky mission to retrieve Rufus from Sam Beck's clutches. The Master of the East Fork had sought out Hartgrove's advice on the matter at the neighbor's place, which was located on the Pigeon River a short distance below Deaver's store. Although Hartgrove was extremely sympathetic to Basil and his personal state of affairs, he did not readily offer up a body of encouragement.

"He's up there jest laying fer ye, Basil. From that devil rock, he'll be a watching ye come up the trail from a mile away. Can't see Beck letting ye leave there alive with the boy neither," Hartgrove pessimistically suggested as he shook his head.

Basil weighed in. "Columbus, I believe Beck's got himself in a real bind now. After what he did to Altha, he knows he'll never be able to show his face again in Haywood or any county in these parts. The law is bound to hound him until he's found and hanged by the neck. He'll have no choice but to vacate this country and head somewhere—like the western territories where the law can't reach him. But even a man like him—do you think he would actually kill his own son?"

"Ain't no doubt, I believe, that he'll kill him. Beck don't want that boy nary bit. He's likely to jest throw him over a cliff fer the wolves and bears to eat. After what ye did to him at Green River, all he keers now is to get back at ye—and ain't goin' be a fair fight neither. He'll take great pains to see to that."

Basil was listening intently and trying to assimilate what he was hearing. Bits and pieces of plans were racing around in his head but that was all there was, just bits and pieces. He still had not gathered enough information nor made the necessary conclusions to devise a coherent strategy to get Rufus back. But before he could offer additional ideas to their conversation or went any further, Hartgrove interrupted his weighty thoughts.

"So, what ye figger? What ye aim to do?" Columbus asked and after hesitating for only a blink of an eye continued, "Ye gotta go, Basil, if ye ever want to see the boy alive agin. Ye gotta go ater him. And I don't aim to leave ye go alone. I'll go with ye!"

Basil was greatly touched by Hartgrove's noble offer. Yet, he held a vivid memory of a recent time when a tenant neighbor had been recruited to ride in support of another one of his adventurous undertakings. And he had brought that man's corpse back to a grieving family. Hartgrove had a wife and young son, and the last thing Basil intended was to add to the population of widows and orphans in Forks of Pigeon. If anyone knew the danger involved in going after Sam Beck, it was this astute farmer he sat with—the same man who had served the Edmunstons so well as their former overseer. Basil had nowhere else to turn for help, but he could not take Columbus with him, no doubt about it. There was no way he could do that.

"No. Won't hear of it," Basil firmly said.

"I ain't asking ye to take me along, Basil. I aim to go, no matter. Yer father treated me well. Ye're as good a man as he is—can tell that already—and ye're a friend. 'Sides, I thought an awful lot of Altha—liked her a sight. I'm going! Don't want to hear no more 'bout it."

"Columbus, it's too dangerous—"

Hartgrove threw his hands up, pointed a finger in Basil's face, and said about as sternly and directly as can be said, "No! No more, I said. Now let's get down to business. It's going take us a good day of riding to get to the devil rock. So I reckon that means we'll need to set out early morning on the day 'fore the twenty-third."

The two determined men plotted and strategized about the trip for a good two hours more. They discussed the mission's necessities, logistics, and especially the tactical options that might be employed against Beck. Before their meeting broke off, they reached firm conclusions on these topics and, most importantly, were of one mind about the overriding strategic goal—getting Rufus back alive.

Chapter 28

The Devil's Business

The Devil's Face Mountain, or devil's rock as Hartgrove and most of the other locals called it, did indeed have a sinister look about it. Early pioneers and settlers that encountered the craggy mountain face—and there were very few who ventured to this extremely remote place—were able to discern from its rocky profile the features of the lord of Hades himself. Even ancient Cherokee Indian lore held that mysterious creatures inhabited the various caves that pocked the mountain's exposed vertical cliffs. The sheer outcropping topped out at almost six thousand feet above the seas and towered some three thousand feet higher than the rocky farming land surrounding Bachelor's Den. Although the mountain was only nine miles or so from the Den, as a crow flies, Basil and Columbus Hartgrove faced a grueling ride of more than twenty-five miles to reach it.

The twenty-second day of December was a blustery cold one with light snow falling and beginning to lay a powdery white coat over the ground. The morning sky offered only gloomy gray light for the two horsemen as they plodded along, bundled in heavy wool overcoats and felt hats pulled down low over their brows. Basil and Columbus rode their horses towards the Devil's Face Mountain along a treacherous wagon path that led them up the headwaters of the West Fork River. It was an extraordinarily steep grade twisting and turning and crossing the river countless times as it rose higher and higher up the mountain.

The men intended to follow this wagon path to the crest of the range that parts the Pigeon and French Broad River drainage basins. At the summit, where the road plunged back downward into another unsettled wilderness beyond, they would quit the rutted trace and veer onto an old Indian trail that wound along the high divide. It was no wonder, the two men held, that Sam Beck chose such a damnable wild place to hide out from the law and other persons he had run afoul with. Few men had enough will or gumption to make the extreme effort and sacrifice to seek him out there.

"He's not in that hell hole alone. He'll have company, he will," Hartgrove commented as he bent forward and close to the horse's head on a steep slope in the wagon path.

"Why do you believe that, Columbus?" Basil asked, although he had a good notion why.

"Ain't very friendly country for one man alone to survive in. Once you git in, it's jest as hard to git out. So's it'd take two of em or more to get in food and water supplies for them and the horses. 'Spect Beck has got a horse with him, don't ye?"

"Yeah, I 'spect so. Don't see how he could get by without one. Say, Columbus, you realize, don't you, if Beck has a passel of allies with guns then we've had it?"

"That won't be no good atall." Hartgrove added. "Might even need this long rifle the Colonel lent me. What ye think, Basil? Don't ye reckon with these pistols and rifles of our'n we can hold our own with a couple of 'em?"

"Reckon so, Columbus, as long as we don't let ourselves get ambushed. It won't do to get careless," Basil offered up while hunching down low into the fierce cold wind.

By late afternoon and with the snow falling harder, Basil and Hartgrove finally reached the gap in the mountain range where the road began its steep descent down the other side. At that juncture they departed the trace and took a narrow, little-used trail that led along the mountain ridges toward the devil's rock, some four or five miles distant. The howling wind gusts and ever-deepening deposits of freezing snow made the going treacherous. In order to advance along some stretches where the precarious shelves were narrow with precipitous drop-offs, they were forced to dismount and walk, leading their horses behind them. Walking and riding and shuffling through the snow, they approached within a mile or so of their destination when darkness made further progress too dangerous.

The two men were able to locate a rocky overhang to camp under where only the windborne snow had a chance of reaching them. After the horses were cared for, Basil and Columbus built a small fire to warm by and then wolfed down some cold food they had packed.

"If it don't let up none, we're goin' have a bad time gitting off this mountain tomorrow," Hartgrove allowed as he slurped down some branch water and savored his next bite of bacon.

"'Spect so, Columbus. Say, I've been thinking. Suppose you should lay back behind tomorrow in case Beck and his friends—if he's not alone—aim to ambush us? Don't want to give them more than one easy target to shoot at."

"Been ciphering on it too. With this here weather I doubt he's seen us coming yet. So Beck may not know there's two of us. Ye may be right, Basil. I'll hang back a good two hunderd yards or so."

Something else was bothering Basil. "How the hell are we supposed to find him, anyhow? Don't want to shoot my gun off as a signal. That way he could storm right up and put an end to me while I reload. Maybe he'll fire a signal." Basil speculated.

"Maybe so. It's a big mountain. But you can ride right up on that rocky devil's head, and I'd 'spect he'll be waiting some'rs 'bout there fer ye. This is the devil's business, Basil. It shur 'nough is."

"Yeah, probably so," Basil confirmed. He was weary and fighting off uncontrollable urges to drop off to sleep. It had not been that long ago since he was bushwhacked in the middle of the night during a sound sleep, so he made a suggestion to Columbus, "I'd feel better if we slept in turns tonight, Columbus. Let's one of us stay awake and on guard against a surprise visit from Beck. He's a desperate man and there's no telling what he's libel to do."

"'Spect that's a good idee, Basil. I'll take the first watch. Go ahead and git yerself some sleep. Ye're goin to need it."

At about this same time a mile or so away in a cave that had eroded out of the devil's rock eons ago, Sam Beck and a cohort sat by their own fire and plotted. Rufus, the poor little boy, lay wrapped in a blanket on the freezing cold, bare-rock floor of the cavern, away from both the men and the fire. The boy, who was not yet able to walk, was shivering cold, frightened, and almost starved to death. He had cried himself out and longed to see what he was never going to see again—his mother's familiar, loving face.

The straw-headed Beck cackled as he and the other man strategized for the morrow's meeting. Beck's nose, which had been severely broken in the fight with Basil, was now permanently disfigured and hideous to look at. His collaborator was a little older than Beck, thirty-five or thereabouts, and not quite so tall. However, he was muscular and strongly built. From the looks of him, he obviously could take care of himself. These two men had bumped into each other from time to time, as they both prowled the Henderson County country in search of ardent spirits, unfortunate females, and a good time. Altha was by no means the only girl Beck had ravaged, and it was not the first time that he had used the wilderness around the Devil's Face Mountain to lay low and hide out from creditors and cuckolded men.

Beck had come up with the idea—this scheme to extort money in exchange for his own son. His partner, although strong and able-bodied, was slow of mind. The man had been enticed by the offer of one hundred dollars cash money from the fruits of the extortion plot, payable only upon a successful outcome. Beck had not bothered to tell his cohort that the price he was demanding for Rufus was a staggering fifteen hundred dollars, about as much as a first-rate negro slave was worth.

"Okay, I tell you what, Israel. I want ye to ride out yonder tomorrow about eleven o'clock and meet Edmunston on the trail 'fore he gits here. Don't ye worry none that he ain't coming. He'll be there fer sure. Ain't got nary doubts 'bout it. Now ye can tell him ye're my mediator or some sech thing," said Beck.

The co-conspirator, whose given name was Israel, replied, "What's that again, Sam? Tell him I'm ye're what?"

"Damn it, Israel! Ye know. Tell him that ye're my go-between and that ye have a message from me."

"Yeah, right. Okay, I got it. What's the message I'm supposed to give him anyhow?"

Beck thought for a minute or so to come up with a message that would be simple enough for Israel to understand and communicate.

"Okay, I want ye to say something like this to him. 'Don't want no trouble, Edmunston. All we want is the money. We'll jest have us a peaceable exchange of the boy fer the money.' Tell him that and then lead him—or he may have someone else with him—so ye can lead them both back to me, you hear? Got it, Israel? And if there are more than two of 'em, fire off yer gun to signal me! "

Deep down, Beck did not relish another battle with Edmunston, or at least anything that resembled a fair fight. The gratifying memory of the knife blade cutting deep into his former wife and her last moments had satisfied his bloodlust for the time being. Though if he could somehow get the drop on Edmunston, he would sooner shoot the interloper boyfriend than look at him. But the money was essential, and he could not afford for the plan to go afoul.

It was all about the money. He needed it to escape to new environs where he could maybe get hold of some public land and make a new start of things. Beck had made an absolute mess of his life so far and it was getting far too hot in the Carolinas for his comfort. He desperately needed the money to make a go of it out West.

"Peaceable, huh. You want to do this thing peaceable—since when, Sam?"

"I want to do it peaceable until I get my hands on that money. After that, if one or other of us gets the drop on Edmunston, let's do away with him—and that boy too."

"Sounds more like it. Ye still aim to do away with the boy?" Israel coolly questioned after Beck had baited his thirst for blood.

"Makes no nevermind to me. He'll just git in the way after we kill Edmunston. Might as well throw him to the bottom of this hellish place. If the fall don't kill him, ain't nobody knows how to git down there to git him, 'cept'n the bears."

"What if he's got some'ns with him? What you aim to do then?"

"Ye're right. Edmunston likely brung someone else with him. Ain't no man in his right mind that'd come out here into this God-forsaken territory alone. But I tolt em in the note that if there be more than two come after the boy, then the boy will be kilt. That's why I want ye to shoot the signal. But Edmunston ain't nary that stupid. He's had a hankering something awful fer that bitch wife of mine—damn her to hell—and the boy. I kin tell ye fer sure now, he aims to get the boy out alive."

"So, if'n there be two of em, what then?" a confused Israel asked again.

"Both us'ns will have guns, won't we? Soon as the baby is give over to Edmunston, he'll be distracted, got it? I'll pull my pistol from a hiding place and shoot Edmunston while he has a'holt of the boy. And ye can take keer of the other'n. It'll be as easy as that, Israel. Got it all thought out in here," Beck concluded tapping his forefinger against the side of his head so the dim-witted Israel would know where all that knowledge was stored. He was proud of himself for having concocted such an ingenious strategy.

But Israel was not entirely convinced that it was a foolproof plan, and he had some trepidation about his own role in the business. "Well, I just hope that other'n won't be much good with a gun. I'm not that fast at the pull and shoot."

Chapter 29

A Goner fer Sure

In the note Beck left at the Andersons' cabin door, he established noon as the time he wanted to transact his dirty business. Basil and Hartgrove were less than two miles away and had planned to leave their encampment twenty or thirty minutes before the set time. That would give them ample time to ride up to the mountain top and find where Beck lurked. To their surprise, as they were saddling up and checking the weapons, a stranger approached down the trail.

It was Beck's co-conspirator, Israel. The stranger pulled to a quick halt when he saw them and bellowed out loudly, "Hello there, men. Ary one of ye be Edmunston?" inquired Israel.

Basil and Columbus were already anxious, but this surprise intrusion raised their nerves to the utmost level. Being naturally wary of the shady character, they instinctively felt for the pistols under their belts.

"I'm Edmunston. Who's asking?" Basil called back.

The underling rode over closer and began relaying the message from Beck, just as he had been told to. "Holt on there now, fellers. Ain't no need to draw them there pistols. Sam Beck sent me as his go-between, he said. He says that he wants the business done peaceable like. All he keers 'bout is yer money. The boy don't mean nuthin' atall to him, he says. Wants ye to have the boy, Edmunston. So foller me, why don't ye, so's I kin take ye to him."

Basil and Hartgrove gave each other questioning looks. It all sounded too easy. Twitching with suspicion, Basil replied skeptically, "Peaceable-like, huh. Don't sound like the Beck I know. How many of you are there, anyway?"

"Jest me and Beck. I'll swear on my mother's grave to it. Ain't no more of you'ns, is they?"

"No, we're alone," Basil answered. He glanced over at Hartgrove who gave him an approving nod and then continued, "Give us a few minutes to finish up here, and we'll follow behind you."

The early winter storm had stopped, and the sky was a brilliant dark blue with the sun shining brightly overhead. It was cold, very cold, and the snow glistened white and sparkly as the sunlight bounced off the tiny ice crystals. The scraggly dormant trees, black balsams, and shrubs that grew on the mountain top were enveloped in a layer of shimmering rime that was beginning to melt from the sun's penetrating rays. Basil, Columbus, and Beck's collaborator, Israel, made the precarious approach to the top of the devil's rock on horseback. Soon, far ahead of them, they could see Beck waiting impatiently with Rufus apparently wrapped up in a little bundle at his feet.

Beck was standing on top of the sheer rock bald which the oldtimers perceived as the head of the devil. The smooth rock surface on which he stood was only about fifty yards wide and no more than thirty deep. Behind him and to his sides, the bald rock head curved gradually downward until it abruptly transitioned into sheer bluffs with a scattering of protuberances. These irregularities were envisioned by the earliest pioneers as the eyes, ears, nose, and chin of the devil himself. The rock face of the devil was indeed threatening in many respects, but the man who was now standing at its peak was even more scary and menacing, Basil believed.

When the three men on horseback were within shouting range of Beck he hollered out for them to halt. Waiting until he saw his order had been obeyed, he then called out to his henchman to come and get further directions. So Israel rode over to Beck, they chatted briefly, and then Israel returned with the new instructions.

"Says he'll make the transfer of the boy fer the money with Edmunston on top of the rock where he's standing. To prove he's unarmed he wants this gentleman to first come over and give him a good search," the henchman explained as he nodded toward Columbus Hartgrove. "At the same time the gentleman can take a look see at the boy to make sure he's still alive. Then the gentleman is to come back here with me while Edmunston goes over yonder to Beck to exchange the money fer the boy. I'll have to check you fer weapons first," he said nodding and looking at Basil, "and make sure you've got the money. That's 'bout the size of it, men. Sound okay to you'ns?"

It was not exactly how Basil or Hartgrove had worked out in their minds this exchange would play out. Yet they could not readily find fault with the plan nor did they have better ideas. "What do you think, Columbus?" Basil asked.

"Don't rightly see another better way of doing it. But I want to keep my pistol with me when I go yonder to check Beck," Hartgrove replied.

They queried Israel about this conditional requirement, and he promptly rode over close to Beck on the rock and verified that Hartgrove could keep his gun. Beck instructed Israel loud enough for all the men to hear. "Ain't no problem if'n Edmunston agrees to let you holt a gun on him, jest in case. Jest tell that there man to come on so's we can git this over with." Beck was certain that upright men like these two he was dealing with would never attempt anything unscrupulous or try to take an advantage over him—being an unarmed man and all.

Basil reluctantly agreed to be held at gunpoint and while he and Beck's cohort laid back, Hartgrove rode over to the devil's rock, climbed up onto its surface, and walked slowly across the trampled snow to where Beck stood some fifteen yards away. Columbus checked the man over good and discovered no concealed weapons anywhere on his body. He picked Rufus up and ascertained that the boy was still alive, although the child had literally turned blue from the freezing weather. Rufus showed no signs of bruising or other ill effects that Hartgrove could detect. After gently placing the boy back down on the ground and making sure he was wrapped against the cold, Hartgrove thoroughly inspected the surroundings and hunted for anything suspicious lying about in the snow. There was nothing out of the ordinary that he could ascertain, and definitely there were no weapons to be found. He only noticed the tracks of packed-down snow from Beck's and Israel's and now his stomping feet. Within ten minutes time he made his search and returned to the spot where Basil and Israel remained on their horses.

"Couldn't find nary thing atall hidden away. It looks safe enough I reckon, Basil. Good luck and git this damn devil's business over with quick-like, ye hear," a nervous Hartgrove urged.

"I will, Columbus," Basil answered as he handed his pistol and rifle over to Hartgrove. Israel searched Basil for more weapons and checked his saddlebags where he found fifteen hundred dollars' worth of bank notes stashed in a sack.

"He's clean and has got the money with him," a puzzled and tense Israel hollered out at the top of his lungs to Beck. The underling had not expected to see so much ransom money and figured he would have some settling up to do with Beck once this dirty business was transacted.

"Okay, Edmunston. Come on!" Beck yelled back.

Basil retraced Columbus Hartgrove's path to the devil's rock while busily making mental preparations for disabling Beck's co-conspirator and then going back after Beck himself. He had no intentions of leaving the mountain top as long as a breath of life remained in that son-of-a-bitch wife killer. But first things first though–he had to retrieve Rufus and make sure he transferred the boy safely into Hartgrove's care.

After tying off Fashion to a scrubby branch, Basil climbed up and walked out on the snow-covered rock surface of the devil's head. He approached Beck cautiously with the sackful of money. Beck bent over slowly, not taking his eyes off Basil, and picked Rufus up out of the snow. The two men glowered at each other as they prepared to exchange paper banknotes for an eight-month-old baby. *This was the devil's work all right,* Basil thought to himself not appreciating the irony of the notion. The two men moved to within arms' length of each other. Basil released his grip on the money bag, and at the same time took a firm hold of Rufus, bringing him close and kissing his cold blue face. For a moment, a brief moment, Basil felt a surge of comforting relief course through his body.

"See, Edmunston. Peaceable and simple as that," the evil man muttered confidently with a feigned smile.

Basil was seething inside and trying hard to keep his cool. But he hated Beck and all that the no-good scamp stood for. The opportunity to slander the man was there for the taking, and Basil unwisely yielded to his inner demons. In reply to Beck he uttered the first thing that came to mind. "That nose of yours is a sight more crooked than the last time I saw you, Beck."

The smile on Beck's face quickly transformed into a smirk, and he countered with a sneering reply, "Think ye're something, don't ye?"

Basil simply ignored him. As he was turning to walk away with Rufus, he saw out of the corner of his eye Beck lunging down to the ground. Buried under the packed snow in a rock crevice was a loaded pistol that Israel and Beck had concealed there. Hartgrove's diligent efforts had failed to find it. Hurriedly Beck took up the gun and pointed it directly at Basil's chest only a few feet away.

With Rufus still in his clutches, Basil was slow to react. Before he was able to make a move in defense, Beck pulled the trigger. At the very same moment that Basil heard Hartgrove's belated warning cry he flinched as Beck tried to fire the weapon. But there was no thundering report from the gun. He did not feel an impact or the pain of a lead ball smashing and ripping through his chest cavity. Strangely, he felt nothing atall. It took but fractions of a second for these considerations to rush through Basil's head before it dawned on him that Beck's gun had misfired.

How lucky can you be? he thought, as he hastily but delicately pitched Rufus into a pile of soft snow. *The gunpowder in the pan must have gotten wet buried under the snow,* he surmised. And that was exactly what had happened. Basil's God, always distant and elusive, had deflected a mortal attempt on his life. An additional indeterminate amount of life had been granted him for unknown reasons. A manner of reprieve it was. And Basil determined to take full advantage of such providential intervention. Still not believing his good fortune, he braced for the charging Beck who was coming straight at him like an angry bull.

Columbus Hartgrove had watched the incident from afar and had not been able to scream out to Basil in time to warn him. Beck's co-conspirator,

Israel, was privy to the plan, of course, and got the jump on Hartgrove. Both men were still on horseback and separated by less than ten feet. While the startled Hartgrove was calling out to Basil, Israel calmly leveled his own pistol at Hartgrove, aimed, and fired. There was no misfiring of Israel's gun, and Columbus could attest to that.

He had tried to duck down and away from his adversary's aim but had not moved fast enough or far enough. The lead ball grazed the right side of his face, breaking a cheek bone and ripping his ear away. There was sufficient force of impact to knock Columbus off of his horse, and he fell heavily and awkwardly to the snow-covered ground. Realizing that Hartgrove was not mortally wounded, Israel reached for his long rifle. He cried out oaths and swore aloud that he would put an end to this damned man with the next shot.

Reminiscent of their previous encounter at the Green River, Basil and Beck crashed down onto the hard rock surface and commenced to wrestling and rolling around in the snow in each other's death grasps. Like two male lions with their teeth and claws bared, they scratched and tore and bit into each other, breathing and roaring loudly while their wild hair flew about in every direction. First one and then the other would battle their way on top and try to land fist punches, but neither could gain enough separation or advantage to deliver an effective blow. Tumbling over and over, again and again, they slashed and tore into each other with their fingernails, tried to gouge out their rival's eyes, and used their teeth in attempts to bite off an ear or finger. With each and every tumble the two combatants moved perilously closer to the edge of the devil's bald head and the sheer drop into the wilderness abyss below.

All the while this horrendous brawl erupted and unfolded, the swaddled Rufus did not remain still. The tiny boy managed to squirm and worm himself free from his cocoon of wrappings and began to slowly crawl after Basil at the precipice's edge. Barefooted and dressed only in a light chemise and drawers Rufus valiantly twisted and wiggled his little frozen body toward the action. He was so pitifully cold and wanted only for Basil to pick him up again.

In the meantime, Hartgrove was in the gun battle of his life—actually his first gun battle. He had seen Israel going for the rifle as he tried to regain his footing. However he was addled and seemed to be blinded in one eye. The right side of his face felt like it was on fire, and the blood poured from the open wound. Amazingly, Columbus had managed to hold on to his own pistol during the fall. Basil's guns that he had been holding were jarred loose somewhere not readily obvious or visible to him. He kept his own pistol firmly in his grasp as he pulled himself off the ground by using his horse's stirrup. Although still stunned and confused, he had sufficient instinct and composure to seek cover behind his horse from Beck's partner. Israel was trying to maneuver on horseback to get Hartgrove in the sights of his long rifle but was having the dickens of a time doing it. His horse was skittish from the shooting, and the damned man he was trying to kill kept trying to hide behind a horse. All he could see were Hartgrove's legs. Israel figured he could not rightly waste his only shot on such an elusive target as he spurred his horse for a better position and open shot.

Back over on the devil's rock Basil and Beck fought to within mere feet of the rim of the cliff. Basil had leveraged his way on top and was attempting to strike a staggering blow against Beck's face but the man was able to shield himself and fend off the punches. Both of them grew extremely tired from their uncommon exertions, and it became almost impossible to keep up the combat. With every remaining ounce of energy in his body, Beck pulled Basil off of him, and once again they were in each other's clutches, wrestling and rolling and sliding still closer to the brim of the scarp. Rufus was continuing to move in that direction too—toward the verge of oblivion where Basil fought desperately for his life.

"Come out so's I kin shoot ye, damn ye," Israel shouted out to Hartgrove.

Columbus had too much on his mind to reply. He himself was frantically conniving to get close enough to his attacker to fire a fatal shot. His head throbbed with a terrible pain, and the bleeding had not let up. As the menacing man circled on his horse, Hartgrove in turn maneuvered his own horse as a screen, keeping it between the two gunfighters. After a minute or so of this tiresome wrangling, Columbus must have had an epiphany. Out of the confused chaos that engulfed him, an amazing inspiration for breaking the impasse popped into his head.

Deftly tucking his pistol under his belt, Hartgrove managed to extract the long rifle from its attachment loops on his horse's saddle without exposing himself. Working quickly he cocked the ponderous gun, held it up with one arm, took quick aim with his good eye, and fired in the general direction of the mounted conspirator. As intended, the loud report of the rifle startled Israel's horse, causing it to abruptly rear back on its hind legs for a brief moment. But those precious short seconds were what Columbus had counted on—all that he needed. As the horse's head suddenly jerked backward, Columbus leaped out from behind his own spooked mount and darted to within close range of his foe on the rearing horse. Before Israel could steady and align himself for the easy open shot, Columbus fired his own pistol directly at Israel's chest. The ball flew true and almost instantly stamped out the co-conspirator's life and his wicked dreams of gaining a quick dollar.

Back on top of the devil's bald head, Basil and Beck had managed to regain their upright postures, and each man was taking turns trying to beat the other senseless. They were both so exhausted and weak—Beck especially, who was still suffering from the debilitating injuries of his previous beating—that the force of their blows had little effect. Standing hunched over and facing each other at the extremity of the devil's head, they both paused for a brief moment and cast anxious glances over the edge into oblivion. Laboring with heaving breaths to suck in more oxygen they frantically continued to probe at each other for an opening or weakness.

By this time Hartgrove, heavily armed with Basil's loaded rifle and pistol, had hurried to the top of the rock. A goodly amount of blood was still flowing from his head wound, and the falling crimson droplets pocked the snow as he approached the brawling scene. Carefully, ever so carefully, he crept and skidded over to where Rufus tottered mere inches removed from the margin of death. After warily eying Basil and Beck, Columbus crouched down, grabbed Rufus, and pulled him away to safety.

In no time it seemed, Hartgrove deposited Rufus in a secure place and returned to face the belligerent warriors. He held his gun at the ready to shoot, while his head throbbed in pain, and he fought off the dizzying effects from his roaring ear cavity. Looking out of the one good eye, he meant to put an end to this fight here and now.

"That's 'nough, Beck! Get yer hands up, or I'll kill ye dead where ye stand," Columbus barked to the defiant scamp and pointed the long rifle at Beck's head. Beck stood within spitting distance of Basil and about that same distance from the edge of the cliff, or the very edge of life. Instantly the harsh realization hit him—*it was all up. It was over.* He was not going to get himself out of this mess now, nor was he going to get Edmunston's money. And that meant no fresh start for him. Surely he would face the hangman for murdering that bitch wife of his. *It was all her fault, though. She had brought it on herself. It was her fault. She was the cause of all of my problems. God damn her.*

And as Beck damned Altha and rationalized the overall nature of his current predicament, he could see that there were few options available to him. He had played out his kidnapping and extortion hand and had lost. It was over. There was only one thing to do. So in those brief seconds that he remained in Columbus Hartgrove's gun sights, he made up his mind how to end the thing.

Suddenly and unexpectedly, Beck gave out a loud screech and lunged directly toward Basil. The two men collided with a terrific impact, as the report of Hartgrove's gun thundered across the rocky mountain top. But Beck's momentum was not broken by the lead ball, and his flying tackle drove both him and Basil clear over the edge of the cliff.

"Nooooo!" Basil shouted, as he and Beck disappeared over the rocky face of the cliff into the abyss and the wilderness of trees and thickets far below. The stunned Columbus Hartgrove looked after them in absolute disbelief of what his eye, his one good eye, had witnessed. *Maybe there is still hope for Basil,* he thought as he crawled cautiously over to the edge of the sheer drop and peered over. What he saw made his stomach queasy and the tears well up in both his good eye and the bad one. It was a good hundred feet to the first vegetation-covered ledge and beyond that a drop of hundreds more to the base of the rock outcropping. *No,* a sobbing Columbus thought to himself as he backed away, *there is no hope atall that Basil could have survived such a fall. He's a goner fer sure.*

Chapter 30

Searching for Closure

Hartgrove was finally able to stem the flow of blood from the side of his head by packing snow against the wound. Then, by fashioning a papoose of sorts, he strapped Rufus to his back and began the long treacherous slog off of Devil's Face Mountain. When a West Fork farmer found him the next day wandering aimlessly along the river, death held both Columbus and Rufus in its stranglehold. One of the families thereabouts treated and dressed Hartgrove's wounds and gave Rufus some much-needed nourishment. Still stubbornly clinging to life, both of them were loaded into a wagon on Christmas morning and hauled down to the Deavers' at Forks of Pigeon.

It was a Christmas surprise unlike any other that Saint Nicholas delivered across the whole world on that Holy Day. The Colonel and his family, although indeed shocked, immediately swung into action. Doctor Allen was sent for to treat Hartgrove's severe head wound, and Julia herself took up the traumatized Rufus and began to care for the poor child as only a mother is accustomed.

The details of Basil's demise, as extracted from Hartgrove, were sketchy. Columbus had been certain that Basil could not have survived the fall. His report came as a horrific shock to everyone, especially Julia. Upon hearing the terrible news the beautiful young girl could not help herself from breaking down into a pitiful heaving and crying hysteria. The tragedy was far beyond her ability to cope. Her secret true love was now gone forever. And he—Basil—had never really comprehended the depths of her love for him.

After the break with Wade Hampton, she had tried, but failed, to explain to Basil her shameful actions. It was because of Basil that she had feigned a romance with the South Carolina gentleman. Basil was always the sweetheart in her romantic dreams. He held the lone key to her heart. She had loved him since that first furtive rendezvous at her father's mill. But due to her own stupidity and childish intrigues she had lost her true love to Altha. And it was all her own fault. Julia knew that. She had driven Basil away from her and into Altha's arms. *Now—now they say he is dead, and he will never know how much I loved him. What have I done?* a crying Julia grieved to herself.

It was a gloomy Christmas evening all around for the Deavers as they gathered in the sitting room adorned with greenery and assorted colorful decorations. The fire crackled and popped, and the aroma of roasting chestnuts filled the air. Hartgrove was no longer with them. Thankfully for him, he had been deemed fit enough to be taken to his own place to recuperate with his family. In the depths of deep depression, Julia sat in quiet distress, as she held Rufus close to her bosom and looked longingly at his sweet face. It was strange how she could see the likeness of Basil in the boy but none atall of Altha. Julia pressed her father to keep Rufus at the Forks until he was fully recovered or until the Andersons came to get him.

With Rufus in her deft clutches, Julia entertained fantastic thoughts of herself being held in Basil's own strong arms. He would hug her tight against his chest and kiss her with the sweetest kisses she could ever imagine. Julia could not get him out of her mind it seemed. She thought of her poor Basil lying all alone in the darkness of the mountain wilderness exposed to the elements. He was lifeless and defenseless and bared to the critters and nature's other voracious mechanisms for consuming flesh and bones. Suddenly Julia became frightened of the dreadful specter, and she turned to her father with a start.

"Father, we must go find Basil. It's just awful leaving him out there in that horrible place rotting away. We must go and try to find him! We must do it!"

Certainly such an idea had merit and had already been run through and processed in the Colonel's astute mind. But not only was he a realist, he also knew the terrain around the devil's rock. If a recovery mission was mounted to find the boy's corpse, it would be nigh impossible for a man to access the base of that rocky precipice where Hartgrove said the body must lie. In reply to his daughter, he tried to ease her away from the notion, "Now, dear, don't ye git yerself all riled up now. Ain't much of a chance atall of discovering the boy's body, as fer as I can see. I'm a'feared we're jest going to have to leave him be." Then with a slight chuckle he added, "And what's this 'we' business 'bout. Ain't nary way ye kin make a ride up to the top of that devil rock, Julia. It be a sight tougher to git to than them berry-picking grounds of your'ns."

However, Julia's determination was manifest, and she was not to be slighted or put off easily. "No, Father! We must try. I know I can ride up there, and I aim to prove it to you. It's not right to just leave him out there to the beasts, and you know it's not right. Besides, it's not like you to just give up on something. You must try. At least make an attempt. Please—please, Father, we must give it a try. Will you?"

Julia's heartfelt pleas had a slight softening effect on the Colonel. He could see and hear the depths of his daughter's grieving and it cut right down to his soul and hurt. And if he was to be truthful about the matter, she had a legitimate point. Furthermore, Colonel Deaver could well imagine the devastation that Basil's father and family would experience as soon as they became aware of their tragic loss. Thomas Edmunston was a dear old friend of the Colonel's. And it dawned on the Colonel as he reflected on Julia's words and searched his own heart that he at least owed Thomas Edumunston a search for Basil's body. After all, if the situation was reversed, he would expect the same. There should be a body to mourn over and to give a proper Christian burial. Closure—that is what the Edmunstons would want, he reckoned. Hell, they all needed a proper closure for Basil's sudden and horrific demise. And, importantly, that's what Julia needed, and apparently wanted.

For sure, the Colonel himself was not about to go off in search of Basil. He suspected rightly that he was a touch too old and feeble to make such a demanding climb up to and around that mountain. But he relented to Julia's wishes and assured her of his intentions to send her brother, Burton, and a posse of men to search the scene and retrieve Basil's body, if at all possible. Also, against his better judgment and after another extended discussion and pleaful tirade from Julia, the Colonel at last consented to allow her to go along with the search party.

Later on that Christmas evening, after Rufus was put to bed and Julia and Maggie had turned in, Colonel Deaver sat down to a most difficult and dreaded task. He had to write a letter to Thomas Edmunston informing him of Basil's death. All day he had pondered what to write and how to compose the letter. So until the wee hours of the morning, he worried with the words and scratched out draft after draft. When finally he felt comfortable that he had come up with something acceptable, he sharpened the nib of his quill pen and etched the hard words that would soon bring so much sorrow to his old friend.

Captain Burton Deaver recruited a few of the Mountain Guards cavalry men who lived in the community to participate in the search mission to retrieve Basil's body. In addition to sister, Julia, whom he intended to keep a close eye on, Burton sent word to Bachelor's Den for Uriah and Lark to come down and join the party. Before setting out for the upper reaches of the West Fork wilds, however, Captain Deaver paid a visit to his good friend, Columbus Hartgrove.

He found his badly injured neighbor resting uneasily in bed. Mrs. Hartgrove had all she could handle caring for the patient as well as minding her young son, William, who was not quite two years old. The doctor had allowed that Columbus's ugly facial wound would not be appallingly disfiguring. However, there was little that could be done about the missing outer ear appendage, which was completely shot off, or the associated loss of hearing. The mountaineer farmer would have to learn to cope with his handicap, and it would always serve as a reminder to him of the devil's business that he and his now dead friend had undertaken.

Hartgrove proved to be very helpful to Deaver, since the real purpose of the visit was to flush out more precise details and ideas on how to execute an effective search. On a small piece of letter paper, Columbus sketched out a diagram of the rock dome where the fight had taken place. Then he scratched a bold X at the approximate point where Basil and Beck had fallen over the edge.

"That be 'bout whur they fell off, Burton, 'pert near here," he said as he carefully marked the spot. "Jest don't see nary way he could've survived that there fall," Hartgrove confidently allowed as they studied his crude map. Shaking his head he went on, "It's least a hunderd feet down to the first outcropping where they would've landed. There's a bunch of trees and a bramble hell growed up over the rock. If ye can climb down to that spot or somehow get round to it from below, them bodies may be lodged up in that thicket. If'n they ain't there, then its more than likely they jest kept on tumbling down that high cliff to kingdom come."

A highly attentive Burton listened closely to the eyewitness account. He and Hartgrove were about the same age and had grown up together around Forks of Pigeon. His knew his lifelong friend could be trusted and counted on, that was for sure, and he took every word for granted while never once doubting the veracity of the story. Burton then furrowed his brow and queried, "You figger we may be able to get out on that first high ledge, Columbus?" Burton asked.

"Don't rightly know fer sure. Never tried it. Never approached the devil's rock from that side. Ye'll have to try and git in there some'rs how though."

Hartgrove went on to explain to Deaver the route they had taken to get to the top of Devil's Face Mountain. Burton had never been up that far, but a couple of the men in the party had. So he felt confident they could find it with little trouble.

"Best ye git off 'bout sunrise if'n ye 'spect to reach the devil's head 'fore night fall," the ailing farmer warned as he uncomfortably shifted positions in the bed. It was the last piece of advice Hartgrove offered to the expedition leader. He figured there was no way that any good was going to come from Deaver's troubles. They were never going to find a trace of Basil in that wild devil's country.

Two days after Christmas, Burton Deaver's search posse made it to the top of the devil's head in one long grueling day's ride. At Burton's urging, Lark had followed close by Julia to help her get past some singularly hazardous stretches of the trail. The rest the plucky girl did on her own. Riding sidesaddle at first she clung to the horse's neck with the tenacity of a starving dog holding onto a bone. Thrown off her horse several times she simply climbed back on with plucky abandon. Eventually however, the girl surrendered to her common sense and, contrary to the strict proprieties of the day, straddled the horse as a man would do. The looks of astonishment and even amusement from the rest of the party were of no matter to Julia. She had promised her father she could do it, and she was not about to fail. Besides, she had to find Basil. She had to get to him before the bears and wolves tore into him and ripped his corpse to pieces. And she had to see him one last time. Julia needed closure of the doomed love affair.

With the temperatures at the higher elevations hovering well below freezing all day long the men had stayed bundled up, as expected. They covered themselves from head to boot with heavy homespun clothes. And for good measure they donned long, wool great coats that were buttoned up clear to their chins to keep out the cold.

Julia thwarted societal mores and strayed from the fashionable riding habit of the day. Under her long riding skirt, she covered herself with not only cotton bloomers but a pair of men's homespun britches fresh off her father's store shelf. Above the waist, she also took a layered approach to stay warm. A chemise, heavy homespun blouse, and plain wool frock coat sealed her off from the West Fork's biting winds. And with Maggie's help Julia had coiffed her long blonde locks into plaits and secured them in a tight compact knot at the nape of her neck. This bunched arrangement was topped off by a coarse black bonnet with a red ribbon streamer tied under her neck. Even these dramatic measures to stay warm proved inadequate that sleepless night as she shivered next to the campfire under two heavy blankets.

The following morning dawned crispy cold as the low winter sun sneaked upward from the southeast. Burton Deaver proceeded to split his posse into several teams and instructed them to begin prowling and combing the mountainside below the rocky cliffs of the devil's rock. It was an extensive area and extremely difficult to move about in. Rock scars had to be climbed and the footing for the horses was too treacherous for their service over much of the ground. All day long, the men and Julia crawled and pushed and hacked their way through dense laurel and rhododendron thickets. Luckily for the searchers, the winter weather had forced the bears and rattlesnakes into hibernation. Otherwise, no man in his right mind would have been fool enough to wade through such a hellish landscape as existed there where the devil himself was said to reside.

Julia surprised her brother and everyone else with the gumption and level of endurance that she exhibited. Where some of the others hesitated, she seemed unfazed and pushed ahead to scale sheer bluffs and shiny across slender rock shelves—all in a desperate hope of spotting the bodies. Lark could not hold her back, and the experienced woodsman was bound to follow her to places where even he felt uneasy.

Towards sunset, Lark and Julia had been able to worm their way out along a narrow ledge to the vegetated area of an expansive rock outcropping. They could not be sure, but they believed this area might be located close to the fall point that Hartgrove had diagramed. Through the dense bushes they fought their way, and scoured every square foot of rocky ground for the bodies. What little daylight remained did not penetrate through the limbs of the thick undergrowth, making it almost too dark to search. But there was just enough light that Julia thought she could make out something unusual a short ways in front of them. Squirming and crawling, she peeked through the stiff branches and was able to discern an obscure, curious form that would have been hard to miss even in this gloomy lighting.

She studied the shape and actually thought it resembled a body. Or at least she could make out what might be the crude outlines of a person. *Could it be him?* she wondered. *Might it be Basil?* Pushing her way through the thickets closer, she was able to see much more clearly. It was definitely a body she saw—a single body—bent grotesquely backward over a rock, face upward and arms spread out behind its head. *Oh no—poor Basil,* she thought as she lost all emotional control and began crying loudly.

Lark heard Julia and quickly worked his way to her side, putting his arm around her and trying to comfort her. "Now, miss. You's gonna be's all right now, miss. Let's has a closer looks at dat body. We's gonna sees if it be Massa Baz. You stays right here, miss." Lark gently released her and crawled a couple more steps over to where he could push the limbs out of the way and have a better look at the face. Almost immediately he recognized that it could not be Basil. The blonde hair for sure meant that it must be Beck. He hollered back to Julia, "It's not Massa Baz, miss! It's not Massa! Dis be's Beck fo' shore." If Lark saw and wondered how Beck came by the huge hole in the side of his head, he needn't have bothered himself. Columbus Hartgrove's frantic shot had been dead on.

An emotional Julia was somewhat addled, but for the moment felt as if she had been granted a brief reprieve. Obviously she held no sympathy for the man whose corpse she had found. He deserved no better and would be left to fertilize the prolific rhododendrons under which she stooped. She and Lark quickly scoured the surrounding area where the other ever-elusive corpse should have been lying. Hartgrove had clearly said that Basil and Beck were locked to each other when they fell. So the two bodies should be close together, unless—unless Basil's body had somehow been deflected or had bounced off one of the rocks and over the ledge, whereupon it would have fallen hundreds of more feet down the precipice. They searched and searched in the proximity of Beck's corpse but could not find poor Basil's body anywhere. The only logical explanation then was that he had gone flying on down the sheer cliff, crashing and bouncing off one rock after another until finally coming to rest in a heap of broken bones and bloody, battered flesh. That was what had happened all right, Julia and Lark sadly surmised. It stood to reason. What a pitiful end it was.

The darkness of night was swiftly enveloping them. It was so dark that Julia and Lark were worried they could not make a safe retreat from the hell they had wiggled into. Slowly and surely they began backing up and working their way out of the tangle of underbrush and down off of that precipitous ledge. And just when they had finally reached a semblance of safety on the steep mountainside, Julia froze still and silent.

Her sudden stiff seizure startled Lark. Julia had heard something—she thought. "Shsssh—did you hear that?" she whispered lowly to Lark.

"No, miss. I not hears nuthin'," the baffled Lark replied.

They both stilled themselves in silence for a few moments and then came a faint muffled sound, "Help. Help. Up here." The message that penetrated the silence of the woods was only barely distinguishable. Julia and Lark could just make out the feeble words over the pulsing sounds in their heads of their own hearts beating.

"Did you hear? You heard that, didn't you?" Julia asked excitedly, looking keenly at Lark. She was confident that she had heard something.

"Yes, miss! Up dare's it! Up dares! It comes from up dares," Lark exclaimed, pointing into the murkiness toward an outcropping above them.

Casting aside all fears of the steep rocky bluff, Julia and Lark began frantically climbing and pulling their way up its steep incline into the murky darkness. It was definitely a human voice they had heard. And the excited Julia knew she was not mistaken. She knew who it had to be.

Chapter 31

A Special Summer's Day

The summer of 1847 was almost spent. It was the season in the East Fork valley when beautiful cool sunshiny mornings invariably gave way to sweltering hot afternoons, often interrupted by thunderous cloudbursts. At Bachelor's Den on this particular morning, all appeared normal from without. The chickens and ducks and guinea fowl meandered to and fro across the barnyard. Around the stables and outbuildings, the slaves and domestic stock milled about. Rows and rows of towering green corn were laid by in the bottoms. Bountiful fields of wheat flourished on the hillsides, waving with the gentle breezes and taunting the Africans to no end. Soon, very soon, their black backs would be bent wielding shearing sickles and thrashing the stiff grasses by hand to extricate the precious seeds. Yes, all outward appearances indicated this to be another normal summer day on the expansive plantation.

Inside the old log cabin, the young master—twenty-one years old now—rose from a chair and stood wobbly on his feet. With the aid of crude stick crutches propped under his arms, Basil Edmunston made slow hopping steps to move his tall frame over to a window. From there he could readily appraise all before him stretching to the East Fork River in the near distance and beyond to the towering mountaintops. It was a sublime view to behold, and one that he appreciated as no one else could.

Shortly however Basil was staring blankly across the fields, lost in deep reflection contemplating his brief tenure in Haywood. His mind raced backward to a time when these very surroundings instilled only a depressing loneliness and gloominess. Not quite eighteen months had passed since his father first met with him here at the farm to explain the immense responsibility that was being turned over to him. He was to become the Master of the East Fork, his father told him, and would thus inherit all of the accountability and duties that high position held. Basil remembered not being sure atall of what he was taking on, whether he even wanted the job, or most importantly, whether he had the capacity to handle the work. There was never a lack of confidence in himself – not then and surely not now. He had never been afraid of anything or anybody. But even his innate self-assurance had not lessened the trepidations and invasive fear of managerial failure that haunted him back then.

As usually happened when Basil entered one of these deep meditative spells, his mind reset to the most recent Christmas past. He would never be able to purge the memories of the tragic events that unfolded during that ill-fated holiday season. Everyone had given him up as a goner for sure. Columbus Hartgrove had stated vehemently that there was no way a man could have survived the fall off of the Devil's Face Mountain. And the scary thing was that everyone had believed Hartgrove. Had it not been for the dogged persistence of Julia Deaver and her emphatic insistence to mount a search to retrieve the body, then Basil would indeed have been a goner.

Against all odds, he had miraculously survived the fateful plunge, and not even he could explain his escape from death's snare. Possibly the fall was cushioned by the stiff limbs of the heavy brush growing on that first protruding rock ledge that he landed on. Or it might have been that the impact was lessened by his landing on top of Beck's body. More likely it was a combination of these two factors that saved his life. And Basil figured there was one more thing. He reckoned that God intervened on his behalf, somehow, to protect him from the devil's imminence and a hellish fate.

Those had been his faint, weak cries that Julia and Lark had heard in the dusky-dark wilderness under the devil's head. Inexplicably he had been able to scrape and crawl and pull his badly broken body off the rock ledge to the steep mountainside. Finding the climb back up the mountain quite impossible given his lack of strength and his broken body, he simply tucked himself into a small shallow cave beneath a rock overhang. There he covered himself with leaves and brush to stay warm, and he kept himself hydrated by ingesting snow melt and ice. But there was nothing to eat, so for five days he lay under the rock and awaited the inevitable.

It was his extreme good fortune that Julia and Lark found him. Burton Deaver's search party carried him down off the mountain—an extremely difficult task in itself—and then he was taken to the Den to recuperate. For weeks it was uncertain whether the Master of the East Fork was going to live. He had sustained fractures in all of the large leg bones, a hip, and several ribs. Fortunately, though, his head had not been smashed, nor had his arms, neck, or back been broken.

Then as abruptly as this unpleasant flashback had pervaded Basil's mind, it was gone. He was jolted back to the present by the awareness of others around him and a familiar tender voice speaking to him.

"Now Basil Edmunston, don't you look something!" Julia Deaver said as she walked over to him and helped him tie a cravat around his stiff collar. "I don't know how I deserve such a handsome feller!" she joked and smiled mirthfully at him.

"How indeed, said the lady's consort," Basil replied, laughing loudly as he broke away from her busy hands to sweep Rufus up into his arms.

"Hello there, my little man. What do you think of this handsome father of yours?"

Basil peered into the boy's warm blue eyes and became lost once again in a deep reflective trance. How close this beautiful, healthy, strong boy had come to not even making it into this world. God had guided Basil to deliver Rufus, magically inspiring and infusing him with the ability to save a baby's life. The boy's mother was saved too. Memories of the wonderful woman Basil came to love for such a fleeting period still possessed him. He had loved her so, that barefooted beauty from the Crab Orchard. Her death had left a jagged cleft in his heart that could never be completely filled, not even by Julia.

Basil blamed himself for Altha's death, just as he continued to carry the burden of Jesse Anderson's demise. It was a compelling reason to stay on in Haywood after the accident. He meant to see that his living Anderson tenants were properly taken care of, and he figured that could not be done from the state university or from Fort Catawba. And as for the deceased Anderson siblings and their mother, Basil saw to it that their tombstones always stood upright and their graves never suffered the encroachment of weeds and briars.

Rufus was another heavy anchor that kept Basil from straying from Haywood. He had always considered the boy to be his own son. The innate bond was formed when he first latched hold of the baby's foot and pulled it from the mother's womb. He had felt the strong attraction at that first touch, and he was intent on securing the bond until the boy at least had a chance to make it on his own. Sometime after Basil's accident, a deal was struck with the grandfather, Josiah Anderson. Through a signed contract between the two men, it was agreed that Basil would adopt and raise the boy in Haywood County and that Anderson would have visitation rights of sorts. This arrangement would be effective until the boy reached his sixteenth birthday. And just as simple as that, Basil became a father and Rufus became an Edmunston.

Julia once again brought him out of his dazed ruminations. "Basil, you still want to take Rufus with you to the church?" she asked, shaking him from his dreams.

"Suppose so. Uriah can drive us in the wagon, and you and Lark can go on ahead in the buggy to the Colonel's house."

That was the plan they had decided on. Julia would go down to her home to dress and then ride on over to the church with her parents. In an hour or so Basil and Rufus would follow and head directly there to meet them.

"I hear Lark outside already, Julia," Basil said as he opened the door and hobbled slowly out to talk with the slave.

"Okay, tell him I'll just be a minute," Julia replied as she frantically finished dressing Rufus.

"How's it going, Lark?" Basil asked as he approached the slave seated in the buggy.

"I be's fine, Massa Baz. How's you feelin' today?"

"Oh, slowly getting better, I expect. Going to be a while though before I can get out in the fields with you and the boys. Delia doing okay?"

"Good, Massa, real good. She says she feels da baby kicking 'round in her belly. Ain't dat somethin', Massa?"

Basil indeed thought it was something. After that runaway business and all he had gone through to keep this slave couple together he sure hoped they would produce plenty of strong and able male offspring.

"That is something all right, Lark. You keep me informed now on her situation. Say, I see you're making some progress on that cabin of yours."

With the mention of this new cabin Lark was constructing, the slave's face lightened up even more. "Yessa, Massa. We's 'preciates you's lettin' me's and Delia builds us da cabin. 'Spects I won't makes much mo' progress on it 'til after harvest time. But I 'spects we's be livin' in it befor' wintertimes. By den we's goin' has us a baby, Massa."

"Sounds real good, Lark. Now you drive slow and careful and get the mistress there safely, hear?" Basil instructed as Julia approached.

Hopping out of the buggy Lark gave assurances to his master, "I be's real careful, Massa. Don't you's worries none. We's gonna git da mistress dare real safe. Yessa, we's shore will."

"Goodbye, Julia. I'll see you directly," Basil said, and he kissed her just before Lark helped her up into the buggy.

"Don't be too long now. I can't wait to see my handsome feller standing tall next to the preacher. I love you, Master Basil."

"I love you, Julia!"

Since rescuing Basil from death's clutches, Julia had fretted over him day and night. Foregoing all thoughts and parental pressures to return to school, she spent the nights at the cabin with Patsy and cared for Basil as his condition demanded. Doctor Allen looked in on Basil most every day and was always accompanied by Julia at his side, as she learned how to change bandages and helped with the physical therapy. The place was a veritable hospital for at least a couple of months until the broken bones began to mend and it was known for sure that the patient would survive. Afterward, Julia rode up to the Den on a daily basis to visit and to offer whatever assistance she could. Included were demanding and sometimes unpleasant chores, such as feeding and bathing Basil and tending to his bodily evacuation functions.

And of course, Julia was left to take care of Rufus, and over time, the connections between them became stronger and tighter. Acting as a nurse and nursemaid had the slow but very positive effect of transforming Julia. She began to shed her youthful narcissistic traits and to mature on a faster track than before. Although her exuberant self and pleasant personality returned after the first few traumatic months, it was tempered by the responsibilities and concerns that came with her newfound duty and adoring attentions paid to both Basil and Rufus.

Moreover, Julia's nursing role began to gradually give over to that of a loving and caring partner. She was finally able to precisely express to Basil the love and deep affection that she held for him—and always had held for him. And she revealed to him that the Wade Hampton business had simply been a childish diversion intended to make him forget about Altha and to lure him back to her. She thought she had lost Basil, and it was all a foolish desperate ploy that had gone horribly wrong, Julia had confided.

Eventually, as Basil's pain began to subside, he would allow Julia to lie next to him in bed to warm him and comfort him. Occasionally, if she was staying over, they would lie next to each other in the dim light of the fire under the quilts and coverlets. While Basil could only lie flat on his back they kissed passionately and hugged as best they could. Julia could caress Basil's face and neck and lay across him with her bosom pressed amorously against his chest. Eventually Basil was able to shunt memories of Altha to the furthest reaches of his mind, and he began to harbor sincere loving affections for the vivacious young woman who now cared for him so. Over the course of many months of convalescence and intimate closeness, Basil fell for his nurse again. And as they grew ever closer to one another, they became desperate to have each other—body and soul.

About an hour after Julia and Lark were gone, Uriah came around with the farm wagon. With the slave's laborious assistance, Basil was able to slide into the back of the wagon with Rufus at his side. Needless to say the jarring ride down the East Fork road was difficult for Basil as he lay on a bed tick with Rufus scooting around all over the place. Every rock that the wheels rolled over sent a corresponding jolt of excruciating pain through his body. When they finally pulled up to the church, it was none too soon for the father and squirming toddler.

Uriah escorted Basil to the church door and left his master there under his own powers. Using his crude crutches, Basil hobbled up the aisle with all eyes in the room trained on him. He could see the extended Edmunston family crowded into a couple of rows on the hard benches. They looked back at him expectantly and with encouraging and pleased expressions on their faces. The smiling preacher, a new one from the Shook's Campground settlement down the Pigeon River a ways, took Basil by the shoulders and helped him find his place.

At last situated in the proper position and trying to stand and catch his breath, Basil looked out at the others in attendance. Good ole Doctor Allen was there with his family. *What a lifesaver the doc had been.* And there was Columbus Hartgrove and his wife. *Sure wouldn't be standing here if not for Hartgrove,* Basil thought. He made eye contact with Columbus, and they both nodded toward each other. Only they knew what a horrific life and death struggle had been waged on Devil's Face Mountain. And there had been no one in the Forks of Pigeon community more surprised and thrilled than Columbus was to learn Basil had inexplicably and mysteriously survived the fall off the devil's head.

The Anderson tenants had shown up—Josiah, Jesse's wife, and Manson and his wife—and were prominent in the audience, as were several more tenants. *It's a nice gesture on their part,* Basil noted. The Osbornes, Catheys, Blaylocks, and many other neighbors from the community had shown up in expressions of respectful friendship and to bear witness to the solemn and joyful formalities.

Basil glanced back toward where his brothers Walter and William and his three sisters were sitting with members of their families. It was a large contingent from Caldwell County that had made the long trek to Haywood for the event. There being a dearth of hotels in Forks of Pigeon, Colonel Deaver was gracious enough to host all of the Edmunstons in his own house and in a couple more small rooms behind the store.

Basil's mother and father were sitting proud and proper in the front row, with their grandson, Rufus, lodged between them. Louisa of all people knew what it was like to live in Haywood County, and she had been extremely sorrowful and worried about her son's plight. For she herself had suffered in the dark mountains for years until Thomas finally had come to his senses and removed the family back to Fort Catawba. Thankfully, Louisa no longer had reason to feel sorry for her son. He had had the good fortune to discover a genuine gem of a girl in the wilds of Haywood.

Basil knew the time was nigh upon them when Maggie Deaver walked through the door and took her seat. All those in attendance watched closely as the matron sat down. And then all eyes turned back in unison toward the church entrance. Much like a hunter's stalk, the crowd fell eerily quiet and still, and every single witness fixed their anxious gaze to catch the first glimpse.

When the door opened at last and Julia appeared at her father's side, the deafening silence erupted into a commotion of astonishment. One and all were so staggered by the visage of the profoundly beautiful young woman at the Colonel's side they instinctively gaped and gulped aloud reactions of *ohhhhhh* and *ahhhhhh.* Although simple and unadorned, the gown Julia wore so elegantly was fashioned from an off-white satin material Maggie had special-ordered from Charleston. Julia's fair skin blended perfectly with the marvelous dress, as did her blonde locks so deftly coiffured and gathered in back. It was no wonder that all eyes were transfixed on her as she slowly made her entrance and paced proudly toward the front.

Basil, thank goodness, entertained no nightmarish dreams of the recent past as he followed each mesmerizing step Julia made. His heart beat faster and faster, and he could hardly breathe. On this very special summer's day, the lovely girl walking toward him was soon to become Mrs. Basil Edmunston. No longer would he be left alone to face the harshness and difficulties associated with making a living in the East Fork Valley. Julia was to become his partner now, and the young couple would share those heavy burdens as the Master and Mistress of the East Fork.

The End

About the Author

Carroll C. Jones was born and raised in the mountains of Haywood County, North Carolina, in the small paper-mill town of Canton. He is a direct descendant of the Hargrove, Cathey, and Moore families who pioneered the Forks of Pigeon region of Haywood County (now Bethel, North Carolina), the setting for *Master of the East Fork*. Jones attended the University of South Carolina in Columbia, where he played football for the USC Gamecocks. After earning a degree in civil engineering, he began an extended career in the paper industry lasting more than three decades. Jones's professional work led him from the Carolina highlands to Brazil, South America, and then back to the United States. Now retired and spending much of his time in Bethel, N.C. with his wife, Maria, he juggles hiking treks and mountain fly-fishing trips with his love of writing. Jones is also the author of three award-winning nonfiction works: *The 25th North Carolina Troops in the Civil War, Rooted Deep in the Pigeon Valley*, and *Captain Lenoir's Diary.*

Coming Soon by

CARROLL C. JONES

The sequel to Carroll C. Jones's *Master of the East Fork* continues the saga of the Edmunston family, who must face the challenges of the American Civil War. It is another historical tale where old characters mature and new ones are introduced, romance blooms, and horrific battles are fought. Also, a new antagonist is presented—that vile human being, Amos Bugg—and a long-suffering feud ensues. Hold your breath and cross your fingers as Carroll tries to dream up a way to whip the Yanks and sort everything out.

CPSIA information can be obtained at www.ICGtesting.com
Printed in the USA
LVOW11s2026281114

416068LV00006B/13/P